CW00520547

Laying Out The Bones

Laying Out The Bones

Kate Webb

QUERCUS

First published in Great Britain in 2023 by

QUERCUS

Quercus Editions Ltd
Carmelite House
50 Victoria Embankment
London EC4Y 0DZ

An Hachette UK company

A CIP catalogue record for this book is available
from the British Library

HB ISBN 978 1 5294 2 128 6
EB ISBN 978 1 5294 2 130 9

10 9 8 7 6 5 4 3 2 1

Typeset by CC Book Production
Printed and bound in Great Britain by Clays Ltd, Elcograf S.p.A.

Papers used by Quercus are from well-managed forests and other responsible sources.

Dedicated to my dear father
John Alfred Webb
2 March 1937 – 17 August 2022
Miss you, Dad.

Day 1, Monday

Sweat was soaking through the back of Detective Inspector Matt Lockyer's shirt. Beside him, DC Gemma Broad was fanning herself with the case file. It was half past nine in the morning, getting hotter by the minute, and it'd been an uphill walk to the lonely burial site on Salisbury Plain.

They were standing where steep banks on three sides formed a miniature valley. Back in February – one of the wettest on record – it had flooded. Torrential rain, sluicing down from the saturated hills, had broken the ground in places, carving impromptu banks as it ran away. It had uncovered large chunks of flint, unidentified military junk and the skeleton of a man.

Out there, miles from anyone else, Lockyer and Broad had taken off the face masks they were supposed to wear at all times.

'About here?' Broad said.

She was standing beside a gnarled hawthorn tree where

the ground had washed away. After that drenched February had come the sunniest May on record. Now, in July, England was in the grip of a heat-wave. It had put highlights in Broad's fair hair – the wispy curls at her temples were almost white. Freckles had come out across her nose, and her cheeks were flushed.

Lockyer nodded. 'He had hawthorn leaves and berries caught up in his clothes, which must have come from that tree and gone into the grave with him.'

'Can't have been much of a grave.'

Beneath the thin soil the ground soon hit chalk, which you'd need a mattock and a lot of muscle to dig into, not a spade and a hurry. It was much the same all over Salisbury Plain.

Lockyer shuffled the crime-scene photographs until he found the headshot. A man's skull with gaping eye sockets, wearing a macabre grin of crooked, tannin-stained teeth.

Possibly the grin of a murderer.

'Chalk's very alkaline,' he said. 'A body can decompose up to three times slower in alkaline soil than in acid, depending on the conditions. Pathologist's best guess is he's been here anywhere between five years and whenever he was last seen.'

There were still strands of hair on the dead man's head, along with the leathery memory of a nose, and other bits and pieces – some of clothing, some of flesh. Scraps of cartilage held his bottom jaw in place.

'And he was last seen . . .' Broad flipped a couple of pages of a stapled sheaf '. . . on the eighteenth of November 2011.

So, he died sometime between 2011 and five years ago? 2015? That's a four-year window, potentially. I guess we should keep that in mind, and not *assume* it happened in 2011.'

Broad was clipped, focused. This was the big one she'd been hoping for, a case their colleagues on the Wiltshire force would be following. The MCIT – Major Crime Investigation Team – had begun an investigation back in March when the body was found by a dirt-bike rider. And even with the various police teams physically isolated from each other in the wake of the pandemic, Lockyer had picked up the buzz when the body was identified. The significance of *this* man, Lee Geary, being found where he was.

He remembered the case clearly. He'd gone straight to Detective Superintendent Considine to argue that the discovery of the body should be treated as new evidence in the shelved 2011 case, and assigned to him and Broad as a cold case. There'd been some debate higher up, but with the MCIT as stretched as ever with live cases, Considine – with reservations – had agreed with him.

Crouching, he ran his fingers across the broken soil by the hawthorn tree. It was parched now, set into hard clods. He broke some off and crumbled it, but there was no hint of a breeze to carry the dust away. Not there, in that sheltered dip of land. It was eerily quiet, and very private. Small wonder the body had lain undiscovered for years.

As Lockyer stood up, something colourful caught his eye. Knotted around one of the hawthorn branches was a scrap of yellow tape. He reached up. Not tape, something much softer. Ribbon, perhaps even silk.

With small beads of sweat along her hairline, Broad was now squinting at a close-up of Lee's skull.

'You can't make out the head wound very well from this,' she said, as the sun dazzled from the glossy paper.

'No,' Lockyer said. 'We need to go and see him.'

'Really?' She sounded surprised.

'Right now he's our only witness.'

'I just thought . . . we've got the post-mortem report as part of the MCIT file.'

'It's always worth actually talking to the pathologist, Gem. They're often more willing to speculate verbally than on paper.'

'Okay. Great.'

'Did you notice the rocks?' he said.

Here and there throughout the hollow the ground had spat up large chunks of chalk and flint. Some had sharp corners and jagged edges, but some, quite naturally, were rounded and bulbous in shape. There was one right at the base of the hawthorn tree. Big and round, perfectly capable of fracturing a skull.

'You don't reckon that's the murder weapon?' Broad said.

'Or it's where he hit his head, having stumbled down the slope,' Lockyer said. 'There's a chance this wasn't murder, since we're keeping open minds.'

'I suppose it's steep enough, if you tripped. But really? Given what happened to the others? And if he just fell, who buried him?'

They'd both read the PM report, and heard the station gossip about one particularly dark detail: the presence of debris in the remains of the victim's airways. It raised the chilling possibility that he'd been buried alive.

'Let's go,' Lockyer said. 'It's roasting down here.'

They climbed to where the view stretched for miles in either direction, to a hazy horizon. Steep ridges climbed up to the high plateau, like the petrified waves of some ancient green sea.

The distant bleating of sheep reminded Lockyer of home. He needed to go to Westdene, his family's farm, straight after work. Needed to check what the hell was happening, if the hospital had called, if his father was coping okay. Or at all.

He made himself focus. Broad turned a full circle, shading her eyes with both hands. A few isolated farms were visible, and the handful of houses of the village of Everleigh to the north.

'He's a long way off the footpath,' she said. 'Could he have been hiking? With a mate? He fell and hit his head, or there was an argument. Either way, the mate panics, conceals the body.'

'But why panic if he just fell?' Lockyer said. 'Why not call an ambulance? Plus there are enough warning signs around here about staying on the path, and not digging.'

They were well into one of the Ministry of Defence's training areas, where past live-fire exercises meant that any stray object you happened across might be unexploded ordnance that could take your leg off. Or worse.

'Plus you'd need a shovel, even for a shallow grave,' he added.

'Metal detectorists?' Broad said. 'They get everywhere, and they've always got spades with them.'

'It's a thought.'

'Something ritualistic?' she tried. 'Aren't hawthorn trees sacred? To, like, druids?'

'I think that's mistletoe.'

Lockyer didn't give the thought much credence, but there *was* something compelling about the grassy hollow with the single gnarled hawthorn tree at its heart. Why not the scrub of blackthorn and bramble that usually grew in such places? It was almost as though it'd been cleared, the tree revealed. Chosen, for some reason, or deliberately planted there.

Skylarks fluttered high above their heads, singing almost manically, as though the heat were getting to them, too. Lockyer looked at the crime-scene photo again. The skull was large, with jutting brow ridges and a heavy, square jaw. He'd been an enormous man. The PM and the original missing-person report had put him at six feet nine inches tall. The bones of his thighs and arms were massive. It was hard to imagine he'd been easy to kill. You'd need to have been completely determined, and not hesitated for a second.

'But are we really thinking this was an accident?' Broad said. 'Got to be linked to Holly Gilbert, hasn't it?'

'Well, it's up to us to prove that, Gem,' Lockyer said. 'Come on.'

He slowed his pace so that Broad wouldn't have to jog to keep up. His legs were the longer by far.

*

The air-conditioning in his old Volvo hadn't worked for years, and after an hour parked in the sun it was like an oven inside, the leather seats scorching. Broad rubbed a tissue across her sweaty forehead, and Lockyer set off too fast, before he'd even got his seatbelt done up, just to get some air in through the windows. The racket made it hard to talk.

'I don't suppose you'll remember when it happened,' Lockyer shouted. 'Holly Gilbert, I mean. You'd have been . . . what? Thirteen?'

'Fifteen, guv,' Broad said. 'And, actually, I went to the vigil.'

'Yeah? How come?' Lockyer had seen it on the local news. Candles in jam jars, and an air of collective outrage that was almost like hunger. Holly's pretty face turned into a talisman.

'I think my mum thought it'd help. We were stuck in the traffic jam that morning, you see. Sat in it for hours. In the end they closed the road further back and turned us all around to get us clear. I was supposed to be going on an end-of-year trip to Alton Towers, catching a minibus from Tidworth at ridiculous o'clock in the morning. When I found out what had caused the hold-up,' Broad shook her head, 'I got a bit obsessed, I suppose. Had some bad dreams. All that time I'd been moaning about missing the bus, Holly'd been lying there, a few hundred metres away. Dying.'

Lockyer glanced at her. 'And did it help? The vigil?'

'Not really. There were loads of people there, wearing T-shirts with Holly's face on, and sending up those paper lanterns that kill wildlife. The press were going around asking people who'd never even met Holly what she'd meant to them. Some action group made a speech about ending violence against women and girls. I suppose I felt I had no right to be there, in the end. Like none of us did, really.'

Lockyer drove on in silence. He remembered it from the local papers. The excited baying when arrests were made, the damning profiles of the suspects, then the disappointment when it all fell apart. Petering out, as news stories do when there's nothing new to add. Largely forgotten after a year or two, except by those who'd loved the victim.

They had an appointment to talk to Lee Geary's sister in the afternoon, so there was time to cool down at the station first, to reread the misper report and the MCIT file. As the Wiltshire force's two-person Major Crime Review team, Lockyer and Broad were based at the county police headquarters, a sprawling 1960s brick building on the edge of the market town of Devizes. Heat shimmered over the car park as they pulled up.

'Bit like *Miami Vice*, isn't it?' Broad said drily, folding her shades into her chest pocket as a large, uniformed officer crossed towards the building, adjusting his belt beneath his beer gut, the armpits of his shirt sopping with sweat.

The station was air-conditioned, apart from the tiny third-floor office Lockyer and Broad shared. No matter how much they peered through the vents, pressed the buttons or thumped it, nothing but warm air ever poured from the unit. Lockyer had put in a request for repair, because Broad was clearly suffering, but in truth he hated air-con. Using electricity to cool the air when the use of electricity was making the world hotter.

He dialled his mother's bedside line in Salisbury District Hospital, gripping the phone tightly, willing Trudy to pick up. He let it ring twenty times or more, sinking inside. He told himself she was probably just asleep, or that the nurses had left the phone, on its retractable arm, out of reach. That her not answering didn't necessarily mean she was worse again.

They were out of the tightest lockdown measures, but the hospital was still very strict about visitors. One per day, per patient, for a maximum of an hour, by appointment. Ironic, given that Trudy had caught Covid-19 in hospital. For several weeks, they hadn't been permitted to see her at all.

Next he rang his father. John was at home alone for the first time ever, and the thought of him all by himself, with his wife in hospital, made Lockyer profoundly uneasy. Like seeing a glass teetering, and knowing he'd never catch it if it fell. John had promised to carry his mobile with him at all times, but he didn't answer. Frustrated, Lockyer gave up. He opened the file on the man whose makeshift grave they'd just been to see.

Lee Geary had been twenty-seven years old when he'd disappeared, nine years previously, in 2011. Last seen on the morning of 18 November by his sister, Karen, at her flat in Salisbury. In Lee's mugshot there were blue eyes beneath those glowering, Neanderthal brows, dark circles under them, and a gaze that was unfocused rather than glaring or aggressive. Stoned, perhaps. He was pale and spotty, with ingrown hairs along his jaw, his scalp shaved to a gingery stubble. The entire right side of his head was covered by a tattoo of a spider's web with a grinning skull at its centre. The irony of that was not lost on Lockyer.

Put plainly, Lee Geary looked like a thug. Not a man you'd want to meet in a dark alley, or an isolated spot on Salisbury Plain. And if you were planning on hitting him over the head, you'd better make damn sure you only had to do it once. Preferably before he saw you coming.

There'd been no form of ID on the body. If he'd had a wallet or anything else in his pockets on the day he died, they'd vanished since. Karen had handed in his toothbrush and razor when he'd gone missing, to provide DNA for identification should he ever turn up in an unrecognizable state. But she needn't have bothered. Lee had been arrested repeatedly from his early teens onwards, before he'd ever met Holly Gilbert or been linked to her terrible death. His DNA was already on the database.

Karen had also provided the Salisbury force with a list of Lee's known associates and hang-outs, all within Salisbury. His hobbies did not include hiking, metal detecting or archaeology. He'd been wearing Nike trainers with no socks when he was killed, synthetic tracksuit bottoms, a grey hoodie and a gold ring in his left ear. He was a townie. Whatever he'd been doing out on the plain, Lockyer doubted he'd been out walking for his recreation. So perhaps he hadn't *gone* there. Perhaps he'd been taken there. The hollow with the hawthorn tree was a quiet, secluded place for illicit activity. Or an execution.

Lockyer put the two photos side by side – Lee's face in life, and his skull as it was now. Teeth that had been hidden behind chapped lips were now bared; the spider's web tattoo had decomposed completely. Nine years was a long time for his death to have gone undetected. A long time for anyone to be left to rot like that, no matter what they'd done in life. A long time for whoever had killed him to think they'd got away with it. And if Lee Geary *had* been buried alive, that hinted at an incredible rage. The deliberate infliction of suffering and terror. An urge to enact the worst kind of revenge.

2

Karen Wilkins, née Geary, lived in a 1990s brick box of a house in Bulford. Once a rural village, it was now sandwiched between two military camps, and the busy A303 roared past a hundred metres or so to the south. The background noise, as Lockyer and Broad got out of the car, was of constant traffic.

Karen's front lawn was parched and almost completely bald. A toddler's pink bicycle lay abandoned on its side; plastic windmills were stuck in a pot of thirsty petunias. Broad rang the doorbell, and looked pained at the answering shriek from inside. She'd carefully removed the expression by the time the door opened.

'You're the police? Come in,' Karen said, without waiting for an answer or asking to see their ID. She was wiry, and wore very little makeup; had a toddler clamped on one hip, and a harried expression – hardly surprising for a woman with two young children, after months of home schooling, when even the nurseries had been shut. The toddler gazed at them suspiciously: more strangers in masks.

Karen led them through to the back of the house, where a kitchen-diner had been extended out over a garden that had already been small. Bi-fold doors were wide open, letting in the heat, and a girl of about five was sitting disconsolately in her paddling pool, every scrap of skin covered by a lurid, sun-proof suit. The kitchen floor was littered with toys, the space next to the sink piled with plastic crockery and Emma Bridgewater spotty mugs.

'Tea? Coffee?' Karen said, as Lockyer and Broad showed their warrant cards.

'Thanks, but we'd better not,' Broad said.

'Oh, right. Covid.'

She ushered them onto a grubby red sofa, deposited the small child on the floor, and perched herself on a stool at the breakfast bar.

'So, you're investigating now? About Lee?'

'That's right,' Lockyer said. 'We're from Major Crime Review.'

'Review? Like, cold cases? Does that mean the other lot's given up already?'

She didn't sound particularly angry, or even surprised. Just flat.

'Well, not exactly,' Lockyer said. 'We've yet to determine exactly how your brother lost his life, whether anybody else was involved, or whether it links to any other cases. DC Broad and I are taking over to see if we can advance the investigation.'

'How he *lost his life*?' Karen echoed. 'Hit over the head, I was told.'

'Well, that appears to have been the cause of death. But he may simply have fallen.'

'Out in the middle of nowhere? What's he supposed to have been doing there?'

'We were hoping you might be able to help us there,' Broad said, with a smile to which Karen didn't respond. 'Do you mind answering a few questions about Lee?'

'Of course I don't. I've been waiting nine years for someone to give enough of a shit to come and ask questions about him— Poppy, I've warned you *twice!*' she suddenly shouted at the kid in the paddling pool, who'd been about to dump a fistful of soil into the water. 'Sorry,' Karen said to them. 'We're going out of our heads in this heat.'

'I know exactly how you feel,' Broad murmured.

'Can you tell us about your brother? What was he like?' Lockyer asked.

Karen thought about it for a moment, then gave a cynical little smile. 'You've seen his police record, I suppose. That picture of him with a skinhead and that God-awful tattoo. The one that was all over the papers? Well, he wasn't like that at *all.*'

'No?'

'Look, Lee was . . .' Karen searched for the right words. 'Let me just spell it out, right? He was as thick as two short planks. But he was a sweet guy. All that stuff – the tattoo, the drugs . . . He was just really easily led. We grew up on a shitty estate and it was way too easy for him to fall in with the wrong crowd. They always wanted to have Lee along if things looked likely to kick off – all he had to do was *loom.*'

Lockyer and Broad exchanged a look, and Karen bridled. 'You don't believe me? You must have access to his school records, and all that? They had him assessed. He had a non-syndromic ID – an intellectual disability. Well, borderline. His IQ was seventy-four and the threshold is seventy, but basically, yeah. He was a sweetheart, though. A gentle giant.'

'So other people got him into trouble?'

'Exactly.' Karen's eyes glittered. 'We got bugger-all help from the state since what Lee had wasn't anything with a name. He had a classroom assistant, who did her best, but he left school without a single GCSE. We tried to get him a job he could stick at – he worked at the big Waitrose for a while, rounding up all the trolleys – but nothing lasted. His so-called mates were always taking him off places when he should have been at work, and in the end he'd get fired. He'd have been all right if they'd just left him alone.'

'So, the things he was charged with . . .' Lockyer checked his notes '. . . possession of class-C drugs, anti-social behaviour, vandalism, and the conviction for burglary?'

'Yeah, well. He did those things, I suppose.' The weariness was back. 'It was just small-town kid's stuff. If we'd been well-off and lived in a nice area, and if he'd looked less like an ogre, he'd have held down a basic job and had a little flat somewhere, eaten cheese toasties for every meal, watched TV and been happy. But we didn't, so he didn't. We lived on a rough estate and he stood out like a sore thumb to all the wrong people.' She thought back. 'That tattoo wasn't even his idea.'

'No?'

'No. A mate of his, Badger – Nigel Badgely – got him pissed one day and took him to get it done. Probably thought it'd be funny. Twat. But Lee wouldn't hurt a fly. Not ever. That's the God's honest truth. He looked like a brute but he *wasn't*. Nothing upset him more than violence, or even just shouting. Confrontation, you know.'

'I'm sorry to hear it was difficult for him,' Lockyer said, struggling to fit the simple soul Karen was describing into the physical body of the man in the photograph. But he'd noticed the softness in Lee's eyes straight away, in spite of the face they looked out from. He'd put it down to drugs, written him off as a thug. Like everyone else, by the sound of it.

Red patches flared on Karen's cheeks, as though she couldn't stand the least hint of pity. 'He did all right. He understood how money worked and . . .' she waved a hand '. . . *life* stuff. But he was gullible. He believed whatever he was told. And he had no initiative. He always looked to other people to tell him what to do.'

She got up, wrenched open a drawer and riffled through it until she found what she was after. 'Here.'

She handed Lockyer a photograph of herself and Lee, sitting at a plastic table in what looked like a branch of Burger King. She had her arms around his massive shoulders – they wouldn't reach all the way. Lee's hair was tufty rather than shorn. He looked younger than he did in his mugshot, and was laughing. Holding a chip as though pretending to smoke it, between fingers like sausages.

'*That* was my big brother,' Karen said, with a catch in her voice. 'All Lee wanted out of life was a plate of food, and for everyone to be happy.'

'Do you mind if I take a copy of this?' Lockyer said.

Karen shook her head, so he took a picture with his phone.

'That's how I know he didn't have anything to do with that girl's death. He'd *never* have hurt her – or anyone else.'

'Not even if someone told him to?'

'No. Not even then.' She was adamant. 'Anyway, he was released without charge. All three of them were.'

'Did he ever talk to you about Holly Gilbert? Or what happened that night?'

'Not much. I asked him, of course. He said he didn't know anything about it, and I believed him. He was always a rubbish liar – didn't have the imagination for it.'

'You were both living in Salisbury at the time, so it's a good twenty miles to where Lee was found. Did he drive?'

'No, he never wanted to learn. Probably for the best.'

'So how did he get about?' Lockyer asked.

'People drove him. He hated being in a car, though. He preferred taking the bus – more room, you see. And walking. He wouldn't think twice about walking somewhere.'

'But not twenty miles? To Everleigh?'

'No,' Karen said.

'Did he know anybody there? Any friends?' Lockyer trod carefully: he wasn't sure how much Karen knew, and didn't want to seed information.

She frowned. 'Not that I know of, but he wasn't in my

pocket, you know? I tried to keep my eye on him, but I had my own life, too.'

'How did Lee come to be homeless?' Broad asked.

'He wasn't homeless – not like that makes it sound.'

The toddler on the rug screamed with sudden ferocity. Karen bent down and hoisted her up, kissing her sticky forehead until she settled.

'Our mum'd died that winter – she had a heart attack out of nowhere. Lee was *devastated*. It was really hard for him to get to grips with. He'd just got a little bedsit of his own off the social, after waiting a year and a half, but he got done for anti-social behaviour after Mum died, and the council chucked him out. I appealed, but he never showed up for the interview.' She looked angry. 'I expect one of his mates had a hand in that. They didn't want him to be independent. They wanted him on a leash, like a dog. Bastards.'

'B'studs,' the little girl muttered.

'Shh, don't say that word,' Karen said. 'Least of all in front of Daddy,' she added, for Lockyer and Broad's benefit.

'So Lee was staying with you?'

'Yeah, off and on. He sofa-surfed a few places – not that he fitted on a sofa.'

Lockyer sympathized. He never slept well on a sofa, and he was only a couple of inches over six feet, and lean rather than meaty.

'I hadn't met my husband then,' Karen went on. 'I was living with another boyfriend and we only had one bed-room. But I was hardly going to turn my own brother out, was I? I did my best.' She searched about on the worktop, found half a banana and gave it to the toddler. 'I tried to help him, but . . . maybe I didn't do a very good job.'

'Lee was twenty-seven, Mrs Wilkins,' Lockyer said. 'He was an adult.'

'Yeah, but he was *vulnerable*,' she said tersely, and Lockyer abandoned any thought of consoling her.

He knew all about self-recrimination. The dark lure of blame, of replaying events, over and over, wishing you'd done things differently. He could have been with his own brother, Christopher, on the night he was killed. Instead he'd chosen to be elsewhere. Knowing he couldn't change that didn't stop him revisiting the decision over and over again.

'And you heard nothing from Lee after you saw him on the morning of November the eighteenth?' he said. 'No phone calls, or texts, nothing like that?'

'No.'

'But he did have a phone?'

'Yeah. Just a really basic one – you know those ones they make for old people?'

'Okay.' Lockyer made a note. 'After such a long time, it might be hard for us to establish exactly *when* your brother died, but—'

'He died that same day,' Karen interrupted.

'What makes you so sure?'

'He went off that morning and didn't come back. He didn't text or call, and he didn't answer when I called.'

'And that was unusual?'

'Unheard of. He was *always* texting me to say he was on the bus, or eating his lunch, or whatever. Always. Every day.'

'It's possible that his phone was lost or stolen.'

'He'd have found a way to call me. He'd have come home, if he could.'

'And you don't think he might have just set off for a walk, out in the countryside?'

'By himself? No way.'

'You're sure?'

'A hundred per cent. He knew Salisbury – it was his comfort zone. New places were daunting for him, let alone big empty fields with no shops or signs, no landmarks he would know. No. If he went there, it was because someone told him to, or took him.'

She pressed her lips to her daughter's forehead again.

'He . . . he *had* been out and about more, that last year,' she said. 'Stopping out. Those new mates of his, Ridgeway and the others. They took him to raves, all-nighters, that kind of thing.'

'Is that how he met Holly?'

'I suppose.' Karen chewed her lip. 'I always asked where he was going, what he was doing. Trouble was, he'd figured out by then that I didn't think much of them. I'd made him wary of telling me things . . . He hated it when I got cross with him.'

'Do you remember any other names on the scene? Besides Ridgeway and Holly Gilbert?'

'No. I've tried, but I'm not even sure Lee told me. There was that girl who was also arrested, but I suppose you know about her. And some guy did come to the flat one day, asking for Lee. He seemed all right, I suppose. Polite. But he never told me his name.'

'And how did Lee seem, before he left on the eighteenth?'

'Upset.'

'Like, angry?' Broad asked. 'Or . . .'

'Nervous. That's a better word. He was twitchy. Had been for a while.'

'And you don't know why? He didn't say where he was going?'

'No.' Karen's eyes gleamed. 'I was in a rush. I needed to get to work. I *wish* I'd made him tell me! All he said was "I have to tell them", or something like that.'

'"I have to tell them"? You're sure about that?' Lockyer said.

'It was something like. I wasn't paying much attention. There I was, trying to dry my hair, and he was pacing about, muttering to himself – can you imagine a bloke his size stomping about a tiny flat? So I – I snapped at him. Told him to calm down, and not make me late. But it was something like "I've got to say something", or "I'm going to tell them."'

She stared into the past. 'I wanted him out from under my feet, so I just said "Good idea. Off you go."'

'It wasn't your fault,' Broad said.

'I know that,' Karen snapped. 'I just wish I'd paid more attention. Made him tell me where he was going, and who with. But then,' she sighed sharply, 'it probably wouldn't have made any difference. Except you might have found him sooner. His . . . body.'

In the pause, the little girl stared solemnly at Lockyer. He stood up and handed Karen his card.

'You've been a great help, Mrs Wilkins. Thank you. If you

think of anything else, particularly any names, please call us.'

She took the card. 'Probably never going to know, am I?'

'We're going to do—'

'Your best. Yeah. But you have to say that, don't you?'

'We mean it,' Broad said.

'What's one more dead druggie ASBO, right? That's what they thought when he went missing – I could see it on their faces. No appeals for information about *him* on the TV news. After what happened to that girl they all thought he had it coming. But Lee was just a big softie. He didn't deserve to get hurt. I just hope—'

Karen broke off, her face clenched by a sudden spasm of anguish.

'I hope they didn't frighten him,' she whispered.

Lockyer thought of the debris the pathologist had found in Lee's airways. The possibility of him being buried alive. If it was true, he hoped Karen would never find out.

'What did you think?' Lockyer asked, as he and Broad drove north, back towards Devizes, along a road flanked by fields of wheat and barley. In the distance, a combine harvester crawled along in a cloud of dust. Rooks sat disconsolately along the telegraph wires, roasting in the sun.

'Well, lockdown was bad enough when it was just me and Pete,' Broad said. 'If I'd been stuck indoors with two little kids like that, I'd have gone completely mental.'

'You're not a fan?' Lockyer said.

Broad gave a little shudder. 'All that mess. And the constant need for attention . . .'

'Oh, I don't know. The kid in the pool seemed pretty relaxed.'

'Probably had heat stroke,' she said, and Lockyer laughed. 'I suppose it's different when they're your own. My cousin always hated kids. She hated going round anyone's house once they'd had babies because they got so boring, and because everything was *sticky* and she said you knew there was either spit, puke or poo all over it. Then she had hers, and now . . .'

'Now her whole house is sticky?'

Broad grinned. 'Spit, puke or poo.' She fell serious, considering. 'Pete wants kids sooner rather than later, he says. But right now I just get this feeling like, I don't know, claustrophobia, whenever the subject comes up.'

Lockyer pulled a face. 'You're, what? Twenty-three?'

'Twenty-four.'

'Well, then, you don't need to be even thinking about it yet, let alone doing it. Take it from someone old enough to be your dad.'

'You're not old enough to be my dad.'

'Technically I am.'

'Well, I don't think of you that way.'

A pause followed, in which Broad pursed her lips and looked away. 'Did you not want to have kids, guv?' she said.

Lockyer didn't answer at once. The way she said it made it sound as though it was too late, but he was only forty-two. *Claustrophobia.* But it wasn't that, exactly. The idea of being a father was simply alien to him. It seemed like something other people did. All that responsibility. Broad had never been to his place, but if she had she might have noticed he didn't even have a pot plant. He'd had a younger brother, though. A brother who'd tried to persuade Lockyer to go out with him on the night he was murdered.

The silence had grown strained.

'The situation hasn't arisen,' Lockyer said.

Broad dropped it. Besides his mother, she alone knew of his feelings for Hedy Lambert, who'd carved a place in his heart and then left, early in the spring, without saying where she was going or for how long. And hadn't been in touch since – until now.

'Anyway,' he said. 'I meant what did you think of Karen's version of Lee?'

'Oh, right,' Broad said. 'Well, it's bound to be rose-tinted, isn't it? She obviously adored him. But isn't that what relatives always say? That it was their mates that made them do it?'

'Sometimes. But there's no arguing with that IQ of his.'

'Doesn't mean he was never violent, though,' Broad said. 'Maybe he got sick of being pushed around at times.'

'And snapped?'

'Exactly. That photo she gave us, though – he was *massive*. Like, properly massive. I can't see how anyone could've carried him up to that hollow if he was unconscious. Or dead.'

'No, you're right. And it's too steep for a four-by-four, even.'

'So either there was a whole bunch of people and they each took a limb, or he walked there,' Broad said. 'I guess there's a chance he went there by himself. If he wasn't out for a stroll, maybe he was running away from someone. That hollow would be a good place to hide. He fell and hit his head, then whoever was after him tried to bury him.'

Lockyer nodded. 'We might know more once we've spoken to the pathologist.'

'Karen said Lee was anxious, and had something he wanted to tell someone,' Broad said. 'Maybe whoever it was didn't like what they heard.'

'She thinks he went there to meet someone,' Lockyer said. 'And I think she's right.'

'But she didn't connect where he was found to Holly Gilbert.'

'No, and let's keep it that way for now.'

Lockyer thought about Karen's parting comment: *I hope they didn't frighten him.* He wondered if she knew who *they* were – if Lee had known his killer. Because three people had been arrested following the death of Holly Gilbert, and now, with the discovery of Lee's remains, all three were confirmed to have died within a few months of Holly. It seemed too much of a coincidence to be anything of the sort. Salisbury Police, who'd led the original investigation into Holly's death, had worked that angle, but found no hard evidence. It had been NFA'd – no further action.

At the end of the day, Lockyer went straight to Westdene Farm. Their flock of sheep and small herd of beef cattle were out to pasture, so the yard was deserted. Nettles and docks were pushing up between cracks in the concrete; a heat haze wobbled above the black tin roofs of the barns, and sunlight bloomed gold across the dusty windows of the house.

Lockyer found his father in front of the TV with a plate of fried eggs on toast. Their two brindled collies lay flat out on the clay tiles of the floor, too hot to bother getting up. Lockyer made himself a cup of tea, since there was no beer in the fridge – though there was fresh milk, which was surprising. In his mother's absence, the uneasy displacement he felt in his childhood home was worse than ever. The farm – the family – had been crumbling at the edges for a long time, ever since his brother's death. But now it felt as though he'd found wide cracks in the basement.

He could hardly bring himself to confront the possibility of Trudy's absence becoming permanent. Didn't know how he or his father would ever get along without her. He reminded himself that she'd been improving, getting stronger.

'How was Mum today?' he asked, once John had put aside his plate and the weather forecast had finished. More sun, no rain.

'Didn't get in to see her in the end,' John said, brushing crumbs from his shirt onto the floor. 'Car wouldn't start.'

'Dad, why didn't you tell me? I could've gone. Or taken you.'

'You were at work. I'd missed our slot by the time I gave up. Rust on the terminals, but a bit of Vaseline sorted it. I'll go tomorrow.'

'*I* was going tomorrow. I've booked in for five o'clock.' It would mean leaving work early, but he usually put in more hours than he was supposed to, not fewer. 'I can go on Wednesday, though, if you want to go tomorrow,' he said.

'No, no. You go.'

'When did you last eat something other than eggs on toast?'

'Nothing wrong with eggs on toast.'

It was hard to argue with that.

'How are you holding up?' Lockyer asked instead.

His father looked at him as though he didn't quite understand the question. 'Sheep still want foot-bathing,' he said eventually. 'Lambs want worming before they go up on Long Ground. Looks like this dry spell's setting in so I might as well start cutting the hay. Need to get that baler sorted out, mind you.'

Lockyer couldn't argue with this, either. There was work to do that couldn't be put off. John could do nothing for his wife except wait for her to come home. If he missed her, if he was worried, he'd internalized it. Like he internalized everything. For the millionth time, Lockyer wished his brother was still there. Chris, with his indefatigable approach to life, his good humour, his knack of making them all feel better.

'You need some help,' he murmured, also not for the first time. It had been a constant refrain since Trudy had been knocked over by a boisterous heifer back in early June. She'd fallen across the corner of a trough, cracked two ribs and suffered a contusion to the stomach wall. They'd kept her in for observation, supposedly for a night or two. Then someone on her ward had tested positive for Covid, and they'd all been quarantined together. Trudy had caught it. Two nights had become seven weeks, and counting. For three of those weeks, she'd been in intensive care. They'd nearly lost her.

Frying eggs and making toast were the limits of John's cooking abilities. Besides that, and apart from when Lockyer brought round a supply of ready meals, he seemed happy to subsist on tea and biscuits. Everything else in the fridge went off and wasn't replaced, and the laundry had soon piled up. It was only when his father had begun to smell that Lockyer had realized how helpless he was without Trudy. He'd come and spent a whole weekend doing the washing.

But the farm was a two-person job, as a bare minimum, even in high summer when the workload on a livestock farm was relatively light. In an ideal world it would be a four-person job. But John seemed to think Trudy would be back at any minute – he had from the moment she'd left. Any suggestion of finding temporary help had been dismissed out of hand.

'I should've booked more time off,' Lockyer said. 'I'll see if I can. Even if it's just a few days. Get that baler sorted.'

But even as he said it Lockyer felt his own treacherous reluctance. He and Broad were due to see Lee Geary's remains at the mortuary tomorrow, and talk to the pathologist.

'You've your own work to do,' John said. 'Besides, Jody says she knows a thing or two to try.'

'With what?'

'The baler.'

Like everything else on the farm, it was held together by orange twine and habit.

'Hang on,' Lockyer said. 'Who the hell is Jody?'

John gave him that vaguely puzzled look again. 'Jody. I told you about her.'

'You one hundred per cent didn't.'

'Well.' He waved a hand. 'You've been on about help. Your mother too.'

Lockyer was astonished. 'I never thought you'd actually *listen*.'

'Ah, well, just goes to show your old man's not completely useless, doesn't it?' He arched his eyebrows wearily. 'Then again, p'raps it shows I am.'

'You're not. I'm just . . . Who is she? Where did you find her?'

'Oh, she just bowled up, heard I was on my own. Malcolm had her last year, for the shearing. Seems a useful sort. Filthy mouth, but she knows sheep.'

'She "just bowled up"?' Lockyer didn't like the sound of that. 'And she's going to help around the house, is she?'

John looked sceptical. 'Doubt it. Seems more the outdoors type.'

'Dad—'

'We're lucky to get *anyone* at such short notice, Matt. And she's taken Chris's old room in lieu, so she won't cost much.'

'She's living in?' A prickle of unease. 'You mean . . . already? She's here now?' He looked around the room for any sign of a newcomer, then remembered the fresh milk in the fridge. 'But you've checked her out, right? References?'

'I told you, Malcolm had her last year. Don't *worry* about it.' John was emphatic. 'The dogs like her,' he added, as though that ought to be enough of an endorsement for anybody.

Lockyer subsided, still feeling the weird disquiet of not being alone in the house when he'd thought they were. 'Well, where is she?' he asked.

'Somewhere about,' John said.

Lockyer went looking, and found her out in the brick-and-flint machine shed, head and shoulders deep inside the Massey Fergusson baler they'd had since before he was born. All he could see was a pair of strong, tanned legs in scuffed rigger boots, and hips in denim shorts.

'Hello,' he said.

There was a clonk of bone on metal, and a muttered 'Fuck,' as she wriggled out.

She was tall and athletic, with tattoos on her shoulders and arms. She wore a khaki vest top and looked fit, with the deep tan of someone who lived outdoors. Her hair was cropped short, black except for a longer fringe, which had been dyed cerulean blue. Lockyer guessed her age at thirty, or thereabouts. She had a thin silver ring in her nose, a strong jaw, and shrewd brown eyes that swept over him in quick appraisal. 'You scared the shit out of me,' she said, wiping her hands on a rag. 'You must be Matt. The copper. Right?'

'You must be Jody.'

'That's me.'

'So, er, you've come to work for my dad?'

'Yep.'

'Living in.'

'Yep again.'

'Right,' Lockyer said. 'Have you . . . Do you—'

'Can I interrupt you there?' Jody said. 'It might save us time if I just give you the potted history. I don't really live anywhere, except with my gran, in Erlestoke, whenever the work dries up. Otherwise I go where there's a job. No ties, and I like it that way. I've got one GCSE – Maths – and I've been on farms all my adult life. I keep myself to myself, I like the work, and I don't make a mess. What else would you like to know?'

'I . . . uh . . .' Lockyer was firmly on the back foot. 'Can you cook?'

Jody laughed. 'A bit better than your dad. I offered to make him my speciality – beef rendang – but he declined.'

Lockyer grunted. 'He doesn't hold with "foreign muck" for the most part.'

'I'll make sure he doesn't get scurvy, don't you worry.'

'Where are you from?'

'Oh, all over the place.' She waved an arm. 'Gran's always been in Erlestoke, though, so this is close to home.'

'Right.' Lockyer was at a loss.

Jody watched him for a while, unbothered. 'I guess you came out to make sure I'm not dodgy, right?' she said. 'Not about to rob and murder your old man.'

'Something like that.'

'Well, you can relax. You're lucky I was free, actually. I was supposed to be working at the Soul Tree Festival down in Dorset all this week, till fucking Covid knocked it on the head.'

'Mind if I ask your full name?'

'So you can run me through the computer?' She grinned. 'Upton. Jody Ellen Upton. You'll find a few things in my dim and distant, but nothing major.'

'Still. Just to be on the safe side,' he said, with a smile. It was hard not to like her.

'Fair enough.'

'Have you figured out what's wrong with the baler?'

'Nah. Well, the pick-up keeps jamming. I've not got to the bottom of why just yet. Probably too late in the day for it now. I love these vintage square balers, though.' She gave the faded red metal an affectionate thump with her fist. 'Built to last. Warms the cockles of my heart to hear an old-school baler banging away.'

'Don't let Dad hear you calling it vintage.'

'Nice to find a farm that hasn't made the move to big bales.'

'Oh, you'll find a lack of progress something of a theme around here.'

'Not necessarily a bad thing. You sticking around? I'll make the rendang, if you fancy it.'

'I'm vegetarian.'

She laughed again, briefly. 'Christ, you're serious? And you a farmer's son?'

'I should get home, anyway.'

He was itching for a shower. Besides, with the smears of machine grease on her burnished skin, and the beginnings of crow's feet at the corners of her eyes, Jody seemed to fit in there far better than he did. He felt strangely deficient.

'Sorry to hear about your mum, by the way,' Jody said. 'Poor thing. Hospital's as bad as prison.'

'Thanks.'

It sounded like she was speaking from experience. Lockyer decided not to ask. 'Well, if you have any problems, or want to ask about anything . . .'

He left a gap that Jody didn't fill.

'I guess I'll see you around, then.'

'Yep. Catch you later.'

After a cool shower and something to eat, Lockyer sat down with a beer and looked at Hedy's postcard again. It had arrived on Saturday, and gave him no more information now than the first twenty times he'd read it. He read it again anyway. *In the truest sense, freedom cannot be bestowed; it must be achieved.* A quotation by Franklin D. Roosevelt – he'd had to look it up. It was written in black Biro, signed *H*, with a single kiss.

She'd been to his place on just one occasion, but she'd spent a week with his parents on her release from prison, during which time they'd been on their one and only date. They'd had their first kiss, then come back to his to make love. That single letter *H* caused him snatches of vivid sensual recall. The fall of her hair across her collar bones and chest, the taste of her skin, her long legs locked around his hips. Then she'd left.

The postmark and stamp were French, the picture a generic one of sunflowers. She must have got out of the country moments before lockdown hit, and was riding out the pandemic on the continent. She'd inherited a house in La Rochelle from Professor Roland Ferris, her old employer, so perhaps that was where she was now.

Lockyer fixed the card to the fridge with a magnetic bottle opener in the shape of a sombrero that his mate Kevin had brought back from a holiday in Spain.

Freedom cannot be bestowed. That was what Lockyer had done – what he thought he'd done, by finding the real killer of Mickey Brown. He'd given Hedy her freedom. So was she saying she needed time to accept it, after fourteen years of incarceration? Or to find freedom of a more profound sort before she could think of anything else? The kind of freedom that was nothing to do with locked doors or barred windows. Freedom from anger, bitterness, fear and regret.

Either way, he read her loud and clear. The card was an acknowledgement of him, and of the fragile bond that had formed between them, in spite of the circumstances. It was perhaps an acknowledgement of the precipitous way in which she'd left. It told him she was safe and well. It was absolutely, positively, *not* an invitation for him to join her.

3

Day 2, Tuesday

With a corpse as decomposed as Lee's the only smell was a faint tang of earth, barely discernible through all the PPE they were wearing. Which was a relief.

Lockyer had seen enough dead bodies in his career to know that unless there was a bullet hole or a knife sticking out, the exact cause of death was usually apparent only to the pathologist. But, with no hair or gore to hide it, the blow to the back of Lee's head was plain to see. It had left a pronounced dent from which fissures spread outwards. Lockyer thought again of his tattoo: a skull in the centre of a spider web. The filthy remnants of Lee's clothes had been removed and stored separately.

'Any theories about the weapon?' Lockyer asked.

The pathologist, Dr Middleton, tilted her head. 'From the size of the depression, something big and round. Nothing with a sharp edge.'

'Baseball bat?'

'Bigger.'

Lockyer thought again of the bulbous chunks of flint found all over the plain. 'Would it have killed him instantly?'

'Possibly, but it's hard to say. He'd have been unconscious very quickly. Dead within a maximum of one to two hours, I'd expect. An injury of this kind would almost certainly have caused a subdural haematoma and put pressure on the brain. Without treatment, he didn't stand a chance.'

'But he might have survived? If he'd got to a hospital?' Broad said.

'It's possible.'

'And he ... he might have been buried alive?' she went on, sounding appalled.

'Again, it's possible. But, if so, it might not have been deliberate,' Middleton said. 'If whoever buried him was in a hurry, they might not have noticed that he hadn't actually died.'

Broad leant closer to Lee's face. It was the first time Lockyer had seen her inspect a corpse. In the bright artificial light of the forensic mortuary they all looked pale, but Broad didn't seemed excessively so, behind her mask and visor. It was a suitably soulless room. The doors of a run of fridges filled one wall, and eight stainless-steel tables ringed the room, each with a sink and drain at one end. The windows had obscured glass, and the air-conditioning was working perfectly. It was blissfully cool in there.

'You reported finding nothing in any of his pockets,' Lockyer said.

'Nothing at all,' she confirmed. 'In a fresher corpse that

might be significant, but with one like this, his possessions could have disintegrated, or been washed away when the flood water moved him.'

'We know where he set off from on the last day he was seen, and we think we know where he might have been heading, but we don't know how he ended up out on the plain,' Lockyer said. 'Are you able to throw any light on that at all?'

'No, but further investigation might. A full examination of his clothes might find pollen, or other palynomorphs. Fibres, mineral particles, that sort of thing. They might tell you where he went in the hours before his death. You could also try to get a sample from his turbinates.'

'I'm sorry, his what?' Broad said.

'Turbinates – tiny frilly bony structures at the top of the nasal passages. They act as filters when we're alive, keeping small particles out of the lungs and trachea. Those particles can sometimes be retrieved after death, even from a clean skull. It's tricky, but it can be done.'

'Well, great.'

Broad gave Lockyer an expectant glance, which he shot down at once.

'Come on, Gem. Forensics like that cost a *lot* of money. We'll have a job getting the super to sign off on it. Unless we can come up with some concrete justification.'

'But the results might give us something concrete,' she protested.

They looked down at Lee's skeleton. Even in his denuded state, he only just fitted on the table.

'Is his size normal?' Lockyer asked Dr Middleton.

'On the borders of being not so, I would say,' she replied. 'Could've been a pituitary imbalance of some sort.'

'Could his low IQ be linked to his size?'

Middleton shook her head. 'Acromegaly isn't associated with learning disabilities. He has got one hell of a brow ridge. Adult-onset acromegaly might have caused the bones of his hands, feet and face to enlarge, gradually. But if there's nothing in his medical records, my guess is that he was just a very large specimen. With not much between the ears,' she said, not unkindly. 'It would have been a hell of a job to bury him.'

'Definitely buried? Not gradually covered by natural means?'

'Hard to say for certain, given the disturbance to the site. But if he died nine years ago, then yes, I'd attribute his state of preservation to having been buried in chalk.'

'He was beneath a solitary hawthorn tree, in a grassy hollow,' Broad said.

'Very folkloric,' Middleton said. 'Close to Stonehenge, by any chance?'

'Not that far away. North of there, near a village called Everleigh.'

'Everleigh . . . I believe there's a site over that way called Giant's Grave.'

'Is there?' Broad's eyes widened.

The pathologist smiled at Broad's dawning intrigue. 'Bludgeoning was one of the ways ritual killing was carried out, historically speaking,' she said. 'Along with garrotting, or cutting the throat.'

'I very much doubt this was a ritual killing,' Lockyer said. Then he remembered the scrap of yellow ribbon in the tree.

'No?' Middleton said. 'Bad luck, DC Broad. For a moment there it sounded quite interesting.'

The mortuary was in Flax Bourton, south-west of Bristol. From there it took them over an hour to get to Warminster, to where Nigel 'Badger' Badgely worked at a branch of KwikFit Tyres.

'Bit of a coincidence there being a mystical site up that way called Giant's Grave, isn't it?' Broad said, as they parked.

'There are loads of places with names like that,' Lockyer said. 'Prehistoric doesn't mean mystical. And, anyway, that's not where Lee was buried.'

'Way to spoil my fun, guv.'

The sun glared from parked cars outside the garage. They were invited to wait in a stuffy reception cubicle, with the stink of rubber and the constant din of pneumatic tyre wrenches, but opted to wait outside in the shade of the corrugated wall.

'Could we grab a cold drink after this, guv?' Broad said. 'Just a Coke or something.'

Lockyer glanced down at her flushed cheeks, her beleaguered expression. He pointed at a Tesco Express across the road.

'Go on,' he said. 'It'll be like a fridge in there. Have as much cold Coke as you want. I'll catch you up on anything interesting Mr Badgely has to say.'

'Thanks, guv.'

Badger was a short, unhealthy-looking man in his late thirties, with greasy hair, several days' stubble on his chin, and the yellow stain of nicotine on two fingers of his left hand. He'd undone the top half of his overalls and knotted the arms around his waist, but the result was less calendar model, more exhausted pit-miner.

'All right?' he said amiably, by way of a greeting. 'What can I do you for?'

'Mr Badgely, I'm Detective Inspector Lockyer, Wiltshire Police.'

Lockyer showed his ID, and Badger paled.

'I'd like to ask you a few questions about Lee Geary.'

Badger squinted up at Lockyer. 'Mind if I smoke while we talk? Only I ain't got long – we're busy today.'

'Looks like hot work.'

'Roasting my bollocks off.' He gave a grin. 'My heart shot off like the clappers when you said who you was just then 'fore I remembered I ain't done nothing wrong. Muscle memory, see.'

'Yes. It's quite the record you have.'

'Just kids' stuff.' He took a long drag. 'Clean as a whistle, these days.'

'How well did you know Mr Geary?'

'Since school. Lee was a good lad, thick as pig shit, but he'd do anything for a friend. Found 'im, have you?'

'Yes.'

'Not alive either, I'm guessing.'

'No. I'm afraid not. It looks as though he died some time in 2011. Did you spend much time with him that year?'

'Here and there, yeah. Can't remember that far back, exactly.'

'His sister doesn't seem to think you were a good influence on her brother.'

'Karen? Nah, not surprised she don't think much of me. I got Lee into some scrapes, back in the day. But I always looked out for him. People can be evil fuckers when they smell weakness. They were always taking the piss, trying to rile him up and get him into fights and that. One time a bunch of 'em had a bet on how much vodka they could get down him before he passed out, fuck's sake. I was the one in A and E with him afterwards, getting his stomach pumped.'

'I heard *you* got him drunk and took him to get that tattoo on his head. The skull in the spider's web.'

'Well, yeah, I did do that. But only so he wouldn't shit himself at the sight of the needle – he wasn't *drunk*-drunk. I thought if we made him look proper terrifying people would leave him alone.' He took another drag. 'Didn't work.'

'I'm shocked,' Lockyer said.

Badger grinned again. 'Never said it was a *good* idea, did I?'

'When did you last see Lee?'

'Christ, now you're asking. Can't remember exactly, but I reckon it was a good few weeks before Karen came round, saying he was missing. You've got to understand what it's like when you're on the dole and drinking a lot, up all night smoking stuff you shouldn't . . . The days sort of blur into one. Back then I couldn't 'ave told you if it was April or Tuesday, most days.'

'Lee's body was found about twenty miles north of Salisbury. Do you have any idea why he might have travelled out there? Or who with?'

'What, like, onto the plain? Nah, sorry, I dunno.'

Lockyer opened the MCIT's brief report and handed a page to Badger. 'This is the list we have of Lee's known associates, from the time of his disappearance.'

Badger scanned it briefly. One of the names was Acid. Another was Eggy.

'Anyone else you can think of?' Lockyer asked. 'Any surnames – or Christian names, for that matter? Anyone you can put us in touch with?'

'Nah. Sorry, mate. I mean, I think Eggy's surname was Egton, or Egley, something like that. But a lot can happen in a decade. People move around, or get put away. I met the missus and went straight, and you can't stay pals with the likes of Eggy once you've got kiddies to look after.'

'I can imagine.'

'I'm sorry about poor old Lee, though. He was never one of the bad ones, just caught up in it all, you know? No way out.'

'Did he have a girlfriend?'

'A girlfriend?' Badger smirked. 'No. I mean . . . he weren't a virgin or nothing. There was always the odd girl who'd come along, take one look at him and think, Now, there's a mountain I'd like to climb, if you get my meaning . . . But I guess it's true what they say 'bout size not being everything, because they never stuck around afterwards. Just used him, they did,' Badger said sadly. He brightened. 'Still, at least he got his end away. More than I can say, back then. Grotty little scrote, I was.'

'Did you ever meet Ridgeway Kingsley-Jones, or Stefanie Gould?'

Badger's eyes narrowed. 'Those were the other two that got arrested when that girl was killed, right?'

'Holly Gilbert. Yes.'

Badger took a final drag, right down to the filter, then ground the butt under his toe. 'I don't remember her. But him . . . He used to get shirty when people asked about his name. I only met him once or twice, at parties and that, but you could tell he was that type.'

'Ridgeway? Which type?'

'The type that likes an excuse to get shirty. I steered clear of 'im.'

'Do you know what he was involved in?'

'Bit more than the usual, I reckon. Maybe more on the supply side, yeah?'

'Did he get Lee involved in anything like that?'

'I dunno. And I'd tell you if I thought it'd get that wanker Ridgeway in trouble, swear to God. But, like I said, I steered clear.' He stared down at his battered shoes. 'Maybe I cocked up there. Maybe I should've tried to get Lee away from him.' He shrugged. 'Too bloody late now.'

'Was Lee ever violent? Did he ever lose his temper?'

Badger was dismissive. 'Lee didn't have a temper to lose. That's a fact. And I never believed he had *anything* to do with that girl getting killed. I said so at the time. Not that anyone took a blind bit of notice of the likes of me.'

'I've been meaning to ask,' Broad said loudly, over the racket of the open window as they drove back to the station. 'How's your mum doing?'

Lockyer fought the urge to reply, *Fine,* and shut the conversation down. It was easier than watching people search for the right thing to say. He'd never known how to respond to sympathy. Beyond Broad and DSU Considine, he hadn't told anyone at work about Trudy's prolonged stay in hospital – and he'd only told them to explain his need to leave early at times, to comply with visiting hours. But Broad had a tendency to say the right thing, and it felt wrong to lie to her.

'I'm not sure,' he said. 'She's not been picking up the phone these past couple of days. I'm going in to see her later.'

'Bet she'll be happy to see you – I was bored to death when I was in for my appendix, and that was only three *days.*'

Lockyer hoped his mother was well enough to be bored.

'Must be so hard not knowing exactly when she's coming out,' Broad said.

'I need to see her doctor, and get some answers. It's impossible to talk to anyone on the phone.'

'I expect they're still pretty busy . . .' Broad trailed off.

'I know,' he said. 'But it's not easy being patient when you're being kept in the dark.'

Broad changed the subject. 'Never heard the name Ridgeway before. Mind you, I knew a bloke at college called Atlas.'

'Seriously?'

'Weediest kid you ever saw.' She laughed.

'Sign of egotistical parents, I've always thought, really "out there" baby names,' Lockyer said. 'Not thinking of the child, just wanting to show the world how exceptional *they* are.'

'Maybe. Or they could just be besotted, and wanting to show that their kid is special and unique.' She gave him a sideways glance. 'You and I being the authority on parenting, of course.'

'Of course.'

Back at the station, with a trace of guilt, Lockyer ran a search on Jody Ellen Upton. The station was quieter than it had ever been, pre-pandemic. Those staff who could work from home were doing so, and the remaining teams were spread out in bubbles, some in old police buildings that hadn't been in use for years. Now, in the heat-wave, the station had a half-empty, school-holiday vibe that Lockyer quite liked. He hadn't set eyes on Steve Saunders, the colleague who liked him least and aggravated him most, in weeks. But he was going to have to, sooner rather than later. Steve had started his career at Salisbury nick. He'd worked the Holly Gilbert case the first time around.

Lockyer soon discovered that Jody had been speaking from experience when she'd compared hospital to prison. She'd served eighteen months for actual bodily harm and possession of a temporary-class substance with intent to supply – probably a legal high of some kind. She'd been convicted in 2011 at the age of twenty-five, which made her thirty-four now, and had been clean ever since. Or, at least, hadn't been caught for anything else. The ABH had been a fight with another woman, who'd ended up with a broken nose. Lockyer could well imagine Jody standing triumphant over a fallen enemy. She'd had the air of a person who didn't back down.

With a start, he noticed she'd been an inmate of HMP Eastwood Park in 2012. Hedy Lambert had been there at the same time. He'd visited her there more than once. At the time of her release his father's depression had been bad and getting worse, but having Hedy around had seemed to help. Lockyer wasn't sure whether Jody would have the same effect, but time would tell.

'Guv?' Broad broke into his thoughts, swivelling her chair towards him. She'd found a desk fan, and her cheeks were a calmer colour than they had been. She'd been studying an OS map. 'I've found that place, Giant's Grave. It's a long barrow, so, like, old, I guess.'

'A Stone Age burial chamber,' Lockyer said. 'Definitely old.'

'Anyway, it's about three and a half miles north-west of Everleigh. And about halfway between that and the village there's another prehistoric site: Old Hat Barrow. I always wondered how the farm had got its name.'

Lockyer sat forward. 'How far is Old Hat Farm from where Lee's body was found?'

Broad checked. 'About a mile. That has to be where Lee was headed that day, right?'

'MCIT officers already went to Old Hat Farm, and spoke to Holly's family. They denied any knowledge of Lee's death.'

'Well – to quote a quote – they would, wouldn't they?' Broad said.

'Have you got the file there? Remind me who exactly lives at the farm.'

Broad checked. 'Mr and Mrs McNeil. He was Holly Gilbert's father. She's no relation.'

'That's it?'

'Apparently. Holly had been living with them for about six months when she died. Before that she lived with her mum. In Surrey, I think it was.'

'Right. Well, let's get everything we can on Ridgeway Kingsley-Jones and Stefanie Gould. If Lee's death is linked to theirs, and if all three are linked to Holly Gilbert's, we need as much detail as we can get.'

'Guv, you do know who worked the case originally? Back in 2011?'

'I know,' Lockyer said, sensing trouble ahead. 'I'll talk to him. Just . . . not today.'

Trudy Lockyer was in a room of four beds attached to a high-dependency ward. It was a monochrome space – white walls, grey floor. The windows were open, and the warm air pushing in was the only soft thing in a room full of metal and plastic. Wearing a plastic apron, gloves and a mask, Lockyer was permitted to sit two metres from his mother. No touching, of course, no hug or kiss.

'How are you feeling, Mum?'

'Oh, not so bad.' She smiled weakly. 'Better than yesterday, I think.'

He knew she was lying. She no longer had Covid and her
blood oxygen was back to normal. They'd all assumed she
was over the worst. Yet she barely had the strength to roll
her head towards him, let alone sit up. His mother's usually
keen eyes were dull, her face slack and colourless.

'I've tried to call you a few times,' he said.

'Have you? Sorry, love. I'm so dozy at the moment. It's
lovely to see you.'

'You look tired.'

'It's very odd,' she murmured. 'I can't seem to get up the
steam to do very much at all.'

'I expect your body's just recovering from the virus,'
Lockyer said hopefully.

'Yes, probably.' She shifted her legs a little, and winced.

'Are you in pain?'

'Just these dratted pins and needles that won't seem to go.'

'Has the doctor said anything about it?'

'Oh, they're going to do some tests, I think,' she said
vaguely.

'Are you eating?'

'Matthew, dear, I'm doing everything I'm told. But I'm
hardly working up an appetite just lying here.'

'But you need to keep your strength up,' he said.

'Don't worry about me. How's your dad?'

'All right, I think. He misses you.'

'I miss him, too. And the dogs.' She blinked slowly. 'Can't
wait to be home.'

'He's got this new girl started. Jody. She . . . seems a character. And she's living in.'

'Good. Simpler that way, I suppose.'

'Did you know about it?'

'Well, I told him to ring around a couple of the neighbours to see if they could recommend someone. Every now and then he does as I say.'

'She's got a record. Been in prison.'

A tiny frown. 'Recently?'

'No.'

'Well, then. I'm sure it's nothing to worry about.' Trudy shut her eyes for a moment. 'You'll keep an eye on them, won't you?'

'Course I will, Mum.'

'Any word from Hedy?'

She'd asked frequently in the beginning but not for ages. She'd liked Hedy; liked even better the idea that Lockyer might have found someone.

'Well . . .' he said, looking out at the bright sky beyond the window. The ward was four storeys up. A row of speckled starlings were jostling and chattering along the dry guttering of the opposite wing. '. . . funny you should ask. She sent a postcard, actually. Doesn't say much – doesn't say where she is, even. But I guess she must be okay. It was sent from France, so . . .' He trailed off, looked back and realised Trudy had fallen asleep. He wanted to reach out and take her hand. He wanted to straighten the sheet, which had got snarled around one of her feet. He wanted to shake her, because it scared him that she couldn't stay awake even for the length of his visit. But he obeyed the rules, and did nothing.

Lockyer spoke to the ward sister, and was told a doctor would come and speak to him, if he was prepared to wait. He found a chair in a lounge area on the other side of the corridor, and stared into space for several minutes, trying to shake the feeling that something was very wrong with his mother. Then took out his phone and Googled Holly Gilbert.

Beneath all the LinkedIn, Facebook and Twitter suggestions, he found several local news pages, dating from June 2011.

A303 Bridge Death Tragedy.

A woman who was killed after being struck by a vehicle on the A303 in the early hours of Wednesday morning has been named as twenty-year-old Holly Gilbert, who lived near Everleigh. Miss Gilbert, a student, is thought to have fallen from the footbridge over the dual carriageway east of the Countess Services. Police have yet to confirm if they are looking for anybody else in connection with the incident. The A303 was closed for six hours while police carried out their investigation, causing long tailbacks in both directions.

Lockyer pictured a teenage Gemma Broad sitting in the eastbound queue, fretting about missing her trip to Alton Towers. A later page had a photo of Holly, which he remembered seeing before. It looked as though it had been taken

on a night out, and had clearly been cropped – a disem-
bodied arm, in a grey suit jacket, was slung around her
shoulders. She was smiling, her big brown eyes sparkling.
She looked younger than twenty, and was very pretty. Long
lashes sooty with mascara; blonde highlights in her glossy
hair; the camera flash glinting from her lip-gloss. The kind
of face the press loved.

Lockyer clicked through a few more pages, containing
little additional information. One said that Holly had been at
Bournemouth University, studying Environmental Science,
another that police were appealing for witnesses: the driver
of the lorry had been discharged from hospital and wouldn't
be facing any charges in relation to the incident. Then the
furore five days later, when the arrests were made. Pictures
of the three suspects on all the front pages: glowering eyes,
sunken expressions; Lee Geary looking every inch a murderer of young women. *Trio of Evil: Police Arrest Three in Tragic
Holly Case.*

From two months later he found a short update reporting
that the inquest had ruled Holly's death as suicide. She'd
lost her mother to cancer less than a year before, and had
alcohol and traces of an unspecified psychoactive substance
in her system. Friends had testified to her dropping off the
radar after the bereavement, missing classes and displaying
out-of-character behaviour.

Still a tragedy, just a less provocative one.

Lee Geary, Ridgeway Kingsley-Jones and Stefanie Gould
had been questioned not as witnesses but under caution.
Lockyer remembered the buzz, the rumours that Holly's

killers had been caught. He remembered the disappointment, even anger, at the coroner's verdict of suicide, but
he didn't know what the evidence against them had been.
Finding that out was a priority. Had they been with Holly at
the time? Had they supplied her with whatever she'd taken?
Another dead druggie ASBO, Karen Wilkins had said.

'Mr Lockyer?'

He looked up with a start.

'I'm Dr Lorne. I understand you'd like an update on your
mother's condition.'

Lockyer got to his feet. 'Yes, please.'

Dr Lorne was petite, with cropped, dark, kinky hair. She
gave him a no-nonsense smile from behind her visor, and
didn't suggest that they sit down.

'Shouldn't she be getting better?' he said. 'Why is she so
tired? And she says she's got pins and needles.'

'Your mother recovered well from the initial infection.
That's the good news. However, she may have developed
a secondary syndrome of some kind, and we'll be running
tests to determine what exactly is going on.'

She held his gaze, and Lockyer guessed she knew more.

'But you think you know what it is?'

'Possibly. There is a condition called Guillain-Barré Syndrome, which occurs when the immune system is upset, often
by an infection, in this instance coronavirus. An overreac-
tion causes the body's own antibodies to attack the nervous
system. Some of your mother's symptoms correlate with those
we would expect to see in Guillain-Barré. Her weakness and
fatigue, the numbness and tingling in her hands and feet.'

'Right. But . . . you can treat it?'

'As I said, we're going to do some tests. If we get a positive diagnosis for Guillain-Barré, we'll begin treatment at once. In the meantime we'll control her pain, and keep her comfortable.'

'She didn't tell me she was in pain.'

'Well,' Dr Lorne lifted her brows, 'she *is* your mother.'

'How long before she's back to normal? And can go home?'

'It's likely to be several weeks yet. She needs to be strong enough to walk unaided, and cope with daily life. Most people make a full recovery within six to twelve months—'

'A *year*?'

'But I must warn you that some people have lasting, or even permanent, symptoms.'

'Like what?'

'Difficulty walking, muscle weakness, pain and tingling. Fatigue.'

Lockyer had to look away for a moment. 'Do people die of this?' he forced himself to ask.

She pulled no punches. 'It can happen.'

'How often?'

'In perhaps five to six per cent of cases. No more than that.'

'Does my father know all this?'

'He didn't ask for the statistics but, yes, of course.'

Lockyer couldn't swallow it. It felt as though the news had lodged in his throat.

Dr Lorne softened fractionally. 'She's in the best place she could be right now, Mr Lockyer. We'll do everything we can for her.'

'Thank you,' he managed to say.

The urge to lay blame was as powerful as it was irrational. If the heifer hadn't barged her, if she hadn't fallen, if she hadn't needed to come into hospital ... Broad had once pointed out to him that fear often manifested itself as anger. Particularly in men. Since then he'd noticed it happening to himself, several times.

'We have your number?' Dr Lorne checked. 'I'll call you with the test results, probably at around this time tomorrow.'

Lockyer looked in on Trudy again before he left. She was as still as the grave.

4

Day 3, Wednesday

Lockyer woke at sunrise and lay listening to the cacophony of birdsong. The night had been sticky – he'd kicked off the sheets at some point. His Victorian brick cottage was attached to the one that belonged to his elderly neighbour, Iris Musprat. They were isolated, backing onto a copse of trees at the end of an unmade track outside the small village of Orcheston. When Lockyer had moved in the place had been completely unmodernized. Before him, a man named Bill Hickson had lived there for the best part of seventy years, and had died in the very room where Lockyer now slept. He tried not to think too much about that.

Lockyer had been fixing it up steadily since moving in, but work had stalled since Hedy's departure.

Mrs Musprat had made a confession to him, at around the same time.

He got up and pulled on some jeans. Went through to the spare bedroom, and looked up at the stain on the ceiling.

He'd uncovered it the previous autumn, by stripping off a layer of paper that had been there for decades. Shortly afterwards, Mrs Musprat had told him the origin of the stain, and now Lockyer had no idea what to do about it.

He found himself hoping it wasn't true – that she had done a terrible thing and kept it secret for such a long, long time. There was only one way to prove it and he hadn't done it yet, because if her story was true there was no way back. He was a police detective: he would have to act on the information. But if there was no proof, perhaps he could just forget about it. He'd been trying to give that option as much oxygen as possible. But he had to know.

He went out to the back garden, to the defunct privy he used as a shed. A few of Bill's old gardening tools were in there. Lockyer grabbed a spade, stepped over the sagging remnants of the back fence, and set off into the trees.

Dawn light sparkled green through the leaves, and the air was earthy-sweet. Lockyer walked until he came to a gnarled yew tree amid the ash, beech, holly and oak. There, before he could think too much about it, he jabbed the spade into the ground and stamped it in hard. The metal scraped against flint and soil. He created a ditch in front of the yew tree, and when it was eight feet long he went back on himself, making it deeper. He was soon sweating, but turned up nothing except roots, chalk, and the odd manmade thing – bits of broken clay pipe, an old-fashioned ring-pull.

When the whole trench was double-depth Lockyer stopped, with a surge of relief. There was nothing there. The tale was just something Mrs Musprat had heard, or dreamt; something that had got stuck in her mind long ago, and retold itself into fact. Instinct told him to quit while he was ahead, but he stamped the spade into the ground one more time.

This time there was a rasping sound that made the hair stand up on the back of his neck. He turned the earth aside and glimpsed something pale, carefully scraped away more soil, until he was sure. A smooth curve of yellow bone. The gentle dome of a forehead. Lockyer crouched, and stared into the near perfect circle of an eye socket.

Any hope of it being fiction evaporated.

He backfilled the trench and walked away. When he reached the garden fence Iris Musprat was there, watching him. Tiny, scrawny, dressed in clothes only a step up from rags, and holding the rope halter of her goat, Desirée. Her frightened gaze took in his muddy spade, and the sweat on his forehead. The moment hung. Then Lockyer went inside without a word.

'You all right, guv?' Broad asked.

Lockyer started. He'd been staring out of the window, lost in thought. 'Yes,' he said curtly.

Broad blinked, turning back to her screen.

'Sorry, Gem. Just . . .' he waved one hand '. . . stuff.'

'It's fine, guv.'

They'd been over to the storage unit at Melksham Divisional HQ first thing, to dig out the original file on Holly Gilbert's death. Lockyer had been reading through it while Broad searched for details on Ridgeway Kingsley-Jones and

Stefanie Gould, but his mind had been pulled away into worries about his mother, and what he'd found in the woods that
morning. That he'd re-covered the bones and walked away,
when the site ought to have blue and white tape around it
by now, and SOCOs performing a full and careful excavation.

'What have you got?' he asked.

'Ridgeway died not long before Lee Geary,' Broad said.
'Injuries sustained in a fall, on the thirtieth of October 2011.
He fell from the top of a multi-storey car park in Salisbury.'

'Which one?'

'Culver Street.'

'I know it. It's not that high – more like three storeys
than multi.'

'High enough, apparently,' Broad said. 'Especially if you
land on your head.'

'He went head first? That sounds like someone helped him.'

'Inquest returned an open verdict. Witnesses reported
seeing other young men in the area at the time, but no one
ever came forward or was identified. There was no physical
evidence of anyone having been up on the roof with him.
Seems Ridgeway had been on the radar with Salisbury Vice
for a while. He'd had contact with some very dodgy people;
at least one dealer with known links to a South London
gang. Thoughts were he was running – or attempting to take
over – a county line.'

'So he might have stepped on the wrong toes?'

'Reading between the lines, that was what they decided.
Efforts to link his death to Holly Gilbert's got nowhere.'

'No handy CCTV footage of the roof?'

'Nope. It was out of order. One camera at ground level caught Ridgeway going in, but nobody else could be positively identified from the images.'

Lockyer studied the photo of Ridgeway Kingsley-Jones. He was good-looking, if on the stocky side, with a broad face and thick neck. There was something cool and contemptuous in his gaze. He didn't look the typical townie drug-dealing type, but assumptions like that were often misleading.

Lockyer turned back to his own desk, where Stefanie Gould's report lay open.

Her grainy photo showed a young woman with long, bleached hair. Her face was a perfect heart shape, with high cheekbones, pale eyes, and an expression of pure fury. She'd died first, of the three, at a music festival on the bank-holiday weekend at the end of August 2011. Drowned in a lake while under the influence of alcohol and amphetamines, her body not found until two days later, during the litter-pick. No evidence of any third-party involvement, and no witnesses, which seemed improbable given the large numbers at the festival. But, then, people got lost in a crowd, especially a crowd that was either high, stoned or drunk.

It was how Lockyer's brother had died, after all. A drunken melee outside a pub. It was how his killer had simply run away, and never been found.

'So,' Lockyer said, 'the three people questioned in relation to Holly Gilbert's death in June 2011 all died within three months of her – if we accept that Lee died very soon after Karen last saw him.'

'I can see why the original investigation tried to link them – we all hate coincidences. But it could be, couldn't it?' Broad ventured.

'A coincidence?' Lockyer said. 'I don't know. Stef's death could've been accidental; Ridgeway's maybe an unrelated murder or suicide, if he *had* got into serious trouble with the wrong people. But I'd be more inclined to agree with you if Lee hadn't been found where he was. A mile from Holly's home.'

'Three murders, then, committed by someone who didn't think Holly killed herself that night? Or who blamed these three even if she did?' Broad couldn't hide a growing excitement.

Lockyer stood up. 'Come on. Let's go to Old Hat Farm, and get a feel for them – tactfully.'

They missed the entrance the first time, and Lockyer swung the car around beside a rusting grain silo, the wheels sending up dust and jackdaws. He turned onto a narrow track. There was no sign, just a single weathered gatepost with a carving Lockyer couldn't quite make out. It looked like *oXo*, with a scalloped line above it, like part of a child's drawing of a cloud. The track cut through a flat expanse of tall thatching straw.

'What do you make of that?' Broad said, pointing at a holm oak up ahead. Long ribbons in every colour trailed from its branches. Some had holed stones or feathers threaded onto them.

'Not a clue,' Lockyer said. 'But I bet somebody in the house does art.'

'Does art?' Broad grinned.

'What?'

'I think you say they're an artist, rather than that they do art, guv. Anyway, it looks more . . . witchcrafty, to me.'

'There was a scrap of yellow ribbon in the hawthorn tree where Lee was buried,' Lockyer said. 'I didn't think it was relevant, but maybe it was.'

A line of poplars marked a shallow stream, crossed via a bridge of old railway sleepers. After that the ground rose gently until the farm came into view: a long house with lime-washed walls beneath an undulating clay-tile roof. From its small windows and low eaves, Lockyer guessed it was very old. It formed one side of a quad of buildings; the rest was made up of a variety of barns, stables and sheds, arranged around a concrete yard. A clutter of brick, flint, wood and corrugated iron that spread away from the house to polytunnels in the distance.

It had a ramshackle feel that Lockyer knew well: a place that was getting by, just about, but not making anybody rich. Not by a long chalk.

Broad swept a dubious glance around the yard as they got out of the car. Lockyer had dropped her home a few times, after Friday-night drinks in Devizes. She and Pete lived in a small, crisp new-build in Semington, on the edge of Trowbridge. It was link-detached to the neighbours by a single garage that was scarily tidy inside. Bottles of car-cleaning products, all in a row.

The front door of the farmhouse was propped open with a brick. Lockyer knocked loudly.

'Hello? Anybody in?'

A hot breeze blew through the house, as though a back door was open as well. On the wall, a large mirror had been painted with the words *Welcome, Traveller. Here is Home.* Somewhere, wind chimes clonked gently. An elderly greyhound appeared and plodded towards them, claws clicking on the uneven flagstones.

Lockyer led the way inside. 'Hello?' he called again, louder.

He headed into the room from which the dog had come: a large kitchen with a low-beamed ceiling and a cavernous inglenook fireplace. An unidentifiable, faintly peppery smell hung in the air. The cupboards and a huge dresser looked hand-made, as did a long refectory table and benches.

'Gem.' Lockyer pointed to a large sketchbook that was open on the table. A messy tray of paints sat beside it, and brushes in a jar of mud-coloured water. 'Art,' he said, and she flashed him a grin just as a woman came in carrying a basket of stinging nettles. She was barefoot, so hadn't made a sound, and when she saw them she pulled up with a gasp.

'Christ on a bike!' she said, with a laugh. 'Hello! Sorry, I didn't hear you arrive.'

It sounded as though she'd been expecting them – or somebody. She looked about Lockyer's age, or perhaps a little older, mid-forties. Fair hair, grey at the temples, fell in unkempt waves halfway to her waist, and she'd lined her eyes dramatically with kohl. The floating folds of an embroidered turquoise dress hinted at voluptuous curves underneath, and long strings of beads and amulets hung down her front.

'Sorry to intrude,' Lockyer said. 'The door was open, and—'

'Oh, there are no intruders at Old Hat Farm,' the woman said, still smiling. 'Only friends we haven't met yet.' The smile widened. 'To borrow a well-worn phrase. Hello.' She took Broad's hand first, clasping it warmly. 'I'm Trish. You don't need those masks here – the fresh air protects us.'

'Detective Constable Gemma Broad,' Broad said, leaving her mask on.

Trish's smile shrank slightly.

'And I'm Detective Inspector Lockyer.' He flipped open his ID.

'You're the police,' Trish said, not offering Lockyer her hand.

'Yes. Sorry about that,' he said.

Trish waved away the apology. 'No, I'm sorry. I was just . . . looking forward to having some new faces around the place. It's been so quiet, what with everything going on.' A pause. 'Well, do sit. Something to drink?'

'No, thank you,' Broad said. 'Best not.'

'Are you sure? My nettle kefir is delicious.' She glanced from Broad to Lockyer, then chuckled. 'Your *faces*!'

They sat down at the long table. Trish dumped her basket by the sink before joining them.

'We were hoping to speak to you about a case we're investigating, which we believe could be linked to the death of Holly Gilbert,' Lockyer said.

Trish took a sharp, involuntary breath. 'You're here about *Holly*?'

'Not exactly. We're actually looking into the death of a

man named Lee Geary. We understand he was a friend of Holly's.'

'Lee Geary? But an officer came to ask about him back in the spring. We couldn't tell him anything.'

'We've taken over the investigation,' Broad said. 'If you wouldn't mind answering a few questions?'

'No, of course I don't mind. I'm just a bit surprised.'

'When did you last see Mr Geary?'

'I don't know exactly. He was here the night . . . Holly's last night. But so were a lot of people. I don't remember seeing him after that.'

'You were Holly's stepmother, is that right?' Broad said.

'I suppose so, but that sort of thing hardly matters when you meet as adults. Holly was Vince's girl – my husband's daughter – but she grew up with her mother. Vince and her mum . . . it was just a fling, really. Vince had no idea Holly even existed until she turned up here. She'd only just lost her mother, and found out about him.' Trish shook her head sadly. 'Poor kid. She was all at sixes and sevens.'

'So she moved in here with you? When was that?' Broad said.

'New Year's Day. That same year she . . . left us again.'

'2011?'

'If you say so. We don't go in for calendars much. Once you learn to pay attention, the earth and sky tell you everything you need to know.'

'That must have been quite an adjustment for you both. A daughter you didn't know existed turning up on your doorstep?' Broad said.

Trish gave her a complicated look – a compound of amuse-
ment and pity. 'Not at all. I'm sure you saw the sign as you
came in. Travellers are welcome here.'

'You mean this is a guesthouse? Like a farm stay?'

'In a way, but probably not the way you mean. Anyone
can come and be here for a while. Old Hat Farm is a very
special place. It has a special energy. People come when they
need to heal. Some stay a day or two, some stay for years.
We never turn anyone away.'

'And people pay you for a room?'

'No money changes hands here. People give back in
whichever way they can, by helping on the farm, say, or
with repairs or housework. Some people give back simply
by letting us see their beautiful souls. But we don't charge
and we don't advertise. We're not a business.'

'So, it's a commune?'

'It's a place where people can come, and be welcome.
It might help you not to try to label everything so rigidly,
Gemma.'

Broad flushed at the use of her first name.

'How do people know about you?'

Trish shrugged. 'They just come.'

'I see.' Broad glanced uncertainly at Lockyer.

'So, you took Holly in,' he said.

'Of course. Happily.'

'She was studying down in Bournemouth at the time,
wasn't she? In her third year. That's quite a distance for her
to travel back and forth.'

'Well, she didn't go back much, once she got here. Two

or three times, was all. She was thinking about taking some time out from it, asking to repeat her final year. The poor thing was so upset about her mum there was no way she could focus on studying. Besides, once she got here she started to see that there are more roads to travel than the one she'd been put on.' Trish sighed. 'If only she'd known Vince from when she was little, she wouldn't have been so lost when her mum died. He had so little time to learn how to be her father. Well. What's done is done.'

'That's very true,' Lockyer said. 'So, what did Holly do here?'

'Whatever she liked. She'd been brought up in a town, though, and wasn't used to getting her hands dirty. It wasn't her fault. You should've seen her face the first time she pulled a warm egg out from under a chicken! Like she'd never *dreamt* of such a thing!' The memory raised a smile. 'I tried to encourage her to express herself, and find a way to let go of her grief. No one here was going to judge her. But from what I could tell, her upbringing had been all about keeping up appearances. It's hard to unlearn things like that. I think she'd have got there in the end, if—'

Trish cut herself off.

'If she hadn't taken her own life?' Lockyer said. 'Did you attend the inquest into Holly's death?'

'No. Vince did, and our Jase. But I – I've never been able to handle things like that. Places like that. And I didn't see what good it would do, me going.'

'Jason is your son?'

'That's right.'

Lockyer watched her closely. 'You know, of course, that

Lee Geary was one of the three people arrested and questioned in relation to Holly's death.'

'Yes.' She looked away, across the room. 'The giant.'

Lockyer and Broad exchanged a glance.

'Did he ever stay with you?' Lockyer asked.

'I don't think so. He only ever came here with Ridgeway.'

'That would be Ridgeway Kingsley-Jones?' Lockyer said. 'You knew him?'

'Yes.' Trish looked uneasy. 'Ridgeway was a troubled young man. He used to spend the school holidays with us, when he was fifteen or sixteen. Then he went on the road. We tried, but . . . he had a darkness in him. The things he'd been through . . .'

'What did his parents think about him coming here?' Lockyer asked.

'I've no idea, Inspector.' Trish put a faintly derisive emphasis on his rank, as though marking him as the minion of a regime that had no authority over her. 'But Lee . . . I don't think he ever stayed, other than kipping the odd night in one of the barns. He came because Ridgeway brought him, rather than in search of anything.'

'Did Holly make friends with the two men? With Lee and Ridgeway?'

'I'm afraid I don't know. Holly had a very . . . magnetic aura. She didn't like being by herself, and she was very pretty, of course. I'm sure she met the boys – she met everyone who came and went, that half-year she was with us. But I don't know that they got especially close or anything like that.'

'Would she have confided in you?' Broad asked.

'Possibly not. She did tell me she'd had a boyfriend at uni, but they'd split up when her mother died. I said that if the relationship had fallen apart the first time it was truly tested, it probably wasn't meant to be. But she was cut up about it.'

'Can you tell me his name?' Lockyer said.

'God, now you're asking . . . Rob something? Look on her Facebook page – he'll have posted on there for sure.'

'Thank you. We will.' Lockyer said. 'Unusual name, isn't it? Ridgeway?'

'It's a good old English name. Anglo-Saxon,' Trish said. 'Names have power, I've always thought. Ridgeway suited his name. He was restless, always going somewhere, even if the path led to high places.'

'What do you mean by that?' Lockyer said.

Trish didn't answer.

'Do you think he was in trouble?'

'I think he *was* trouble. He wasn't a bad person – I don't believe anyone is, deep down. It's all just defensive layers. But some people are dangerous for others to be around. The combination of a personality like Ridgeway's with gentler, more malleable ones . . .'

'There are indications that Ridgeway was involved in drug-dealing at the time of his death.'

'I don't know anything about that,' Trish said evenly.

'Do you think he was likely to take his own life?'

'No. But, then, Ridgeway had things he kept to himself. That anger of his. Anger can mask a lot of other things.'

'It can,' Lockyer agreed. 'Do you believe Ridgeway or Lee was involved in Holly's death?'

'Involved? No. I mean, they were the last people to see her alive, but . . .'

'But you're not in any doubt that Holly took her own life?'

Trish didn't answer at once, but was firm when she did. 'No. I'm not in any doubt. Vince . . . Vince had questions. But he felt the loss more, of course. To me it just seemed like she was carrying an awful lot around inside her and, in the end, it broke her.'

'Do you mind telling me how you make a living here?' Lockyer asked. 'Are you actually farming?'

Trish smiled enigmatically. 'Yes, in a way. We live off the land.'

'You're self-sufficient?'

'As much as we can be. We only have forty-three acres so we grow a few specialized things. Vince and Jase sell their woodwork, and there's the honey, too. And the farm shop up the road is interested in stocking my kefir. We're hand-to-mouth, but our mouths are never empty.'

'Can you think of anything else in regard to Lee Geary's death? Anything you saw, or heard, around that time?'

She shook her head. 'Like I said to the other officer, Lee wasn't one of ours, not really. A pity, though. Anyone could see his heart was as big as his feet.'

'Would you be able to give us a list of everyone who was staying here at the same time as Holly?' Lockyer asked.

Trish's face fell. 'No. Sorry. I can't.'

'Or you won't?'

She was unabashed. 'Both. We had so many people here, that year. Especially around the solstice, when Holly . . . left us. We held a gathering of thanks and rebirth, to welcome the sun. I could give you some names, but they wouldn't be any use to you.'

'It might be better if we decide that.'

'I said I could, not that I would,' she said, without rancour. 'That's not what this place is about. We welcome, we heal, and we don't judge. And we definitely don't give out names to the police. No offence.' She stood, signalling that their time was up.

'You said your husband and your son went to Holly's inquest,' Lockyer said.

'Yes, that's right.'

'We'd like to speak to them, too.'

Trish took her time. Lockyer was getting the impression that she was the gatekeeper of Old Hat Farm. In spite of her serenity, and her genuine warmth, he suspected not much went on there that she didn't know about.

'I wish you wouldn't,' she said eventually. 'It really upsets Vince to talk about Holly. But if you must, he's with the bees.' She looked amused again. 'I hope neither of you is allergic to being stung. The heat makes them tetchy. Go out through the yard that way. You'll see the hives.'

'Thank you, Mrs McNeil,' Lockyer said.

'Trish, please.'

*

Back out in the punishing sunshine, Broad turned to Lockyer with a sceptical expression. 'What did you make of all that?' she said.

'I'm not sure. She clearly knew Ridgeway well. Maybe she knew Lee better than she's letting on.'

'"The giant", she called him.'

'Well, I expect Lee's size is what most people remember about him.'

'Yeah, but the way she said it . . .'

'Don't get too carried away with your ritual theory, Gem. The countryside isn't all like *The Wicker Man*.'

'She seemed pretty far-out to me, guv. And can they really be living off the land? I mean, *only* that? How do people like that buy a place like this in the first place? You'd have to sell a shedload of nettle kefir.'

'Maybe it was in one of their families from way back,' Lockyer said. 'Maybe they have past lives as stockbrokers. Who knows? It *is* possible to live off the land, even in this day and age.'

'Well, if you say so,' Broad said. 'Next time we go to the pub, though, I'm going to try paying by letting the barman see my beautiful soul.'

Lockyer smiled. 'I'd be very careful who you make offers like that to, Gem.'

She looked away, abashed.

'Quite a strong Stevie Nicks vibe, didn't you think?' he said. 'I bet she was a fan.'

'Who's Stevie Nicks?'

Lockyer glanced at Broad to see if she was joking. She wasn't.

'Never mind. I did notice something, though. She didn't ask how Lee died. Or where. Or when. She didn't ask *anything.*'

Broad thought about it. 'Maybe whoever came out from the MCIT told her?'

'Maybe. Let's check that.'

They walked past a small flint barn with open gable ends, an old machine shed very like the one at Westdene Farm. Big bunches of herbs hung drying from the rafters. Built onto it was a timber lean-to with a metal roof. The door was padlocked.

Lockyer pointed it out. 'I thought there was no such thing as intruders here?'

'That's all well and good until someone nicks your lawnmower.' Broad's expression turned diffident. 'Lockyer's another Anglo-Saxon name. Did you know?' she said. 'It means "locksmith". I went through an ancestry phase a while back.'

'So much for nominative determinism, then.'

'No. I don't believe in it either.'

Lockyer was careful not to react. Broad was five foot two at best, and sturdily built. She was also very fit, but nicknames were rife in the police. She was sometimes called Laptop. Cursed with an easy blush reflex, she always reddened when she heard it. Lockyer knew better than to say anything about it. There was a fine line between banter and bullying. So far, he didn't think it had been crossed. His own nickname was Farmer Giles, which sounded innocent enough until you discovered it was Cockney rhyming slang for 'piles'. A pain in the arse.

They walked past the polytunnels, in which rows of fruit and salad crops were sweltering, then across a stretch of ground covered with scrubby wildflowers. One plant in particular seemed to dominate – some kind of woody herb, covered with purple-blue flowers. It was everywhere, and Lockyer recognized it as part of the complex smell in the kitchen. The whole meadow was alive with bees.

A man was crouching by the hives, holding an earthenware jug. He wasn't wearing any kind of protective suit or visor, just combat trousers cut off at the knees, a faded T-shirt, and what looked like home-made leather flip-flops. Lockyer noticed shallow dishes of water on the ground here and there.

'Excuse me,' he said. 'Vincent McNeil?'

They showed their ID when Vince looked round. A ladder of deep wrinkles climbed his forehead. He had aquamarine eyes, startling in his tanned face, and several days of salt-and-pepper stubble. Lockyer could read nothing in the look he gave them. It was neither measuring, nor friendly, nor hostile.

'Could we talk to you for a moment, please?' Lockyer said.

Vince stood up very slowly and came towards them.

'Let's move away,' he said, his voice a bass rumble. 'The heat stresses the bees. They're angry.'

'Shouldn't you have a suit on, or something?' Broad said.

'They know me,' he said.

A bee landed on Broad's arm and she flinched, preparing to swat at it.

'Don't,' Vince said softly. 'Just keep still.'

Broad peered nervously at the bee, which had its back end in the air and was vibrating its wings. 'What's it doing?'

Vince bent closer. 'Fanning. They'll all be at it inside the hives, trying to keep the queen and the young cool. They've been gathering water all day. I was just topping up the dishes. Not fun for them, this heat.'

'How long is it likely to . . . stay?' Broad said.

'He's just confused,' Vince said. 'Any second now he'll realise he's not where he's supposed— There.'

The bee took off. Broad looked relieved.

Vince was a tall, well-built man. Strong hands with scarred knuckles. He walked them back to the entrance of one of the polytunnels. 'What's this about?' he said.

'We're investigating the death of a man named Lee Geary.'

'Again?' Vince's face gave nothing away.

'Yes. He was questioned in relation to your daughter's death.'

The quality of Vince's silence changed. It was the silence of a held breath, of something not being said. 'I'm aware of that,' he said, in the end. 'But anyone who knew Lee knew he wasn't responsible. He was just a child, in a lot of ways. How did he die?'

'That's what we're trying to establish.'

'Well, I'm afraid I can't help. Like we told the other two, we hadn't seen him here for a long time. Not since Holly—' He broke off.

'Lee never came back here, after Holly died?' Broad asked.

'None of those three did.'

'You mean Lee, Ridgeway Kingsley-Jones and Stefanie Gould? Would they have been welcome?'

'Everyone's welcome.' A trace of irony. 'But perhaps they'd have thought twice about it.'

'Why's that?' Lockyer said. 'They were cleared of any involvement in her death, after all.'

'The police failed to find any *evidence* of their involvement. That doesn't mean they weren't involved.'

'You think they were?' Silence. 'Did they have some reason to want to harm her?'

'No,' Vince said. 'Doesn't mean they didn't. Ridgeway was . . .' His eyes narrowed. 'Ridgeway always wanted more.'

'You mean he wanted more from Holly? More than she was prepared to give?'

Vince was silent again. 'I can't speak for what Ridgeway wanted,' he said eventually. 'I know Holly didn't feel that way about him. But she was . . . The last time anyone saw her, she was getting into his Land Rover with the other two.'

'When was that?'

'Late. The night of our solstice party.'

'You saw her get into the car with him?'

'No, but plenty of other people did. I'd seen her earlier, and she was fine. A bit drunk, but not out of control. She was full of smiles, having a great time. Then I'm expected to believe she found her way onto that bridge, when she'd never even been to Amesbury, and . . .' He bit back whatever he'd been about to say.

'We're sorry to have to ask you about something so painful,' Broad said.

'I only knew her for six months,' Vince said. 'But I knew her in my *bones*. She was my own flesh and blood. I hadn't realized what was missing until she came and found me.' He looked away. 'Why are you asking about Holly? How can Lee Geary dying have anything to do with what happened to her?'

Lockyer took a risk. 'Mr Geary's body was found not far from here. A mile or so out on the plain. Do you have any idea what he might have been doing in the area?'

'No.'

'Did he come here at all?'

'I already said, no. Not since that night.'

'All right. Well, if you think of anything that might be useful, even if it doesn't seem relevant, please call us. We asked your wife for a list of people who were here at the same time as Holly—'

'She won't give you one.'

'No.'

'Neither will I. Not that I could – a lot of people come and go, and most only ever give a first name. That's how we like it. Anyway, how could a nine-year-old list be any use to you?'

'We think Mr Geary died that same summer. Not long after Holly. Just like Ridgeway and Stefanie.'

Vince took this in. 'Ridgeway was mixed up with the wrong sort of people,' he said. 'He probably got Lee mixed up with them, too. Maybe Lee was on his way here – or trying to find us again. Maybe he needed a place to stay.'

'How did you hear about Ridgeway's death?'

Vince left it a moment too long. 'Grapevine,' he said. 'People bring us news.'

'And it's just you, your wife and your son here, at the moment?'

'No, Melody and Pascal, too. Backpackers.'

'Could we speak to them?'

'I can't stop you, but there's no point. They're Australian, only came to the UK last year, and they'd have been at primary school the last time Lee was here. In any case, they're not here right now. Jase has taken them to Devizes.'

'We'd like to speak to your son, too. Perhaps you could ask him to give us a call.'

'Jason doesn't have a phone. None of us do.'

'We'll come back another time, then,' Lockyer said. 'When might be good?'

'There's no schedule here,' Vince said, 'but Jase doesn't leave the farm very often. He's in the workshop most days.'

'Did he get on well with Holly?' Broad asked. 'It must have been a big adjustment for him, suddenly finding out he had a sister.'

Another of Vince's inscrutable silences followed. He studied Broad for so long that she shifted uncomfortably, squinting up at him against the sun's glare.

'Jason loved Holly,' he said eventually, then turned to head back towards the beehives.

As they drove away Lockyer thought of the ribbons trailing from the holm oak, and the scrap of yellow ribbon in the hawthorn where Lee was buried. *Very folkloric.* Saying nothing to Broad, he wondered if there could have been something ritualistic about his murder. *The giant*, Trish had called him. To Lockyer, his death still smacked of vengeance, but the style of it . . . From what he'd just seen, the style of it was very Old Hat Farm.

5

Day 4, Thursday

Detective Superintendent Christine Considine looked at Lockyer over the top of her steepled fingers. It was an expression he knew well. It was the one she got when she was deciding whether or not to give an inch.

'A full forensic examination of the remains will cost a fortune, Matt,' she said.

'This is a murder investigation, ma'am. I'd say it was justified.'

'Are we completely sure it's murder?'

'I thought you put me on this case because you knew it was,' Lockyer said. 'And because there are strong links to Holly Gilbert, and the deaths of the other two suspects in that case.'

'Not knew, suspected,' she demurred. 'I agreed to put you on the case to prove it one way or the other. We all want closure on the Gilbert case – you know how convinced Salisbury were that there was foul play.'

'I'm not going to be able to prove it if I can't look for evidence.'

'What do you make of it so far?'

Lockyer chose his words carefully. 'I'm as sure as I can be at this stage that Lee Geary wouldn't have gone out onto the plain on his own for no good reason. He had a learning disability, and he was a townie. Somebody either took him there, chased him there, or he was trying to get to Old Hat Farm again.'

'Why would he do that?'

'I don't know yet. Vince McNeil suggested he might have been looking for a safe place to stay, if he was running away from something going on in Salisbury. Lee was anxious the day he disappeared, and the last thing he said to his sister was that he needed to tell someone something.'

'That doesn't explain why he went out onto the plain. The farm's not that hard to find, is it?'

'For somebody like Lee, yes, quite possibly. He didn't have a smartphone, and you can't see it from the road.'

'So you think he wanted to speak to someone at Old Hat Farm? Got lost? Didn't make it?'

'Or he did,' Lockyer said.

'And somebody didn't like what he had to say?'

'Vince McNeil doesn't believe that Holly killed herself. He clearly blames Ridgeway, and maybe the others by extension.'

'He'd hardly tell you that if he'd gone on a killing spree to avenge her. A killing spree there's no real evidence of yet.'

'Perhaps he thought we'd find out anyway, if he's never

made a secret of it. And the pathologist believes Lee *was* actually buried all these years.'

'She's not prepared to stand up and say that in court, though.'

'Lee's death wasn't accidental. I'm sure of it. Even though everyone we've spoken to agrees he couldn't be held responsible for what happened to Holly.'

As he said it, Lockyer remembered something else Karen had said about her brother: *He always looked to other people to tell him what to do.* Did that mean Lee would do *whatever* he was told? Even if it meant violence – however much he'd hated it? Lockyer couldn't decide, just then, what that possibility said about his guilt or innocence.

Considine raised her eyebrows. She had a piercing gaze. They'd worked together for a long time, and Lockyer trusted her, but these days she was hamstrung by the need to make their ever-decreasing resources stretch as far as possible without snapping.

'Well,' she said, 'I expect the finer points of criminal responsibility go out of the window when your daughter – or anyone you love – has been killed so horribly. What are they? *Good-Lifers*? Actual farmers?'

'Not quite. Very ... New Age-y, I suppose. Mother Earth will provide, et cetera. And protect them from Covid, apparently.'

'Oh, really?' Considine snorted. 'Well, we can't police people's beliefs. More's the pity.'

Lockyer had checked the MCIT file as soon as they'd got back from the farm: details of the manner and location of

Lee's death *had* been discussed with Trish McNeil back in the spring. It allayed his suspicions about her not asking, but he still thought it odd that she apparently hadn't shared the information with her husband. Vince had seemed to assume that Lee had died recently.

'Trish McNeil was friendly enough,' he said. 'Vince was . . . not cagey, but distant. *Very* self-controlled. Both of them were unfazed by our questions, and adamant that they hadn't set eyes on Lee since the night Holly died. But I definitely got the impression they knew – or at least thought – plenty more than they were saying. I can go back and talk to the son, Jason, as well. But . . .' Lockyer spread his hands.

'You need forensics.'

'If we can prove Lee *did* go to Old Hat Farm around the time he died, we can prove they're hiding something.'

'And if what they're hiding are a few lockdown raves and a bit of marijuana?'

'Old Hat Farm has an oak tree full of ribbons and tokens. I found a scrap of ribbon in the hawthorn tree where Lee was buried.'

Considine maintained her steady scrutiny.

'If we can't get anything from Lee's body, it'll be hard to prove what happened to him,' Lockyer said. 'Right now I expect the coroner would return an open verdict, same as with Ridgeway. But someone might have helped Ridgeway off that roof, and dragged Stef into the water, and that same someone might have coaxed Lee out onto the plain. If we don't look closely enough . . .'

'All right,' Considine said at last. 'Full forensic analysis of what's left of him. But if that doesn't make the picture any clearer, I won't be throwing good money after bad.'

Lockyer got up to go. 'We might need a warrant to take comparative samples from Old Hat Farm.'

'I'll sort that.' Considine cleared her throat. 'How's your mother? Coming home soon?'

Lockyer turned. 'Uh . . . no, ma'am. Doesn't look like it.'

A flicker of sympathy in her eyes. 'I'm sorry to hear that, Matt. If you need some time—'

'No. Thank you, ma'am.'

Broad looked up hopefully when Lockyer returned to their airless little office.

'Full forensic on Lee,' he said.

'Brilliant, guv,' she said, with a wide smile. 'Just before you get on the phone, I found Holly's ex-boyfriend on Face-book. His name's Robert Heywood.'

She turned her screen for Lockyer to see.

Holly's profile page had been memorialized; it had remained live as a place for people to leave messages, and look through photos of her. *In memory of Holly Gilbert*. There was a long string of messages on her wall, the most recent only a month old. Most featured emojis of broken hearts, flowers and tears. How anyone could hope to express a genuine emotion like that, Lockyer had no idea.

'Hang on a tick.' Broad clicked a few times, bringing up the original picture that Holly had cropped for her profile image – the same one the local press had got hold of when she died. The grey sleeve around her shoulders belonged to a sulky-looking lad with bloodshot eyes and his blond hair combed forwards. 'That's him,' she said.

'Did he write anything on there after Holly died?'

'Just this. "Cant believe ur gone. Miss u Golightly x".'

'Effusive.'

'Well, they *had* broken up, before she even went to Old Hat Farm. This is his page now, all babies and weddings.'

'Bang on time. They'll be hitting thirty about now. See if you can find a phone number. I want to know if he's got anything interesting to say about Holly's state of mind, and the "out of character" behaviour mentioned at the inquest.'

'I've already put in a request for a transcript of the inquest.'

'Good.'

'One other thing, guv,' Broad said, as he turned away. 'This most recent message on Holly's wall, it was posted on the twentieth of June, the anniversary of her death. This year. And there's been one every year. They're from a girl called Nina Thorowgood. This is her.'

Broad clicked on the profile. Nina had long pink dreadlocks, and piercings in her lip, septum, tongue, and the bridge of her nose. She was gurning at the camera, but it couldn't hide her lustrous olive skin and delicate bone structure.

'She's not friends with any of the Bournemouth Uni lot,' Broad said.

'What's she written?'

'Some fairly generic stuff about spirituality and fighting the powers-that-be. Her page is all cannabis leaves and links to various parties and festivals. But look at the first message she posted on Holly's wall, that summer of 2011. "They stole from you and then they stole YOU from US. Fuck all liars and thieves. Fly free, magic heart."'

Lockyer read it twice. 'Sounds to me like Nina had something she wanted to say.'

'Looks the kind of girl who'd fit right in at Old Hat Farm, don't you reckon?'

'See if you can find her, Gem, and we'll ask.'

'Will do, guv. Someone I haven't been able to find is Jason McNeil, Vince and Trish's son.'

'No record?'

'No. But he's not just not on our database, he's not on *any* database. Electoral register, DVLA, social media, he's nowhere. Doesn't exist.'

Lockyer sat down and leant back in his chair. 'That's interesting, don't you think?' he said.

In the canteen, Detective Inspector Steve Saunders paused with a fish-finger sandwich halfway to his mouth, his face registering shock at seeing Lockyer standing there.

More than ever, since lockdown, they'd pursued an unofficial policy of avoiding each other as much as possible. Prior to that, Saunders had taken every opportunity to pick holes in Lockyer – and, by extension, Broad. He'd shouted the loudest for Lockyer to face a disciplinary after the arson case involving his friend Kevin. When that hadn't happened, he'd made it his mission not to let anyone forget about it. Least of all Lockyer. But then Lockyer and Broad had caught the real killer in the Ferris case, and got Hedy Lambert out of jail. That had seemed to go some way towards mollifying Saunders. Or perhaps he'd just read the room and realized that the general attitude towards Lockyer had thawed.

'Farmer Giles,' he said, taking a big bite of the sandwich and talking around it. 'Do you mind? I'm eating.'

'No, I don't mind,' Lockyer said, deliberately misinterpreting him.

Saunders grunted. He was a big man, square-set and sandy-haired. His face rested naturally into an expression of cynical contempt for the world, but from working with him on the MCIT before the falling-out, Lockyer knew that behind it all he was a good detective, and straight as a die.

'Spit it out then,' Saunders said.

'I wondered if you'd be willing to talk through the Holly Gilbert case. At a time to suit you.'

Saunders put down his sandwich and wiped his fingers. 'Yeah, I heard you'd been put on Lee Geary's skelly. Sounded to me like it should've been a live case, not handed over to you and the Laptop.'

'Lee was buried about a mile from Old Hat Farm. Where Holly Gilbert lived.'

'I know,' Steve said.

Lockyer sighed inwardly. 'You interviewed Lee, and the other two.'

'Yeah, I did. I also heard the MCIT wasn't completely convinced Geary was murdered.'

'No, but I am.'

Suspicion narrowed Steve's eyes. 'You trying to say we missed something back then?'

'No. The picture's . . . unclear. But if Lee and the others were killed in revenge for Holly, I need to know what happened to her. I need to know if they *were* to blame. So it would be useful to pick your brains about the original case.'

'Why should I help you? You're not a team player – you've made that abundantly clear.'

'Must be a hell of an effort lugging this grudge around with you, Steve.'

Saunders shook his head. 'Easy as pie. I don't like bent coppers.'

'But you do like a solid clear-up,' Lockyer snapped. 'I've read the file. You were the one pushing hardest for Ridgeway and Stef's deaths to be linked to Holly's, even when it was NFA'd after the inquest. And I think you were right.'

Saunders considered it. 'All right. I'll pop up for a chat.'

'Thank y—'

'If you'll admit – just between us, here and now – that you fudged the evidence for your mate in that pub fire.'

Lockyer held his gaze. 'I might not be a team player, Steve, but I'm not bent. And I'm not an idiot.'

With that he gave up, and walked away.

Until the forensics came back on Lee all they could do was accumulate as much information as possible on the people linked to Holly, dead and alive. Robert Heywood, Holly's ex-boyfriend, was easy enough to find: he had accounts on every social media platform.

Since the outbreak of the pandemic the police had been encouraged to interview by phone wherever possible. Lockyer didn't like it. He preferred to see people's reactions to his questions, and to being approached by the police in the first place; those tiny changes in expression and posture that could speak so loudly. But phoning did save a lot of time, and with someone like Rob, who was not in any way a suspect, he supposed it did no harm.

'Holly went nuts after her mum died,' Rob told him. 'I mean, I know she was sad. Anyone would be. But she turned it all on me, you know? Nothing I did was good enough any more. She didn't want to go out, didn't want to stay in – didn't want to do anything. And I couldn't say anything right – like it was all my fault.'

'Do you remember when you last saw her?' Lockyer asked neutrally.

'When she dumped me. End of term, a couple of weeks before Christmas.'

'And her mother had been dead for how long, by then?'

'A month, I guess. Something like that.'

A month. The grief would have been fresh, still barely understood, let alone processed. And her boyfriend had expected her to be getting over it.

Rob cleared his throat. 'Look, all right, I was a bit of a dick back then,' he said. 'But I was twenty-one. I just wanted to get pissed and be *cool*. I had no idea what she must've been going through, or how to help.'

Lockyer thawed fractionally. 'And you didn't see her during the Christmas holidays at all?'

'No. I don't even know where she spent that Christmas. She didn't have any other family, so maybe a friend's place. I – I hope she didn't just go home and sit in an empty house.'

Rob was quiet for a moment, as the very real possibility of that sank in. Lockyer heard the dawning realization of just how badly he'd behaved.

'Then after that she hardly seemed to be around at all. I didn't get in touch with her. I never even asked her how she was doing. But I thought I was winning the break-up, you know? Keeping my distance.' He took a breath. 'I should've called her.'

'How long were you together?'

'About a year. Holly was great,' he said. 'What's this all about, anyway? She – she jumped off that bridge, right? It messed her up, her mum dying like that. Her dad was killed in a motorway pile-up when she was little, so she'd already had that to deal with. She and her mum were really close.'

Lockyer wondered when and how Holly had found out about Vince being her biological father, and how she'd then located him. One thing becoming abundantly clear was that Holly had needed a new circle. She'd needed a new family. Perhaps desperately.

Dr Lorne rang him at half past five to talk about Trudy's test results. 'I'm afraid we *are* looking at Guillain-Barré, as I discussed with you yesterday,' she said.

A fist clenched in the pit of Lockyer's stomach. 'When will you start treatment?'

'We've already started. I think it might be better if you

and your father didn't come in for the next few days. Trudy's very fatigued.'

'Have you asked her whether she wants us to come in?'

'No, but it's about optimizing her chances of recovery, Mr Lockyer. And reducing the risk of any new infections.'

'But she doesn't like being by herself.' And must be frightened, he thought but did not say. Anyone would be, as they slowly lost the use of their body. It was an unbearable thought. Karen's comment about Lee echoed in his head: *I hope they didn't frighten him.*

'Well,' Dr Lorne sounded irritated, 'I can only give my recommendation, as her physician.'

Lockyer went straight to Westdene after work, determined to speak to his father about it. The house was empty. He pulled off his tie, dumped his jacket on the newel post and went upstairs to his brother's room. He knocked – which felt odd – and put his head around the door. There was Chris's bed, messy and unmade. There was his bedside table, usually empty but now sporting a dog-eared book, reading glasses, and a travel clock.

It was profoundly strange for the room to have a new incumbent. They'd cleared it of all Chris's personal things a long time ago, but still, it would always be his room. Lockyer could still see him sprawled on the bed, face crammed into the pillow, in denial of it being morning. *I'll pay you three trillion quid if you'll let me stay in bed.* He waited to feel outraged, but it didn't happen.

He was halfway down the stairs again when he saw Jody

at the bottom. The look on her face was of suspicion ready to tip into anger.

'Sorry,' he said. 'I was looking for you. Or Dad.'

'Did you find either of us in there?'

'No. Sorry. Look, I wasn't trying to pry, I promise. It's just . . . that's my brother's room. Used to be.'

'Yeah. I know.' She softened. 'Christopher, right?'

'Yes.'

'Got stabbed on a night out twenty-odd years ago.'

She said it like it was a snippet of news, just something she'd heard. None of the tentative sympathy people tended to use if they mentioned it. No anticipation – or assumption – of his feelings. It shocked him. But, again, the outrage he expected to feel didn't come. Just the ache of old grief, his constant companion.

He carried on down the stairs. 'That's right.'

'Must have been bloody awful for you all.'

'It was.'

'What kind of arsehole does a thing like that?'

'I've been trying to find out ever since.'

'No one was ever caught?'

'Not yet. It was a brawl. Chris just . . . got caught up in it.'

He heard the flat tone of his own voice, felt the tightening of his throat. The outrage. Even now.

'The police found the knife a few streets away, dumped in a bin. They raised a DNA profile from it, but there was no match in the system. Still isn't.'

'But you can keep looking?'

'Course. But there might never be a match.'

'Shit. That's the kind of thing that could drive you mental.'

'Yeah.'

'Well. Your dad just told me to take one of the empty rooms, so I did.' Jody gave him the swift appraisal he'd seen before. 'Want me to switch?'

'No, it's fine. It's probably a good thing.'

'Cool.'

She went through to the kitchen and Lockyer followed, again forced onto the back foot by her lack of deference as a guest. By how relaxed she was. The total absence of British awkwardness. It was quite impressive, and refreshing. There was a salty tideline of dried sweat on the back of her black vest. She took a big bottle of lemonade from the fridge and drank straight from it. Several huge gulps.

'God, that's better.' She wiped her mouth and stifled a burp. 'I'm basically a wasp. As long as you put in sugar and water, I'll keep buzzing.'

'Is my old man around?' Lockyer asked.

Jody took another gulp before putting the bottle back in the fridge. 'Yep. We've been worming the lambs. Jesus, though, they're a wriggly bunch. Except the two tame ones.'

'Yeah. Mum bottle-fed them.'

The two rejected lambs had lived in a cardboard box by the Rayburn all through March, making the whole kitchen smell of sheep. Trudy never gave them names, but she babied them all the same. The thought of it made Lockyer miss her intensely.

'We're just taking five,' Jody went on. 'You coming out to help?'

Lockyer was still in his suit, but it was an old shirt, and he could borrow any of the many generations of boots that cluttered the utility-room floor, since he and his father had the same-size feet. 'Can do,' he said, rolling up his sleeves.

The farm's fully weaned lambs had been rounded up and penned, and were being treated with a worming solution. John had the tank strapped to his back and the dosing gun in one hand. The sheep were funnelled single file into a narrow run. John dosed the front five, while Jody prevented them escaping backwards. Then she opened a gate at the front to let them back out into the field, and marshalled the next five in. Westdene's adult ewes knew the drill, and barely batted an eyelid, but the lambs weren't sure what was going on. There was a lot of bleating and scattering – they got panicky in the run, and tried to climb out.

Lockyer took over at the front gate, which was hardly strenuous but saved time. Surreptitiously, he watched Jody work. She was calm, and handled the sheep with no more force than was absolutely necessary, even when lambs escaped, trampled her feet or, in one instance, peed on her leg.

'Thanks for that, matey,' was all she said.

After a while Lockyer took the tank from his father, who was flagging. The first lamb he dosed got its tongue above the nozzle and spat it all out.

Jody grinned at him. 'Out of practice?'

'Maybe,' he said, embarrassed. In truth, it had been years since he'd done it. By the third lamb, he'd remembered the knack.

'You can take the boy out of the farm . . .' Jody said.

They got into a good rhythm, working in companionable silence.

Suddenly, the sun dipped below the hill and shadow swept over them. Lockyer blinked, his eyes struggling to adapt to the sudden loss of light.

'That's them, then,' John said, as the last lamb bolted from the pen. 'I'll stick the kettle on.'

Jody went over to the trough and splashed a few handfuls of water onto her urine-spattered leg. Then she took off her boot, swilled it out and emptied it onto the grass.

'Made your dad an Asian tuna salad for dinner last night,' she said, drying her hands on the seat of her shorts.

'Don't tell me he ate it?'

'Fresh chilli, sesame seeds, sprouted grains and all. What can I say? I outdid myself.'

'You really did,' Lockyer said. 'Now if you can just figure out a way to get him to talk to me, that'd be great.'

'I'm not a fucking magician.' She grinned. 'Besides, he does talk. Just not with words.'

Lockyer grunted. 'Some things need words.'

It should have been uncomfortable talking to a relative stranger about his dad, but perhaps because Jody was clearly a person who didn't do uncomfortable, he wasn't either. He hesitated, but realized how much he needed to talk to someone about it all.

'Has he spoken to Mum today, do you know?'

'No. I mean, I don't know.' She produced a packet of tobacco and rolled a cigarette. 'Want one?'

'No, thanks,' Lockyer said.

'Right. "Goody Two Shoes" – remember that song?'

'Except I *do* drink. And Adam Ant is a bit before your time, isn't he?'

'Nah. New wave, post-punk. It's a classic.'

'God, that's refreshing,' Lockyer said. 'If my DC was here, she'd ask if you used to play it on your gramophone.'

'Kids, eh?'

Jody took a long drag, and turned her head away to exhale. 'I know I should quit. But I'm down to five a day and you've got to die of something, right?'

Lockyer winced at that. 'Yeah.'

'What's with being a veggie, then? Seen too much of the business end of farming?'

'Something like that.'

'These animals of yours lead a pretty great life,' she said. 'Right up until they don't.'

'They're not mine. And, yes, they do. It's just personal preference.'

'You could go more ethical, on a farm this size. Go organic. Use a small, local abattoir, one that's taken every possible stress-minimizing measure. More and more people want to know their meat was produced with the minimum of horror, and in a way that isn't going to turn the planet into a fiery hell.'

'Come on,' Lockyer said. 'You've met my dad. He's old school. What you're talking about is the sort of thing my brother would have tackled.'

'Why not you?'

'I'm a police officer.'

'Right. Seen my record yet, have you?'

'Yes,' he admitted.

'Not bad enough to fire me on the spot, then?'

'As long as tobacco's the only thing you still smoke.'

'Really? Not even a tiny bit of weed?' She looked at him, all innocence, then chuckled. 'I'm kidding! Not on the premises, Scout's honour.'

'What was the fight about?'

'The ABH? Bloody ridiculous. Waste of everyone's time, charging me for that.'

'You broke the other woman's nose.'

'She had it coming.' Jody arched her eyebrows. 'So, are we good?'

'Yeah. We're good.'

'This place does have that whole end-of-an-era feel about it.'

'Thanks,' Lockyer said wryly.

'Don't get me wrong, I love it. But . . . I dunno.' She took a drag. 'I used to dream about getting my own farm. I spent a couple of years stalking places that were coming up for auction, and I'd see it all the time – farms in Wales and Devon and all over that had gone to rack and ruin. And always, in one of the rooms, there'd be an abandoned zimmer-frame in a corner, right? Like whoever had lived there had just kept on going as the place fell down around their ears, right up until the day they dropped.'

'That's depressing as hell.'

Lockyer thought of Bill Hickson, who'd lived in his cottage before him. And of Iris Musprat. And of himself, with no family once his parents had gone. Getting old, struggling, with no one to notice.

'Really?' Jody looked surprised. 'I've always loved it – that they just bloody well kept on keeping on. No surrender.' She finished her cigarette, stubbed it out and slipped the dog-end into her pocket. 'I guess when your mum's home things are bit livelier around here?'

'Not much, to be honest. But it has a pulse, at least.' Lockyer squinted up at the sky above the hill, where swallows were feasting on high-flying insects. 'But they won't leave,' he said. '*He* won't leave. I don't even think he's happy here any more. I don't think either of them has been happy since Chris died.'

'It's not just stubborn for stubborn's sake, though, is it? Like you just said, you're a police officer.' Jody nodded at the house. 'He's a farmer.'

'So what's going to happen if my mother can't farm any more? What's going to happen if she can't cope? They can't afford—'

'Oh, I get it,' Jody interrupted. 'You're a planner. You like to feel in control.'

'I just . . . I don't see how—'

'Of course you don't. Don't suppose your folks do, either. You're just going to have to wait and see. Keep on keeping on.'

'You're not a planner.'

'Hell, no.' Jody looked away. 'I used to be, but every last

plan I ever made went to shit. So I stopped. Things got a lot easier after that. I recommend it.'

Lockyer shook his head. 'Anarchy.'

Jody laughed. She stood up from the wall and stretched her arms behind her back.

'Well, I'm looking forward to washing the sheep piss off me. Not to mention sinking a pint. Staying for dinner? It's bangers and mash. Or fried eggs, in your case.'

'No, thanks. But I'll come in. I need to at least try and talk to Dad about what the doctor said.'

When Lockyer got home, after a stilted, unproductive talk with his father, he walked back out into the woods. Midges dithered in the twilight beneath the trees. Lockyer stood beside the grave he'd uncovered that morning. The bones belonged to Róisín Conlan, who'd died in 1964, in the attic of the house where he now lived. Lockyer hadn't fact-checked anything Mrs Musprat had told him yet. Nothing that would flag in a search history. But the problem was impossible to ignore, and he really had tried. He stared down at the broken ground, frustrated by his own indecision.

He'd never once seen Mrs Musprat go into the woods. When she was in the back garden she kept her eyes down, focused on her goat or her laundry, or whatever else she was doing. But he didn't suppose she'd forgotten about Róisín for a minute of the fifty-six years that had passed. Her confession had probably been brewing for decades, perhaps even from the very day it'd happened. Just waiting for Bill Hickson to die, and the opportunity to arise.

Again, she was waiting when Lockyer finally walked back. 'You found her,' she said.

It wasn't a question.

Lockyer gave a single nod, and for a second Mrs Musprat's face crumpled in dismay. As though she'd also been hoping it was a bad dream from years ago. She fiddled with a piece of paper, hands shaking. 'What are you going to do?' she asked.

'I don't know,' Lockyer said. 'I wish you hadn't told me.'

'Time she had a proper grave,' she murmured. 'Rosie was a Catholic. They set store by that kind of thing. I always knew that, but . . . We *couldn't* say! Bill would've hanged for murder, most likely, else died at the hands of that husband of hers.' She swallowed. 'I just never thought I'd be in the firing line. Can't you . . . keep my name out of it?'

'They're going to want to know how I found the body, Mrs Musprat.'

She was trembling. 'The ground spits stuff up,' she said hopefully. 'I've seen it on the news. Bodies lie there for years and years, and no one knows about it. Till they do.'

'Forensics will know if the bones have been deliberately dug up. And unless we tell them who it is, it's unlikely they'll ever make an identification after all this time. Róisín still wouldn't get a proper burial. Her family still won't find out what happened to her.'

She thought about this. 'You could investigate—'

'You mean pretend I don't know anything? Waste police time and resources making a show of finding out? You're talking about perverting the course of justice.'

'Justice?' she echoed. 'What's *justice*? Folk don't get jus-tice – that's how Rosie ended up dead! Weren't no *justice* about it.'

'I cannot reveal the location of that grave without bringing you in!'

'But I did nothing wrong!'

'Concealing a death, and preventing the lawful burial of a body are crimes! You must have known.'

'No! I only helped Bill to . . . And it was so long ago—'

'There's no statute of limitations on criminal offences in this country.'

'Then say nothing. Forget I ever told you.'

'I can't. I wish I could, believe me.'

She drew in a shaky breath. 'I can't go to jail. I *can't*! It'd be the death of me.'

He heard the raw terror in her voice. 'It might not come to that. Maybe just a fine, or a suspended sentence. Maybe nothing at all.'

'But can you say for sure?'

He couldn't. And the maximum sentence for what she'd done was life imprisonment.

'Please,' she whispered. 'I can't face it. Please don't tell.'

He hated to hear her supplication. 'What about her family?' he said. 'Her proper burial?'

Silence.

'Christ.' Lockyer ran one hand over his face. 'Look, I *have* to call it in. I'm a police officer. I've already put my job on the line by delaying.'

Mrs Musprat looked haunted. She handed him the piece

of paper, a black-and-white photograph. Lockyer couldn't make it out in the failing light.

'That's her, on the left,' she said. 'That's Rosie.'

She turned away, and went indoors.

In the dazzling light of his kitchen, Lockyer studied the picture. A row of four young women on a sunny day, their hair curled and pinned, their outfits tailored in at the waist. One was wearing white gloves, another had patent leather shoes. He wondered where they'd been going, all dolled up. The woman on the left had fair hair, and was taller than the others by a couple of inches. She was looking across at her friends and laughing, her chin lifted. It was a lovely smile. Lockyer looked at her sunlit face and noticed the bones underneath it. The skull he'd seen, clogged with earth.

He fixed the picture to the fridge, next to Hedy's postcard, and in that moment felt a wave of longing for her. He'd doubted Hedy for years. Doubted his own judgement around her, doubted everything she'd ever told him. He'd even been convinced, for a while, that she was a murderer. He'd been through hell with his feelings for her, and it had burnt away all the uncertainty. Now he trusted her more than he trusted himself, and wished he could talk to her about this. She saw things clearly, and she didn't dissemble. He took out his phone and stared at her name in his contacts, then put it down and went up for a shower.

The ground spits stuff up, eventually . . . Bodies lie there for years and years, and no one knows about it . . . Mrs Musprat was right about that. Like Lee Geary, in the secluded spot his killer had chosen. Turning to bones for almost a decade, his sister left in an agony of ignorance, just like Róisín Conlan's family. So many years. He could hardly imagine how difficult that must be. Far worse than the person responsible for harming a loved one escaping justice, and he knew full well that that was bad enough.

They stole from you and then they stole YOU from US. Did Nina Thorowgood also blame Ridgeway, Stef and Lee for what had happened to Holly? Had someone – or more than one person – done something about it? *Folk don't get justice.* More often than not, Iris was right about that, too.

6

Day 5, Friday

It took Lockyer and Broad a while to find their way onto
the bridge from which Holly Gilbert had fallen. It wasn't
a road bridge, or even a footbridge. It was – bizarrely – a
bridleway, a relic of a bygone era that began, more or less
invisibly, not far from the retail shed in Amesbury where
they'd parked the car. It then travelled out of town along
a residential alleyway, before branching northwards to the
bridge across the A303.

The bridleway linked Amesbury to a forgotten hamlet
called Ratfyn, then disappeared. You couldn't drive to
the bridge, and it wasn't signposted. Lockyer took Vince
McNeil's point straight away: it wasn't a place you were
likely to stumble across by accident. You'd need to know it
was there, and as far as anyone knew, Holly hadn't known
Amesbury at all.

They walked out to the centre of the bridge, with four
lanes of traffic thundering beneath their feet. There were

vertical metal railings either side, reaching to Lockyer's shoulder and Broad's eye-level, if she craned.

'Wouldn't be easy to climb over these,' Broad said. 'I guess that's the idea.'

'But not impossible, if you were determined.'

Lockyer looked along the road to where Holly's body had ended up. She'd fallen onto the front of a seven-and-a-half-tonne box lorry, travelling west at approximately sixty miles per hour. The collision investigation report concluded that Holly had been pinned between the cab and the container by the vehicle's forward momentum, and carried along for a hundred metres or so. The driver had understandably panicked, and jackknifed across the central reservation onto the eastbound carriageway. The lorry had come to a halt on the flat bridge across the River Avon, at which point Holly had been thrown clear. Mercifully, there hadn't been anyone coming east at that moment.

It had happened at a quarter to four in the morning. Holly's body hadn't been found until almost midday.

'There must have been traces on the lorry,' Broad said quietly. 'How come it took them so long to find her?'

'They didn't know to look. It was dark, still an hour before sunrise, even at that time of year. First response's priority was to close the road and get the driver to hospital. It was only when he regained consciousness that he said he thought he'd hit someone.'

'Poor bloke.'

'Yeah.'

'No cameras on the bridge, of course,' Broad said.

'No. Or covering this stretch of road. And this was before dash-cams were really a thing. Nobody saw her up here, and nobody saw her fall.'

They were quiet for a moment. A massive artic pummelled by beneath their feet.

'Come on,' Lockyer said. 'Let's see if we can get to where they found her.'

They crossed back to the town-side of the bridge, and found a series of footpaths at river-level. Following the most likely one, they passed beneath the A303. Exchanged a quick look when they hit a fence with a *Private Property* sign, and climbed over.

The river widened between banks of flowering grasses. Willow trees trailed their silvery leaves in the crystal clear water. It would have been idyllic, if it hadn't been for the vibrating roar of the road right behind them.

'I've driven along here loads of times and never noticed how pretty it is,' Broad said. 'It must have been gorgeous before the road was built.'

'There's been a road here more or less as long as there've been people,' Lockyer said. 'It's just ... mutated.' He consulted the diagram in the collision report and went to stand in the spot where Holly was found, then turned to look at the crash barrier of the road above. 'It was summer then, too,' he said. 'So all this long grass would have hidden the body.'

'But it wouldn't have made any difference to her, would it?' Broad said. 'Them not finding her right away?'

'Hopefully not.'

Lockyer looked down at the papers again, this time at Holly's post-mortem report. The injuries from the impact of the lorry had been catastrophic. The pathologist's findings all pointed to her having died if not on impact then within moments of it. And she'd certainly been alive when she went over the railings. What was less clear was whether or not she'd been conscious.

There was an anomaly: a head wound. The pathologist hadn't been able to say what had caused it, other than a hard impact with something flat, which could have been the ground. The skin had split to the bone and it would have bled profusely. The blow had also caused a bleed inside the skull, putting pressure on her brain. But there'd been a vital response around the wound – inflammation and bruising. That, and the size of the subdural clot, suggested that the injury had occurred at least two hours prior to Holly's death. The report suggested that, had she still been conscious, she would have been behaving erratically. Perhaps seeming groggy, and slurring her words, perhaps mistaken for being drunk.

Lockyer studied a picture of Holly's clothing, removed and bagged for evidence. Jeans; a blue sequined vest top; white Converse trainers. All covered with blood.

The head injury made it no more or less likely that Holly had deliberately killed herself. It might have caused her to lose her bearings, and engage in risky behaviour. It might also have made it more difficult for her to walk, and climb vertical railings. It might have killed her, eventually, if the lorry hadn't got there first.

'So the coroner was sufficiently convinced that she might have wandered off, found the bridge by chance and climbed over,' Lockyer said. 'Suicide, either premeditated or precipitated by confusion caused by drug use and the head injury.'

'But how did no one at the solstice party notice she'd hit her head?' Broad said. 'Even if she just tripped and fell, it would have bled all over the place.'

'Depends how much they'd all had to drink. Or what they'd taken. Plus, it might have happened *after* she'd left the party.'

'What time did she leave?' Broad asked.

'Not sure.' It would be in the transcript somewhere, but he didn't have it to hand.

'Why did it take them five days to bring in Ridgeway and the others?' Broad said.

'Holly had no ID on her when she died. Not even her phone. It was only when Vince reported her missing that the connection was made.'

'Did they ever find her phone?'

'It's not mentioned anywhere. But we need to go through everything more thoroughly. Pin down the details.'

'Because she wasn't likely to go off somewhere without it,' Broad pressed. 'People just don't – least of all people under thirty.'

'Depends. She might not have been thinking clearly. And if she *was* planning on killing herself . . . who knows?'

Broad squinted around at the romantic landscape, and Lockyer knew she was ready to leave. Being there clearly didn't have the same resonance for her as it did for him – he always liked to visit the scene, to get a feel not just for the place but for the crime. And, at a remove, for the people involved. He was already more convinced that Holly hadn't jumped. Or, if she had, that she hadn't been alone at the time. Could drugs and a head injury have made her do something as risky as try to balance along the railings? Had Holly been that kind of person – the type to take a dare? She'd been looking for a new life, new friends, a new family. He wondered just how hard she'd been trying to fit in.

'Have you got the satellite map there?' he asked.

Broad opened her phone and handed it to him. The bridleway didn't even lead directly to the cottages: it turned east and ran parallel to the dual carriageway for half a mile or so before joining the lane. The walk looked just long and boring enough for him to bet that the residents of Ratfyn took the car into town. He glanced at Broad, who was exuding patience.

'Let's get back,' he said, to her visible relief.

'Back to Old Hat Farm?' she said. 'And Jason McNeil?'

Lockyer knew she was itching to find him – a man with no online presence whatsoever. She was young enough to doubt the very existence of such a person. But Lockyer wanted a better grasp of the whole picture before they went back. He wanted to understand why Lee Geary and the others had been brought in for questioning about Holly's death, why they'd been released, and why a verdict of suicide had been reached. What might have convinced somebody otherwise.

'No, to Melksham nick. Let's dig out the interviews of our deceased threesome.'

The storage unit at Melksham Divisional HQ was considerably better organized than many in the county, so it didn't take long to locate the taped interviews of Ridgeway Kingsley-Jones, Lee Geary and Stefanie Gould. They bought lunch in the cafeteria before heading back to Devizes, where the only free media room was stuffy and smelt of sweaty socks.

Broad gave a sigh. Lockyer took pity on her. 'Take all the written reports somewhere cool and read right through them,' he said.

'You sure, guv?'

'Go on, Gem. We'll soon run out of air with both of us in here.'

'Okay. Thanks.'

Lockyer got as comfortable as he could in a squeaky swivel chair with a permanent arse-print. Everything they'd heard so far pointed to Ridgeway as the ringleader of the gang, and to Stef and Lee being the *known associates*. But he put Lee's tape into the machine first. It was his death they were investigating, and he was keen to see this gentle giant, who'd looked like such a brute but wouldn't have hurt a fly.

The picture flickered to life, and there he was. Lockyer felt the same peculiar pang as when he'd looked at the photograph of Róisín Conlan – the subtle shock of seeing in life a face he'd already seen in death. Hunched over, Lee still looked far too big for the chair, the table and the whole room. His legal brief was wedged between him and the wall, looking profoundly uncomfortable. The video was a little grainy but Lee's expression was clear enough. Hands clasped in his lap, he peered up from beneath his jutting brows with the eyes of a frightened child.

The interviewing officers introduced themselves. DI Brent, whom Lockyer had never met, and DS Steve Saunders, whom he very much had.

'You look nervous, Lee,' Brent said, after the preliminaries. 'Have you done something to be nervous about? Something you don't want to tell us about?'

Brent's arch, hectoring tone immediately put Lockyer on edge. Hadn't they known about Lee's learning disability? Shouldn't he have had an appropriate adult to sit with him? But then, Lee's low IQ had scraped over the official threshold. No concessions had been made for him; he'd been given no extra help.

'No,' Lee said, in a voice that boomed even though his tone was meek. 'I don't . . . I don't know.'

'You don't know?' Brent echoed.

Lee shook his head miserably.

'Let's start from the beginning, shall we?' Saunders said. 'We've brought you in today to talk about Holly Gilbert. Holly was last seen getting into a vehicle, belonging to Ridgeway Kingsley-Jones, at Old Hat Farm, on the night of the twentieth of June. Also seen getting into that vehicle were you, Ridgeway, and Stefanie Gould. Can you confirm that this is correct?'

'I don't know.'

'You don't know?'

'I . . . What day was that?'

'We're talking about the night of last Monday, going into the morning of Tuesday, June the twenty-first. It was the night of the party at Old Hat Farm for the summer solstice.'

'Yes.'

'Yes, you got into a car with Holly Gilbert, and the other two individuals?'

'No.'

'No?'

'It's a Land Rover. He doesn't like it if you call it a car.'

'Who doesn't?'

'Ridgeway. He says it isn't a car, it's a utility vehicle.'

DI Brent said, 'Are you trying to be funny, Mr Geary?'

Lee looked across the table at him, face creasing in thought. After a moment, he shook his massive head again.

Saunders pushed on: 'So, Holly was in the utility vehicle with you, and you left the farm together?'

'Yes.'

'Where did you go next?'

'I . . . I don't know.'

'You don't know.'

'Could I . . . please could I have something to eat?'

'No,' Brent snapped. 'What happened to Holly, Mr Geary?'

Lee sat in silence.

Saunders leant forwards. 'Mr Geary, are you aware that Holly Gilbert is dead?'

'What?' Lee's face crumpled again. A look of blank incomprehension, followed by a rush of renewed fear. 'Wh-what do you mean? Why is she dead?'

Lockyer watched the rest of the tape with one hand clamped tightly around his jaw. It ought to have been obvious, even if they'd had no background intel, that Lee was barely capable. Saunders was more patient than DI Brent, trying to pick his way around the huge holes in Lee's comprehension with very limited success. Unless Lee was a brilliant actor – which Lockyer seriously doubted – it was clearly news to him that harm had come to Holly. Nobody had bothered to tell him, and he obviously wasn't quick on the uptake.

Anger kindled in Lockyer's gut.

'What were you doing at the party, Lee?' Saunders asked. 'Were you selling drugs?'

'I was . . . There was a barbecue,' Lee replied. 'I had a jacket potato.'

Disgusted, Lockyer ejected the tape with more force than was necessary. They'd had to interview him, of course: he was one of the last people to see Holly alive. But allowances ought to have been made. A soft interview room, his sister present. *I hope they didn't frighten him.* But Lee had looked like a thug, so he'd been treated like one.

He watched Stefanie Gould's interview next. She slouched back in the chair with her arms folded, glowering at Brent and Saunders. A tight sweater had been scissored off above her navel. She wore it with skinny jeans and no bra, and sat with her knees wide apart, her body language a blatant challenge to the two men sitting opposite her, daring them to look at her. Days-old makeup was smudged around her eyes, and her hair was a wild, bleached mane.

Saunders and Brent put the same initial questions to her as they had to Lee, but where he'd been slow, Stefanie was quick. Too quick.

'Why are you asking me all this?' she snapped, then enunciated each word precisely, as though they must be stupid: 'I already told you, I don't know what happened to Holly. She got out of the Landy at the end of the track. She never even came to Amesbury with us.'

'Why would she do that?'

'How the fuck should I know? She was probably tripping and—'

'She'd taken drugs?'

'I don't know, Officer,' Stefanie said, again with that deliberately insolent enunciation. 'But she might've. And no, I hadn't taken anything and no, I wasn't selling anything, either. All I know is one minute Holly was coming along for the ride, the next she was kicking up a fuss and wanted to go back. Ridgeway hit the brakes and out she got. Back home to Daddy. End of.'

'What were you planning to do in Amesbury?' Saunders asked.

'Drive around, see some mates. I dunno.'

'Not visit Darren White, then?'

'Never heard of him.'

'Mr Kingsley-Jones's vehicle was captured on CCTV, parking outside Mr White's address in Amesbury, at two twenty-five on the morning of the twenty-first.'

'If you say so.'

'You and Ridgeway exited the vehicle and went inside.'

'Look, mate, I'd had one too many sherries, right? All I know is we went to see some mates of Ridgeway's. I've no clue who they were.'

'Mr White is a known drug-dealer. Was he supplying drugs for you and Ridgeway to sell?'

Stefanie raised her eyebrows nonchalantly. 'Doesn't sound very likely, Officer.'

'It's about ten miles from Old Hat Farm to Amesbury. A drive of around twenty minutes. Witnesses have reported seeing you leaving the farm, in Mr Kingsley-Jones's vehicle, with Holly Gilbert and Lee Geary, at approximately one thirty. What were you doing during the other forty minutes?'

'What forty minutes?'

'The unaccounted forty minutes between you leaving Old Hat Farm and the time the vehicle was seen parking outside Mr White's address.'

'No idea.' Stefanie sat forwards. The neckline of her sweater sagged perilously low. Lockyer suspected she knew, and didn't care. 'I wasn't driving, was I? I was just having a nice ride-along, listening to some music, thinking happy thoughts.'

'Do you know how Holly Gilbert came to be on a bridge crossing the A303 at a quarter to four that same morning?'

'Nope.'

'Were you with her on the bridge?'

'Nope.'

'Were Holly and Ridgeway an item?'

A short, sharp sigh. 'Nope. I think he might've shagged

her once or twice, but they weren't exactly exchanging rings. Holly wasn't his type.'

'What's his type?'

'Someone with an edge.' Stefanie sat back again, crossing one ankle over the opposite knee. 'I bet Holly still had teddy bears on her bed. Ridgeway likes women with a bit more experience, know what I mean?'

'Someone like you?'

'Well, you said it, Officer, not me. What? Am I *your* type, or something? Is that what you're trying to say?' She smiled nastily. 'Sorry to disappoint you, but I don't screw pigs. You'll just have to put me in your spank-bank.' She pointed at the camera. 'Is that what the little home movie's for?'

'Miss Gould—' Her legal counsel attempted to rein her in.

'*What?*' She rounded on the poor man, and he shrank back.

'Holly sustained a head injury in the hours before she died,' Brent said. 'How did that happen? Did she and Ridgeway argue? Perhaps up on the bridge?'

'Are you deaf or something?' Stefanie said. 'I already told you Holly never came to Amesbury. I'm trying to say it clearly for you. She – got – out – at – the – end – of – the – track. She – did – not – come – with – us. Are you receiving me?'

'We've been through all the CCTV, Miss Gould,' Saunders said. 'No other vehicles left Old Hat Farm and travelled south to Amesbury, either via the A338 or the A345, between half past one and three forty-five that morning. Only Ridge-way's Land Rover.'

'So?'

'So how did Holly get from Old Hat Farm to the A303 if she wasn't in that vehicle with you?'

'I don't know. Perhaps she flew, on her little glittery fairy wings.'

'A young woman has been killed, Miss Gould. This isn't a game.'

'And I'm not playing.' Stefanie jabbed the table top with her index finger. 'She wasn't in the Landy with us. She got in, freaked out, got out at the end of the track, and went back. End of.'

'What did she freak out about?'

'No fucking clue.'

'Nobody else reports seeing her get out of the vehicle, or returning to the party.'

Stefanie pushed her hands into her hair in frustration. 'Oh my God. She got out at the end of the track. Haven't you been there, for fuck's sake? It's a long track, and it was dark. Of *course* nobody saw her.'

'Nobody saw her rejoin the party, either.'

'Perhaps they did, and they're just not saying. This may come as a shock to you, Officers – and I'm sorry to have to break it to you – but not everyone enjoys talking to useless fucking *wankers* like you!'

Brent and Saunders asked Stefanie the same questions a few more times, circling around, trying to trip her up, but even though she got more and more enraged with them, she never wavered from her story. Lockyer made a mental note to check other road routes between the farm and Amesbury, but from memory, Brent and Saunders were right: only two roads went south from there, one on either side of a wide, empty stretch of the plain, much of which was MoD danger area. The A338 went through Tidworth, and the A345 passed Durrington. Both were military towns; both, undoubtedly, would have been well covered by CCTV.

He moved on to Ridgeway's interview, checking his date of birth in the file as he hit play. Ridgeway had been twenty-five at the time. He sat with his arms folded, upright but relaxed. None of Stefanie's aggressive sprawl or Lee's cringing anxiety. Lockyer saw straight away that Ridgeway was far better equipped for keeping secrets, and his cool, than either of the others. His beard hid the shape of his mouth, but his eyes had the kind of opaque neutrality that Lockyer instantly distrusted. He spoke in an accent that veered between Home Counties and Somerset drawl, never quite alighting on either. But he told the same story as Stefanie: that Holly had initially left the party with them, but had changed her mind.

'When can I have it back, by the way?' he said.

'Have what back, Mr Kingsley-Jones?' Brent asked.

'My Land Rover. Having no means of transport makes it very hard to go about my business.'

'And what is your business, Mr Kingsley-Jones?'

'Bit of this, bit of that. I'm a consultant, of sorts.'

'Oh? And what do people consult you about?'

'This and that. So. My ute?'

'We'll get it back to you as soon as we've finished with it,' Saunders said, as deliberately unforthcoming as Ridgeway.

'Hair on the passenger seat is a visual match to Holly Gilbert's. We're having it tested.'

A minute shrug. 'I expect it's hers. She'd been in there often enough.'

'We also found blood on the back seat,' Saunders said. 'We're having that tested as well.'

'I expect it's Holly's.'

Ridgeway hadn't moved at all. His expression hadn't changed.

After a pause, Brent said: 'Can you explain how Holly's blood came to be in your vehicle, Mr Kingsley-Jones?'

'Well, I'm not squeamish, and neither was Holly.' The trace of a smile. 'We had sex. She got her period. It was messy.'

'I see. And when was this?'

Ridgeway shrugged. 'Not sure. We had quite a lot of sex, Holly and me. Every time I rocked up at Old Hat there she'd be, ready and waiting. Do you know, now I come to think about it, I reckon she had a crush on me?'

'The bloodstains in your car are fresh.'

'It's not a *car*. And it was quite recent – the sex with all the blood.'

'So the blood didn't come from a head wound Holly sustained shortly before her death?'

'No. The blood came from her snatch.'

'We'll be able to verify that, Mr Kingsley-Jones,' Saunders said. 'Menstrual blood is quite distinct from venous blood.'

Lockyer had no idea if that was true, or a bluff.

'Knock yourselves out,' Ridgeway said.

'Do you know how Holly sustained the injury to her head?'

'No, I don't. She was fine when we set off from the farm. She was fine when she got out again, just before we reached the road.' He thought for a moment. 'There was some cloud cover by then, so it was very dark. Perhaps she tripped. Fell over and hit her head.'

There was no feeling at all in his tone, and if it was a deliberate tough-guy act then it apparently came quite naturally to Ridgeway.

'Where is Holly's phone, Mr Kingsley-Jones?'

'How the hell should I know?'

'Why did she get out, and go back?'

'No idea. She was kicking up a fuss about something.'

'About what?'

'I don't know. She was rat-arsed, and dialling up the drama. You know how girls get.'

'Where were you going, when you left Old Hat Farm?'

'To round up a few mates in Amesbury, and head over to Stonehenge. The party at Old Hat was a little . . . low-key for me.'

'But you didn't go to Stonehenge. You stayed at Darren White's address until six a.m.'

'What can I say?' Ridgeway spread his hands. 'Best-laid plans. But – here's the thing – if I'm supposed to have somehow got Holly onto that bridge and chucked her off it at – what time was it? Four in the morning? – then how come I was at Darren's until six?'

'Your *car* was at Darren White's until six,' Saunders

clarified. 'The back gate to the property isn't covered by CCTV.'

'But the front is, so you've probably got footage of me and Stef going in. Any sign of Holly in that footage? I'm going to guess not. Because she wasn't with us.'

'Where was Lee Geary? He doesn't get out of the car either.'

'Fast asleep in the back. Past his bedtime.'

'Or perhaps you'd dropped him off before you got there, him and Holly. The traffic cameras lose sight of you for about forty minutes before you arrive at Darren's.'

'Holly was still at the farm. Lee was asleep in the back.'

Ridgeway's calm was impenetrable.

'Did you assault Holly, Mr Kingsley-Jones?' Brent asked tonelessly. 'Did she fight back? Did you have to hit her? As I understand it, a lot of women avoid having sex during their periods.'

Ridgeway looked amused. 'With *you*, maybe, but that's not been my experience. Like I said, Holly wasn't squeamish. And I sure as shit didn't need to rape her.'

'Did you realize you'd gone too far, and leave her with Lee with instructions that he get rid of her?'

'Now you really are having a laugh. You've met Lee, right? About the most complicated instruction I'd trust him to follow is to breathe out after he's breathed in.'

'Not that complicated, though, is it? Take Holly onto the bridge, throw her off. Job done. He looks strong enough.'

'He could carry the two of you in one hand, and I could chuck him under the bus right now, if anything of the kind had actually happened. I could go with your theory, and say it was all Lee. That he didn't mean to hurt her, doesn't know his own strength, that kind of thing.'

Finally, Ridgeway moved. He leant forwards, put his elbows on the table and looked at each of the officers in turn.

'I could tell you he watched me giving it to Holly and wanted in on the action. Got overexcited.' He smirked. 'But it'd be bollocks. I left Holly at the farm, a bit pissed, a bit stroppy, but perfectly fine. And you're never going to prove otherwise.'

At the end of the day Lockyer drove directly to Salisbury. Grey clouds were clotting the sky, and it finally looked as though the weather might break. He'd watched the interviews right through a second time before leaving, noting down the things he wanted answers to.

Stefanie and Ridgeway had both described Holly as being upset, as they'd set off from the farm. It smacked of a cover story, something they'd cooked up to explain why Holly supposedly got out of the Land Rover before it reached the road. Without witnesses, in the dark, it would be hard for anyone to prove that she hadn't. Plus, the fact that she'd got into the car in the first place explained away any forensic evidence of her inside it.

But had it not occurred to Ridgeway that their journey would be clocked by traffic cameras and other CCTV along the route? That any other road users – and there wouldn't have been many at that time of night, midweek, on a rural road – would be traced and eliminated? Why not simply say that Holly had run off once they'd got to Amesbury, instead of denying that she'd made the journey at all, when his was the only vehicle in which she could've got there?

It niggled him. It seemed a foolish story to tell, when the question of how else Holly had supposedly got to Amesbury was coupled with the fact that nobody had seen her return to the party. However drunk or high people had been, *someone* would have seen her – and remembered. He took Stefanie's point that people who'd been partying all night where drugs were freely circulating probably hadn't been keen to talk to the police about it. Then he checked his assumption: there was no evidence it had been a drug-heavy event. A young woman had died, and not everyone saw the police as the enemy. Some had been willing to give statements, and all had reported last seeing Holly getting into the Land Rover.

What bothered Lockyer was that if the version of events Ridgeway and Stefanie had told wasn't true, it seemed stupid to tell it. And if Stefanie was hard to assess, through her barely bottled fury, Ridgeway wasn't. And he hadn't seemed stupid at all.

Muted reflections glanced up from the hospital floor.

'Hi, Mum,' Lockyer said quietly, sitting down at the required distance. Trudy lay motionless. Lockyer couldn't tell if her sleep was peaceful, or just involuntary. The hospital still had its hush, in spite of the many machines to which his mother was now connected. He watched her with a leaden feeling. If she had been awake, he wouldn't have known what to say to make her feel better. He'd never been any good at that. Gemma Broad could express sympathy for a total stranger, and they'd know at once she meant it. But when he tried it sounded fake, however genuine it was.

He checked around the room. The other patients were either also asleep or had their flimsy headphones on, watching TV.

'Mum ... I've found an unmarked grave in the woods behind my house. A woman called Róisín Conlan. She died in my attic, decades ago. And I'm not sure what to do about it.'

Laying it all out like that, Lockyer almost laughed. It was absurd. And it certainly didn't sound like any kind of dilemma.

'I don't think it was murder. Just a horrible sequence of events. But between them they certainly concealed a death, and prevented a lawful burial. Those are crimes. And now Iris is terrified.'

He watched the shallow rise and fall of Trudy's ribs.

'I wish you'd wake up and tell me what to do.'

But he suspected he already knew what she would say: that when people put off a decision, they already knew what they should do. It was only a question of working up the guts to do it.

It was not up to any individual, let alone a police officer, to decide the value of a case; to apportion – or withhold – justice when a crime has been committed. There was the law, and there was due process. It was that simple. Or it ought to have been.

Iris Musprat had no family that Lockyer knew of. He'd never seen anyone come to visit her. If she'd had friends – and even the most insular of people usually picked up one or two – they were long gone. He knew she'd cared a great deal for Bill, but he was gone too. She'd lived in her half of their building since before Lockyer was born, her habits ingrained by all the long, lonely years, and there was something obscene about the idea of her being forced out of there, and taken to a police station. Maybe put into custody, maybe charged. But if he did nothing, and it was later discovered, the very best Lockyer could hope for was the end of his career.

'I wish she hadn't told me,' he muttered.

At home, he ate a lazy supper of beans on toast. There was no point in searching the web for Róisín Conlan. She'd died in 1964, and Mrs Musprat had been vague about her family, and whether or not she'd even been reported missing. There'd be nothing about her online, unless – the thought caused him a pang – relatives were still searching for her; contacting missing persons forums, or reaching out to people of the same name on social media, if they looked about the right age.

Lockyer slammed his plate into the sink and paced. Her having no surviving family wouldn't make what had happened to Róisín any less wrong, but the thought of anyone missing her all these years, and trying to guess what had happened to her, was atrocious.

He ought to have been thinking about Lee Geary and Holly Gilbert. He ought to have been turning over everything they'd learnt so far, and looking at it from all angles. Frustrated, Lockyer shoved his feet into his boots and went out to walk. It was what he'd always done when he couldn't sleep, or when he needed to order his thoughts.

Salisbury Plain was riddled with human burials. The bones of a hundred generations lay cut into the chalk, beneath blankets of turf and wildflowers. What was one more skeleton? One more person, left nameless by the passage of time? Lee Geary might so easily have become another, if the flood hadn't unearthed him. His sister Karen might have lived out her life never knowing what had become of him. When Mrs Musprat died only Lockyer would know where Róisín Conlan lay. He *couldn't* leave her to become one of the nameless many. For a minute he toyed with the idea of waiting until Iris Musprat died before 'accidentally' finding the bones somehow. But it wasn't good enough. She was a tough old bird, and might – he hoped – live for years yet.

He couldn't wait that long, and neither could Róisín.

Lockyer climbed onto Orcheston Down. The plain stretched out all around him, just visible in the low light. Further than he could see, beyond the River Avon to the east, was the expanse of plain that led to Everleigh, and the place where Lee Geary had died.

There was a barbecue. I had a jacket potato.

Something about that simple statement tore at Lockyer's heart. Those words, if nothing else, convinced him that Karen had been right. People had taken advantage of Lee, made use of his physical strength and his gullibility. Abused him, essentially. He'd set off that final day with something to say to someone. Someone at Old Hat Farm? Someone else altogether? By then Ridgeway was already dead. Whoever it'd been, Lockyer was gut-certain about two things: it had been about Holly Gilbert, and it had got Lee killed.

7

Day 8, Monday

The day dawned rainy, with a fitful breeze.

'Everything all right, guv?' Broad asked, as they hurried across to the car.

'Yep.'

'Isn't this temperature bliss?' she said.

'I don't know about bliss, but it makes a change.' He backed the car out of its parking space. When he'd left on Friday, Broad had still been reading though the transcript of the inquest, and the original file on Holly Gilbert. 'Find anything?' he asked.

'Well, nothing revelatory . . .' Broad turned a few pages in her notebook. 'Two of her friends from university gave evidence at the inquest. A girl called Jess, and a bloke called Dean. They said that once Holly moved to Old Hat Farm, after that Christmas, she basically ditched them. Started experimenting with drugs, staying up all night, not turning up to tutorials, that kind of thing. Apparently she just laughed when they suggested she see a grief counsellor.'

'She thought she'd already found the answer,' Lockyer said.

Broad flipped a page. 'From the toxicology report, the hallucinogen in her blood was a chemical called Salvinorin A, which has a similar effect to LSD. It used to be found in a number of legal highs, until it was banned by the Psycho-active Substances Act in 2016, not that *that* stopped people taking it. The effects can be acute, but are short-lived. It gives you a twenty-minute trip. Tests indicated that Holly was well on the way to having metabolized it out of her system.'

'So she wasn't tripping when she went off the bridge.'

'No. More to the point was the amount she'd had to drink. Her blood alcohol was ninety-five milligrams. At those levels you'd expect a loss of inhibition, impaired judgement and motor function, and possibly a right sad-on.' Broad coloured faintly. 'I mean, if she was depressed, it could have made it worse.'

'Nothing in the PM about struggle bruises?'

'No. I had another read-through, and she did have some small bruises on her forearms, and a larger one on her thigh. Nothing out of the ordinary, though, consistent with a rowdy crowd on a dance floor, and maybe a fall.'

'The fall in which she might have hit her head? Time-wise?'

'Time-wise, yes. But nothing conclusive of the chain of events.'

'Of course not.'

'Anything from the interviews?' Broad asked.

'You should watch them,' Lockyer said, 'since it's as close as we're going to get to speaking to any of them in person. Stef Gould was a seriously angry young woman – the type who wouldn't cooperate with the police even if gangsters snatched her mother. And Ridgeway was a piece of work. Calm, clever, not at all fazed. I wouldn't trust him as far as I could throw him. They both insist Holly got out of the car at the end of the farm track, and didn't go to Amesbury with them.'

'Then how's she supposed to have got there?'

'Exactly. And Lee . . . Well, you watch and see.'

'I'm a bit surprised the coroner returned suicide rather than an open verdict, or misadventure,' Broad said. 'Salisbury'd had to let Ridgeway and the others go because of a lack of evidence, but *someone* drove Holly to Amesbury, and they never came forward. Then there's the head wound nobody saw happen . . .'

'I know,' Lockyer said. 'I guess with her grief, the drugs and the alcohol, on balance, however she got to the bridge, it's probable that she jumped.'

'But you don't think so?'

'Do you?' he asked.

'I think . . .' Broad said '. . . I think she probably did. But that doesn't mean no one else was involved, or that somebody didn't blame Ridgeway for it. And the other two.'

'I agree. Holly was in a vulnerable state, and Ridgeway wasn't a good person for her to have got close to.'

At Old Hat Farm, Lockyer took a lungful of petrichor – the smell of rain on parched ground. He'd always loved it.

This time their knock at the farmhouse door was answered by a teenager in dungarees, her hair done up in bunches.

'Hi! I'm Melody,' she said, with a strong Aussie accent.

'We're looking for Jason McNeil,' Lockyer told her, showing his ID.

'Jase? Why? What do you want with him?'

When they didn't reply, she pointed vaguely at the barns behind them.

'He'll be in the workshop, I reckon.'

'Thanks,' Lockyer said.

They peered into a few of the outbuildings until they heard a radio muttering quietly, and followed the sound to a single-storey building, long rather than deep, with stable doors at intervals along the side. Inside there was a rich smell of cut wood. Twenty feet of workbench had been built against the back wall, with shelves above and a huge array of tools: chisels, saws, planes and hand drills, in neat runs of size; everything from a tiny steel toffee-hammer to a huge, spherical mallet.

Vince McNeil was hunched over the bench, squeezing a neat line of hot glue along two scrolled arms of wood. He looked round at them without surprise, then returned to his work.

'Be with you in a tick,' he said, in that deep, rumbling voice. 'Just need to get this clamped.'

'Take your time,' Lockyer said.

He liked people to think they had all the time in the world:

it communicated that there was no point in them stalling. But he doubted any such strategy would work with Vince, who seemed like a man who only ever moved at his own pace.

'What's that going to be?' Broad asked, when Vince had finished tightening the clamps and turned, wiping his hands on a rag.

'A bookcase. That's the cornice.'

'Your wife mentioned that you and your son make things to sell,' Lockyer said. 'How does that work, without phones or the internet?'

'We don't have phones, but I doubt she ever said we weren't online. We have a laptop, mostly for the woodwork business. I used to sell at flea markets and car boots, but it's actually much less polluting to do it this way.'

'And here we were, thinking you were completely off-grid.'

'If we could be, we would be,' he said easily. 'But we have to make ends meet.'

'We were hoping to speak to your son,' Broad said, 'but he seems as invisible in real life as he is online.'

Vince looked amused. 'Being online isn't a legal requirement, you know. Anyway, I expect you searched for Jason McNeil, did you?'

'Well . . . yes.'

From outside came the sound of footsteps.

'Jase is real enough,' Vince said, as a man ducked in through the far set of doors, carrying a length of scaffold board. Hurriedly, he added, 'Please, talk in soft voices to begin with.'

Seeing Jason, Lockyer understood why they hadn't found him by searching for Jason McNeil. He was in his early thirties, lean and mid-height, with the muscled arms of years of manual work. He was also black, and wore his hair in short braids, tied into a spiky bunch on top of his head. Whoever his biological parents had been, they weren't Trish and Vincent McNeil.

Jason looked up sharply, visibly startled. His eyes flicked from Broad to Lockyer and back again.

'Jason,' Vince said, in a low tone, 'these are the police officers I was telling you about.'

Jason put down the board and came towards them. Something in the cautious way he moved made Lockyer hesitate to say anything. As though he might disappear again.

'How can I help you, Officers?' Jason said.

The strangeness of his approach seemed to have knocked Broad off her stride.

'Er,' she said, and Jason's night-dark eyes focused on her. 'We'd like to talk to you about a man named Lee Geary. We understand he was a regular visitor here, at one time. We're investigating his death, which we believe occurred approximately nine years ago, and . . .'

Broad trailed into silence, because Jason was smiling at her. Not a mocking smile, or a slight, polite smile, but a wide, disarming smile that lit up his face.

'Um . . .' Broad said.

'Carry on, Officer,' he said.

'That . . . that was the same year Holly Gilbert died.'

The smile faded, and when Lockyer spoke, Jason flinched.

'Did you know Mr Geary?'

Jason's eyes slid away from Lockyer's. 'Yeah, I knew him. Not well. I – I tried to look out for him, when he was here.'

'In what way?'

'He used to hang out with Ridgeway and his girlfriend. They weren't always nice to him.'

'Do you mean Stefanie Gould?'

'Yeah. Her.'

'So you didn't like them much?'

'They had jagged edges, the pair of them,' Jason said. 'I steer clear of people like that.'

'How often—' Lockyer began.

'Sorry, could we please talk outside?'

Jason headed for the door without waiting for a reply. Lockyer and Broad exchanged a look, but Vince turned back to his work, untroubled.

It was still spitting with rain outside. Jason walked to the middle of the yard and stood with his eyes shut for a moment. They followed him, and Lockyer noticed the subtle changes in his posture as the tension ebbed. Shoulders dropping, jaw softening.

'Better,' Jason said, opening his eyes. 'It upsets my dad to talk about Holly.'

'When you say your dad, Vince isn't your birth father?' Lockyer said.

'You spotted that, did you?' He sounded amused. 'No. But I was still just a kid when I turned up here – in my teens, but only just. Vince and Trish took me in. They didn't have children of their own.'

'Can I ask your full name?'

'Jason McNeil.'

'Your *given* family name?'

Jason said nothing, and Lockyer noted the resolute quality of his silence.

'All right,' he said. 'How about when you first came here?'

'Must have been . . . 2000? 2001?'

'And your previous family?'

Jason looked uncomfortable. 'They . . . I was better off without them.'

Lockyer couldn't imagine having to grow up without the love and security his family had given him, but he'd seen enough cases of neglect and violence within the home to know that it wasn't always best for a child to stay with their parents. It was telling that the McNeils had taken in the young runaway instead of calling social services. They clearly thought of themselves as living outside normal procedures like that.

'How did you feel about Holly?' Broad asked. 'Finding out you had a sort of step-sister must have been an adjustment.'

Jason turned to her, a trace of that wonderful smile tugging at the corners of his mouth. Lockyer saw treacherous patches of colour creeping into Broad's cheeks.

'Holly was great,' he said. 'I mean, she was in a bit of a mess. She'd lost her mum. Lost her way. But she was solid gold, really.'

'How old were you, then?' Broad asked.

'About twenty-four, twenty-five.'

'And you got on well? No . . . friction?'

'Course not,' Jason said. 'Holly was Vince's natural daughter. No way could I resent them wanting to get to know each other.'

'Was she a mature twenty, would you say?'

'More mature than *I* was at her age, perhaps. But girls generally are, right?'

'They tend to be,' Broad said, with a tiny smile of her own.

'Holly was easy to like,' Jason said. 'I mean, I know she was only here six months, but it felt like I'd known her for a long time. Some people you do just *know*, right? You feel close to them. It's like you recognize them.'

'So you were upset when she killed herself?' Lockyer asked.

'She didn't kill herself.'

'You don't think she jumped?'

'Not of her own accord. Holly can't have had any idea how to find that bridge, and she didn't want to kill herself. She was so . . . alive.'

'She was obviously going through a lot at that time.'

'Not by then,' Jason said. 'In the early days, maybe. But by summer she'd accepted her grief. She could see the other side of it – that was what she said to me. It'd stopped feeling like some . . . *chasm* she'd never get across. And she was so full of beans, man. She was indigo and gold. Just like you.'

He addressed this to Broad, who looked bewildered, and blushed again.

'In my experience, grief isn't linear,' Lockyer said. 'It sort of . . . comes and goes, in waves.'

'Yep,' Jason agreed. 'And by then Holly knew that whenever

the tide came in, it would go out again, eventually. Trish taught her that.'

'What do you think happened to her?'

'I think she went to Amesbury with Ridgeway and the other two, and whatever happened after that, she didn't just jump. They knew more than they ever said, you can bet your life on it.'

'Did you see her get into Ridgeway's Land Rover at the party?'

'I wasn't at the party.'

'Oh? Where were you?'

'I . . . I don't do well in a crowd,' he said. 'Too many people, too many voices, all coming at once.' He shut his eyes again briefly. 'It messes with my head.'

'You get claustrophobic?' Broad said.

'No. It's hard to explain.'

'So, what? You stayed in the house?'

'No, I cleared out altogether. Went to see some friends.'

'Where was that?'

A pause. 'Avebury.'

'Wasn't it crowded there as well? At the solstice?'

'Not like here.'

'How many people came here?'

'You'd have to ask my folks. It was usually three or four hundred, something like that.'

'An event that size needs a licence,' Lockyer pointed out, to which Jason pulled a face.

'Leave it out.'

'Do you know what drugs Holly took?' Lockyer asked.

Jason didn't reply.

'There was a hallucinogen in her system at the time of her death, as well as alcohol.'

Again, silence.

'Look, we're not interested in bringing any kind of drugs charges here – let alone ones for drugs taken almost a decade ago. We're just trying to understand Holly's death. Her state of mind, what she might have taken, and, more importantly, who might have supplied it to her.'

'She tried a few things. Nothing heavy.' Jason looked troubled. 'I think she was trying to tap into her spiritual side. Find a better understanding of things.'

'And is that the kind of thing Ridgeway used to sell?'

'He was into harder stuff – coke, amphetamines – but he wouldn't have brought any of that here. Vince and Trish wouldn't have it.'

'Did you ever buy from him?'

'No.'

'Really?'

'What – because I'm black I must be snorting and smoking all kinds of shit?'

'That's not—'

'I don't even drink.' Jason tapped the side of his head, raising one eyebrow. 'Believe me, there's enough crazy going on in here already.'

'When did you last see Lee Geary?'

'I don't know. Whenever he last came here with Ridgeway, before the party. But I couldn't tell you when that was.'

'Not at any time after that? You're sure?'

'I'm sure.'

'Holly and Ridgeway got close, didn't they?'

Jason's reaction to this was visible. He tensed, his nostrils flaring. 'Physically, perhaps,' he said tersely. 'But that's all it was. Holly was an only child, and she'd been brought up very . . . straight, you know? Homework before supper, fish on Fridays. All a bit safe. She was only twenty, and Ridgeway had that bad-boy thing girls go for. But she was getting the measure of him. Figuring out there wasn't anything to find behind the hard-man act – just a selfish prick.'

'Smart girl.'

'Yeah. She was.'

'Did she have her own room here?' Broad asked. 'Or is it all, like, dormitories?'

'Dormitories?' Jason echoed, with that grin again. 'Old Hat isn't a doss-house, Officer. But say it again.'

Broad looked puzzled. 'Say what again? Dormitories?'

'Yeah,' Jason said. 'It's like orange sorbet, that word – you're giving me sugar cravings. Yes, Holly had her own room. Want to see it?'

'Yes, please,' Broad said stiffly, as though she suspected she was being laughed at. But Lockyer thought he was beginning to understand.

Jason led them into the house, up a turning oak stair and along the narrow corridor to the room at the far end. 'Vince doesn't like stuff being moved around in here,' he said, as he let them in.

'We won't touch anything,' Lockyer assured him. He knew the score there. The strangeness of Jody's things in Chris's room, even though they'd long since removed all his stuff. Her reading glasses on the bedside table, her pyjamas on the floor. The ineffable air of the sacred that a loved one's room acquired when they died.

Holly didn't have teddy bears on her bed – Stefanie had been wrong about that. Just a colourful throw and a cushion with a crocheted cover. The room was quite bare, but a mirror in an elaborate frame hung on one wall. Lockyer took a closer look. It had been carved from a single piece of gnarled wood, its natural kinks coaxed into intertwined fronds and whorls, so that the whole thing was reminiscent of seaweed, and polished to a lustrous sheen.

'It was the most amazing tree,' Jason said. 'A yew. Must have been hundreds of years old when it fell.'

'You made this?' Lockyer guessed.

'Best one I've ever done.'

'And you gave it to Holly?'

Jason smiled. 'I made it *for* Holly.'

'Is this all of her stuff?'

A nod. 'She turned up here with a backpack of clothes and not a lot else. Said that was all she needed.'

Lockyer wondered what had become of the clutter of books, music, trinkets, accessories and junk that most people, especially girls, accumulated. He made a mental note to find out, if possible, where it had all ended up. Any electronic devices she'd owned, in particular. Reflected in the mirror he saw someone coming over the bridge on a quad bike, towing sacks of chicken feed in a trailer. As she reached the yard, Lockyer recognized Trish McNeil.

Broad crossed to a small desk in one corner. It had a shallow drawer, and she slid it open. Inside was a tangle of necklaces, pens and joss sticks, and a stack of Polaroid photos. Broad touched her fingers to the top one, then jumped at the sound of a voice.

'Please don't touch that,' Vince said, his tall figure filling the doorway.

Broad snatched her hand back. 'Sorry.'

'It's all right. I just . . . it's just . . .'

Vince crossed to the desk and gently slid the drawer closed. He looked wretched. Lockyer was struck by that, given that nine years had passed and he'd had Holly in his life for just half of one. *I knew her in my bones*, he'd said before. *She was my own flesh and blood.* Vince turned to them. He couldn't disguise the intensity of feeling in his bright blue eyes, and for a second Lockyer saw something darker underneath. Some regret that bordered on desperation.

'It's strange, when you lose someone. The places where she was . . . where she *should* be . . .' Vince trailed off, as though he didn't know how to explain. 'I was her father, but I—'

'You didn't fail her,' Jason said quietly, as though he'd heard it before. He took hold of Vince's upper arms. 'You did *not*.'

'But I didn't keep her safe.'

Trish called up the stairs. 'Vince? Jase? Are you up there? What do you want for lunch?'

Lockyer waited, but neither Vince nor Jason replied straight away. The two men shared a long look.

Then Jason called, 'Just coming, Trish.'

The four of them creaked back down the stairs without speaking. When Trish saw them she hesitated, but only for a second.

'Oh! Hello. Are you staying for lunch?'

'No. But thank you,' Lockyer said.

'You've been up to Holly's room, I take it?'

'Your son kindly offered to show us.'

Trish's face revealed nothing, but there was no mistaking the atmosphere in the room. A subtle tension between the three of them.

'I'm not sure I understand how that'll help you,' Trish said eventually. 'Isn't it Lee Geary you're supposed to be investigating?'

'We are,' Lockyer said, deciding to leave it at that and see what kind of reaction it got.

The answer was none. Vince crossed to the kitchen table and sat down, lacing his fingers in front of him. Trish watched him for a second, then looked back at Lockyer.

'Holly's death was a tr—'

'Don't call it a tragedy, Trish,' Vince rumbled.

Trish bit back whatever she'd been about to say. She took the tomatoes to the sink and began to wash them. Neither of them seemed to have anything to add.

'I'll just go and switch everything off in the workshop,' Jason said.

Lockyer and Broad took their leave and caught up with him halfway across the yard.

Jason rounded on them. 'Look, I know they act weird

when it's about Holly, but don't go reading into it, okay? Holly coming here . . . Trish tried her best, she really did. But it was difficult for her. She never let Holly see it, but I could tell.'

'How could you tell?'

'Her – her voice changed colour whenever Holly was in the room.'

'What do you mean?' Broad asked.

'Jason,' Lockyer said, 'do you have synesthesia?'

'Not a detective for nothing, then,' Jason said wryly. 'Most people have never heard of it.'

'I don't pretend to fully understand it. But I gather it can be overwhelming, at times.'

'It's my superpower and my kryptonite,' Jason said. 'That's what Vince said, when I was still a kid.'

'Why do you think Trish found it hard to have Holly here?'

'I dunno. But I guess . . . They never had any kids of their own, right? There was some issue there. Trish has had miscarriages. But I guess they'd got used to the idea. They had each other, this place, me. Then it turns out Vince *did* have a kid, and he loved her from the second he met her. I guess I can see how Trish might've felt left out.'

'Do you think she resented Holly?'

'Resented her? No way. Trish isn't like that. She's, like, the most generous person I've ever met. But for the longest time it was just her and Vince. Then, all of a sudden it's her and Vince and Holly, and she just . . . she didn't get any say in it, I guess.'

'Vince was obviously very upset when Holly died.'

'He blamed himself. He was the one who let Ridgeway keep coming here, you see. Trish wanted to keep him at arm's length. The things he was doing – I mean, we didn't know, exactly, but we heard things. People were wary of him. But Vince said how would it help to shut him out, right? To turn him away, when this had always been a safe place for him.'

'So Vince blamed Ridgeway and the others for Holly's death?'

'He blamed himself,' Jason repeated. 'I'd better get back in, and help them out.' He glanced at Broad. 'Say dormitories one more time?'

Broad looked uncertain. 'Dormitories.'

Jason smiled, and, as if she couldn't help it, Broad did too.

Back in the car, after a thoughtful silence, Broad said, 'Why on earth did he keep asking me to say dormitories?'

'I guess he likes orange sorbet,' Lockyer replied.

'I don't have the first clue what you're on about. And what's that illness you said he had?'

She sounded ruffled, so Lockyer stopped teasing. 'Synesthesia. It's not an illness. Just something some people have. The senses get cross-wired in certain ways, so some sounds might be experienced as a taste, or a colour, or a smell. Or certain colours might have a smell, or whatever. There are various different kinds. Some people taste music. Or hear fragrances.'

'That sounds mad.'

'Hard to imagine, I guess, if you don't have it. But it's real. Lots of people have a mild form and don't even realize it, but people with intense synesthesia can get overwhelmed by it.'

'Like Jason and crowds.'

'Yeah. I imagine that if you experience voices as colours, or as tastes, then a large group of overexcited people must be riotous, from a sensory point of view.'

Broad was silent for a while. 'He said I was indigo and gold. Like Holly.'

'And when you said dormitories, he tasted orange sorbet.'

'That's just bonkers,' she said, but Lockyer thought she sounded just a little bit pleased.

'Better than being snot-green and tasting of ear wax, right?' he said.

She laughed. 'Yeah. That's kind of more how I see myself, actually. How come you know so much about it, guv?'

'There was a programme on Radio 4 a while back.'

'Right. I was probably watching *Love Island* at the time. No. Don't say anything.' Broad held up a hand. 'I already hate myself.'

Lockyer smiled.

'I got a good look at some of the photos in Holly's drawer before Vince chased me off,' she went on. 'One was of Jason and Holly, a selfie. She's holding the camera and smiling at it, and Jason has his forehead against hers, his eyes shut, and this expression . . . Well, it could have been a wedding picture.'

'Sleeping together?'

'If they weren't, I reckon Jason wished they had been.'

The rain had stopped and the road was drying, but the car still skidded as they rounded a bend and nearly went head-on with a tractor. Heart thumping, Lockyer crawled onto the verge to let it pass.

'So, why do you suppose he wouldn't tell us his real name?' Broad asked. 'Hiding something?'

'Could be. Or hiding *from* something.'

'Like what?'

'People he used to know – his birth family, even. If they were violent, or abusive.'

He thought of his childhood friend, Kevin, whose father had always had one dodgy deal or another on the go. Kevin had never been able to stand up to Bob, or disentangle himself. Now the older man was in prison for arson and insurance fraud, and Lockyer had shielded Kevin from being prosecuted alongside him. It was what had got him moved from the MCIT to cold cases. But Bob was still managing to send out tentacles, to rope Kevin in.

'And the way they just shut down, when we came back from Holly's room,' Broad said. 'That was weird, wasn't it?'

'My guess is they've got lots of things they're carefully *not* saying to each other,' Lockyer said. 'Let alone to us.'

'Things we need to find out?'

'Trouble is we won't know that until we know what they are. I'd like to get them all in, one by one; off that farm and out of their comfort zones. Push them harder. But we need more to go on first.'

'We need those forensics.'

'We do,' Lockyer agreed. 'Lee being found a mile from their place isn't enough. Ridgeway and Stef dying, too, *could* just be coincidence. Chaotic lives, just as Trish said. We need to *know* Lee went there before he died. Then we can try to find out what he wanted to tell them.'

The sky had turned bright white as the sun fought its way through. Lockyer pictured Vince McNeil's steady aquamarine eyes, and the hidden things behind them. The scale of his grief over Holly, the guilt Jason had mentioned. Trish, sidelined by his relationship with his long-lost daughter. The beautiful yew-wood mirror Jason had made for Holly. *Jason loved Holly*, Vince had said. Lockyer wondered how deep those feelings had run, whether they'd been platonic, or, as Broad had extrapolated from the photo, something more. He recalled how Jason had recoiled at the mention of Holly and Ridgeway together.

Then he thought of another yew tree. Human bones beneath it, scattered with earth and skeleton leaves. A sixty-year-old secret.

'You okay, guv?' Broad said.

Lockyer realized he was staring at nothing. 'Yeah.' He put the car into gear and lurched down from the verge.

8

Leaving Broad to dig for intel on the three permanent residents of Old Hat Farm, Lockyer drove himself to Culver Street car park in Salisbury. Built of brown brick, it was as fundamentally ugly as only a multi-storey car park can be. He drove up to the top floor. Checking the file on Ridgeway's death, he walked to the exact spot from which he'd fallen, stood at the tubular metal railings, and looked down.

It was, as Broad had suggested, high enough.

A good fifteen-metre drop. Fifty:fifty, perhaps; you *might* survive the fall, albeit with serious injuries. At no point had anybody come forward to describe Ridgeway as suicidal, or as having any issues with his mental health. If you genuinely wanted to kill yourself, would you choose to jump from a height that might not kill you? It seemed unlikely. And Ridgeway hadn't come across as the cry-for-help type, who'd make an attempt if he didn't intend to succeed.

Lockyer looked at his own hands, gripping the warm, grubby railings. The bars were horizontal, perfect for climbing over. He flexed his fingers. And if you were climbing over, you'd grip the top rail, exactly as he was gripping it now. He checked the report. Fingerprints had been lifted from railings, but none had belonged to anyone on the database, including Ridgeway. Apparently nobody had attached much significance to that.

From there he drove to Salisbury nick and signed out the CCTV evidence, which had been retained after the coroner's open verdict. Checking his watch, he knew he should head straight back to Devizes, but when he hit the first round-about on the ring road he found himself going right around it, and heading towards the hospital. His father would be there now, visiting Trudy. Perhaps there, away from the farm, they might talk. Lockyer didn't know what he wanted to say, exactly, or what he wanted to hear. But the way he and his father routinely said nothing was starting to feel like a weight pressing down on him.

He spotted his father's battered but indestructible Toyota Hilux in the car park, but before he'd got out of his own car he saw John over by the pay station. Jody was with him, typing the registration number into the machine and tapping a card. They walked over to the Hilux together, and even though Jody was doing most of the talking, John did respond now and then. She bumped him gently on the arm with her fist, and he almost smiled. Then she climbed into the driver's seat, and once John was settled beside her, reversed deftly and swung the car away.

Lockyer made sure they didn't spot him. The sight of them was inexplicably wounding. A snapshot of his own failings. It shoved him into a memory of Chris's last Christmas, in

1999, when the four of them had been together. John, notoriously cynical about the whole rigmarole and impossible to buy presents for, had been saying for weeks that he didn't want anything.

'Come on, you grumpy old git,' Chris had said. 'You know you'll only sulk if we really don't get you anything.'

'I'd be bloody delighted if you didn't,' John replied, retreating into his armchair and refusing to make eye contact.

'Oh, John—' Trudy said.

'No, no,' John cut her off. 'It's a waste of time and money that none of us have got.'

'I reckon I can spare a few quid to make you smile on Christmas Day,' Chris said secretively. His face had been ruddy from being out in the weather all day and then sitting too close to the fire, a touch of puppy fat still softening his jawline.

'What are you planning?' Lockyer asked him later.

'That's on a need-to-know basis.' Chris grinned. 'You?'

'Shirt, probably. Or a jumper.'

Chris rolled his eyes.

On Christmas morning John unwrapped Chris's present and stared at it in silence. It was a framed certificate: platinum membership of the Grumpy Old Gits Society, which was an actual society, it turned out, based in Oadby. After a moment John laughed. Actually *laughed*, shaking his head at Chris, who shrugged a shoulder and said, 'Misery loves company.'

John opened Lockyer's shirt with a nod of thanks, and

Lockyer had sat, feeling flat, until he realized he *envied* his little brother. That knack of his for getting it right, for finding a way to reach people. Trudy understood. She squeezed his shoulder as she got up to baste the potatoes.

Sitting outside Salisbury Hospital just then, the feeling was exactly the same. Lockyer left a minute later, feeling – not for the first time – surplus to his own family.

'Vince McNeil's done time,' Broad announced eagerly, when Lockyer got back.

'Tell me,' he said, slumping into his chair.

'He was sent down in 1990 for aggravated arson and two counts of manslaughter. Served seven of a nine-year sentence, released early on parole in '97 for good behaviour.'

'Manslaughter?'

'Yep. Two people died in the fire, Paul and Diane Simm. It was their house. I can't get the original file from that far back, but I found something in one of the online news archives. Mr and Mrs Simm were Vince's girlfriend's parents. He'd had a major falling-out with them.'

'Then how the hell did he get away with manslaughter?'

'They weren't meant to be there. They were supposed to be staying overnight in London. He thought the house was empty.'

'And the jury believed that?'

'They did, because he was obviously repentant, and because the girlfriend was also in the house. Imogen Simm. Treated for smoke inhalation but otherwise unharmed. She was meant to have been away with her parents – it was her birthday treat, but they'd come back early because Imogen got ill.'

'1990? So, before mobile phones. Imogen wouldn't have been updating her boyfriend on her whereabouts every five seconds.'

'And he wouldn't have been able to track her.'

'Any idea what the falling-out was about?'

'Well, reading between the not-too-subtle lines of the newspaper piece, Imogen was only just seventeen, Vince was nineteen. The Simms were well-off, Vince was . . . from the wrong side of the tracks. His whole family were known to the police. Perennial truant, dropped out of school early, and seems to have dedicated himself to a life of petty crime – he'd been hauled up for glue sniffing, shop-lifting, vandalism, that sort of thing.'

'What was it Jason said yesterday? About teenage girls being drawn to the bad boys?'

'Yeah. It's definitely a thing,' Broad said. 'Not with me, mind you. I was in the Venture Scouts. Too busy getting my orienteering badge to think about boyfriends.'

Lockyer tipped his chair back and stared out at the ash trees. He remembered Vince's particular stillness, and now thought he recognized it. He'd seen that resolute serenity in other ex-convicts. They developed it in prison, at first as a way to save face and mask any emotions that could make them a target – fear, depression, desperation. After a while it became ingrained, almost a part of their personality. Revealing nothing of themselves to the outside world: a way of creating privacy in a place where there was none.

Hedy had had that stillness, too, though in her case it pre-dated prison.

Of course, that didn't mean those emotions weren't still there. Under the surface.

'Still, I reckon—' Broad began to say, but cut herself off.

Lockyer looked round. Steve Saunders was standing in the doorway, wearing a full-face visor, with a battered-looking policy book in one hand.

Lockyer sat up abruptly. 'Steve.'

'Farmer Giles, Laptop.' Saunders gave an ironic nod. 'As you were. I'm not coming in, so you'd better make it quick before my feet get tired.'

Broad scrabbled for her notebook and pen. Lockyer knew she was nervous of Saunders, and his routine antagonism.

'Er,' she said. 'You were one of the investigating officers in—'

'Yeah, yeah. Holly Gilbert. Ridgeway Kingsley-Jones. I've read through my notes, so get on with it.'

Lockyer cut to the chase. 'Did you have any doubts that Holly's death was suicide?'

'Yes. I did. Mainly because Ridgeway was a cocky little twat, and I wanted him behind bars. And I knew he was lying about Holly not travelling to Amesbury with them that night.'

'Did you check *all* other vehicles heading south on either road that night?'

'Yep.' Saunders leant against the doorframe. 'There were only sixteen. We traced them all, and the stories all checked out. None of them had been to Old Hat Farm, or even heard of it.'

'There's always the possibility that whoever drove Holly down there took a more circuitous route.'

Saunders looked sceptical. 'Far more likely that the story about her staying at the farm was bullshit.'

'Agreed. Why do you think Ridgeway and Stef lied about that, when it would have been so easy for you to check it?'

'Dunno. Not as clever as they thought they were.'

Saunders paused to consider this, perhaps remembering that Ridgeway *had* been clever. 'Or they panicked, when Holly went off that bridge,' he said. 'Came up with the idea of denying she'd gone with them, and stuck with it.'

Broad cleared her throat. 'Um, what about if she'd come from the *other* side of the bridge?'

'Nah. The bridlepath just joins the unclassified lane to Ratfyn. It's a dead-end to the west, and joins the Porton Road roundabout to the east, which is covered with cameras.'

'And nobody went through there that night?'

'Not a soul.'

'The blood in Ridgeway's Land Rover,' Lockyer said. 'It was Holly's?'

'Yes. But it was . . .' Saunders glanced uncomfortably at Broad '. . . it was from her period, like he said. And her hair was on the back seats as well as the front. She'd obviously been in there more than once.'

'So you had to let them go.'

'No grounds to hold them,' Saunders said. 'It wasn't enough that we couldn't find another vehicle Holly might have travelled in. We lost track of them for about forty minutes on the journey, during which time Holly could have got out anywhere; plus Ridgeway and Stef had alibis for the time she actually hit the lorry.'

'Darren White backed up their story?'

'As did others who were at his place that night – none of them exactly upstanding members of society, but still. There was no physical evidence that any of them had been on that bridge with Holly. And there was no real motive for them to have hurt her.'

'Stef clearly didn't like her,' Lockyer said.

'Stef didn't like anyone. But she wouldn't do anything without Ridgeway's say-so, and *he* had no motive we could prove.'

'Could it have been something to do with his dealing?' Broad ventured. 'Holly was going to shop him, or something?'

'Why would she, though? If she didn't like his line of work she'd hardly have been shagging him.'

Broad scribbled something in her notebook then looked up, tapping her pencil on the page. 'What do *you* think happened that night, DI Saunders?' she asked.

He put his head on one side. 'I think she got in the car with those three, and went to Amesbury. She was pissed – they probably all were. Or high. I reckon something went wrong in the forty minutes before they turned up at White's. Maybe Ridgeway assaulted her. Didn't want to let her being on the rag spoil his fun. She got the knock on the head. He needed rid of her. So, either he left her hidden somewhere, unconscious, and slipped out the back of Darren's to chuck her off the bridge, or else he left her with Lee, and that bloody idiot did what he was told. He was obviously scared shitless of Ridgeway, and we weren't ever able to get a coherent account of the night out of him.'

'By all accounts Lee wasn't a violent person,' Lockyer said.

Saunders grunted. 'He didn't need to be. Ridgeway did the violence; Lee just followed orders. Maybe they convinced him she was already dead.'

Lockyer considered this scenario. It was all too plausible, except for one thing: Lee's obvious confusion in his interview, when they told him Holly was dead. According to Karen he'd been a rubbish liar. *Didn't have the imagination for it.*

'And Holly's family knew all this, presumably?' he said.

'They had a family liaison officer, who wouldn't have named names, of course, but I expect the McNeils knew exactly who we'd arrested. There'd been all those witnesses at the party, as well.'

Broad had been leafing through the transcript of the inquest. 'And the pathologist testified that the first head wound *could* have been survivable,' she said. 'So the McNeils would have heard that.'

'Yeah. They could've saved her, if they'd taken her to hospital.' Saunders left a beat. 'So what are you thinking? Vigilante killings? Her family, or some other boyfriend, out to settle the score?'

'It's a hypothesis,' Lockyer said. 'Isn't that what you thought at the time?'

'After a while,' Saunders said. 'At first I didn't think anything of it when Ridgeway went off that roof. Vice had

had their eye on him – they were pretty sure something was about to go down. But they couldn't make an arrest. Couldn't ID any suspects, or prove that anyone else had been up on the roof when he fell. So it all went cold. But . . . I dunno.' He folded his arms. 'Do you know what my first thought was, when I heard he was dead? I thought, Serves you bloody right, you piece of shit. You know, for Holly.'

Lockyer and Broad exchanged a quick look.

'And that got me thinking,' he went on. 'If that was how *I* felt about him, barely knowing Holly . . .'

'Then the people who'd loved her would've felt it tenfold.'

'Exactly. So I raised it with Brent, but he had no time for hunches.'

Lockyer thought he heard a trace of self-mockery in Steve's tone. He'd always supposed Saunders didn't have the time or imagination for hunches either, but perhaps he'd been wrong.

'We'd done our best to prove that they were with Holly that night, and got nowhere,' Saunders said. 'After the suicide verdict, he didn't want it back on his desk.'

'But it's in the file?' Broad said. 'The possible connection between the deaths is in the file?'

'Yeah,' Saunders said. 'I went to Ridgeway's funeral, see. Thought I'd see who else showed up. And guess who didn't show up?' He gave it a second. 'Stef Gould, who worshipped the ground he walked on. So I thought I'd look in on her, see what she was up to.'

'And you found out she'd drowned,' Lockyer said.

''S right, down in Dorset. They'd dealt with it, and it

was never treated as a suspicious death, so it didn't make a ripple in Salisbury – pardon the pun. When Lee Geary went missing as well, Brent finally started listening. But we couldn't trace Lee. The great lump just evaporated into thin air. We had no proof of foul play with Stef, and the fortnight we spent reviewing the evidence in Ridgeway's case turned up nothing new. So, no further action. Again.' He shook his head. 'It never sat right with me.'

'Doesn't sit right with me, either,' Lockyer said.

Saunders straightened and stood away from the door-frame. 'Yeah, well. Good luck making a concrete link between the three of them.' He sounded almost sincere.

'But you think they were murdered?'

'Yeah. Don't you? Specially now Geary's turned up with his skull bashed in. And no way did Ridgeway jump off that roof, cocky little gobshite. Thought he was the dog's bollocks, he did.'

'Someone at Old Hat Farm, you think?'

Saunders pulled a face. 'Dunno. I mean, they'd have motive, but I never got that vibe off them. 'Cept maybe Vince – he's like the bloody sphinx, that one. But there was no evidence, not with Ridgeway or Stef. Anyone who'd loved Holly had a motive, and it seems like plenty of people did. Plus that farm is basically a revolving door for drifters and weirdos.'

'Yeah,' Lockyer said. 'Okay. Thanks, Steve.'

The big man put his hands into his pockets, shifting his weight. 'If someone did kill Lee Geary, well, they shouldn't've,' he said.

'Isn't that generally true, with murder?'

'Some more than others. But killing Lee'd be like . . . killing a Labrador for fetching a stick.'

And with that, Saunders turned and walked away.

Later in the day Broad had a reply to her most recent Facebook message to Nina Thorowgood, the woman who posted on Holly's memorial page every year. She'd been trying to persuade Nina to talk to them. The reply read: *Just get lost, pig*.

'But she hasn't blocked me,' Broad said cheerfully. 'I think she's warming to me.'

Earlier in the week she'd gone on a drive-by of Nina's registered address, a flat in Frome. There'd been nobody at home, and a neighbour had said that Nina was often away all summer, migrating between festivals and protest camps, and only came home in the autumn.

'Fair-weather crusty,' Broad remarked. 'Mind you, *I* wouldn't want to spend all winter in a tent, either.'

'Keep at her,' Lockyer said. 'I want to know what she meant about Holly being stolen.'

Broad nodded, then went down a rabbit-hole trying to find background on Jason McNeil without knowing his date of birth or his real name. She ended up scrolling through missing persons for anyone meeting his description. There were hundreds, and they had no idea if Jason had even been reported missing.

'Knock it on the head, Gem,' Lockyer told her. 'See if you can find out if Holly had a computer, and where it ended up.'

He went back to the media room to watch the CCTV from

Culver Street car park. The relevant footage was bookmarked. There were no images from the top storey, but a camera in the pedestrian entrance vestibule at lower street level had been working. It had been knocked askew – probably deliberately – so that it took in a section of the door, stairs and wall, rather than the ticket machine it was supposed to protect. Grainy and flickering, the camera had definitely been on its last legs. But Ridgeway was recognizable as he came in. He looked over his shoulder, inadvertently giving the camera a full-face shot.

Lockyer wound back and rewatched it a couple of times, then hit pause on the clearest image. The whites of his eyes gleaming, mouth set in a bristling line as he checked behind him. Tension in every inch of his frame. He didn't look half as steely or nonchalant as he had in his interview about Holly. *Cocky little gobshite.*

'Who were you meeting?' Lockyer murmured. 'Whose cage had you rattled?'

He hit play and let Ridgeway carry on up the stairs. The last climb he'd ever make.

Less than a minute later someone followed him, wearing a sweatshirt with the hood pulled up to shield their face completely. Not even a glimpse of nose or chin, and nothing remarkable about their height or build. Male, from their shape and posture. The man reached for the handrail to pull himself up, jumping straight to the third step and then to the first landing where the stairs turned. The springy, elastic movements of a young, fit person. Lockyer wound it back and watched again and again.

The man wasn't wearing gloves, and as he grabbed the rail the sharp contrast in skin tone between the back of his hand and the palm caught Lockyer's eye. It suggested that the man was black. Like less than one per cent of the population of Salisbury.

Lockyer knew that SOCOs had got a partial palm print from the rail, but that it hadn't matched anyone on the database. The investigation had concluded that this man might be a contact down from London, a foot soldier for whoever was running the county line, with whom Ridgeway was known to have been in contact. Maybe he'd been sent to kill Ridgeway. Or maybe he was just a guy who'd been to a late showing at the pictures and was heading back to his car. It had been twenty past one in the morning, but the car park was open twenty-four hours.

Lockyer was about to switch off when he realized he hadn't reached the end of the bookmarked footage. He let it play on. Two minutes or so later the door opened again, and a single foot in a white trainer was set inside. The person it belonged to stayed outside, in darkness. They hovered, as though undecided, then moved away and let the door slam shut again. Lockyer wound it back, hit pause. The trainer – the foot – was *massive*. He went back to the footage of the unidentified black man to make a comparison, and saw that he was right. The third figure's shoe was at least twice the size of the man in the hoodie's.

Perhaps he'd been told to stand guard to prevent anyone following – which he'd singularly failed to do. Lockyer doubted he'd have cocked it up on purpose: he wouldn't have known what was about to happen to Ridgeway, and he wouldn't have wanted to let him down. No identification made by a glimpse of a trainer would ever stand up in court but, for whatever reason, Lee Geary had been there that night. Lockyer wondered whether the sound of Ridgeway hitting the tarmac had been what had made him turn back at the door.

9

Day 9, Tuesday

Lockyer's phone buzzed as soon as he reached his and Broad's office in the morning. He waved it urgently at her when the number came up as the Cellmark laboratory.

'What – already?' she said.

They'd expected to wait weeks, not days.

'DI Lockyer,' he answered.

'Oh, hello,' said a young, male voice. 'This is Dr Paul Griffiths. I thought I'd call with an interim report, because we've had a couple of what might be quite useful early results with samples taken from Mr Geary's clothing.'

'You have my undivided attention.'

'I've been working on the palynomorph analysis. Mr Geary was carrying a rich and varied plethora of pollen and mould spores, which is what I'd expect when a body has lain on or in the ground for a long period of time. However, I found one particular species in such profusion that I thought I'd track down an identification first and foremost.

It doesn't fit the typical pollen profile of the topographical area where he was found, and it wasn't something I recognized immediately. The body is covered with pollen from the *Salvia divinorum* plant.'

'*Salvia divinorum*?' Lockyer echoed.

Across the room, Broad tapped it into her computer.

'Yes. Also known as Seer's Sage, or Leaves of Prophecy, and various other nicknames. It's a hallucinogenic. They've used it in Mexico for centuries, for rituals and ceremonies and what-have-you.'

Broad turned her screen towards him, pointing urgently. *Salvia divinorum* was a woody herb, with purple-blue flowers. They'd both seen it recently, growing in profusion around the McNeils' beehives at Old Hat Farm. Lockyer thought at once of the bunched sheaves they'd seen hanging to dry in the machine shed.

'When you say Geary was covered with that particular pollen,' Lockyer said, 'could it have been carried on the wind?'

'It's unlikely. The plant is insect-pollinated, not wind-borne. Given the sheer quantity of it, I'd say Mr Geary must have been in actual physical contact with it – a lot of it – shortly before he died. Is that helpful?'

'Immensely.'

'Oh, good.'

'You mentioned two things you'd found?'

'Yes. We also found smudges of a hard, encrusted substance on the back of Mr Geary's trousers. A colleague of mine is still running tests, but the best guess at this stage is that it's a polyurethane reactive adhesive. A hot-melt glue.'

The significance of it hit Lockyer with force. 'The kind you'd have in a glue-gun?'

'Useful again?'

'Very. Thank you.'

'Glad to help. I'll send the full report once we've completed it.'

As soon as he'd hung up, Broad jumped in.

'Salvinorin A – the hallucinogen Holly had in her system?' she said.

'Don't tell me. It comes from *Salvia divinorum*.'

'Yep. The leaves can be chewed fresh, or dried and either smoked or made into a drink,' she read from her screen. 'That's what they're growing at Old Hat Farm, isn't it?'

'Not only growing, but processing, I'd say.'

'So we can bring them in, right? It's an illegal substance now, even if it wasn't when Holly took it.'

'And there's hot-melt glue on Lee's trousers.'

'Like Vince McNeil was using?' Broad said. 'So we can prove Lee went to Old Hat Farm before he died. We can prove they're lying.'

The sun was fierce again that day, the office already heating up. Broad brushed a lock of damp hair back from her forehead, literally at the edge of her seat, ready to start making arrests.

'Let's just . . . hang on a second,' Lockyer said.

Broad started to say something, then changed her mind.

'We know they're lying about Lee not visiting the farm before he died,' he went on.

'Exactly!' Broad burst out.

'But people lie for all sorts of reasons, Gem. We don't know that they killed him.'

'But, guv—'

'At the moment they're talking to us. Jason in particular. If we go in mob-handed, and start arresting them – which at this stage could only be on minor drugs charges – how long do you think that's going to last? Vince in particular. I've met men like him before, and I'm willing to bet he could sit out a six-hour interview without saying a single word. Wouldn't even break a sweat.'

'So, we do nothing with what we've found out?'

'No, but we finish getting background. We haven't looked at Stef's death yet, or found out anything about Jason. And I want to talk to Karen Wilkins again. Once we've done that, we go back and try to get each of them alone.'

'But not at the station? Not under caution?'

'Look . . . We need to keep them on side, for now. And we need to make sure we ask the right questions.'

She still seemed doubtful.

'Just trust me, Gem. Let's make sure we've assembled as much of the picture as we possibly can. I want another look around that farm and I don't want to have to apply for a search warrant. So we need them to let us in.'

'Keep our powder dry? That sort of thing?'

'Exactly that sort of thing. Any joy with Holly's laptop?'

'Yes and no. I spoke to Steve again. He said she definitely had one – they collected it as evidence when she died.'

'Anything on it?'

'He says not much. Nothing to confirm or deny the

suicide theory. He said there was a video message from her mum on there, "a sort of deathbed thing", but that it wasn't especially revealing. "Gruelling", apparently – his term, not mine.'

'I'd still like to see it.'

'I thought you would, so I asked where the laptop ended up, after the inquest, and he doesn't know.'

'Brilliant.'

'I'll try and track it down in storage, but it was most likely returned.'

'Who to? Holly didn't have any other family.'

'Old Hat Farm, then?' Broad said.

'They never mentioned it.'

She shrugged. 'No, but we never asked. Vince did say they had a computer, right? Maybe they're using Holly's.'

'Something else to ask them about next time.' Lockyer got up. 'I'll update the super. At least I can tell her the forensics were worth the money.'

Back at his desk, Lockyer clicked open Stefanie Gould's inquest report. He'd skimmed it before, and there wasn't much to it – none of the grey areas that surrounded Lee and Ridgeway's deaths. Hers was death by misadventure: she'd gone swimming at night, in open water, while under the influence of drugs and alcohol. Whether there'd been a crowd of people with her or no one at all, nobody had been willing or able to say. She'd been found by a litter-picker, tangled in reeds, at the close of the festival. The lake had been ring-fenced with more of those easy-to-climb horizontal railings, and the *Danger – Deep Water* signs would have been far too easy to ignore in the dark.

Nobody seemed to have missed Stefanie during the final day of the festival. If she'd been there with a group of mates, they'd either not cared where she was or had assumed she'd headed elsewhere.

There was absolutely no way to know whether or not anyone had helped her drown.

No way to know if someone had held her under until she'd stopped kicking. It wouldn't have taken long: she'd been under the influence, and, for all her ferocity, she'd been slightly built. Not much to her. She must've been terrified in her final moments, realizing that she couldn't save herself, and that nobody was coming to rescue her. The postmortem had found no obvious marks of restraint on her arms, head or neck, just the scattered bruises of a person who'd spent a few days partying and sleeping on the ground.

Something had caught Lockyer's eye and he read back through until he found it: Stefanie had died at the Soul Tree Festival. He'd heard it mentioned before, very recently.

He swivelled his chair towards Broad.

'Gem, in all the forensic excitement, I forgot to tell you that Lee was at Culver Street the night Ridgeway died,' he said.

She frowned. 'That wasn't in the report.'

'No. The footage wouldn't have been good enough for a positive ID. You can't see his face, but I'm *sure* it's him. He puts his leg through the door and there's his foot, the size of a loaf of bread.'

Broad smiled fleetingly. 'You don't reckon *he* threw Ridgeway off?'

'No. In fact, I think what stopped him going in was that he heard Ridgeway hit the deck.'

'Christ.'

'And I think . . . I think perhaps he saw whoever *did* help Ridgeway over those railings.'

Broad thought about that. 'And you don't mean he saw some random drug-dealer from London, do you?'

'You're right. I don't. Come on, I'll show you.'

Towards the end of the day Lockyer went in search of DI Saunders, and found him, unsurprisingly, in the canteen, with a cup of tea and a packet of three Bourbon creams. Without asking, Lockyer dragged out the chair opposite him, and sat down.

'What's new?' Saunders said, dunking one of the biscuits and eating it whole.

'The message from Holly's mum on her computer,' Lockyer said. 'Can you remember what it said?'

'Like I told your Girl Guide, not a lot.'

'Her name's DC Broad.'

'I know that, but I'm trying to wean myself off calling her Laptop. I nearly snorted my tea when she came and asked me about a laptop.'

'I suppose that's progress. Of a sort.'

'Ah, take your head out of your arse, Lockyer.'

'The message?'

Saunders ate the other two biscuits. 'There was nothing

in it that'd help you, as far as I can remember. She was obviously getting near the end. All I remember is it was pretty harrowing. She says goodbye, says a whole lot about how unfair it all is, a ton of regrets, et cetera et cetera. Some of it made no sense at all.'

'Did she tell Holly she was adopted? Or who her real father was?'

'No. The only really interesting thing was how many times Holly had watched it. Tech told us.'

'How many times?'

'Over two hundred.'

'Jesus.'

'Yeah. She was seriously missing her mum.'

'That would have been more useful in building a case for suicide, rather than murder.'

'Yeah,' Saunders said ruefully. 'We disregarded it in the end.'

'Still, it'd be useful to see it ourselves. If we can find it.'

Another of his expressive grunts. 'Best of British.'

'Do you remember what make it was?'

'Acer, perhaps. Maybe Dell. Nothing fancy. Very girly, though – pink, with band stickers all over it.'

'Okay. Thanks.' Lockyer got up, but paused. 'You were right, back in 2011. Trying to link the deaths. Good job you were paying attention, or it'd probably have been missed.'

'Turn it in, Lockyer. Kissing my arse isn't going to make me forget what you did.'

Again, Lockyer hesitated. 'And you'd never break the rules? Or bend them – even for a mate who you know is fundamentally innocent? Not responsible?'

It was the closest he'd ever come to confessing.

Saunders gave him a steady look. 'No. I wouldn't. "Fundamentally innocent"? Christ, this isn't a bloody philosophy class, mate. Court is where they wring their hands and quibble about motive and mitigation. But not here.' He jabbed one finger at the laminate table top. 'Here we find out the facts. Who did what and how, end of. Then we send them on their merry way, into the criminal justice system. That's the job. And if you're in any way confused about it, you shouldn't be in it.'

Lockyer was rattled. 'I'm not confused about it, Steve.'

He didn't sound convincing to his own ears.

Saunders's response was a snort of derision.

Lockyer sat with his dinner on the shaded back step of his house, trying to follow a podcast about the statistics of the pandemic. Blackbirds carolled as the evening cooled.

He'd texted his friend Kevin, but hadn't had a reply. He'd rung his mother's bedside phone three times, and got no reply. He'd reread Hedy's postcard, and written her a WhatsApp message: *Are you at the house in France? I don't know where to picture you. I would love to hear your voice right now.* Then carefully deleted every character.

He'd sunk three beers, and was contemplating a fourth. He decided to go for a walk, then changed his mind. It usually helped him sort his head out, but right now, it felt like dropping the ball. Eventually he stepped over the remains of the fence between his garden and Iris Musprat's, and knocked at her back door.

She opened it cautiously, peering up, owl-eyed.

'Can I come in for a minute?' Lockyer said.

Iris tugged the laddered arms of her cardigan down over her wrists and stepped back.

Her kitchen looked much as Lockyer's had before he'd pulled out every last thing and scraped the years of dust and grease from the walls. She'd run an antiques and curios shop in her younger days, and the shelves of a huge dresser were heaving with clutter. Everything wore a brownish toupee of dirt.

He was reminded of what Jody had said, about people just carrying on as best they could until they dropped dead. *No surrender.*

They sat down at the rickety table.

'What happened to your husband, Mrs Musprat?' Lockyer asked.

She hardened at once. 'He's not buried out in the woods, if that's what you're asking.'

'No, not at all. I was just interested.'

She eyed him a moment longer. 'Jebel Akhdar, 1959.' She snorted at his blank expression. 'Sidney deserved better than to die in a war no one's even heard of,' she said. 'Out in Arabia. He was a sapper. Clearing mines.'

'You must have been very young.'

'Widow at twenty-five. I had his army pension, but it wasn't much. Mum said I'd have the baby to remember him by, but I lost that an' all.'

'I'm so sorry, Mrs Musprat.'

She tutted. 'Don't bother feeling sorry for *me*.'

'Is that when you moved in here?'

She nodded. 'With Sid's folks, to begin with.'

'And was Bill already living next door?'

'He was. His mum'd died when he was only a nipper, so it was just him and his old dad, who up and died the same year as Sid. Bill had never wed.'

Lockyer pictured Bill and Iris. Two people, still young, who must have been desperately lonely. Living side by side in cottages away from the rest of the village.

'How did Bill meet Róisín?' he asked.

'Why do you want to know?' she said. 'I want to know what you're going to *do*. Bang me up? Because I'm too old – I won't survive it.'

'Please, Mrs Musprat.'

She fetched a bottle of Bell's from the sideboard and two glasses from a shelf. Sloshed out two measures and took hers in one.

'Paddy Conlan was building an extension on the back of their place. Bill was a navvy – they had him round to dig the foundations. Paddy was too grand to get mud under his nails by then.'

'He'd made money?'

'Ha! He'd got it, all right, but not by any fair means. Came down here 'cause he fancied himself as lord of the manor.'

'A crook, then?'

'To his bones. Links to all the wrong sorts of people. He was a bookie and a money-lender, none of it above board. And twenty years older than Rosie, fresh off the boat from Dublin, green as grass. Shame for any woman to get herself married to a man like that, but for Róisín . . . Crushing the life out of her, it was. You never saw her without a cut lip or a black eye. She'd wear these high-necked blouses, but I'd get glimpses of the bruises underneath.'

Iris poured more whisky for herself. 'I reckon he'd have killed her one day, just for the fun of it. Like a cat with a mouse, he was, letting her go then fetching her back. Sending her out with us girls for the day, only to punish her when she got back. Sweet to her one day and vicious the next.' She shook her head. 'Sent her half mad, it did.'

'I can imagine.'

'Paddy said he'd finish her if she ever ran away, and you'd better believe he meant it. He always had his spies in the village, keeping an eye on her. Small wonder she fell in love with Bill, who was as mild as the milkman's pony.' Iris stared down at her empty glass. 'He'd have laid down his life for her. I suppose he did, by letting her come here.'

'She ran away?'

'No.' Iris looked haunted. 'That was the thing – he let her go. Laughed at her. Said, "Go on, then, and see how far you get." She and Bill only had a minute or two before that bastard worked out where she'd gone – or before someone told him.'

'So, what was the plan?'

'Plan?' Iris snorted. 'No time for a *plan*. Rosie was frantic, said she couldn't take it any more. So we just . . . hid her.'

Iris was right. It wasn't a plan. It was a dead-end, quite literally. Lockyer knocked his whisky back in a single gulp. It wasn't his usual drink, but the heat of it felt good.

'Well?' Mrs Musprat demanded. 'Are you going to dig her up? Call your lot in?'

'What did you think would happen?' he asked sadly. 'She deserves a proper burial, just like you said. Her family deserves to know what happened to her.'

'Her parents'll be long dead,' Iris said.

'How old was Róisín when she died?'

'Twenty-four, twenty-five.' Iris thought back, her wizened fingers straying towards the bottle. 'She had a brother and sister, a little younger than her – showed me a photo of them once. Twins, they were. Blond as angels. They'd be seventy or so, now. Rosie and the sister were forever sending letters back and forth . . .'

Lockyer shut his eyes. A sister who'd written regularly would remember her clearly. Might have spent the past fifty years missing her, desperate for news. 'Christ,' he muttered.

'I'll . . .' Iris began '. . . I'll be dead before long. Just wait till then.'

'What? Why? Are you ill?'

She gave him a withering look. 'I'm eighty-six.'

'My great-grandmother lived to be ninety-eight,' Lockyer told her.

'Well, I'm not going to,' she said, almost defiantly. 'I'll write a letter about it all, and leave it for you to find. You can open it once I'm gone.'

Iris blinked. Age had stolen the blue from her eyes. Neither of them spoke for a long time.

She leant forwards. 'How can it be a crime, what I did?'

she said. 'We thought we were helping Rosie. Keeping her safe! And afterwards I just . . . I couldn't betray Bill.'

In her haunted stare he saw undiminished guilt.

'What was done was done out of love,' she said. 'How can that be a crime?'

'Countless crimes have been committed for love.' Lockyer sighed. 'What was her maiden name? I'll need it, if I'm going to find her brother and sister.'

'I can't remember.' Iris's voice shook, and Lockyer suspected she was lying to him.

'Try,' he said firmly. 'And anything about them – where they lived, what they did. Anything like that.'

'You mean to turn me in, then?'

Lockyer didn't reply.

'I thought . . .' she hesitated '. . . I thought I could trust you.'

She stayed at the table as Lockyer left.

He went home, his head crowded, and before long heard the TV come on next door. The tinny mirth of people neither of them would ever meet. Stories like Iris's were commonplace, he reflected. Everyday stories of love and tragedy, of life and death. Sidney Musprat, caught by a mine, his blood draining into the sandy ground of Arabia. Bill Hickson's mother dying while her only son was still small, her name – her death – barely remembered now. And those without a partner, without a family, without children of their own, ended up alone. There were always some. Slipping out of life, solitary and unnoticed, leaving a tragically defiant walking frame in the corner of a room.

Lockyer thought of his brother, twenty years dead. Who might Chris have married? What might his kids have been called? The nieces and nephews Lockyer would never have, the grandchildren his parents would never have. And he saw with sudden clarity that he was on the exact same path as Iris Musprat and Bill Hickson. He was no different. His parents would die, when their time came, and he would be alone. He'd work out his career in the police, and then retire – to what? Tending a garden nobody ever saw? Getting a dog to take on his walks? It seemed inevitable. Whether or not it was too late, it felt as though it was, and he wondered, only then, if he was punishing himself for what had happened to Chris in subtler ways than he was conscious of.

Or perhaps this was just how life went for some people. *Did you not want to have kids, guv?* Broad's inadvertent use of the past tense, hinting that she saw the inevitability of it, too. Perhaps that was why he was being hamstrung by an inconvenient loyalty to Iris Musprat. Why he was apparently risking his own good name to protect her, just as he'd done for Kevin. Like he would have done for Chris. Perhaps for any member of his shrinking family, for any person he loved, any kindred spirit. *If you're in any way confused about that, you shouldn't be in the job.*

He picked up his phone, wrote: *Will you be back, Hedy? At all, I mean?* And hit send before he could rethink.

10

Day 10, Wednesday

After a couple of hours' sleep snatched near dawn, Lockyer headed to Westdene before work. The ground was dry, all trace of the rain gone. Thistledown scudded on a hot breeze, and he found his father on the yard, loading a posse of their biggest ram lambs into the trailer.

'Off to Frome with these,' he said, as Lockyer reached him. 'Fella wants breeding stock – he's picking 'em up from the auction pens.'

'Good price?'

John gave a rueful twitch of his eyebrows. 'It'll have to do.'

'Want me to come with you?' Lockyer thought it might be a good time to talk, just the two of them in the pick-up, unable to escape from one another. 'I'll drive, if you like?' he said.

'Shouldn't you be at work?'

'I can stay late.'

'No need. I won't be long. You help the girl with the baler.'

'It's still not working?'

'She's got it more or less sorted,' John sounded impressed, 'but the feed's still iffy.'

'Have you spoken to Dr Lorne this morning?'

John creaked open the driver's door and climbed in. 'They said they'd call.'

'Did they say when?'

'No.' John squinted at his own gnarled fists on the steering wheel for a moment, then reached out and patted Lockyer's hip awkwardly. 'Don't go on, son. She'll be home soon, right as rain, you'll see.'

Taken aback by this sudden display of affection, Lockyer didn't reply. He watched through the dust, biting back his frustration, as the pick-up bumped away down the track. *No, she won't,* he wanted to say. *She might not come home at all.*

He followed the sound of the tractor to where Jody was inching along a row of hay, turning in the seat to watch the result. A few bales were dotted behind her, but she hadn't got far. When she saw him she knocked the tractor out of gear and jumped down.

'Thought I'd fixed this old fucker,' she said, 'but it's still not right. You've just missed your old man.'

'Seems like the two of you are getting on all right.'

'Yeah, course. He's good as gold. I took him in to see your mum the other day – he'd had too much sun, didn't feel like driving. He was a bit wobbly afterwards, so we sat in the caff, had a chat.'

'A chat?' Lockyer echoed. He felt that subtle hurt again, that intimation of failure. His father didn't do chat.

'Yeah. Horrible to see a bloke like him in that place. But he's doing all right, I reckon. It's just the total opposite of his natural environment, isn't it? The white walls and that smell, everything made of metal or plastic . . . Shakes him up, I guess.'

'I'd better sort out putting you on the car insurance.'

She flashed a grin. 'Oh yeah. Forgot about that.'

'But he's all right? My dad?'

'Can't you ask him yourself?'

'Apparently I literally can't,' Lockyer said. 'Not in any way that he'll answer, in any case.'

'But you *know* your dad – and your mum. You know what their lives are, what they're going through. Right? And they know you're here for them. So why're you trying to turn it into something it isn't?'

'What do you mean?'

'Look, haven't you ever wondered if the reason you and your dad don't have a lot to say to one another is that there isn't anything much that needs saying?'

Lockyer blinked.

'No? Never occurred to you? I mean, I'm willing to bet there isn't much either of you is thinking or feeling that the other doesn't fundamentally get, right? You seem to worry about some rift between the two of you.' Jody shrugged. 'To me it looks like the complete opposite. You and John are basically the same person – and that person isn't chatty. So why are you fighting it?'

Lockyer had no reply. But he felt better for hearing it. 'Thank you,' he said.

'Don't mention it.'

Jody looked down at the stubbled ground. Then they spoke simultaneously: 'I actually wanted to talk to you about—'

'I was wondering if I could ask you about—'

'You go first,' Jody said. 'I've made my speech.'

'When we first met, didn't you mention something to me about the Soul Tree Festival? The one down in Dorset?'

'Yeah, probably. That's where I'd be now, if it wasn't for the sodding virus.' She grinned mischievously. 'And I'm not the only one missing a good knees-up. I thought about heading over to Charmy Down the other week.'

In defiance of lockdown regulations, thousands of people had gathered at an illegal rave on the old airfield at Charmy Down, just north of Bath.

Jody's smile widened at Lockyer's expression. 'It did look like a laugh.'

Lockyer was sceptical. 'By the end people were dancing on the verge alongside the A46, in broad daylight, with no music.'

'Yeah.' She laughed. 'You can't kill the vibe.'

'Have you been to the Soul Tree Festival before?'

'Every year since it started, back in the nineties.'

'So you were there in 2011?'

A tiny pause. 'I guess so. Working, like normal. Well, working *and* having fun. Why?'

'It just came up in a case I'm working on. A woman called Stefanie Gould died there that year.'

'Yeah. I remember hearing about that. Poor Stef. I mean, she was a cow, but that was awful.'

That jolted him. 'You *knew* her?'

Jody gave him a look. 'Yeah. Just from festivals, parties, that kind of thing. She was usually at Soul Tree, but I didn't see her there that year. Then I heard she'd snuffed it.'

Lockyer picked up a trace of tension in Jody, the first he'd ever noticed. He thought back through what he knew about her, and hit upon something.

'You were arrested for possession with intent of a temporary-class substance that year, 2011. A legal high,' he said.

'So what?' She'd started to look pissed off.

'Was it *Salvia divinorum*?'

That startled her. 'Why do you want to know?'

'I'm investigating the death of a man named Lee Geary. He was killed that year, along with Stef, and a man called Ridgeway Kingsley-Jones. They all had links to Old Hat Farm. Have you ever been there?'

Jody squinted away across the field, then flicked him a hard look and turned to climb back into the cab. Lockyer took her arm, which was a mistake. She wrenched it free. 'Get the fuck off me!'

'Okay, okay! Sorry. Look, Jody, I'm not interested in your past or what you were involved in then. I'm really not. I'm just asking for your help. Please.'

Jody glared at him. 'What kind of help?'

'Did the SD come from Old Hat Farm? Have you been there?'

'I've been there,' she said grudgingly.

'I promise I'm not remotely interested in bringing drugs charges against anyone there. Least of all from back then. But four people died that year, and I need to work out why.'

'*Four* people?'

'A girl called Holly Gilbert, too. I think all four deaths are connected.'

'Sally D never killed anybody.'

'I know that,' he said.

'I heard Ridgeway was taken out by some Lambeth gangster.'

'It's possible, but I don't think so. Did you know him?'

'He was just a face, you know? On the scene. Someone you could buy shit from. I steered clear, as a rule. He felt like bad news.'

'And Lee Geary? Ever meet him?'

Jody looked blank.

'But you knew Stef. How did you meet her?'

'*Around*, like I said.' She rolled her eyes, then relented. 'They used to have these parties at Old Hat Farm, for the pagan festivals. Old Hat, New World they were called. The matriarch there is an old-fashioned Gaia type.'

'What's a Gaia?'

'You know – hairy armpits, Earth-mother type.'

'Trish McNeil?'

'Yeah, that's her. She was a sweetheart, though, made everyone welcome. But she hated anyone bringing hard stuff onto the farm. Nothing chemical, she always said.

And definitely no morphia. Just plant-based stuff, nothing harmful.'

'Heroin comes from a plant. So does cocaine.'

'Yeah, but *Salvia* is just sage leaves, right? It's *natural*, not processed.'

'I fail to see the difference, but go on.'

'Go on, what? What else do you want to know?'

'Are you still in touch with the McNeils?'

She shook her head. 'No. It was just . . . in a past life.'

'But you met Stef at one of the parties there?'

'Yeah, probably. I think so.'

Lockyer wrestled his phone from his back pocket, and pulled up a picture of Holly. 'Did you ever meet this girl? She was staying at Old Hat in 2011, and was at the solstice party that summer.'

Jody peered at the screen. 'This is the other girl who died?'

'Yes. Do you recognize her?'

'No.'

He fetched up Lee Geary's terrible mugshot instead. 'What about this one?'

'Christ. No.'

'Okay. Well, how about at Soul Tree that year, the year Stef died?'

'I already told you, I didn't see her there. I was working most of the time.'

'What work did you do?'

'Checking bags on the gate, patting down the females, that sort of thing. A daily six-hour shift, then you're free to go and party.'

'Did anyone else you'd seen at Old Hat Farm come in while you were on the gate? Any faces?'

'Not that I remember.'

Lockyer deflated. 'Okay. Never mind. Thanks, Jody. I'm sorry to have pried into all this.'

'Don't mention it,' she said, putting her foot on the plate and swinging herself up again.

But, for a second time, she changed her mind and jumped down. 'Look, I've probably got some pictures of it.'

'Photos?'

'Yeah. I took a camera everywhere with me back then. Took some official photos for the Soul Tree website, shot some videos, that sort of thing. I was trying to build up a portfolio,' she said self-mockingly. 'Thought it might get me somewhere.'

'Could I see them, please?'

'I suppose. I deleted loads, only kept the good ones. But I can fetch them from Gran's, if you want.'

Lockyer's pulse picked up. 'Thank you. How about from Old Hat?'

'Not so much,' she said. 'I'll look, but no one was going to buy pictures of an illegal party, were they? I stuck a few clips on YouTube – they're probably still there.'

'You were at the Old Hat, New World party in June 2011?'

'Yeah.' She was quiet for a second. 'Just search YouTube – I bet there are loads of videos on there from Soul Tree and Old Hat.'

'Thanks, Jody,' he said again.

'You're not going to use anything I've said against the McNeils, right? You swear?'

'About the SD? No.'

'Because . . .'

'What?' Lockyer asked

'No . . . nothing. They're good people, okay? Don't go after them just because they're different to you.'

'That's not how I operate,' he said. 'What was it you wanted to talk to me about, anyway?'

Jody looked away again. 'I should get on, but . . . yeah. Might be better while your dad's out.'

'What might be better?'

'Easier if I just show you.'

Without another word she reached in and killed the tractor engine, then set off towards the house. Curious, Lockyer followed. She led him upstairs to Chris's old room, shot him a look and tipped her head at the bed.

Lockyer shifted uncomfortably. After a moment, Jody rolled her eyes. 'Don't flatter yourself. Not that.'

'What, then?' he said.

She bent down, grabbed the foot of the bed and heaved it about six inches forwards from the wall. It was a single, with a heavy wooden frame and a tall headboard. It had probably been there since before either Chris or Matt Lockyer was born.

'Your dad's been giving me cash,' Jody said. 'I hate having cash – far too easy to nick. So usually, when I'm in a strange place, I stick it behind the headboard.'

'Right?'

'Well, have a look.'

Still confused, Lockyer went and peered behind the bed.

Shreds of dusty cobweb, a chip in the plaster, a shrivelled, balled-up tissue. And, fastened to the back of the headboard with a drawing pin, a plastic bag of pills.

His stomach lurched. He glanced back at Jody and she raised her hands.

'Nothing to do with me. Swear on my life.'

Lockyer looked at the pills with the dawning, unavoidable realization that they must have been his brother's. His hand shook as he reached for them. Jimmied the pin for a second before giving up and just wrenching the plastic free. He examined them. Pale-blue 150mg tablets, stamped with a thumbs-up symbol. There were maybe seventy or eighty in the bag.

'Is this ecstasy?' he said.

'That'd be my guess.' Jody folded her arms. 'Anyone else been staying in here?'

'No,' he said dully. 'Not since Chris.'

'Right.'

'This is too many for personal use.'

Jody rocked on the balls of her feet. 'I wasn't sure what to do about them. Thought about flushing them but, you know, me and plans. Be just my luck for you to find one in the pan, or walk in while I was doing it, and send me packing.' She hitched a shoulder. 'Then I thought they might be yours.'

'*Mine?*'

'You were in here the other day, after all. Snooping around.'

'I wasn't sn—'

'Yeah. Anyway, now I've got to know you a bit, nothing

about you screams disco-biscuits.' She chewed her lip. 'Then I thought about just forgetting I'd seen them, but I figured you'd probably want to know. What with it being your brother's room. And you being a plod.'

Lockyer nodded silently. Heat was flooding his insides, making his head pound. Was it embarrassment? Anger? He couldn't tell. And he couldn't look Jody in the eye.

'Well,' she said, 'best get back to work.'

He was still staring at the bag of pills when he heard the tractor rattle into life and the baler clunking. From the window, he watched as Jody made steady progress across the field. Behind her, a twist of breeze lifted the dust in a spiral, up into the hot air. Clutching the bag of pills, his head both empty and far too full, he stood there with the *thump-thump-thump* of the machinery matching the hard beat of his heart.

At work he made a strong cup of tea, opened YouTube and searched for Old Hat Farm. Jody was right. Twenty-eight videos had been posted of various gatherings there over the past twelve years or so. They varied in length from fifty seconds to twenty-five minutes. He clicked on the shortest, which was called *Third Eye Open*, and had been posted the previous summer by someone called DelilahXXOO. A girl was sitting cross-legged in a field of blue flowers – Lockyer recognized the *Salvia divinorum* field near the beehives. She had her eyes closed, her hands palm-upwards on her knees, and was smiling beatifically.

'I can feel it,' she said eventually, without opening her eyes. 'Do you feel it?'

The video ended there. Lockyer wondered if she'd taken SD, and it had started to kick in. A higher state of consciousness – or just a chemically induced one. He scrolled down the list, checking how long ago each film had been posted. Only two were tagged from the summer of 2011. One was called *Solstice Fun*, the other simply *Sunrise*, both posted by JoJoNomad, which Lockyer assumed was Jody's online handle.

He clicked on the first: six minutes of slow panning footage, shot at night. A stage lit up with strings of lights, on which a band with at least ten members was performing a strange mix of chanting and singing, beneath a hand-painted banner. A crowd of people were half dancing, half just swaying; oil drum fires blazed in the background, wafting smoke past the camera. On stage, the lead singer put her hands in the air. 'Hail to the eternal spirits of the sky,' she intoned. The crowd obediently raised their arms.

It was difficult to pick individual faces out of the moving mass, or to say exactly where the party had been held, since neither the farmhouse nor any of the barns ever came into shot. Lockyer guessed it had been filmed on a proper camera rather than a mobile phone, purely because of the time and date stamp embedded in a bottom corner of the frame, ticking up the seconds. He watched it right through again, without seeing anyone he recognized.

The second video was of the sunrise. By that time Holly had been dead, lying smashed on the riverbank beside the

A303. People who'd survived the night sat in rows in a field of trampled grass, staring silently into the east as light bled across the sky. Somebody was playing a soft, steady rhythm on a tabla; spliffs and sharing cups passed from hand to hand. Lockyer spotted Trish McNeil to one side, looking serene, wearing a white dress and flowers in her hair. She was the only person he knew. There was nothing to disprove Jason's claim of not having been there, and wherever Vince had been, he hadn't been caught on camera.

Lockyer made more tea, refusing to think about the tablets Jody had found in Chris's room. They were still in his car. He felt an aimless resentment, because he had enough on his plate without having to sort out his little brother as well. But Chris was dead. Long gone. He didn't need *sorting out*. Lockyer should have flushed the pills down the toilet at the farmhouse and forgotten about them, instead of bringing them into his life. Into his memories of Chris. Because sorrow lurked beneath his anger, a treacherous sensation, as if he'd lost some other part of his brother. A part he hadn't even known.

Chris had got drunk at the age of fifteen. Driven by a hunger for adulthood, experimentation and discovery, he and Joe Cameron, his best mate, had swiped a litre bottle of vodka and taken it to a barn. Downed the lot. What they'd discovered, predominantly, was that drinking so much vodka made you puke your guts up. It was a phase Lockyer had largely bypassed – the rebellious drinking and smoking. During Fresher's Week at university, when it'd seemed mandatory, he'd drunk himself sick once or twice. But that had been plenty. He hadn't gone back for more, over and over, like most teenagers did. Like Chris had.

As Chris had lain on his bed after that vodka, limp and sweaty, retching periodically into a bucket, Lockyer – eighteen at the time – remembered thinking that lessons would be learnt. It had been, he now realized, a very middle-aged thought for him to have. Not to mention woefully optimistic. Chris had always liked a drink or six. It was one of the reasons Lockyer hadn't gone on his eighteenth-birthday pub crawl. He'd known they'd all be plastered from early in the evening, and pretty much insensible by the end. Falling about in crowded places, slurring, talking shit. Already, by the age of twenty-one, Lockyer would rather have been anywhere else. So that was why he hadn't been there when Chris was stabbed. The very specific way in which he'd let his brother down.

But pills? Ecstasy? He'd had no idea Chris was into that. And not just into it, apparently, selling it, too. The thought made his skin crawl. Had he had pills with him on his birthday binge? Had he taken any – dealt any? Had he been high when he'd waded into the brawl outside on the pavement, believing he could sort it out, and make everyone get along? Was *that* why? Chemical confidence? The anger flared again. Chris's post-mortem hadn't included a tox-screen – why spend the money when he'd had a four-inch knife wound through his ribs?

Lockyer realized he was sitting with his fists clenched, staring at nothing. Across the room, Broad yawned. There were blue smudges under her eyes, which was unusual. She normally looked so fresh she made Lockyer feel like a ruin. 'You okay, Gem?'

She made a face. 'Just about. I can't sleep when it's this hot at night. Can you?'

'I've never been much of a sleeper.'

'Right. I don't know how you function. Two broken nights and I feel like I've been lobotomized. I mean, I'm fine for work, guv,' she added hurriedly. 'I've had about four gallons of coffee.'

'I know you're fine for work.'

She stifled another yawn. 'When do you think we'll get those pictures from your friend, then?'

Lockyer had told her about Jody as a potential source of intel. He'd left out the part about her probable history of selling SD for the McNeils. Living off the land, indeed. 'Not sure.'

He'd forgotten to ask, and that bothered him. The discovery of the pills had emptied his head, made him even more distracted.

'I'll call her later. She said she'd have to get them from her grandma's house, so I might need to drive her.'

Lockyer resolved to get rid of the pills as soon as he got home.

He ran a search on YouTube for the Soul Tree Festival. Literally hundreds of videos came up. With a sigh, he found a quiet room to call Karen Wilkins instead.

'Yep?' was the curt reply, when she picked up.

The toddler was screaming in the background, and muffled sounds told him Karen wasn't sitting still. He pictured her with the phone clamped between shoulder and ear. Multi-tasking.

'Mrs Wilkins? This is DI Lockyer.'

'Poppy, give that back. Give it back to her. *Do as you're told!* DI Lockyer,' she said, breathlessly. 'What is it? Have you found something?'

'I believe I'm beginning to get a clearer idea of what might have happened to your brother. I just wanted to check a couple of things with you, if you have a minute?'

'I *never* have a sodding minute, but fire away.'

'I wanted to ask about Ridgeway Kingsley-Jones, one of Lee's new friends.'

'That's one word for him. Have you found him?'

'In a way, yes. Ridgeway actually died in unexplained circumstances shortly before Lee went missing.'

There was a loaded silence at the other end of the line. Karen took a sharp breath. 'You can't think Lee had anything to do with—'

'No, I—'

'Because I told you, he wasn't violent. Not ever, and—'

'Mrs Wilkins—'

'Karen,' she interrupted impatiently.

'Karen. I don't think Lee was involved at all. But I do think he was there when it happened.'

'What? When was this? Look, whatever those arseholes were mixed up in, I'm telling you, Lee was just—'

'Karen, I know. I *know*.'

A pause. 'Okay.'

'You told us before that Lee had been worried about

something – agitated – before he finally went off on the eighteenth. I think seeing what had happened to Ridgeway might've been what upset him. Can you remember exactly when Lee started to seem upset?'

'No. I just don't know – I'm sorry. He was in and out . . . I didn't see him every day.'

'That's okay. Can you tell me whether it was days or months before he went missing?'

'Definitely not months. More than days. I guess two or three weeks? I mean, I'd been asking him, "What is it? What's wrong?" I told him he could trust me, whatever it was, but he – he obviously didn't.'

'He might not have wanted to put you in any danger by involving you.'

'Oh.' Her voice wavered.

'Ridgeway died on the thirtieth of October 2011. That's eighteen days before Lee set off from your flat, and didn't come back. Does that sound as though it would tie in with his unsettled behaviour?'

'Yes. I guess it would.'

'You also said that one of Lee's new friends came to your flat looking for him. Can you remember whether that was before or after he became agitated?'

'I can't be a hundred per cent sure, but I'd say it was after. Nearer to when he went missing.'

'Did you tell Lee that someone had come looking for him?'

'Yes, I would have done. Especially then, with him so het-up.'

'Can you describe the man who came looking for Lee?'

'Not really. Youngish. In his early thirties, I guess, though I find it harder to tell black people's ages. It was on TV the other day that white people often think young black people are much older than they really are.'

'So, a black male in his twenties or thirties? Can you tell me anything else about him?'

'God, I only saw him for twenty seconds. He had his hair in those braids, you know, close to the scalp, with gaps in between.'

'Cornrows?'

'Yeah. He wasn't especially tall, or fat or thin. But he was quite nice-looking. And polite.' Something clicked. 'You know who it was, don't you? Did he kill Lee?'

'As soon as I know anything for certain, I'll tell you. I give you my word. Do you think you'd recognize the man if you saw him again?'

'I don't know. Maybe?'

'Okay, I'll keep that in mind.'

The only problem with that was that they didn't have a photograph of Jason McNeil. Or whoever he really was.

Karen interrupted his thoughts. 'How did Ridgeway die?'

'He sustained fatal injuries in a fall from the top of Culver Street car park,' Lockyer said. 'I believe he was pushed.'

'Christ. I was only there yesterday. Did whoever it was go after Lee, too? Because he was a witness? Was it drugs?'

'I don't want to speculate at this stage, Karen. But thank you. You've been very helpful.'

He walked back to the office slowly, thinking she might

have been right. It might actually be a case of witness elimination. They might have got carried away in trying to connect Lee and Ridgeway's deaths to Holly Gilbert's. And Stefanie's drowning could be unrelated to any of it.

Lee *had* been to Old Hat Farm shortly before his death, but perhaps the McNeils were lying about that for other reasons. Perhaps they simply liked to keep the law at arm's length. Or perhaps they'd seen what had happened to Lee, and were too frightened to speak up. Perhaps they'd been threatened. Perhaps the black male who'd been at Culver Street car park and had gone to Karen's flat looking for Lee hadn't been Jason McNeil. Perhaps Lee had run to Old Hat Farm as a place of safety. Even Jody, who certainly wasn't afraid to speak her mind, had described the McNeils as good people.

And perhaps whoever Lee had been running from had simply tracked him to Old Hat Farm. He wouldn't have been hard to follow.

Aside from yawning, Broad had spent the morning trying to find out what had happened to Holly's belongings – including her mother's house, and her missing laptop. At the age of twenty Holly naturally hadn't made a will, so Broad had the idea of locating her next of kin and asking whether, in the final six months of her life, Holly had spoken to them about any of the goings-on at Old Hat Farm. After his conversation with Karen Wilkins, Lockyer had a sneaking feeling that they were wasting their time, but when he got back to the office Broad had the particular energy that immediately told him she'd found something. Excitement did more for her than any amount of caffeine.

'I've got something quite interesting, guv.'

'I'm all ears, Gem.'

'So, Holly's mum was Imogen Gilbert. She married Graham Gilbert in 1992, when she'd just turned eighteen. Holly was less than a year old then, so I guess Graham brought her up as his own until he died in a road accident in 1999. Holly was only eight, must have been devastating.'

'Yes?'

'Well, look at the dates, guv. 1990, Vince is jailed for setting fire to his girlfriend's house, with her in it. 1991, Vince's daughter, Holly, is born.'

Lockyer saw what she was saying. 'And the girlfriend's name was Imogen. Imogen Simm.'

'Yep. Vince was arrested the day after the fire, and remanded in custody after that. So Imogen must have been pregnant when it happened.'

'Jesus.' He let it sink in. 'Do you think he knew? Was *that* what he was trying to do – get rid of her *and* the baby?'

'I don't know. Must have made it interesting when Holly turned up on his doorstep all those years later, though.'

'Interesting is one word.'

'But that's not the *really* good bit.' Broad was clearly enjoying herself. 'I contacted Surrey Council. Everything went to Holly in Imogen's will, but probate hadn't been granted by the time Holly died. There were only eight months between the deaths of mother and daughter. The council had to use a deceased-estate research company to track down Holly's next of kin. I've just been on the phone to them.'

'They found a relative?'

'Yes, they did. An aunt.'

Lockyer frowned. 'A sibling of the stepdad – of Graham Gilbert?'

'Nope. A maternal aunt. Imogen had a younger sister. Patricia.'

Broad waited for him to get it.

'You don't mean *Trish*?' he said.

'Patricia McNeil, née Simm. Trish was Holly's aunt. And she inherited a nice little three-bed in Guildford, which, according to Land Registry . . .' she turned back to her computer screen and clicked a few times '. . . she sold in the spring of 2012 for five hundred and thirty-two thousand pounds.'

Lockyer tipped his head. 'Quite the pay day.'

'I *knew* there was no way they were running that place by selling honey and weird drinks.'

'And SD, don't forget.'

'Yeah, but a half-million-pound cash injection can't have hurt, can it? And don't you think it's weird they never mentioned that Holly was Trish's niece?'

'Yes,' Lockyer said. 'Unless they didn't know.'

'What do you mean? How could they not have known?'

'Jason and Trish both said that Vince had had no idea he was a father until Holly showed up. Maybe Trish didn't know she was an aunt, either. Maybe Vince had other girlfriends.'

'But Vince must have known as soon as Holly said who her mother was. And they've all known since Trish inherited the house, right? So why hide it?'

Broad raised her eyebrows, waiting.

Only minutes before, Lockyer had been questioning how hard they were looking at Holly's family, and reminding himself that it was *Lee's* death they were investigating. Now he was changing his mind again. 'All right,' he said. 'We'll go back and ask them. But carefully. Let's not march in there and throw a grenade. I want to know who knew what, and when.'

11

They found Trish first, in the chicken run behind the farm-house where the ground was scratched to dust. She was shovelling mucky straw into a wheelbarrow. Flecks of chaff had stuck to the sweat on her chest, and the pungent stink of chicken shit was in the air, but she smiled in greeting. As if they really *were* welcome.

'Officers,' she said. 'I think you're starting to like it here.'

'Hot day for yard work,' Lockyer said.

'Ah, well,' Trish said. 'That's animals for you. They still need looking after, no matter how hot or cold it is.'

'I know. My family farms,' Lockyer said.

She cast an appraising eye over him. 'I didn't think you were the usual office type. Although I expect you mean the kind of farm where most of the residents get eaten?'

'I'm afraid so. Even the sugar beet.'

Her necklaces clattered as she delved back into the hen-house. 'What can I do for you today?' she asked.

Lockyer cast a quick glance at Broad. She'd thrust one hip

out and propped her arm on it, resting her weight as though literally wilting in the heat.

'Why didn't you tell us you were Holly's aunt?' he said.

Trish froze, then glanced back at them fearfully. 'Who told you?' she said tersely.

'Nobody. Finding things out is a big part of what we do.'

'Evidently. Even when it's not remotely relevant to your case.' Trish threw a scoop of muck into the barrow. 'Please,' she said. 'Please don't tell Vince and Jason.'

Broad looked bewildered. 'Surely Vince must know already.'

'He knows,' Trish said. 'He just doesn't know that I know.'

'Would you care to explain that?' Lockyer said.

'Not really.'

There was a long pause. Lockyer broke it. 'Well, we can always just go and ask Vince—'

'No!' A touch of desperation. 'All right. I didn't know until after Holly died, and the solicitor got in touch with me about the house.'

'You didn't know your sister had a daughter called Holly?'

'No. We weren't in touch. Not for years and years. I knew she was pregnant, but I left before she had the baby. Went travelling. And Vince was . . . different back then. He was in a lot of pain. Emotional pain. I knew he hadn't been faithful to Imogen. I never thought for one moment that Holly was her kid.'

'Really? Even though she was exactly the right age?'

'Like I said, Vince had other girlfriends. He – and Holly – told me her mother's name was Susan Gilbert. And Holly didn't bring any photos with her – not that she showed me, anyway.'

'Why would they hide that from you?'

'I suppose it was Vince. Trying to protect me.'

'Protect you from what?'

'I . . . He . . .' Trish didn't look them in the eye. 'Look, Vince was Imo's boyfriend to begin with, right? Back when we were kids. I mean, we were both in love with him, but I was only fifteen. He never looked twice at me back then. But after the fire . . .' She looked up at last, eyes haunted. 'After that, of course, I didn't see him for years.'

'You're going to have to help me out here, Trish,' Lockyer said.

'I left as soon as I could. Never saw my sister again. Never wanted to. We always . . . we *hated* each other. I know people say you don't hate your family, not really, but we were like oil and water. And after what she'd done . . .'

'What had she done?'

Trish carried on as if she hadn't heard the question. 'I turned sixteen soon afterwards, and went off backpacking. I was gone years. Imo went to live with our grandmother – she was always her favourite. Took after our mother. Little Miss Prim and Proper . . . in spite of having a kid at the age of seventeen.' Bitterness had crept into her voice. 'They didn't try very hard to persuade me to stay, and when I left I never told them where I was going.'

'Where did you go?' Broad asked.

'Here, there and everywhere,' Trish said. 'Working in bars, picking fruit. Just to meet people really. I had money. Our dad . . .' At the mention of him she faltered. 'Dad had taken out a life-insurance policy. It was more than enough to pay for the kind of life I wanted to lead. Simple, clean.' She looked around, squinting into the harsh light. 'Eventually, when I was ready to come back, I used it to buy this place.'

'And then you married the man who'd killed your parents. And almost killed your sister,' Lockyer said.

'Vince never meant to hurt *anyone!*' Trish said. 'He never *would*. Not even back then, when he was off the rails. That's what my parents used to say about him.' A humourless smile. 'As though living life on rails was a good thing.'

'They were possibly just concerned for their young daughters.'

'Maybe, but they created the problem. Trying to split them up, being so horrible to Vince – if they'd just let it run its course, he'd have seen what Imogen was really like. She was selfish . . . manipulative. But she had him hook, line and sinker for a while. He was besotted. So when *we* got together – and I know it was years afterwards, but still – I just couldn't bear to think of them together. Vince and Imo. Couldn't stand being reminded of it. It was easier to just not talk about it. Let it heal over.'

'I thought acceptance and non-judgement were the route to healing?' Broad said.

Trish nodded, downcast. 'They are. I never said I was the finished article.'

'So, what you're saying is that Vince kept the identity of Holly's mother from you because you were insecure about his past relationship with your sister?' Lockyer said. 'Really?'

She shot him a resentful look. 'Don't belittle other people's experiences, Inspector.'

'I wasn't. It's just you strike me as a strong, self-assured sort of person.'

'Everyone has a weak spot. Imogen's mine. Or she was.'

Lockyer tried to think it all through. 'Holly turned up out of the blue, you said. Did she not tell you both straight away who her mother was?'

'I think the whole out-of-the-blue thing was a bit staged, truth be told.'

'You mean, you think Holly and Vince had been in touch prior to that?'

'Not long before, but yes. Holly must have found him somehow, and I suppose he asked her not to mention whose daughter she really was.'

'How do you know Vince and Imogen hadn't been in touch all that time?'

'Because they *hadn't*,' she said emphatically. 'He'd have told me, and he would never lie about that – about *her*. Not to me.'

'So do you think Holly knew who *you* were? That you were her aunt?'

'I don't know.' Trish looked troubled by this. 'If she did she never said anything to me.'

'I suppose she couldn't, if she'd agreed to conceal her mother's identity. So, once she'd died and you found out she was your niece, why didn't you go to Vince with it?'

'I thought, What's the point? I mean, he was grieving. He'd loved Holly from the moment they met – she was his flesh and blood. And she was so easy to love. There just never seemed to be a good time to bring it up,' she said. 'It wasn't like Imogen was even alive ... Like we were going to run into her at Holly's funeral, or anything like that. It didn't seem worth mentioning.'

Lockyer was certain he wasn't being told the full story. 'Not even when you inherited her house?' he said. 'When you sold it for all that money?'

Trish paled. 'Vince doesn't know about that. Please, don't—'

'He doesn't know you've got half a million in the bank?'

'We haven't! Not any more. I look after all the finances, and I didn't tell him. I've just been topping us up with it for the past nine years. The roof needed repairs, and the parties always cost more than they make. We got a new laptop, and the quad bike. Some better tools for the workshop. When we had to stop selling the *Sa*—'

She pulled herself up short, looking anxiously back and forth between them.

'The *Salvia divinorum*?' Lockyer suggested.

'You – you know about that?'

'We do. But it doesn't have to be relevant. Unless it proves to be relevant.'

'We stopped selling it when it was made illegal,' Trish asserted. 'That hit our income.'

'Yet you still grow it. An awful lot of it,' Broad said.

'It just grows here, now,' Trish said. 'There was no need to uproot it. It's just a herb. The bees love it.'

'And the stuff you've got drying in the barn?' Broad pressed.

Lockyer didn't want them sidetracked by the SD. 'Like I said, we're not here about that,' he said. 'What make was the new laptop you bought?'

'What? It's a – a Toshiba.'

'What had you been using prior to that?'

'I can't remember. Why on earth does it matter?'

'We're trying to find Holly's old laptop. Do you know where it is?'

'No. I never saw her use one. Perhaps she didn't bring it here.' Trish seemed to gather herself. 'But you're here about Lee Geary,' she said. 'Aren't you? *Why* are you poking your noses into our lives like this? We've done nothing wrong!'

'Well, it's because we still think Lee's death might be linked to Holly's. And it's because we know you're lying to us.'

She blinked. 'About what?'

'Lee Geary came here shortly before his death, in the autumn of 2011.'

'But . . .' She looked perplexed. 'He didn't.'

'We can prove that he did.'

'I never saw him again after that solstice. I swear on my life. It's not like you could miss a great lump like him around the place.'

'How do you know Vince and Jason didn't see him?'

'Because they'd have told me.'

'You're certain of that?'

'Yes. We don't keep secrets from each other.'

'But that's just not true either, is it, Mrs McNeil?'

She fiddled with the dustpan handle. 'I need to get on,' she said quietly.

Lockyer and Broad left her to it.

They spotted Vince and the two backpackers in a field near the stream, between the farmhouse and the road, working between neat rows of vegetables.

'Could we hang on for one second?' Broad said plaintively, as they reached the shade of the poplars. The trace of a breeze whispered through the leaves there. 'The trouble with this weather is that it almost never happens, so we don't get the chance to acclimatize,' she said. 'Poor Merry hates it – I've ordered one of those gel mats you put in the freezer.' She saw Lockyer's puzzled expression. 'Then you put it under their bed, to cool them down.'

Merry was her Jack Russell terrier. Broad occasionally – illicitly – brought him into the station. 'Might get one for myself,' she added. 'Pete won't have a fan going at night – the noise keeps him awake. I took him for a swim in the river last night.'

'Who? Pete?'

Lockyer struggled to picture Broad's very vanilla boy-friend doing any such thing.

Broad smiled. 'No, Merry.'

Lockyer nodded back towards Trish. 'What did you make of that?'

'Weird as hell,' Broad replied. 'I mean, how long were Holly and Vince planning on keeping up the fiction that her mother was some random woman called Susan? Forever?'

'It's something to ask Vince,' Lockyer said.

'And didn't Trish have a right to know? Her sister was *dead* . . . Did no one tell her that, either?'

'I agree,' he said. 'I get that they were estranged, but still . . . There has to be more to it than Trish being insecure about marrying her sister's ex.'

'Has to be,' Broad agreed. 'I mean, does anyone hate their sister that much? I thought the deal with siblings was that you had to love them, even when they drove you mad.'

'So did I.'

Lockyer felt a flicker of anger, and the unpleasant sensation that was nearly shame at the thought of Chris and his dealing. All followed by a flush of dismay. 'But perhaps when that relationship breaks down, it *really* breaks down,' he said.

'She said they both loved Vince, and then he went and killed their parents,' Broad said. 'I can't imagine what that must have done to their heads.'

'Well, she seems to have forgiven him,' Lockyer said.

'And then some. It almost sounded as though she blamed her parents for what happened.'

'And the sister. "What Imogen did", she said. And ignored it when I asked what she meant.'

Broad squinted thoughtfully. 'Thing is, guv, how does any of this get us closer to finding out who killed Lee Geary?'

'It gets us closer to finding out who these people really are, and how they all connect. What they have to hide and how good they are at it.'

'Do you believe her? About Lee?' she asked.

'Almost. Yes.'

'Me too.'

'Unless she's a very good liar.'

Broad was clearly flagging. Lockyer had borrowed a squad car with functioning air-con, and almost suggested she go and wait in it. But she'd hate the implication of being superfluous, and he wanted two pairs of ears to hear what the McNeils had to say for themselves.

Vince and the two young Australians had been picking caterpillars from rows of brassicas. The plants had been carefully netted but the butterflies had been undeterred.

'What are you going to do with them?' Broad said, peering at the writhing mass in the bucket with a shudder.

'Chickens love 'em,' Vince rumbled, meeting Broad's horror with a gently teasing smile, his eyes a glimmer of electric blue.

'Don't you like butterflies?' Broad said weakly.

'Of course. But not as much as I like having food to eat through the winter.'

Lockyer thought of the money Trish probably still had in the bank. It must take a long time to spend half a million pounds on the sly, even with a roof to repair and a new computer. Yet here was Vince, thinking they might conceivably go hungry if his cabbages failed.

'How did Holly find you, Vince?' Lockyer said.

Vince's face clouded. He cast a glance at the backpackers, then moved further away and reached for a flask of water from the quad bike, which was parked alongside.

'Trish doesn't seem to know,' Lockyer pushed.

Vince frowned. 'You've been talking to Trish about Holly?'

'We have.'

Lockyer sensed Broad's unease. Probably wondering if he was going to give the game away, and tell him that Trish knew Holly was her niece. But he wasn't planning to. Until such time as they related to a crime, their secrets were their own.

'Of course, there are tracing agencies people can use,' he said, 'but she'd have needed your name to go on. Did Imogen tell her?'

Vince picked up a rag and wiped the sweat from his face. Giving himself plenty of time to answer, Lockyer thought.

'In a way,' Vince said. 'After her mum died, Holly found letters she'd stashed away. Letters I'd written to her from prison, years back, before I learnt to let go. Imogen never replied to any of them, but she kept them. I guess that means something.'

'Did you try to contact Imogen when you came out of prison?'

'Yes, and if I'd known about Holly, I'd have tried a lot harder. But I respected Imo's wishes. I didn't want to force anything . . .' He trailed off, staring into Lockyer's eyes as realization dawned. 'You know,' he said. 'Don't you?'

'We know it was Holly's grandparents who died in that fire. And that your girlfriend, Imogen Simm, who was also in the house, was pregnant with Holly at the time.'

Vince's gaze slid away across the dusty field to where the land rose sharply, in the north-west, up to Pewsey Hill. 'Smoke inhalation,' he said eventually. 'The fire was right below the Simms' bedroom. Imo's was on the other side of the house. And I had no idea she was pregnant.'

'Would it have made a difference?'

'The house was supposed to be empty. Nobody was supposed to get hurt. It was a – a cry for help.'

'That doesn't really answer my question.'

Vince said nothing.

'They charged you the next day,' Lockyer said. 'No bail, and you remained in custody after that. I guess the case against you must have been pretty watertight.'

'Haven't you read all about it?' Vince said neutrally.

'It's virtually impossible to locate case files from thirty years ago. Especially if the case was closed.'

'Ah,' he said, and Lockyer wasn't sure he was going to add anything else. Then: 'Yeah, it was pretty watertight. I was just a stupid kid. I used one of my own T-shirts to light it. Stuffed it into a bottle of Jack Daniel's covered with my fingerprints, shoved it through the cat flap. It set fire to the door curtain and went from there. But the whiskey never caught. So the part of the T-shirt that had been *inside* the bottle didn't get burnt.' A complicated expression flitted over his face. 'Rookie mistake,' he said. 'Should've soaked the fabric first. But perhaps it was for the best, me getting nicked. I was a loose cannon back then, so angry with the world about the crappy hand I'd been dealt. I'd already been in a lot of trouble. The police were delighted to get their hands on me.'

'The Simms had said you couldn't see Imogen any more,' Broad said. 'Was that the reason?'

'They hadn't just said it, they were physically enforcing it. Imo was basically being kept prisoner. By then she hated them as much as I did.' He blinked. 'Or, at least, I thought she did. I thought we were going to get married.'

'What did you hope to achieve by setting their house on fire?'

Vince flashed Broad a lupine grin. 'I don't think you can apply that kind of logic to a lovesick teenager, when nothing will *ever* be as important as getting who they want.' He fell serious again. 'Looking back, I don't blame the Simms for not wanting me anywhere near their daughter. But prison was the making of me. I learnt about consequences. I learnt patience. I learnt not to let other people dictate the way I felt, or what I did as a result.'

'You learnt control,' Lockyer said.

'Yes. And I'm not talking about being able to bottle up a feeling. I'm talking about not being made to feel it in the first place.'

'Did you have counselling or something?' Broad asked, and Lockyer noticed the way Vince's face softened fractionally when he looked at her. The innate, perhaps old-fashioned chivalry it implied.

'I did, but not from a shrink.' He took a swig of water. 'I met a bloke called Mitch Dolton, in shop. He taught me woodwork. Terrifying man, but only on the surface. Dolton was on a life term. He wasn't ever getting out, and he knew it. He taught me how to just . . . be.'

'Jason told us you and Trish haven't been able to have kids of your own,' Lockyer said.

Vince fixed him with a level stare, and said nothing.

Lockyer knew he'd crossed a line. It was none of their business. 'Sorry,' he said. 'I didn't mean to pry.'

A slight narrowing of Vince's eyes. 'Didn't you?'

'No more than I have to.'

'No more than you have to for what?'

'To find out what Holly meant to you. And what you might've been prepared to do for her. Before she died, and afterwards.'

'I've told you, she meant the world to me. I don't understand why you feel the need to test that.'

Lockyer decided to be frank. 'We're trying to work out whether you might have killed for her.'

Vince didn't move a muscle.

'Because we know Lee Geary came here on or about the day he disappeared. We can prove it. And then he ended up dead just a mile away. What we don't know is why he came here; although I have a couple of theories.'

'Oh?'

'One is that somebody here believed he – or, rather, Ridgeway Kingsley-Jones – was responsible for Holly's death. And when Lee understood what had happened to Ridgeway, and to Stef, he got scared. So he came here to try to talk that person out of doing the same to him.'

More stillness. More silence.

'He was a simple, trusting sort of person. Not the brightest. It probably didn't occur to him that he was offering himself up on a plate.'

Not even a flicker of emotion changed Vince's expression.

It was impossible to read him. If Dolton had taught him that, it was an impressive trick.

'You reckon you've got proof he came here?' Vince said. 'But do you have any proof that he was *attacked* here? Because if you think, for one second, that anyone here would've wanted to harm a gentle soul like Lee Geary, then you're way, *way* off the mark.'

'So you didn't blame the three of them for Holly's death? Directly or otherwise?'

'I blamed Ridgeway. We all know what he was like. And damage had been done to Stef that made her dangerous. The anger in her . . . I recognized it. But I had nothing to do with their deaths. Neither did Jason – or anyone here, for that matter.'

'You know that for certain?'

'I do.'

'But you were here that day? The eighteenth of November 2011?'

'As far as I know. But I never really know what day it is.'

'And you maintain that you never saw Lee Geary that day? Or on any other day since the solstice party?'

'I do. But it's a big farm. If he *did* come here, he left again without talking to any of us.' A pause. 'What's your other theory?'

'I'd prefer to keep that to myself,' Lockyer said.

Vince stared off into the distance again. 'Seems to me that if whoever killed Ridgeway was coming for Lee as well, they might have followed him here,' he said, 'forced him out onto the plain, somewhere quiet, and attacked him.'

He and Lockyer exchanged a long look. Neither man blinked.

'Well,' Broad said, breaking the tension, 'thanks for talking to us, Mr McNeil. Do you know where we might find Jason?'

'Workshop, most likely.' He turned back to the vegetables. 'Knock. Don't just burst in on him.'

They walked back towards the yard, their shoes covered with dust. Lockyer was distracted by the notion that there was something in what Vince had just said. Or perhaps in the *way* he'd said it. Something had snagged his subconscious. He noticed as they approached the workshop that Broad was quiet, too. 'You all right, Gem?'

'Yeah. Just a bit hot.'

He hesitated. 'Want to sit this one out? Go and hang out in the air-con?'

She raised a smile. 'Thanks, but I'm too curious to know what colour I sound today.'

'All right. That's twice Vince has warned us to approach Jason softly. What do you think would happen if we just barged in?'

Broad looked uncomfortable. 'Only one way to find out, guv.'

I've got enough crazy going on in my head already, Jason had said. For the first time, Lockyer wondered how literally to take that. Whether, when he was overwhelmed, he had a tendency to snap.

But when they reached the shed and heard Jason at work,

Lockyer was reluctant to cause unnecessary trouble. He knocked, and tried not to sense guilt in the subsequent silence.

'Yup,' came the call from inside.

Jason was at the bench, stripped to the waist and wearing jeans cut off at the knee. A T-shirt hung at one hip, pushed through a belt loop. His torso had long, lean muscles. Flecks of shavings and sawdust were caught in the scatter of hair on his chest, and his skin was gleaming from the heat. Broad's eyes widened, perhaps because it was so much darker inside than out.

'You're back,' Jason said, smiling as though genuinely pleased. 'Come to sweet-talk me with some more choice words, DC Broad?'

Broad looked a tiny bit flattered. 'Not exactly.'

'Shame.'

Jason turned. He had a huge, round-headed mallet in one hand and a chisel in the other. Behind him on the bench were the beginnings of another sinuously carved frame.

'Is that for another mirror?' Broad asked.

'Eventually. If I can coax the right shapes from it.'

'You don't work to a design?'

'No more than the tree did. I follow the lines it gives me. I try to make it the shape it *wants* to be. If that doesn't make me sound like a total knob.'

'No,' Broad said. 'It sounds like the sort of thing an artist would say.'

It was Jason's turn to look subtly pleased.

'That's quite a weapon,' Lockyer said, nodding at the

mallet in Jason's hand. It was short-handled, its head a ball at least eleven or twelve centimetres in diameter.

'Carver's mallet,' Jason said. 'Vince made it when he was inside. It's turned from a single piece of hornbeam. He wanted ironwood – that's traditional. *Lignum vitae*. But it costs a lot more. Her Majesty's prison service wouldn't stretch to it. I think the hornbeam's better, anyway. Perfect weight and bounce, perfect balance.'

He put the chisel down and hefted the mallet head into his palm. It made a meaty smack.

'What does it weigh?' Lockyer asked.

'About eight hundred grams, maybe a little more.'

'Why does it need to be so big?'

'The weight means you can use less muscle, the short handle lets you get up close to the work, and the round surface means you can keep your eyes on what you're carving. The mallet doesn't have to be square to the chisel. You'll still hit it true every time. It's all about precision.'

Jason put it down on the bench behind him. 'But I don't suppose you're here to talk about woodwork.'

'Not really,' Broad said.

Lockyer thought he heard the trace of an apology in her tone. It made him uneasy. It was one thing to like a suspect objectively, another, far more complicated, to really *like* them. He knew that well enough from experience.

'You mentioned before that you don't drink alcohol, or take any recreational drugs,' he said. 'Is that because of your synesthesia?'

'Yeah, mostly. I've tried a few things in the past but,

man . . .' He drew the word out, shaking his head. 'The chaos in my brain. Just wasn't worth it.'

'Does that include the *Salvia divinorum*?'

Jason pressed his lips together. 'Right, so you know about that?'

'You're not exactly taking steps to hide it.'

'Well, it's just a plant. Not illegal to grow it.'

'It is if it's for human consumption,' Lockyer said.

'We don't grow it for human consumption.'

'So . . . the stuff that's drying in the barn? Who's that for? The chickens?'

Jason twitched his head slightly, not meeting Lockyer's eye. For a second Lockyer thought it might be a tell, but then: 'If you could avoid saying that word, Inspector, I'd really appreciate it.'

'Which word? Chickens?'

Another flinch. 'Yeah.'

'You live on a farm, with a lot of ch– poultry, but you can't stand to hear the word?'

'Only when *you* say it. It's like . . . burning rubber.'

Lockyer almost apologized. 'Would you mind showing us the shed next to the drying barn, please? The one that's locked?'

'Yeah, no worries.' Jason reached for a key from a hook on the wall. 'Walk this way.'

The workshop had been stuffy, but had at least been shady. Outside, the sun had the brute force of a hammer.

'Holly took SD the night she died,' Lockyer said, as they walked.

'I know.'

'Have you ever tried it?'

'Yeah. It's not for the easily spooked.'

'What's it like?' Broad asked.

'Short, but fierce. For about a quarter of an hour I thought I was made of smoke. When I started to come down I wanted to die. Just briefly. It was . . . There was something *terrible* about it. Like I didn't exist, and everything was a lie.'

'Sounds awful,' Broad said, with feeling.

'I only tried it the once. Other people have different responses to it, but it's by no means a party drug. It's more about accessing parts of your mind that are normally closed to you. If you really want to know, you could always try some.'

'Are you trying to sell drugs to a police officer?'

'Never said anything of the sort,' Jason pointed out, reasonably enough.

'You're very open about it all,' Broad said.

'Well, you asked. And you know it grows here, and that we used to sell it. I'm guessing you're not going to nick me for having taken it once, years ago. So no point being cagey, is there?'

'I guess not,' Broad agreed. 'How did Holly react to it?'

'You mean, what did she experience? Only she knows. Only she *knew*.' He corrected himself. 'Some things are difficult to describe. She always came down hard, afterwards.'

'She took it more than once?'

'Yeah, more than once. I didn't like that.' They'd reached the shed. Jason looked down at Broad, turning the key over and over in his fingers. 'But you can't tell people not to do it,' he said. 'They have to decide that for themselves. Get past it.'

'Doesn't sound as though you have much faith in your own product,' Lockyer said.

'Not *my* product, man,' Jason said, with a roll of his head.

He undid the padlock, pushed open the door and stepped back to let them in.

The lean-to smelt richly of creosote. It had a corrugated-iron roof, and was roasting inside. There was a rough-hewn bench similar to the one in the workshop, but smaller. On it were a set of electronic scales, a large pestle and mortar, a cardboard box of small Ziploc bags and a label maker. In another box were the finished articles: sealed bags in neat rows, each containing ten grams of dried, crushed SD leaves. The labels bore an emblem of a rainbow wearing a ten-gallon hat, and the name *Sally D*. Exactly what Jody had called it. Lockyer picked one up for a closer examination, then gave Jason a significant look.

'See, there.' Jason pointed to the label. 'At the bottom. "Not for human consumption".'

'Come off it,' Lockyer said.

'Makes it legal,' Jason said easily. 'Like I said, you can't stop people wanting to take stuff like this. And better this than something worse.'

'Holly would never have heard of it if you hadn't been growing it here.'

Jason folded his arms. 'Yeah. Well, maybe. But it didn't do her any harm.'

'No? It didn't help push her towards Ridgeway Kingsley-Jones? Sounds like he was peddling worse things. Maybe Holly had got a taste for experimenting by then.'

Jason rubbed one hand along his jaw. 'She wasn't taking anything she got from him.'

'How do you know?'

'He wouldn't have dared give her anything. Vince would've skinned him.'

'But who knows what they got up to, away from the farm? That might be why she went off with them the night of the solstice. Don't you think?'

'No. I don't.'

'So why *did* she leave with them that night? When the party was nowhere near over?'

'I don't know. I only wish . . . I only wish she hadn't.'

'Right. I was forgetting. You weren't here. Would you have tried to stop her, if you had been?'

'Yes. Of course. He was an arsehole.'

'Must be terrible to think you could have saved her.'

Jason's stare turned glassy. 'Yeah.'

'You were in love with Holly,' Lockyer said, 'weren't you, Jason?'

Jason took a moment before answering. His deep-brown eyes were fathomless in the low light. 'Yeah. I loved her.'

'But that's not the same as being *in love* with her. That must have been far harder – watching her get close to Ridgeway, falling for him. Knowing they were sleeping together . . .'

At this, Jason suddenly put his hands in front of his face, palms inwards. It was such an unexpected gesture that it silenced Lockyer. The younger man brought his hands down slowly, inhaling deeply. 'Sorry,' he muttered. 'Helps me reset when – when I need to.'

'She went off with the three of them that night, and left you behind,' Lockyer said. 'And then she died. Or was killed. Did you want revenge, Jason? Justice? Anyone would, I think. For someone they loved.'

'Why are you asking me about this?' he said softly.

Lockyer changed tack. 'Did Holly ever talk to you about her family? Her mother . . . or her mother's relationship to her father?'

Jason folded his arms. 'Sometimes.'

'Did she tell you what Vince had done? Why he'd gone to prison?'

'That he'd started the fire that killed her grandparents? Yeah. She told me that.'

'Did she tell you Trish was her aunt?'

'Yeah.'

'Right. So it was only Trish who was kept in the dark.'

'I wasn't happy about that. I hate secrets. But Vince said it'd upset her, and he doesn't do anything lightly. He'd *never* hurt Trish. And neither would I.'

'Didn't it strike you as odd?'

'Odd? Yeah, you could say that.' He chewed his lower lip. 'I don't know how come they got together. Maybe Vince wanted to explain about the fire, or maybe Trish went looking for him, wanting an explanation. Anyway, there was obviously forgiveness. And love can grow out of extreme events, right?'

'So I've read. Still, seems strange to lie to Trish about something like that. Even after Holly's death.'

'Everyone who comes to Old Hat Farm has got something they want to leave behind,' Jason said. 'Something to forget. That's what Trish says. Could be something small, could be something huge, but whatever it is, she won't let it follow them here. That's the deal. And I guess, for her, it's to do with her sister.'

'What did you want to forget, Jason?' Lockyer asked.

Jason had learnt a measure of Vince's stillness. He let the silence drag before he spoke. 'Everything from before I got here. I'd seen stuff no kid should see.'

'Where were you on the eighteenth of November 2011?'

'That's the day Lee died?'

'Yes. And he came here before he died.'

'Says who? I wouldn't know, anyway. I wasn't here.'

'Where were you?'

'Away. Visiting some friends.'

'Are these the same friends you were visiting the night of the solstice party? In Avebury, I think you said?'

'No. Different ones.'

Lockyer took out his notebook. 'If you give me some names, I can check it with them. Rule you out altogether.'

Silence.

'Why didn't you mention it before?' Broad asked. 'That you weren't here, I mean?'

'I forgot. We don't go in for dates much round here.'

'We'd gathered that,' Lockyer said. 'But now you've had

a chance to reflect, you're sure it was the eighteenth that you were away?'

'Yeah.'

'I'm going to need at least one name.'

Silence.

'What is it, Jason?' Lockyer asked. 'Why are you trying to hide your real identity?'

'*This* is my real identity.' A slight tremor in his voice.

'I don't think so. Or, at least, it wasn't always. Who are you? What are you hiding from?'

Jason's expression was bleak. 'It can't follow you to Old Hat Farm.'

Lockyer shook his head. 'Not that simple, I'm afraid.'

'It's going to have to be.'

'We *know* Lee Geary came here just before he died. And we know you blamed him for Holly's death. Him and the other two. An alibi would really help you out, Jason.'

'I already told you—'

'A convenient trip to see anonymous mates isn't good enough.'

'I wasn't here. If – if Lee came here, I never saw him. And I didn't lay a finger on him.'

Lockyer took out his phone and opened the camera. He wanted to check with Karen that it had been Jason who'd come looking for Lee. There was the Polaroid of him that Broad had seen in Holly's room, but the chances of them being allowed to take that were nil.

'Mind if I take your picture?' he said. 'Just for our—'

Jason's hands came up again at once. 'Yes, I mind. Don't!'

Unsurprised, Lockyer put his phone away. 'We've a habit of finding these things out, Jason. What don't you want us to know?'

'You? I don't want *anyone* to know.'

'You mean the McNeils?'

Jason seemed to waver, but at that moment Broad stumbled to one side.

'I might just—' she said, as she slumped against the workbench and crumpled to her knees.

'Gem?' Lockyer was startled. 'Are you okay?'

She didn't look up. Her cheeks were puce, her lips ashen. Before he could react Jason was on his knees beside her, taking her arm. 'Are you faint?' he said.

'It's just . . . the heat . . .' she said weakly. She gave him a round-eyed, panicky look, starting to hyperventilate.

'It's all right,' Jason said. 'I've got you. Nothing bad is going to happen, I swear. You just need to cool down. Dehydrated, probably.' He looked up. 'Come on,' he said to Lockyer, and they helped Broad to her feet. She swayed.

'Oh, God. I might be sick.' She sounded appalled.

'Puke away,' Jason said. 'You should see me when a migraine kicks in.'

'Really?'

'You've seen *The Exorcist*, right?'

Broad managed a weak smile. They led her slowly outside, into the deep shade of the machine shed where there seemed to be more air, and sat her down on a stack of old fence posts.

'Hang on there,' Jason instructed. 'I've got an idea.'

He went off, and Lockyer sat down beside Broad, feeling the awkwardness of inadequacy. 'How are you doing now?' he said.

'Yep. Grand,' she said, keeping her eyes closed. Her face was now marble white, and clammy. 'I'll be fine in a sec, guv. Sorry. It was so stuffy in there . . .'

'No need to apologize.'

He sounded as stiff as the wood they were sitting on, but couldn't think what to say to make her feel better. Jason reappeared, carrying a slopping bucket of water, and for a second Lockyer wondered if he planned to pour it over Broad's head.

'Kick your shoes off,' he instructed.

Uncertainly, with the air of having strayed beyond the normal bounds of a working day, Broad did as he said.

'Now plop your feet in there.'

'Christ! It's freezing!'

'Yep. That's the point. The blood is closer to the surface in certain parts of the body. So if you can cool them down, it'll cool the rest of you, too. Like an elephant's ears.'

'So you're saying my feet are like elephant ears?'

Jason laughed. 'Exactly. Here, try this on the back of your neck, as well.' He dunked his T-shirt in the water, wrung it out and handed it to her. 'Now,' he said, standing back. 'Say elephants again.'

'Elephants,' Broad said, glancing up at him. A little colour had returned to her lips.

Jason looked at her wonderingly. 'Orange sorbet.'

Lockyer couldn't tell if it was true, or if he'd said it to

make Broad feel better. Whether he was actually flirting with her. The possibility rankled slightly. He needed Broad focused on the case, and didn't like the idea of her being manipulated. If that was what was happening.

Once Broad was steadier she dried her feet and put her shoes back on.

'I'll take you home,' Lockyer said.

'Thanks, guv. Sorry.'

'It's fine.'

'I feel a right prat.'

'Well, don't.'

Lockyer looked at Jason, as they turned to go. 'Thanks for your help.'

'Don't mention it.'

'Don't go anywhere, will you?' he added.

The car's thermometer was reading thirty-seven Celsius when they returned to it. The interior was like an oven. Lockyer got the air-con blasting, and they waited in the shade while it got to work. Broad was still very quiet. When the car was bearable he drove her home, through Devizes and out to Semington.

'It's this one, isn't it?' Lockyer said, indicating at what he thought was the correct turning.

The new estate was only small, but the streets, the houses, all looked the same to him.

'Fieldfare Drive,' he said, trying to fix it in his memory, and wondering why developers so often named places after the wildlife they'd made homeless.

'When we bought it, Pete thought that meant fare from a

field,' Broad said. 'Like, food. From a field. For weeks I didn't have the heart to tell him it was a bird. Especially since I only knew that because you'd told me.'

'Did I?'

'Yeah. Last winter. Don't you remember? We saw a load of them when we were driving somewhere.'

'Okay. I just never thought you bothered to remember stuff like that.'

'Are you kidding? I'm always hanging on for your next nature note, guv.'

'Right.' He glanced her way. 'You must be feeling better, if you've got the energy to take the piss.'

'Yeah. A bit.'

After a pause, Lockyer said, 'What food do you think Pete would find in a field?'

Broad laughed. 'Pizza. As long he had his phone.'

They pulled up outside number seventeen. In spite of the air-con, Lockyer's shirt had stuck to his back during the drive. He tugged at it as he got out and went round to help Broad, but she was already out, shutting the door and adjusting the waistband of her trousers. She looked profoundly uncomfortable.

'I'm fine now, guv. Honestly. You get off.'

'Well. If you're sure. Got your keys?'

They hadn't been back to the office for her to collect her bag. Or her bike.

'No. But Pete's still working from home, so he'll be—'

As she said it the door opened, and Pete appeared. Medium height, medium build. Medium value as a human being, as far as Lockyer was concerned. He drummed up a smile that Pete didn't return. Instead, he wore a faintly long-suffering expression, chino shorts, a polo shirt and a garish watch that had probably cost money but not nearly enough. His face still had the soft edges of a man not yet come of age. Whatever the opposite of rugged was. Merry looked far more pleased to see Broad – the little dog came out wagging all over, and milled happily around her feet.

'Matt,' Pete said, by way of greeting. Hands in his pockets. 'What's all this?'

Lockyer tried not to clench his teeth too visibly. 'Gemma wasn't feeling too great.'

'It's just the heat,' Broad said stiffly.

Lockyer suspected she sensed his antipathy towards her long-term boyfriend, and decided to try harder. But Pete didn't make it easy. If he was at all concerned about his girlfriend, he didn't let it show.

'Wait – what?' he said, holding up both hands to halt Broad's sluggish progress across the block paving. 'What kind of not-great? Like, Covid not-great? Have you got a temperature?'

'No,' she said. 'It's just *the* temperature, Pete. We'd been out in it for a while.'

Pete shot Lockyer a look that questioned the wisdom of that. Lockyer returned it coolly.

'Well, you'd better go straight up to the spare room, and stay in there until we're sure it's not the virus,' Pete said.

Broad made a face. 'It'll be roasting in there.'

'It'll be cooler than standing about in the sun,' Pete said, looking at Lockyer again. 'You won't mind if I don't ask you in?'

'Not at all,' Lockyer said, meaning every syllable. 'Feel better, Gem. Drink lots of water.'

'I will. Thanks for the ride home, guv.'

'Want me to pick you up in the morning?'

Broad glanced at Pete, who was still keeping his distance. Apparently, he wasn't about to offer to drive a potential Covid case anywhere. 'Thanks,' she said. 'That'd be great.'

She continued her solo traipse inside, with Merry at her heels, and Lockyer got back into the car before he was tempted to say anything else.

12

At home in the slowly simmering evening, Lockyer took out his phone. His message to Hedy hadn't been opened or read. She could've changed her number, for all he knew. He regretted sending it – his sudden, probably unwelcome, display of vulnerability.

Chris's bag of pills was now on the kitchen table. He'd planned to flush them straight away, but hadn't. Even though he hated the sight of them, they seemed too important to discard.

Then he remembered a time when Chris, who'd rarely had a cross word for anyone, had snapped at him, 'Fuck's sake, do you not know how to knock?' Scrambling up from the bed, cheeks flaring, hair damp and scruffy from a shower.

Taken aback, Lockyer had grinned. 'Sorry, mate. But you should do that *in* the shower, not afterwards.'

'I wasn't—'

Chris had looked away, not meeting Lockyer's eye. Not embarrassed but angry, which Lockyer hadn't understood.

'Mum wants to know if you're in or out for dinner,' Lockyer said. 'Moody git.'

'I'm a moody git?' Chris shot back, looking up at last with his irrepressible grin.

Now Lockyer wondered. Had he been hiding the pills? Or siphoning some off to sell later? He couldn't remember if Chris had gone out that night. Had his rare flare of temper been fear, at almost being caught red-handed? Around that time Chris had started acquiring new things. Just quietly, without showing them off, like he usually would. An MP3 player. New boots. Hubcaps for the elderly VW Polo they shared.

'Birthday money from Nan,' was one explanation he'd given.

Or that he'd done some extra shifts at the pub.

Lockyer felt like an idiot, furious to have been duped like that – he'd never even considered that the money might be ill-gotten. But worse was how shaken he felt, like he'd built a house on shifting sands. Knowing he'd been lied to by his little brother hurt more than he'd have thought possible.

He messaged Jody, and when she replied, he grabbed his car keys and opened the front door to find Mrs Musprat hovering there. A tiny, wizened figure in ratty clothes, nevertheless possessed of a certain dignity.

'Carey,' she said, with a birdlike nod of her head. 'That was Rosie's maiden name. I remembered it. And the younger sister was Gráinne.'

'Graw-nya?' Lockyer attempted to echo the pronunciation.

Mrs Musprat held out a scrap of paper. 'I wrote it down

'cause it's a funny spelling. One of those Irish words that makes no sense.'

Lockyer took it. 'Thanks.'

'Can't fetch up the brother's name at all.' With that, she turned and left.

Lockyer fastened the scrap of paper to the fridge, with the photo of Róisín. He looked closer, suddenly realizing that the slim figure on the right was Iris. A plain but finely chiselled face, with a delicate nose and chin. A self-conscious smile, as though she wasn't used to being photographed. All four looked happy. A moment of pleasure plucked from long spells of loneliness, pain and mundanity. He wondered whether every photo ever taken was, to some degree, a lie.

Like the violent thug portrayed in Lee Geary's mugshot. *Like killing a Labrador for fetching a stick.* Even Steve Saunders, a man not overly blessed with empathy, had known that Lee wasn't to blame. But could you call a man innocent if he *had* been involved in a murder? Lee had been big and strong enough to knock Ridgeway out cold, and take Holly to a hospital rather than throwing her off the bridge, if that was what he'd done. But if he'd done it because Ridgeway had threatened to kill him, and he was terrified? Because he wasn't capable of knocking *anyone* out cold? Because they'd told him Holly was already dead, and he'd believed it? Could someone with the vulnerabilities of a child be held any more responsible than a child?

The bitter injustice of Lee being bludgeoned to death hit Lockyer anew. And the fact that the lasting official record of him was a photo in which he looked like a monster made it just that little bit worse.

He collected Jody from Westdene and drove her the five miles to Erlestoke. She was still in shorts and a vest – it was warm enough, even at nine o'clock – and filled the car with the smell of wet hair and freshly showered skin. July was about to give way to August, and the weather reports were predicting a spell of tropical nights, when the temperature wasn't expected to drop below twenty degrees between dusk and dawn. He wondered how much sleep Broad would get, and whether she was still confined to the spare room. At least, he thought sourly, if she stayed there she could have a fan on without disturbing Pete.

Jody didn't seem bothered by any amount of heat. From what Lockyer had seen, she worked on regardless, sweating but un-slowed.

'I'm surprised you don't have a car,' Lockyer said, 'being the no-ties, go-where-the-work-is type.'

'I used to have one. Used to have a lot of things.'

'How do you get around? Especially out here.'

'Start walking,' she said, offhandedly. 'Before long there's a bus, or a lift. My regulars are normally fine to come a couple of miles to pick me up.'

'So you hitchhike?'

She put her bare feet up on the dashboard. 'Next you're going to tell me it's not safe.'

'It isn't.'

'Ninety-nine per cent of people are completely fine. I did

meet a wrong 'un once. That ended in a lay-by with my boot in his bollocks. I've always carried since then, and I've had no issues.'

'Carried what?'

'My knife.'

Lockyer glanced across. 'Please don't tell me *anything* else about it.'

She laughed.

Lockyer fell into thought, trying to remember seeing any vehicles at Old Hat Farm, other than the quad bike Trish had bought with money from the sale of Imogen's house. He didn't think he'd seen any others, though there were several barns they hadn't explored yet. He couldn't remember whether the original 2011 investigation had mentioned any, and wondered how Jason had got around, *if* he'd been the man on the CCTV at the car park in Salisbury, and *if* he'd gone to look for Lee at Karen's flat. Jason had been absent the first time they'd visited Old Hat Farm – taking the backpackers into Devizes. But taking them how, exactly?

Jody pushed her fingers through the shock of blue hair over her forehead. The colour was growing out a little, the black beginning to show at the roots. 'So, how's the investigation going? Have you found out what happened to that girl, yet?'

'No. But I can't talk to you about it. Sorry.'

'Just like on TV, right?'

'Not much about modern policing is, but that part's right.'

'Have you calmed down about your brother's pills yet?'

'I was always calm.'

'Really? Because for a moment you looked like you might pop a blood vessel.'

Lockyer said nothing.

'Look, I know you're a copper, but a few Es doesn't make him Pablo Escobar, does it?'

Lockyer felt that unfamiliar intimacy again, the space opened up by her plain speaking. 'No. But I didn't know he took anything like that. And I thought I knew everything about him.'

'Come on,' Jody said. 'Nobody knows everything about anyone else. Ever. Do they?'

'I thought I did. He knew everything about me.'

'Course he didn't. I mean, he obviously knew you well enough not to tell you about the sweeties . . . But everything you thought? Everything you felt? No way.'

'How did he even get hold of that shit?'

'It's not difficult. Anyone can get hold of it.'

'Enough to start dealing?'

'I guess he wanted some extra cash.'

'But that's . . . It's *not* okay. He loved the farm. He had everything he needed.'

'Maybe he didn't think so. He was *eighteen*, and we all do stupid shit at eighteen.'

Lockyer thought about it, trying to make it sit right when it absolutely wouldn't. 'I suppose I thought we didn't have any secrets. Not big ones, anyway.' He took a breath. 'What if he wasn't happy? Maybe he wanted to leave the farm.'

'What if he did?' Jody said, more gently. 'Neither of you can do anything about it now.'

There was a covered veranda at the back of Beryl Upton's black-and-white cottage, where she'd been sitting in a rickety swing chair. Having got them both a glass of orange squash, she went back to her spot and resumed crocheting.

'I'll only be a sec,' Jody said to Lockyer, swinging herself up the wooden stairs. 'It's just 2011 you want?'

'Yes, please,' Lockyer said.

He went outside and sat in a plastic patio chair, keeping a safe distance from Beryl. The garden was tranquil, full of soft grey twilight. An apple tree was hung with bird feeders, and a thrush sang loudly from the top branches.

'Comes every night, he does,' Beryl said. 'I like to think the poor buggers in the prison can hear him.'

Invisible behind the trees across the road, HMP Erlestoke was a sprawling Category C complex bigger than the village itself. It was the prison where Vince McNeil had done his final year of time: a year of reintegration training, having served his sentence for arson and manslaughter elsewhere. For killing Trish's parents. Lockyer was struck again by the unlikelihood of their situation. Other people's relationships often only made sense to them, but still. This one clanged like a cracked pot. Had Vince been trying to atone by devoting himself to one of the sisters? Had he been so lost that he'd attempted to go back in time, somehow, to start forwards again?

'It's not such a bad prison to be in,' Lockyer said to Beryl. 'There are far worse, believe me.'

She grunted her agreement.

'Funny, my Jody making friends with the likes of you,' she said. 'A *policeman*.'

'Is it?'

'Well, she's a good girl, but she's had a rough time of it. Never did like rules, you see.' She gave him a grin. 'Never could resist a challenge, either.'

Lockyer was saved from having to answer by Jody's reappearance. She handed him a tiny memory card in a plastic case. 'Everything I didn't delete is on there,' she said.

'Thank you.'

'What's all this?' Beryl asked.

'Nothing you need worry about.' Jody smirked. 'I'm helping the policeman with his enquiries.'

Beryl laughed. 'There's a turn-up, eh?'

'Pint?' Jody said to Lockyer. 'The George and Dragon is right next door.'

Lockyer pocketed the memory card. 'Good idea.'

Back at home, Lockyer stared at Iris Musprat's spidery pencil letters on the scrap of paper. *Gráinne Carey*. He knew he was treading water, summoning the guts to make the call, because he couldn't do what she asked of him. By the time Iris died, Róisín's brother and sister might also have gone, without ever knowing what had happened to her. Without ever being able to let go of their loss. But then he remembered the fear juddering through the old woman's skinny frame. *I thought I could trust you.*

After a while he moved, snatched up Chris's pills and flushed them down the toilet. There was absolutely no point keeping them – he could hardly confront Chris with them, after all. Then he went onto Facebook and found Joe Cameron, Chris's best mate, one of the group of lads who'd been with him the night he was killed.

Lockyer hadn't seen or spoken to Joe since the funeral, but he was instantly recognizable in his profile picture, in spite of a receding hairline and a fatter face. Lockyer opened a direct message. *Hi Joe, hope you're keeping well. I know I've not been in touch for a long time, but would you be up for meeting me? I'd appreciate it. It's about Chris.*

Then he went out walking, on one of the chalk tracks that ran for miles across the plain to places that didn't exist any more. He was trying to rid himself of the feeling of waiting when he didn't know what for, trying to escape a growing sense of helplessness, and the loneliness he'd felt since Hedy's vanishing act, since Trudy had stopped answering her bedside phone, and Jody had shown him the bag of pills in Chris's room. He needed to clear his mind, somehow, if he was going to see the Holly Gilbert case clearly.

Lockyer walked two and half miles to Copehill Down, an empty village built by the MoD for training purposes. He sat down on the prickly grass, staring at the black outlines of homes nobody had ever lived in, nor ever would. The sky glowed faintly with distant stars, and the silence, once he'd caught his breath, was complete. There was something deeply eerie about the place, even though he knew nobody was there, looking back at him. Only bats and foxes. The village was a sham, a stage set, as unreliable as a person who pretended to be someone they weren't.

He felt he'd touched upon something then, but when he tried to follow the thought it simply circled around to Chris. To having been lied to. To not knowing who his brother really was, and why that should make him feel as though he hardly knew himself.

Broad emerged from her house as Lockyer pulled up the following morning. Merry tried to follow her out, and she had to wait until Pete came and took the dog's collar, none too gently.

'All okay?' Lockyer said.

'Yeah, fine, thanks. Merry's in the doghouse, though.' She made a comic face. 'Went digging in the neighbour's veggie patch this morning. So far so normal, except I'd left the garage door open and he ran straight back in when I called him. Up onto the sofa, covered in mud. We've just had it cleaned.'

'Ah. Bad dog.'

'Just dog.' She was quietly defensive. 'Pete never had pets, growing up. Anyway . . .' she took out a bottle from her bag and held it up '. . . coconut water. Great for rehydration. No more dramatic swooning from me.'

'At least we know what to do, if you do go again.'

'Yeah.' She looked away. 'Stick my feet in a bucket and call me an elephant.'

'That's not what—'

'No, I know. I'm just . . .' A shrug.

Just making light of it, Lockyer thought. Because Jason McNeil was charming, talented and very good-looking, and Lockyer suspected she'd started to care too much about his good opinion. He thought about saying something – perhaps warning her.

'This heat-wave has to end soon,' he said lamely. 'Else the papers'll run out of headlines.'

'I'm not sure the weather got the memo about that,' Broad said, gazing out at the parched verges and turgid green canal as they drove into Devizes.

'I've got Jody's photos and videos from the Soul Tree Festival,' Lockyer said. 'I thought you could make a start on them. There are reams of clips on YouTube as well. I'll join you as soon as I get back.'

'Where are you going?'

'Old Hat Farm – don't look so disappointed. It'll be brief. I have a couple of things I want to ask. And to see.'

'It's been a couple of days since I pestered Nina Thorow-good,' Broad said. 'I'll give her a chivvy-up, too, see if she's changed her mind about talking to us.'

First of all, Lockyer ran a DVLA search and found only one vehicle registered to Old Hat Farm: a motorbike belonging to Vince. And it had a SORN – a sworn-off-the-road notice. He rang Steve Saunders.

'Cars?' Steve echoed. 'Must have, mustn't they? Living right out there?'

'But did they in 2011? Do you remember?'

'Not off the top of my head, but I already told you, we checked all the vehicles clocked heading south the night Holly died—'

'This isn't about the night Holly died.'

A pause, in which Lockyer could sense Steve's curiosity.

'All right, Farmer Giles. I'll get back to you.'

Lockyer checked his phone as he went back out to the car. Joe Cameron had read his message but not replied. Lockyer fought to stifle his impatience. There was no way to make anybody talk to him. His message to Hedy was still unopened, and he thought that meant he could delete it before she ever saw it. He sat silently in the car for a moment, undecided.

The yard at Old Hat Farm was quiet: no sign of the backpackers, or sounds of work going on in any of the sheds. A shout from inside the farmhouse answered his knock. Trish was at the kitchen table, wearing thick-framed glasses, a laptop in front of her – ordinary silver, not pink – and a messy stack of paperwork to one side. It was incongruous to see her doing something so conventional. She shut the computer when he came in, and her smile was far more guarded than before.

'Detective Inspector,' she said, getting up. 'Back again.'

'I'd have phoned instead, if I could.'

'Ah, well. There you have me. What can I do for you today?'

'Just a couple more things I'd like to ask, if you don't mind.'

Trish sat down again, and gestured for him to do the

same. Lockyer bashed his knees on the table as he stepped over the bench. 'Seems quiet here today,' he said.

Trish shuffled the paperwork into a neater pile. 'They're all out strawberry picking. My back can't hack it these days. Still, gives me a chance to balance the books.'

'When we first met you gave the impression that this wasn't a place for anything as mainstream as accounting.'

'Nothing mainstream about knowing we'll be able to heat the place through the winter.'

'But you will, I'm sure. You must have some of Imogen's money left.'

Trish blinked, then dropped her gaze. 'Yes. Some,' she murmured.

'That money makes you very uncomfortable, doesn't it, Trish?'

'Having secrets from my family makes me uncomfortable.'

'So tell them.'

'It's not that easy, Inspector. Vince didn't want me to know, and I respect that. What did you want to ask?'

'Do you have any cars? Does anyone here?'

'No. Did you know that road traffic in Wiltshire alone accounts for the release of about fifteen hundred kilotonnes of carbon dioxide into the atmosphere every year?'

'Not this year, surely.'

'No, well, even a pandemic can have a silver lining,' she said.

'How have the others got to wherever they're strawberry picking?' Lockyer asked.

'They walked into Everleigh and the farmer picked them up in his trailer.'

'Do you have a tractor? Any agricultural vehicles?'

'No. We do it all by hand – or we get help. Why are you asking?'

'The first time I came here, you told me Jason had taken Melody and Pascal into Devizes, to go to the bank. How did he take them, exactly?'

'He went with them to show them the way. Walked to the main road, and caught the bus into town.'

'What about in 2011?' Something else occurred to him. 'How did Holly get here?'

'She had a little red something or other. Vauxhall Nova, I think it was.'

'What happened to it?'

'She gave it away.' An approving smile.

'She *gave* it away? Who to?'

'Just some people who'd been staying here. They got word someone had fallen ill, and had no way of getting up north in a hurry. So Holly just gave them the keys. Said she didn't need it back.'

'That was generous of her.'

'She'd learnt how great it feels to do something like that for a person in need.'

'What about the motorbike?'

'You mean Vince's Harley? What about it?'

'Does he still have it?'

'Course. He adores it. But he doesn't ride it any more – nearly went head-on with an idiot in a Range Rover one day, out in the lane. It really shook me up. But it's still out in one of the sheds.'

'Does Jason know how to ride it?'

'He doesn't have a licence. Anyway, the bike's been mothballed for ages. It burnt through so much oil, and the engine was always threatening to seize. I doubt any amount of kicking'd get it started now.'

'But it was still on the road in 2011?'

'I think so. I can't remember. Why do you want to know?'

'Trish, can you tell me anything about where Jason was before he came here? Or even just his given name?'

'No.'

'I know you don't want people's pasts to follow them here, but hiding things doesn't make them go away.'

'If he has another name I don't know it. I've never asked.'

'And he's never spoken to you about it? About what he was running from?' he asked.

Her expression became haunted. 'Bits and pieces. Nothing you need to know about. Nothing to do with Lee Geary, or with Holly.'

'Trish—'

'Did you know that young black men are *ten times* more likely than young white men to suffer a psychotic episode?' she interrupted. 'And four times more likely to be sectioned? It's true. And do you know why? Because of the steady drip, drip, drip of discrimination and deprivation they're subjected to all their lives. All the aggression, from micro to life-threatening. Every single day. Just think about that, Inspector. Think about what that *means*. Every time someone called them a name at school, every time they were passed over for a job, every time their guilt was wrongly supposed by the police . . . It causes trauma on levels so deep we can barely even grasp it.'

'I don't think—'

'Coupled with the fact that most young people of colour grow up in urban areas, like Jase did, with all the mental-health implications of being completely out of touch with the natural world. Then throw in the sensory overload of synesthesia . . .'

'You're saying that Jason was breaking down when he got here?'

Trish thought before she answered. 'Close to it, I think. But Jason is a phoenix, Inspector. The world burnt him to nothing, and he came back stronger. He's good, in spite of it all. Generous, honest, loving. Wherever he touches a life, he makes it better. So whatever he did before, whatever you think he might have done, it doesn't matter.'

'But I do need to know who he was before, and what he was running from.'

'He was running from chaos,' she said.

'You love him very much.'

'Like everyone who really knows him.'

'Including Holly.'

'Yes, including Holly.'

'But perhaps she didn't love him in the same way he loved her. That can be very painful.'

In the silence the tap dripped into the sink, and the ancient greyhound sighed in its sleep. Lockyer saw an old, remembered pain in Trish's eyes – one that he recognized. She nodded, just once.

He stood up. 'My interest in Jason's involvement in all this has nothing to do with him being black.'

'No?' Trish fired back. 'Are you sure?'

'Mind if I look around the other barns before I leave?'

'What for?'

'Curiosity. I'd quite like to see the Harley.'

'Help yourself, Inspector. We've got nothing to hide.'

As he turned to go a photo caught his eye, pinned to an overloaded cork board. It was of Vince and Trish, apparently taken without their knowledge. They were walking through the blue blaze of *Salvia* flowers, Vince gazing off to one side, Trish looking up at him, smiling. Reaching for his hand.

'Do you have a photo of Jason I could take a copy of, please?' he asked, knowing it would get him nowhere.

Trish's face hardened. 'No. We don't go in for photos much, around here.'

'What about this one?' He gestured at the cork board.

She hesitated. 'Holly took that.'

Lockyer found the motorbike beneath canvas in a rickety hay barn. There was a thick layer of chaff and bird shit on the tarp, but the bike underneath was gleaming. It wasn't the monster chopper Lockyer had been expecting, just a normal, upright roadster. An open-face helmet hung from one of the handlebars, black, with spikes of red lightning down the sides. The bike looked roadworthy to Lockyer's inexpert eye, but it was completely surrounded by dusty junk that clearly hadn't been moved in ages. Lockyer's tracks, as he'd clambered through, were the only ones.

The Harley might not have been ridden for a long time, but in 2011 Jason would have had access to it. It wasn't hard to learn to ride a motorbike, and he needn't have bothered with a licence. Plenty of young men didn't.

Lockyer made his way to the workshop, ducked inside and looked closely. There were two clear workstations, where Vince and Jason could work side by side. Two glue-guns, both unplugged and cold, the sticks of glue solid and waxy. Lockyer picked up the huge carver's mallet that Jason had been using. The one Vince had made in prison. He swung it into his palm, and the impact jarred right up his arm. *Something big and round*, the pathologist had said, of whatever had made the fatal dent in Lee Geary's skull.

The brick floor had been worn smooth by generations of feet. The joints held the crumbling remnants of old mortar, and years of trampled-in dirt and sawdust. Lockyer grabbed a screwdriver, crouched down and scraped between two bricks, clearing it all away. The joint went right down to the earth. A floor like that was inherently absorbent. A floor like that was very hard to clean thoroughly. Jason was usually on the farm, usually in the workshop. Lockyer wondered if he had in fact been in it on 18 November 2011. The day Lee Geary had come calling.

His phone buzzed with a message from Broad. *Bingo, guv.*

In the musty darkness of the media room, Broad scrolled the video back and hit play again. A sunny afternoon at the Soul

Tree Festival; a field crowded with people, tents and flags. The muddy grass was littered with dropped things: paper cups, bits of costume, the odd stray welly. Steam billowed from food stalls, music was playing, and in the distance a circus troupe were up on stilts, juggling hoops. Jody had taken a slow panning shot of the scene, stopping to zoom in on people who were particularly colourful or outlandish. Like a girl dressed as Hello Kitty, wearing pink biker boots with a six-inch platform sole, who was eating candy-floss, and waved at the camera.

'There.' Broad paused it, and pointed. 'See?'

Lockyer looked closely. Behind Hello Kitty girl, hunched against the side of a mac 'n' cheese van, was a lithe young black man, with a sculptural face and his hair in cornrows. A motorcycle helmet was resting on his feet. Black, with spikes of red lightning down the sides.

'Yes. That's Jason,' Lockyer said. 'Karen told me the guy who came looking for Lee had cornrows, and I've just seen that helmet at the farm. He borrowed Vince's motorbike.'

'But he hates crowds.'

Broad sounded disappointed, and Lockyer knew she'd been hoping Jason McNeil had had nothing to do with any of it. He'd been hoping it himself. He liked Jason, who seemed both thoughtful and genuine. Lockyer thought back to his assertion to Trish, earlier, that his suspicions had nothing to do with the colour of Jason's skin. Her instant riposte: *Are you sure?* But, if anything, Lockyer had been hoping to be able to clear Jason. The last thing he wanted was to be accused of racial bias. He despised that kind of prejudice, especially within the police force.

'So I guess he must've had a good reason to go to that festival,' he said.

Broad let the film play again, and the whole time Hello Kitty was waving and eating her candy-floss, Jason stayed huddled into himself, staring first in one direction, then in the other.

'He's looking for someone,' Lockyer said.

'Stef Gould,' Broad murmured. 'But do we really think he deliberately *drowned* her?'

'Well, it's not actually that difficult to drown someone accidentally. But I think we need to ask him – on the record this time. Look at the date. This footage puts him right there, at the scene, hours before Stef died. Hell of a coincidence if he's just there to party, isn't it?'

'He just didn't seem the type.' Broad was subdued. 'Doesn't say much for my ability to read people.'

'All sorts of things can misdirect, Gem. Not least people who are *really* good at coming across well.' With a nasty little jolt, Lockyer thought of Chris as he said it.

'So, we bring him in?' Broad said.

'Soon. First I want Forensics in the workshop.'

'Is the super likely to sign off on that?'

'I'm going to convince her. Is there much more of that to go through?'

'I've done all of Jody's video footage, but there are a couple of hundred of her photos to look at. And then the YouTube stuff – thirty-four people uploaded videos from that year's festival.'

'Keep looking, then. I'll come and help once I've spoken to the boss.'

Lockyer laid it all out for the DSU via a video call. The carver's mallet. The fact that Lee Geary possibly saw Jason at the car park where Ridgeway died. The fact that he'd just seen, with his own eyes, Jason at the Soul Tree Festival on the day Stefanie Gould had died. Jason's open admission to having loved Holly.

'If we can get prints from Jason, we might be able to match him to the partial palm found at the car park,' he said. 'That would back up what I saw on the CCTV.'

'Is he likely to volunteer his biometrics?' Considine said. 'Because you haven't got enough to arrest him yet, or for me to grant permission to take non-intimate samples.'

'No. Jason McNeil does *not* want anyone to know who he used to be.'

'And Geary having gone to the farm shortly before his death doesn't prove he was killed there.'

'But the glue on his clothes puts him in the workshop, and the guns would have to have been in use for it to have got onto him. So he saw at least one of the McNeils that day. If Forensics can give us the scene, that would be enough to arrest Jason. Lee was killed there, then driven to the deposition site,' Lockyer said, with a small misgiving.

A motorbike wouldn't have been any use on that terrain in late autumn. From the ruts he'd seen near the burial site, even a four-wheel drive would've struggled. Trish had bought the quad bike and trailer with the money she inherited when Holly died but, given that Surrey Council had been forced to use a tracing service to find her, it seemed unlikely that probate would have been granted, or the house sold and the money paid over, by the middle of November.

'So, a forensic sweep of the workshop?' he pressed. 'I'd bet my life we'll find something in there.'

Considine took a second. 'All right. Do it.'

13

Day 12, Friday

In the morning, Lockyer watched from his car as two paper-suited SOCOs – Wiltshire Police scenes of crime officers – taped off the workshop at Old Hat Farm and carried in their kit. Jason, who'd been working, was crouching to one side with his arms wrapped around his knees, like a child. Trish came marching out of the farmhouse, her dress fluttering behind her.

'Hey! You can't just—' she said, then seemed to run out of breath.

There was no sign of Vince.

Lockyer got out of the car, and Trish made a beeline for him. He tried to read her face as he showed her the search warrant. Outrage, certainly, but perhaps something else underneath.

'Why are you doing this?' She crumpled the paper in her hand. 'Why can't you just leave us alone? We've been helpful. We've cooperated!'

Lockyer retrieved the warrant. 'And I'm grateful.'

'What exactly do you expect to find in there? A body under the floor?'

Lockyer glanced at Jason, who was well within earshot of the exchange. 'I expect to find blood, Mrs McNeil. Lee Geary's blood.'

Trish recoiled, struck dumb by his candour. She glanced, wide-eyed, at Jason. He was staring pensively at the concrete yard, as though reading the cracks and the meandering ants.

'Well, you won't find it.' Her voice cracked. 'Please . . .' she whispered. 'Please, Inspector, don't take my boy. He's a good man.'

She was shaking, and Lockyer couldn't help feeling sorry for her. 'You know, don't you?' he said softly. 'You know what happened here.'

Mutely, she shook her head.

'We will find out. And if Jason has done what I think he has, then I'm very sorry.'

Lockyer went closer to the cordon to wait. Twenty minutes later, one of the SOCOs put his head out. 'DI Lockyer? You might want to take a look at this.'

'Want me to suit up?'

'No need. Your DNA'll be all over the place already.'

Inside, he was temporarily blinded. They'd blacked-out the windows, and the SOCO was holding a UV lamp.

'There,' he said.

A mottled patch of spectral blue glowed on the floor in front of the workbench. Spots and spatters of it went up the nearby wooden leg of the bench.

'Is that what I think it is?' Lockyer said.

'First indications. From the pattern I would say blood, rather than a clean-up effort with bleach or any other substance that might react with the luminol.'

'It looks like a lot?'

'A significant amount.'

'Will it give us DNA, after so long?'

'Nine years?' The SOCO considered it. 'It's possible. Time and the lab will tell.'

'You've bagged the big mallet? Good.'

Lockyer crouched beside the blue patch, trying to picture Lee Geary's final moments. Only a very strong man – a very sure man – would let someone of Lee's size see it coming, which was probably why the blow had been to the back of his head. And only someone with Lee's learning difficulties would have turned their back on a person they thought had killed twice already, imagining they could just walk away. Or had he been trying to run? Grimly, Lockyer wondered if Lee had realized his mistake in going there. If he'd panicked.

He went back out to the yard, squinting. 'I need you to come in and answer some questions, Jason,' he said.

'And if I don't?' he said softly.

'Then I'll be forced to arrest you. At which point, I will have the right to take your fingerprints, photograph and DNA.'

Jason shuddered. His eyes had the dangerous intensity of a cornered animal. 'All right,' he said.

'Thank you.'

Lockyer turned, and saw Vince watching it all from the window of Holly's bedroom.

Lockyer sensed Broad's discomfort as they sat down opposite Jason in one of their dingy interview rooms. It bordered on embarrassment, in fact. There was none of Jason's smiling appreciation of anything Broad said, and she, in turn, barely looked at him. In shorts and a sleeveless T-shirt, Jason sat with his arms folded, too still to be relaxed. He did not fidget; he did not look around. Broad started the recording, and they all introduced themselves.

'Mr McNeil, you're being questioned under caution in rela-tion to the death of Lee Geary, on or around the eighteenth of November 2011. You have been offered legal counsel, and have declined at this stage.'

'The fewer people in here the better,' Jason said.

'Is it all right for us to address you as Jason?'

'Yep.'

'We understand you suffer from synesthesia, Jason. Do you need any extra help or support during this interview as a result of your condition?'

'I don't *suffer* from it. And no, I don't need any help. Thanks.'

Broad laid three photographs in front of him. 'For the tape, I am now showing Mr McNeil items ten through twelve, images of Ridgeway Kingsley-Jones, Stefanie Gould and Lee Geary. Could you please tell us when you last saw any of these three people?'

Jason looked for a long time, and Lockyer wondered if

pictures had the same sensory impact as seeing a person in real life; what Jason heard, what he smelt or even tasted when he saw their faces.

'Jason?' Broad prompted him.

'As far as I can remember, it was sometime in the spring of 2011,' he said. 'April or May.'

'And where was that?'

'At home. Old Hat Farm.'

'What were the circumstances of you seeing them there?'

'Ridgeway came to see Trish and Vince. He stayed with them a lot when he was younger.'

'And the other two?'

'They went wherever Ridgeway did.'

'So it was just a friendly visit?'

'Yeah.'

'They weren't, for example, collecting a supply of anything to sell?'

'Nope.'

'Where were you on the eighteenth of November 2011?'

'I was away.'

'Away where?'

'I went to visit friends. In Swindon.'

'I see,' Lockyer said. 'Were these friends from a long time ago, Jason? Friends from before you went to live at Old Hat Farm?'

'Yes.'

'Is that why you don't want to tell us their names?'

Jason didn't reply.

'Are they the same friends you went to see on the

twentieth of June that year, when a party was held at Old Hat Farm for the summer solstice?'

After a long pause, Jason said, 'No. That was someone else.'

'How did you get to Swindon?'

'Walked down into Everleigh and caught the bus.'

'Why not take the motorbike?'

'What?'

'Vince McNeil's Harley Davidson. You'd borrowed it before.'

'No, I – I took the bus. I don't have a licence.'

'We know that, Jason,' Lockyer said. 'But we also know that doesn't stop you using the bike when you need to.'

'No. I don't.' Still very composed, but with that empty look of fright in his eyes.

'You're going to need to tell us who you were with on the eighteenth, Jason. Because without an alibi, it makes it even more serious that you're lying to us.'

'What? I'm not—'

Broad interrupted him. 'Did you attend the Soul Tree Festival, in Dorset, on the twenty-eighth of August 2011?'

Jason snatched a quick breath. 'No.'

'Is that because of your synesthesia? You mentioned before that crowds bother you. That you find them over-whelming.'

'That's right.'

'Same reason you left Old Hat Farm during the summer solstice party, earlier that year.'

'Yeah.'

Broad flicked a quick glance at Lockyer, then brought out a series of three stills from Jody's footage, blown-up and centred on Jason. 'I am now showing Mr McNeil items seventeen through nineteen. These images are from video footage shot at the Soul Tree Festival on the twenty-eighth of August 2011. Can you confirm that the man in the photograph is you?' she said.

A shiver went through Jason as he stared at the glossy prints.

'For the tape, Mr McNeil has not responded, verbally or otherwise,' Broad said, in a clipped, officious way.

'We believe it *is* you, Jason.' Lockyer tapped the photo. 'It certainly looks like you. And I've seen that motorcycle helmet in the barn at Old Hat Farm, along with Vince's Harley Davidson motorcycle. Stefanie Gould died at the Soul Tree Festival that same day. She drowned in the lake. Did you see her there?'

'No.'

'In the footage, you appear to be looking for someone. Were you looking for Stefanie?'

'No. I – I wasn't there.'

'You *were* there, Jason. Did you see Stefanie Gould?'

Silence.

'Did you follow her to the lake? Did you kill her, Jason?'

'*No.*'

Lockyer signalled to Broad, who brought out another still, this time black-and-white, and worse quality. It was the best angle they'd managed to get. No face this time, just a figure of Jason's height and build, a hand with black skin.

'I am now showing Mr McNeil item sixteen. This image was taken from CCTV footage recorded at Culver Street car park, in Salisbury, in the early hours of the thirtieth of October 2011. Is that you, Jason?'

He shook his head. 'No.'

'You weren't in that location, at that time?'

'No, I wasn't.'

'Whoever this person is, he's suspected of being involved in the death of Ridgeway Kingsley-Jones, who fell from the upper storey of the car park shortly after this image was captured.'

'It's not me.'

'Forensic investigators were able to recover a palm print left by this person on the handrail as they went up the stairs. Would you be willing to give us your handprint for elimination purposes, Jason?'

'No.'

'Why not, if the person in the image isn't you?'

'I have the right to decline,' he said shakily.

'You do,' Lockyer said. 'At the moment. Did you see Lee Geary at Culver Street car park that night, Jason?'

A flicker of puzzlement. 'No.'

'It was dark, I suppose. But Lee *was* there, and we believe he saw you. We believe he witnessed Ridgeway's fatal fall. We believe he thought that *you* were responsible, Jason.'

Silence.

'For the tape,' Broad said, 'Mr McNeil is shaking his head.'

'Where were you that night, if you weren't at Culver Street?'

'I was home. At the farm. Vince and Trish will back me up.'

'I'm sure they will.' Lockyer decided to change tack. 'Jason, what do you think happened to Holly Gilbert on the night she died?'

At this, a spasm of anguish crossed Jason's face. 'I don't know.'

'But you have a theory. Do you blame Ridgeway, Stef and Lee? That was what you said to us in an earlier conversation at Old Hat Farm.'

'Yes, I blame *him*. Ridgeway. He took her away that night. She went with them to Amesbury, and then what? She's on the motorway, smashed to pieces? And we're expected to believe she *jumped*?' He swung his head from side to side. 'No way, man. No *way* did she jump.'

'She'd been drinking and taking drugs. You told us yourself that *Salvia divinorum* can cause intense feelings of disconnection. You told us she always came down hard from it. She was grieving, and she'd suffered a head injury—'

'And how do you suppose she got that?' Jason burst out. 'Who gave her that injury?'

'You're suggesting it was Ridgeway Kingsley-Jones?'

'Of *course* it was him.'

'Had you seen Ridgeway display violent behaviour towards Holly before? Or towards anyone else?'

A pause. 'No.'

'Then what makes you so sure?'

'Because I knew him. I saw how people reacted to him. Vince did too, and Trish. They only let him keep coming because Vince thought it was better to have him on the inside, pissing out. Even Trish kept him at arms' length, and she's about the most forgiving person I've ever met.'

'Lee and Stefanie seem to have been very loyal to him.'

'Yeah, because they were scared of him, not because they liked him. He'd got inside their heads.'

'So, you think there was some kind of mishap? That wherever they went after they left the farm, Holly hit her head, and instead of taking her to hospital they dropped her off the bridge onto the road?'

Jason shut his eyes as though to block out the image. '*Mishap*,' he muttered. 'Nah. He hit her. Or knocked her down. Probably tried it on and wouldn't take no for an answer.'

'You're talking about a sexual assault?' Broad said. 'Do you have any evidence to back up that allegation?'

'No. I don't have any evidence to back up that allegation, except what my gut's telling me. Except what I know about Holly, and what I know about *him*.'

'Were you and Holly sleeping together? Either at the time she died, or prior to that?'

Jason looked up with a slow-turning emotion in his eyes that Lockyer couldn't pin down. Different from the fear. 'Just once,' he said. 'She wasn't my girlfriend.'

'But you wanted her to be? You were in love with her?'

'Yeah.'

Lockyer's phone buzzed, and he glanced down – he was waiting to hear preliminary results on the samples from the workshop. Sure enough, the email was from Cellmark. He scanned it quickly.

'Okay, Jason,' he said. 'Here's the thing. We know Holly meant a great deal to you. You really cared about her, so her death must have been very hard for you. It must have been equally hard to see the people you believed were responsible escape any kind of justice. We know you were on the spot the day Stef Gould died. We suspect – and a matching handprint will prove – that you were also on the spot when Ridgeway died. That gives you means, motive and opportunity in *both* of their deaths. I also suspect that you went looking for Lee Geary at his sister's flat, in Salisbury. We have a witness who saw you there, and may be able to identify you. Forensic traces on Lee Geary's clothing put him in your workshop at Old Hat Farm very close to the time of his death. And we've found a large quantity of human blood on the workshop floor.'

'Blood? What? I – I don't know anything about that!'

'I think you do. It'll take longer for the lab to confirm it's Lee Geary's blood, but I predict that they *will* confirm it.'

'I don't know anything about it! I wasn't there!'

'Right. You were away, seeing friends. In Swindon.'

'Right.'

'Come *on*, Jason. Give me a single name. A single person you saw in Swindon that day, who can back up your story.'

Breathing hard now, Jason didn't reply.

'How did you move Lee off the farm and out onto the plain? He must have weighed twenty-two, twenty-three stone. Maybe more.'

Silence. A knot had appeared between Jason's eyebrows.

'It was pretty cold-hearted of you to drown Stef, if she

was just a hanger-on, like you said. Or was that an accident? Were you trying to get her to tell you something, Jason? Like what really happened to Holly, or where you might find Ridgeway?'

'I never saw her! Not after that spring – way before any of this!'

'Nobody was going to miss Ridgeway much, I grant you. But Lee Geary? He was harmless. Just a child, in a lot of ways. Hardly deserved to have his head smashed in. Mind you, the railings on that bridge are pretty high. Shoulder height, for most people. It wouldn't be easy to lift a girl over them, especially if she was struggling. So is that what you think – that it was big, strong Lee who actually threw her over?'

'*Yes!*' Jason burst out. 'Yes, I think it was him that threw her over! But I *didn't* kill him – or any of them!'

'Alibi, Jason. Right now.'

The silence hung.

Lockyer cleared his throat. 'Jason McNeil, I'm arresting you on suspicion of the murder of Lee Geary, on the eighteenth of November 2011.'

'No! Wait!'

'You do not have to say anything, but it may harm your defence if you do not mention when questioned something which you later rely on in court. Anything you do say may be—'

'All right!' he cried. 'All right, stop!'

'—given in evidence,' Lockyer finished. 'Do you understand? Jason?'

'Yes!'

At Lockyer's side, Broad was radiating tension. He sensed it too: a confession was coming. Jason put up his hands, as they'd seen him do before. Hovered them in front of his face for several seconds, palms inward, before lowering them. Exhaling. Lockyer waited it out.

'All right,' Jason said, at length. 'I – I went after them for a while, okay?'

'Went after who?'

'Ridgeway and the others. I just wanted to make them tell me the truth! All that *bullshit* about Holly getting out at the end of the farm track. About her not even going to Amesbury with them. And then the coroner calls it suicide, and we're expected to just *accept* it? Move on with our lives? Let that bastard Ridgeway carry on doing whatever he wants, like Holly was *nothing?*'

'So what happened when you found them? Did they refuse to tell you what you wanted to hear? Must have been infuriating, since that was the only way you were ever going to know for sure.'

'*No.* It wasn't like that! I never saw Stef at that festival, I swear it. Look, I went because someone at Old Hat told me she'd be there. She said she *always* saw Stef there. So I went, and I looked for her, but it near enough drove me *mad.* All those people, all that noise . . . I stuck it out for a few hours, but my head was a mess. I couldn't even ride the bike afterwards, to get home.' He glanced at them each in turn. 'I had to push it about a mile up the road, and sit somewhere quiet for a bit. There were, like, thirty thousand people there. I never saw Stef! And I never touched her.'

Lockyer exchanged a short look with Broad. He read doubt in her face, but whether she doubted Jason's guilt or his innocence, he couldn't tell.

'Tell us about that night at Culver Street car park,' he said.

'I followed Ridgeway there. I just wanted to make him admit what he'd done.'

'And an empty car park in the middle of the night is a pretty good place for an interrogation,' Broad said.

'Right. Except I obviously wasn't the only one thinking that. I got up there just in time to see them chuck him over the rails.'

'Who? Who did you see?'

'I don't know who they were. One black guy, one white. Looked nasty, so I just legged it. They weren't the kind of people you want setting eyes on you while they're about their business, you get me?'

'Do you think you could identify them from photographs?'

'Maybe, yeah. But I'm not that stupid.'

'If you could identify known associates of Ridgeway, it might help corroborate your story.'

'Might also get me buried.'

'Tell us about Lee Geary.'

'After Ridgeway died, Lee was the only one left who could tell me what had happened. And I figured he wasn't the brightest. He might be easier to—'

'Intimidate?'

'Yeah. So I went to his sister's place, trying to find him.

But I wouldn't have killed him, would I? Not if he was the only one left who knew the truth about Holly.'

'I don't know,' Lockyer said. 'Perhaps Stef had already told you what you wanted to know, because you'd held her head underwater until she did. Perhaps Ridgeway also told you, right before you let go of his ankles.'

'Come on, man! That's not *me*! That's not who I am!'

'But we don't know who you are, do we, Jason? Or where you're from. We don't even know your real name.'

There was a long pause. Jason hunched forwards and knotted his hands together, his long, elegant fingers clenching and unclenching. Lockyer thought of his intricate wood carvings, jarred by the idea that the ability to kill in cold blood might dwell side by side with the impulse to create such beauty. Then he remembered the carver's mallet.

For a few seconds, Jason's eyes roamed the drab corners of the room.

'On the eighteenth of November 2011, I was at my brother's funeral, in Swindon,' he said. 'I didn't want to go, but my mum begged me to. She kept texting, kept trying to call.'

'Trish informed us that none of you have phones.'

Jason looked shamefaced. 'I have a burner. Only Mum knows the number. I keep it hidden in the workshop. Please don't tell the McNeils – don't tell them where I was! They don't know I'm still in touch with any of my family. We all agreed it would be better that way, so there's no chance of my cousins ever finding me.'

'They're bad news?' Lockyer said.

Jason rolled his head, neither confirming nor denying.

'We'll have to check up on this, Jason,' Broad said. 'We'll need your mother's contact details. And her name.'

Jason reeled off her mobile number by heart, and gave her address, which was in a rundown part of Swindon, near the station.

'Her *name*, Jason,' Lockyer pressed.

It seemed to get stuck in Jason's throat. Lockyer wondered how long it had been since he'd told anyone.

'Chantelle Stevens.'

'And you attended whose funeral on that day?'

'Benjamin Stevens, my brother. Not just that one day, I stayed for a while. To help Mum.'

'And *your* given name?'

'W-William Jason Stevens.'

Lockyer met his eye. 'Thank you.'

He gave Broad a nod. She reached for the tape recorder.

'Interview suspended at ten fifty-five,' she said, then clicked it off.

'So what happens now?' Jason asked.

'You'll be released under investigation until we wait to hear whether it's Lee's blood in the workshop, and whether your alibi can be corroborated.'

'So I can go?'

'Almost.' Lockyer stood. 'Once we've processed your arrest.'

'But . . . No, hang on – I've *said* I was at Culver Street. You don't need to check that's my handprint. I'm telling you it is, so you don't need to take—'

'You're still a suspect in a murder inquiry, Jason. We need your prints and DNA.'

Jason hung his head, shut his eyes.

'What are we going to find?' Broad asked him gently.

'I . . . It's not . . .' He swallowed. 'Nothing.'

'Then you've got nothing to worry about,' Lockyer said. 'And if you're telling us the truth about Lee and the others, you'll be released without charge, and your DNA will be removed from the database.'

Jason remained in his seat.

'Are you going to cooperate, or do I need to ask some colleagues to step in and assist us?'

Jason stood. He looked exhausted. 'No more people. No more talking.'

Lockyer opened the door to usher him through. A thought occurred to him. 'Just one other thing, Jason. The person at Old Hat Farm who told you you'd find Stef at the Soul Tree Festival. You said it was a woman?'

'Did I?'

'Yes. You said, "She always saw Stef there." Can you remember her name? Or what she looked like?'

'I can't think of her name. She came a few times. She was all front. Armour-plated, but raw underneath. Not that you'd want to cross her – she'd lamp you before she asked you to explain. Boudicca. That's who I thought of, whenever she came around. Blackest hair I ever saw on a white girl.'

'Jody Upton?'

'Yeah, that was it. Jody.'

*

Jason gave no trouble as his samples and photograph were taken. Once he was in the squad car and on his way home, Lockyer and Broad climbed the stairs back up to their poky office.

'What do you reckon?' Lockyer asked, since Broad was uncharacteristically quiet.

'Well, I guess if his alibi checks out, it can't have been him,' she said.

'This is all assuming Lee died on the eighteenth, or very close to it. What's to say they didn't keep him there a few days? Take his phone from him?'

'Why would they do that, guv?'

Lockyer spread his hands. 'Waiting for Jason to come home? I don't know.'

'How are we *ever* going to prove that? And we've nowhere near enough evidence to charge him for Ridgeway or Stef.'

He gave her a sideways look. 'You sound relieved, Gem.'

'Maybe a tiny bit,' she confessed. 'He seems like a nice person, that's all.'

'He does. But that can't be a factor,' Lockyer said firmly.

'I know, guv.'

'I want a cast-iron alibi before we de-arrest him. Not just his mum saying, "Yeah, he was here." I want to know exactly when and where the funeral of Benjamin Stevens took place. I want the names of people who saw Jason there, and I want their statements. Let's get on it before he's reunited with his phone.'

'Yep.' Broad sat down at her computer and smacked the space bar to rouse it.

Lockyer was about to bury himself in paperwork when a call came up from the front desk.

He was surprised to find Trish McNeil standing on the top step outside, from where she'd apparently shouted in to the desk sergeant that she wanted to speak to him. Lockyer supposed Devizes must seem like a seething mess of virus-laden humanity, compared to Old Hat. He wondered how long it'd been since Trish had left the farm. She seemed on the verge of tears.

'Let him go, Inspector,' she said, in place of a greeting.

'Let's go and stand in the shade at least,' Lockyer said. He led her over to the ash trees.

'Vince told me to wait at home but I couldn't. You *have* to let him go. He hasn't done anything wrong! And he can't cope in places like this. People in his face, closed-in spaces . . .'

'Actually, I'd say he coped very well with the interview.'

Trish blinked. 'When can he come home? You've no right to hold him, if he hasn't been arrested—'

'But he *has* been arrested, on suspicion of the murder of Lee Geary.'

She looked stunned. 'But – but he wasn't even on the farm that day! He never even *saw*—'

'But you *did* see Lee, Trish? Is that what you're trying not to say? Is that why you're so sure which day it was, and that Jason was away at the time?'

'No, I—' Trish's face crumpled. She put her hand over her mouth; he heard, muffled: '*Fuck.*'

'Talk to me,' he said. 'It'll be better in the long run.'

'I saw him, all right?' she said. 'Lee came to the farm that day. I was doing the chickens, and I saw him come across from the beehives, and go into the workshop. I was going to go over and say hello, ask what he wanted ... I mean, I never expected to see *any* of them again, after Holly. But I saw Vince talking to him, and then he just left. Before I could even go over. I swear to God he just left.'

'By himself? You didn't see anyone else with him or following him?'

'No, he was by himself.'

'What did he want?'

'He wanted ... Look, he bought some Sally D, all right? He told Vince he wanted to see things clearly. That's something Ridgeway used to say to people – take SD if you want to see clearly. Lee was going to go out onto the plain to take it. That was what he said.'

Lockyer could hardly believe what he was hearing. 'Why the hell didn't you say any of this before?'

'Because we didn't want to be involved! And it didn't look good for us, did it? The SD. We had no idea what had happened to Lee or how he came to *die*. So we thought what did it matter that he'd come to the farm beforehand?'

'It mattered a great deal! You've lied, and obstructed a police investigation—'

'It wasn't like that! It's just ... people like us ... with the Sally D and Vince's record. And Jason—'

She cut herself off, looking down at the shrivelled remains of last year's leaves.

'And Jason not being who he says he is,' Lockyer finished

for her. He took a moment, thinking it through. Lee, tripping out on SD, falling into that hollow and hitting his head on a rock. Ending up under the tree, where leaves and twigs and eventually soil covered him. It was possible.

'There was a scrap of ribbon in a tree near to where Lee died,' he said. 'Do you know anything about that?'

Trish's brows knotted. 'I don't know where you mean.'

'A hollow about a mile south of the farm, where the land starts to rise. The centre of it is hidden from view, and there's a single hawthorn tree there.'

'Yellow ribbon?' she whispered.

Lockyer nodded.

'We – we used to have gatherings there, sometimes. At Imbolc – one of the fire festivals – to welcome the coming of spring. We'd have a bonfire, and a big cook-up, make offerings to the Celtic goddess, Brigid.'

'And Lee came to one of those? He'd been there before?'

'Yes. It could even have been that year.'

Lockyer was silent as this sank in. The possibility that he'd been trying to solve a murder that had never happened. A *series* of murders that had never happened – or, at least, could never be proven. A heaviness settled on him. Then came a rush of anger. 'If this is true then you've wasted a *lot* of police time and money.'

'Well, I'm sorry for that,' Trish said stiffly, 'but it's not *our* job to do your job.'

'I could charge you with obstruction.'

'But not with murder! That's not who we are.'

'Jason just said the exact same thing, but I don't feel I

know who any of you are, least of all Jason. And perhaps you don't know who he really is, either.'

Trish was firm. 'I know who he is now.'

'Why is he so frightened to admit to his past that I had to arrest him before he'd tell us his name?'

'I don't know. And, in any case, what does it matter? Who we are as children is not who we are as adults. And I'm not just talking about age. I'm talking about growth. Inner growth. What matters is who we are now. What we do now. That's why people leave their past at the gate when they come to Old Hat Farm.'

'I'm afraid I don't agree with you. And neither does the law.'

'Oh, what does the bloody law know?'

'There's no statute of limitation on crime in this country, Trish. Do you think gangsters and abusers should be allowed to live out their lives on Spanish beaches as long as they've come to realize that what they did was wrong?'

'That's completely different.'

'It's one hundred per cent the same.'

'No, it *isn't*. A determined devotion to – to cruelty and depravity is *not* the same as a mistake made once, in the chaos of childhood.'

'I'm afraid, in the eyes of the law—'

'Like I said, what does the law know?' she said bitterly. 'What's the point of punishing someone who's already changed? Who is already rehabilitated? Who's now a – a positive presence in the world?'

Lockyer considered this for a moment. 'Generous,' he

said. 'That's a word I've repeatedly heard to describe you, Trish. Forgiving. Kind.'

'So what? I'm glad.'

'I'm wondering what your sister did that was so bad you never saw or spoke to her again. Not once, in all the years until she died.'

'Imogen.' Trish sucked the word in as though it'd hit her in the ribs. 'I didn't come here to talk about that. About *her*.'

With a visible effort, Trish pulled herself together. 'Just let Jason go. He was nowhere near Old Hat when Lee Geary came that day, and he sure as hell didn't kill him.'

'Is there anything else you haven't told me? Anything at all about Lee Geary, Ridgeway or Stef?'

'No. But surely those were accidents? Or suicides.'

'Perhaps not.'

'We don't know anything about them. And you can't arrest Jason for Lee – he has an alibi.'

'Do you know what his alibi is?'

Trish recoiled. Then: 'He went to see his mother. It was his brother's funeral that day.'

'There's another one, then,' Lockyer said, with a shake of his head. 'Another secret that isn't a secret at all. Jason asked us not to tell you or Vince that he was seeing his family. He said you didn't know he was in still touch with them. But you *do* know. Just like *they* still think you have no idea Holly was your niece.'

He remembered an impression he'd formed, early on, that not much went on at Old Hat Farm without Trish knowing.

'You've arrested him,' she said. 'So . . .'

'So we've taken his prints and DNA, yes.'

Fear flashed across her face. 'Will you let him go, though?'

'Jason left just before you got here. We sorted him a lift home.'

Trish's obvious relief at hearing this soon cooled, given how long it had taken him to tell her. She turned to go, but looked back. 'There's no way that blood is Lee Geary's.'

'You seem very certain of that.'

'That's because I saw him walk away that day. And he wasn't bleeding at the time.'

'Can anyone back you up on that, Trish? Anyone else who was at the farm that day?'

'Actually, I don't think anyone was staying at the time.'

'Right.' Lockyer sighed. 'Don't let Jason run off. It'll be much worse for him if he does.'

Trish ignored that. 'There was a guy called Fitz who stayed with us a couple of summers ago,' she said. 'He thought he was handy at woodwork; nearly took his thumb off with a chisel. That bled like a geyser. I expect that's what you've found.'

'And I suppose you stitched it up yourselves, and we'll find no record of this Fitz attending any hospital for the injury.'

'No. It was bad. Vince took him to Minor Injuries, in Andover.'

'On the Harley?'

'In Fitz's car. The hospital should have a record of it. It was in August, I think, the year before last. His full name was Jim Fitzmorris.'

With that she walked away, seeming so certain that Lockyer was inclined to believe her.

Which would mean they were back at square one, wondering whether Lee Geary had simply walked out onto the plain that day, taken *Salvia divinorum* and fallen. With a sinking feeling, Lockyer realized they might be grasping at smoke. They might never be able to verify Lee's innocence, or what had really happened to Holly. That he was powerless to prove any of it.

14

Lockyer got straight onto the phone to Andover Hospital, having given Broad a quick rundown of everything Trish had said.

She looked crestfallen. 'So if Jason's alibi checks out, and what they're saying is true, we've got nothing. Right?'

'That's about the size of it, Gem. But I want it watertight before we let it go.'

'Yes, guv,' she said, with a nod. 'I suppose it was only ever a theory that Lee believed Jason was coming after him. We never knew it for sure.'

'No,' Lockyer agreed. 'But Lee left his sister's place that morning in a state because he wanted to tell someone something. And then he went to Old Hat Farm.'

'But we don't know that he went *straight* there,' Broad reminded him. 'Maybe he went there after seeing somebody else, and telling them whatever was on his mind. Maybe he wanted the SD to help him process whatever that other encounter was.'

Lockyer mulled that over in silence.

Broad cleared her throat. 'The DSU's going to be pretty annoyed about all the forensics.'

'Yes. She is.' He sat back in his chair, looking up at the ceiling for a minute. 'Just because Jason wasn't there that day it doesn't mean one of the other McNeils didn't harm Lee,' he said. 'They must *all* have blamed those three for Holly's death. And we know Vince was especially cut up about it. We've only got Trish's word for it that Lee bought SD then left the yard alone.'

Lockyer thought of the photo he'd seen in their kitchen: Trish looking up at Vince and reaching for his hand. He thought of her continued pretence of ignorance about Holly's parentage, even nine years after her death. Because Vince had wanted it that way.

'She'd say anything to protect Vince,' he said. 'I think they'd *all* lie to protect each other, and what they've got there.'

Andover Hospital rang back to confirm Trish's story. Jim Fitzmorris had been treated for a penetrating laceration to his hand on 30 August 2018. He'd been referred for orthopaedic surgery in Basingstoke. Then Broad, having spoken to Swindon District Council, confirmed that Benjamin Stevens, Jason's brother, had been buried on 18 November 2011.

'I checked Benjamin's record,' Broad said. 'It's a long as your arm. Burglary, assault, concealed weapons. Suspected of gang involvement and county lines. He died of knife wounds.'

'Have you got hold of the mother yet?'

'I've left a message.'

'Keep trying her.'

'What about Jason's – William Stevens's – record, guv? Anything on the PNC?'

'No.' Lockyer turned the screen to show her. 'Not a single thing.'

'That's weird, isn't it? Given how stressed out he was about us checking?'

'All it means is that he was never arrested, or charged, for whatever he did.'

'Or maybe it was just his *family* he was trying to hide from us – or hide *from*,' Broad suggested, with a note of tentative optimism. 'He mentioned not wanting contact with his cousins, and his brother was clearly mixed up in all sorts. Maybe he's just scared of *them*. And doesn't want them finding out where he is.'

'Could be,' Lockyer conceded. 'So let's not leak his whereabouts. But we need the full story. This is a setback, but let's focus on Jason's alibi, and on those blood results.'

'And if it checks out? And it's not Lee's blood?'

'Then I'm going to have to tell the DSU and brace myself for a kicking. A Covid-safe, socially distanced kicking. But still.'

After lunch Lockyer went to find Vince. Trish tried to turn him away. 'Haven't you caused us enough grief for one day?' she said.

'It's either here or at the station,' he said, impatience getting the better of him.

'Vince isn't having a good day.'

'I'm sorry to hear that. But you've lied and obstructed this investigation from the beginning, and I'm sick of having my time wasted. So where is he, Trish?'

With a jerk of her head she indicated the stairs. Lockyer knew at once where she meant.

Vince was sitting on the side of Holly's bed, holding a pale-yellow T-shirt, his face ravaged. With a jolt Lockyer recalled seeing his own father in that exact pose in Chris's room, not long after his death. Gripping one of his jumpers in his fists.

Vince looked up as Lockyer approached. 'What the fuck do you want?'

'I want to know what you and Lee Geary talked about when he came here.'

Vince turned to squint at the bright square of the window. 'He said he wanted some Sally D. He had things on his mind that he needed to sort out.'

'Did he say what those things were?'

'No. And I didn't ask him.'

'Did he say anything about Jason? Or Holly?'

'No. Well . . . he said he was sorry about Holly. Sorry for our loss. It was the first time I'd seen him since it happened. He said he hadn't hurt her – swore it, in fact.'

'Did you offer him a place to stay?'

'No.' Vince frowned. 'Maybe I should've, but no. I didn't blame him for what had happened, but I didn't want him around, either . . .' He trailed off, slowly smoothing the fabric of the T-shirt between his fingers and thumbs.

'You seem to spend a lot of time in here,' Lockyer said.

'It's the last place to be near her. My girl.'

'Do you think it's hard for Jason to see how much you miss Holly? After all, he's been in your life for a lot longer than she ever was. But you loved her at once, because she was yours. Perhaps you loved her *more*.'

Vince gave him a look so hard that Lockyer almost stepped back. 'Jason isn't that kind of petty, jealous, *small* person, Inspector. He's better than that – he's better than all of us.'

'Has he ever told you about his life before he came here?'

'Not in detail. But when I told him about mine I could tell he recognized a lot of it. The abuse. The fear. Having to be someone you're not, just to survive.' Vince shook his head minutely. 'That kind of thing stamps itself on you. You get this hard place inside you that sometimes has a mind of its own. But not Jase. Whatever he went through he's managed to . . . cast it off. I mean, I might make things, but Jason *creates*. He's an artist. And it's the same with people. I get along with them, but Jason gets to *know* them.'

'What do you mean?'

'I don't expect you to understand, but I *admire* him. He's the kind of person I wish I could be. And he knows I love him. We're family.' He fixed Lockyer with another glare. 'Now get lost. This is Holly's place.'

Later on, Lockyer messaged Joe Cameron again, and this time his brother's friend replied at once: *Yeah alright knock off at six can meet for swift half.*

Lockyer went straight back with a venue. Then, without thinking, he clicked on his message to Hedy. Still unopened;

still unread. He tapped and held until the option to delete appeared. Hesitated again, then deleted it. If she'd changed her number without telling him, that was that. The postcard she'd sent was just her way of saying goodbye. It had been almost six months since she'd left. Six months since they'd made love, that one night, before she'd run. There was nothing whatsoever to be gained by hanging on, replaying in his memory the two or three precious times he'd made her laugh.

He met Joe at a new, entirely soulless pub called the Milk Wagon, which nestled alongside the busy A350 just south of Melksham. Lockyer found a table outside and ordered a pint. Joe appeared minutes later. He had the very average physique of a man who spent most of every day sitting down, a pleasant enough face, but a slightly unfriendly expression. In spite of the Facebook photos, Lockyer had half expected an eighteen-year-old lad to come swaggering in, at once self-conscious and over-confident. That was how he still saw Chris, after all.

They didn't shake hands. He gave Lockyer an appraising look.

'Thanks for coming, Joe,' Lockyer said. 'You keeping well?'

Joe ordered a lager when the waitress brought Lockyer's pint. 'Didn't think I'd ever hear from you again,' he said, skipping the small-talk. 'To what do I owe the pleasure?'

There was a slight barb in the question. Lockyer suspected Joe had always found him lofty and disapproving. He supposed he might've been, at times.

'I wanted to talk to someone who was close to Chris. Someone who knew him as well as I did. And maybe better than I did, in some ways.'

'Okay.' Guarded but curious now.

'Not that we weren't close,' Lockyer said, 'but I guess a brother isn't the same as a best mate.'

'Near enough with you two, I always thought,' Joe said.

Lockyer took a long swig of beer.

Joe lit a cigarette. 'What's this about, Matt?' he said.

'Joe . . . was Chris happy?'

'Course he was happy. Your brother was *always* happy.'

'He was always cheerful. But that's not the same thing, is it?'

Joe blew smoke to one side, narrowing his eyes.

With a surge of impatience, Lockyer jumped the gun.

'I know about the pills. The ecstasy.'

Joe turned sharp. 'What pills?'

'Come on, Joe. You of all people must've known what he was up to. And I'm not here in any kind of official capacity. I just . . . need to understand.'

Joe smoked in silence for a bit. 'You found his stash, I'm guessing. I had a quick look for it at the wake. Didn't want your folks to find it and freak out.'

'It was pinned behind the headboard.'

'Right. Should've thought of that.'

'So, you were both involved? Why, Joe?'

'Why do you think? Money.'

'Chris had money.'

'Come off it. *Money.* Not scratching around for a few quid

to buy a pint at the end of the week. He was saving up to go travelling.'

'*Travelling?*'

'Yeah. Did he never say?'

'No. Travelling where?'

'Dunno, don't think it mattered. Couple of years, he was planning. "If I'm going to be stuck on the farm for the rest of my life, then I'm going to see some of the world first." That's what he said.'

It was a kick in the guts. Lockyer looked down at the table as the words sank in. 'I thought he loved farming,' he muttered. 'I really did.'

'Well, it wasn't like he hated it, or anything. It was just, well, you'd left, hadn't you? So he knew *he* couldn't. I guess he felt trapped. But, look, he'd have come back. He was only eighteen, for Christ's sake. Nobody wants to be told at eighteen how they're going to spend the rest of their life, do they?'

'I suppose not. But why didn't he tell me any of this? I'd have understood.'

'You wouldn't have understood about the pills.'

'No. He didn't need to sell drugs. There were other ways he could've saved up.'

'What? A Saturday job at the garage? He'd have been thirty before he'd made enough for a round-the-world ticket.'

'I'd have helped.'

'Really?' Joe said baldly. 'He thought you'd try to talk him out of it. He wanted to go while he was still young, and I was already selling a bit of this and that so—'

'So you suggested he come in with you?'

'He *asked* to come in with me.'

'You could've said no.'

'Why would I? I was making more money than anyone else we knew. I was doing him a *favour*. He already liked dropping an E on a night out. It was no big deal.'

'It could have landed you both in prison. Or hospital.'

'Yeah, Dad. But it didn't.'

'No. It ended with Chris bleeding to death outside a pub in Chippenham.'

'That wasn't anything to do with the pills.'

'Had he taken any that night?'

'Look—'

'*Had he?*'

Lockyer couldn't keep the tension out of his voice. It was the bitterness of only finding out now, twenty years after Chris's death, what had actually happened to him and why. His anger, yet again, was at least half with himself, for having put his brother in that position, and been unaware of it.

'Was he dealing?' he said. 'Was *that* what the fight was? An altercation with a rival, or a supplier? Jesus Christ, Joe, was the stabbing *deliberate*?'

'All right, keep your voice down!' Joe said. 'No, that's not what the fight was about. Nobody was pissed off with us, or out to get us. There was no altercation, for fuck's sake. He wasn't dealing that night, all right? It was just his birthday party.'

'But had he *taken* any? Was that why he waded into the

fight, thinking he could get everyone to just kiss and make up?'

Joe turned his bottle of lager, smudging the condensation on the glass. 'He'd dropped one,' he said, 'we all had but, like, hours before. At the start of the night. It would've worn off by the time he—'

'You're sure about that?' Lockyer snapped.

Joe glared at him. 'I'm sure Chris would have tried to break up that fight even if he'd been as sober as a bloody judge. That's just what he was like, right? Natural-born Scout leader.'

'Yeah, but he wasn't stupid. And it was such a *stupid* thing to do – bringing a smile to a knife fight. It's always bothered me how idiotic that was.'

'Look, Matt . . .' Joe leant forwards across the table, softening. 'We were pissed as farts. Maybe still a tiny bit high. I was inside, I didn't see it happen, but if Chris had known someone had a knife he wouldn't have gone *near* it. Would he? It was just a random fucking catastrophe. Wrong place, wrong time.'

'Maybe.' Lockyer got to his feet.

'Now, hang on, don't go blaming me,' Joe said. 'If I'd been outside, I'd have stopped him.'

'I know.' Lockyer guessed, from Joe's sudden aggression, that he blamed himself, at least in part. He felt the same guilt. 'I know you would, Joe. Thanks for meeting me.'

I don't expect you to understand, but I admire him. He's the kind of person I wish I could be.

Lockyer heard Vince's words again as he sat sweating in

the car. But Lockyer *did* understand, because that was how he'd felt about his brother. He'd wished he could be more like Chris – his optimism and lust for life, his ability to communicate and get along with people. To be the life and soul. But a person who dealt drugs? Who lied to those closest to them, and got themselves killed because they were so out of it they hardly knew what they were doing? That was hardly a person Lockyer could admire.

He was halfway back to Orcheston before he realized how badly he didn't want to be alone with what he'd just learnt. Swinging the car around in the wide concrete splay of a tank crossing, he went to Westdene instead. The collies greeted him; he put his head around the living-room door and saw his father crashed out, still in his overalls. He was whimpering in his sleep, hands twitching. Unhappy sounds. He looked old and worn-out.

Lockyer knelt beside him and squeezed his arm.

John jerked up, blinking rapidly. 'Matt?' he said.

'Sorry to wake you, Dad. You were dreaming.'

'I was.'

John looked down at himself, brows beetling. Fiddled with a button that had come undone. It didn't seem as though he was going to say anything else, so Lockyer stood up to go. A hand on his arm stopped him, gripping hard. He looked down into his father's frightened eyes. 'Are you all right, Matt?'

Lockyer was startled. In recent years, depression had made John turn ever further in on himself. However much he loved them, he rarely remembered to wonder, or to ask, if other people were okay.

Lockyer gave his stock answer: 'I'm fine, Dad.'

'But are you *really*?'

The firm grip and insistent stare didn't waver, as though the answer mattered. It caused Lockyer a sudden spasm of deep unhappiness.

'When am I ever?' he said quietly, truthfully. 'But I'll be okay. You don't need to worry about me.'

'Course I bloody do,' John mumbled. He yawned enormously, eyes sliding shut again. The hand on Lockyer's arm went slack.

Lockyer swallowed hard. 'Dinner won't be long, Dad. I can smell it.'

'Perfect timing,' Jody said, when he appeared in the kitchen. She plonked a block of Cheddar and a plate in front of him. 'Grate that, would you?'

'All of it?'

'Yep. I'm making Parmigiana. Needs plenty of cheese.'

'Isn't it usually mozzarella?'

'Really?' Her eyebrows shot up. 'You want to quibble about the recipe when you're getting your dinner cooked for you by a woman who's been up since five a.m., and has been frying aubergines for forty-five fucking minutes?'

Lockyer conceded the point. 'No.'

'Good. Mozzarella was a stretch too far for the Co-op down the road.'

'Am I allowed a beer while I grate?'

'Maybe.' She grinned. 'Depends how quickly you work.'

They drank and chatted while the dish came together. The sun dropped behind the house, and her skin almost glowed in the artificial light. For some reason being bossed around by her helped Lockyer forget about Chris dealing drugs and wanting to leave the farm, and about the dead-end Lee Geary's case seemed about to hit.

'Your dad's been asleep since four o'clock,' she said, when the food was ready. 'Reckon I ought to wake him?'

'Oh, definitely. He'd hate to miss a meal.'

'Hang on, then.'

She cracked an egg into a pan on the hotplate, swearing when it spat oil onto her hand. 'I've worked out he'll eat basically anything as long as it has a fried egg on top,' she said. 'Funnily enough, frying an egg was about the only thing my own dad taught me to do.'

'Did they live around here when you were growing up?'

'No. Somerset.'

'Farmers, I take it?'

'God, no. Dad's a deputy head at a secondary school. Mum's a GP's receptionist. But I worked out early on that I was better with animals and machinery than I was with people.'

She carefully flipped the egg. 'And I'm not going to talk about my childhood, or why I have a room with Gran and not my parents. Just so's you know.'

Lockyer fetched plates. 'You're pretty cagey for someone with so many opinions about other people.'

She was unperturbed. 'Tell me to mind my own business, and I'll do exactly that. Now, let's eat. I'm *ravenous*.'

John shuffled to the table with bleary eyes and his hair standing up in tufts.

'What do you reckon?' Jody asked, when he'd had a few mouthfuls.

'You always get the yolk just right,' John said, to which Jody gave a bark of laughter.

When the food was finished they left John in front of the TV. Jody fetched a blanket from the back of a chair and a six-pack from the fridge.

'I'm going out to the machine shed to watch the bats,' she said. 'You coming?'

'To watch the *bats*?' Lockyer echoed. 'All right.'

They sat with their backs to the wall, facing south-west across a black swathe of rising ground that met the pale sky in a crisp line. Bats were already flitting silently from their roosts in the old tiled roof, spiralling into the twilight. Jody opened two beers and passed one to Lockyer.

'I've always loved bats,' she said, resting her arms on her bent knees.

'Really?'

'Yeah. So flippin' fast. They have sonar. And have you ever held one? They weigh nothing. All those skills, not to mention a tonne of folklore, in such a teeny, tiny package.'

'Jody, how many beers have you had?'

'A few, Dad.'

Lockyer smiled wryly. 'That's the second time I've been called that this evening.'

'Yeah? Who else have you been trying to parent?'

'An old friend of my brother's. The one who got him into selling the pills. He was with Chris the night he died.'

Jody took her time to answer. 'What did he say about it?'

'He basically said I'd trapped my brother here by going away to study, then into the police. I'd left the farm, so Chris couldn't. He was trying to get the money together to run away. That's what the pills were about.'

'To run away?'

'Travelling, for a couple of years. But who knows if he'd have come back?' Lockyer took a drink. 'I thought we could talk to each other, but I had no idea he felt that way. That he wasn't happy.'

'Come on,' Jody said softly. 'That's not what it meant.'

'No?'

'No! It meant that he was eighteen and starting to . . . flex his wings, and all that guff. Look, wanting to go travelling, shag someone on a beach and take a bunch of pictures of the sunset does *not* mean he planned to turn his back on you all. It doesn't mean he didn't want to be here in the long run.' She looked across to check he was listening. 'I know your brother was, like, the golden child; the one who turned grey skies to blue around here. But nobody can be like that all the time, can they? Not unless they've got a serious deficiency of some kind.'

'I just . . . I guess we weren't as close as I thought. The first time he had something important going on in his life, and he couldn't tell me about it.' Lockyer tipped his head back against the wall. 'I suppose there must have been signs that I missed. Maybe he tried to tell me, and I didn't listen. I really . . . I basically failed him.'

'That again?' Jody heaved a sigh, then was quiet for a while.

'Did you know,' she said, at length, 'there's a place in Mexico, called Pomuch, where families take their relatives' bones out of their tombs every year to give them a good clean?'

'What?'

'It's true. Once a year they pop the box, and out comes Granny's skull, or Uncle Geoff's leg bones or whatever. They give them a buff-up, say whatever they need to say to them, then pop them back in for another year.'

'Okay. Seems weird.'

'But that's *exactly* what you're doing, Matt,' she said. 'Can't you see it? It's like when a family keeps their kid's room the same for decades after they've died. Trying to hang on. Trying not to let them go.'

'But surely you can understand why—'

'I understand *why*. But it doesn't make the person any less gone. Do you think your brother'd be happy to know you all fell apart when he died? That you still sit around, laying out his bones and stressing about who he was and why he died and what it means?'

'No,' Lockyer had to concede. 'He was always more of a live-for-the-moment sort of person.'

'There are you are, then.'

'Except I don't seem to have any choice *but* to think these things.'

'There's *always* a choice. He's gone, and it sucks, but stick to the facts. Miss him, be sad about losing him, but don't make it all about *you* – that's just ego. What happened wasn't your fault. You're you, and he was him, so you *couldn't* have done things differently – and you can't change a damn thing now. You *loved* him. That's all that matters. Just let the rest go, for Christ's sake.'

It was probably good advice. Lockyer had no idea if he'd ever manage to take it.

'It's not easy to—' he faltered.

'I never said it was *easy*. But you at least have to *try*.'

'Who did you lose?' Lockyer asked, on instinct. He was very aware of Jody beside him – the physicality of her. Lean muscle and bone, sun-kissed skin with trace scents of cooking. She was staring up at the sky with a naked vulnerability he'd never seen before.

'I had a little boy,' she said eventually. 'He got ALL. Acute lymphoblastic leukaemia. Died two days after his third birthday.'

'Jody . . . I'm so sorry.'

'Don't be.' She turned towards him, smiling tremulously but with real warmth. 'Far and away the best three years of my life. He was my little jack rabbit – up on his feet from the word go, practically. And always climbing. God, if I took my eyes off him for one second he'd be hanging off a shelf, or something.'

Her eyes caught the light from the back door of the farm-house. Shining.

'Then he started to get tired and dizzy. Then the nose-bleeds . . .'

'Jody.' Lockyer was at a loss. 'What was his name?'

'Danny,' she said. 'Danny Alexander Upton.'

'Good name.'

'Yeah.'

'You used to have a lot of things,' Lockyer said. 'That's what you said to me. You meant Danny.'

'Yeah. And the life I thought I was going to lead after he was born. Got myself a flat, a car, a job. I thought that was what a kid needed, but it wasn't. All he needed was me, and a bit more luck than he was dealt.'

'I'm so sorry.'

'But when he was gone I – I got rid of it all. All his stuff, the flat, the car. No point trying to hang on to any of it. And there was no way I could've carried on, being reminded of him every day. That hurt *way* too much. The world'll kick your heart to pieces, if you let it. I decided not to let it.'

'Boudicca,' Lockyer murmured, the alcohol loosening his tongue.

'What?'

'Boudicca. The barbarian queen. I heard someone call you that today.'

'Oh, yeah? Who?'

'Jason McNeil.'

'Jase? The guy from Old Hat Farm?'

'You told him where to find Stef Gould. At the Soul Tree Festival, back in 2011.'

'Did I?'

'Apparently.'

'Well, there you go. I always liked Jase.' She frowned. 'He didn't hurt Stef, did he?'

Lockyer didn't think twice about his answer. 'No, nothing like that.'

'Thank fuck for that. Did you find anything useful in my pictures?'

'Yes, we did.' Lockyer searched her face. 'You've helped so much.'

Jody started to say something else, but stopped. She registered his scrutiny and seemed to weigh it up. To consider it. Then she uncoiled her arms and turned her body towards him, leaning in until their faces were inches apart. With the hint of a smile, she waited for him to close the distance.

15

Day 15, Monday

Lockyer spent Saturday nursing a hangover and doing his best to avoid thinking about Jody. They'd lain on their backs for a long time afterwards, each lost in thought, watching the sky until it got too dark to see the bats. Then, as the temperature finally began to drop, Jody had kicked herself upright and yanked on her clothes.

'Better get to bed. I'll be up again in a couple of hours,' she said. 'Night, Matt.'

He hadn't managed to get in a reply other than 'Night, Jody.'

Now he was left wondering if he'd messed up something good. A friendship, and the best thing to happen to the farm in years. And also with the nagging sensation of having been unfaithful to someone he loved – even though that person had left him months ago.

He went to the hospital and sat with his mother for the permitted hour, listening to the steady bleep of the machines on the high-dependency ward. Trudy's skin had a waxy, bloodless pallor, and she didn't wake. Tears burnt in the back of Lockyer's throat, a premonition of the pain to come if she died.

From Salisbury he drove back to Bulford to update Karen Wilkins. She was quiet for a long time after he'd outlined the possibility of Lee having gone to the hollow, a place he knew, to take *Salvia divinorum* in search of wisdom. The possibility of him having fallen and hit his head.

A crease appeared between her eyebrows. 'That just doesn't sound like Lee.'

'I understand,' Lockyer said. 'But perhaps he'd discovered some new things that year. Going to Old Hat Farm, and hanging out with Ridgeway . . .'

'I suppose.' She didn't sound convinced. 'Are you sure that's what happened?'

'No. But it's one possibility.'

'He said he wanted to see someone – that he had something to tell someone.'

'I'm still doing everything I can to find out who and what that was.' Lockyer handed her Jason McNeil's new mugshot. 'Is this the man who came and asked to see Lee that day? This is a recent photo, so he would've been younger at the time.'

Jason had already confirmed that it'd been him, but just for the sake of completion, and because Lockyer was curious about whether or not Karen would remember.

'I . . . think that's him . . . I mean, it definitely *could* be. His hair's different but, yes, I think so.' She handed the photo back, looking sad. 'He's got a lovely face. Did he . . . could he have had anything to do with what happened to Lee?'

'I thought so for a while, but this man was not in the area at the time Lee disappeared.'

'Oh. But was he the one Lee was running from? The reason he went and bought this drug you're on about?'

'When I know for sure, so will you. I promise.'

Lockyer didn't want to go home, to Róisín Conlan's bones and his circling, toxic thoughts about Chris, so he headed into the station instead. Heat blasted up from the tarmac. Lockyer supposed Broad would be keeping cool somewhere. Taking Merry for a swim, perhaps. He realized he much preferred to picture her out and about with her dog than at home with Pete.

The only useful thing he managed to find out that afternoon was that the partial palm print lifted from the handrail at Culver Street car park was not a good enough match to Jason's to prove he'd definitely been there that night. There were several points of convergence, but not enough. Jason had already admitted to being there, and it was just as well. He'd explained what he'd been doing, and what he'd seen, but whether it had been the truth or a way to dismiss his presence at Soul Tree as well, Lockyer wasn't sure. Instinct told him it was the former. But his instincts had been wrong before.

Towards the end of the day Lockyer drove to his friend Kevin's house. In the last days of winter Kevin had rung him, asking for help – no doubt with some dodgy situation engineered by his father. For the first time in his life, Lockyer hadn't taken the call. He'd felt both guilty and defiant about that. The last time he'd helped Kevin it'd almost cost him his job. He couldn't keep doing it.

Since then, lockdown had made it easy not to see Kevin, but they'd hardly spoken either. Perhaps some tacit agreement that Kevin was on his own this time. Twice divorced, he was lolling in a deckchair when Lockyer pulled up outside an ex-local-authority semi in the village of Netheravon. His kids were leaping in and out of a sprinkler, squealing. Scrawny, wearing his years of hardship and anxiety on his face, Kevin looked up at the sound of the car door. He didn't smile, and for the first time ever, Lockyer wasn't sure of his welcome.

'Matt,' Kevin called. 'Thought you'd died of the virus. Long time no see.'

'Still alive,' Lockyer replied. 'You?'

'I've had it. Felt like shit for a couple of weeks, and now I'm thick as mud and can't stay awake for more than two hours at a time.'

'Back to normal, then.'

They eyed each other for a second, then Kevin grinned. 'Sit down. Grab a beer.'

Lockyer stayed for two hours, catching up. Then – as he suspected had been his main reason for coming – he told Kevin about the ecstasy.

'Ah, don't sweat it,' Kevin said. 'So Chris sold a few pills, so what? I've done that, and far worse besides.'

'It's not the pills, exactly.'

'It's that he wanted to leave?'

'Yeah.'

They watched the kids cavort. The smell of wet, trampled grass was everywhere.

At length, Lockyer said, 'Did he ever say anything to you about it?'

'Me? No, course not.'

'I think I should tell my parents. It might help explain why he waded into that fight.'

'What the fuck is the matter with you? No. Don't tell them.'

'But it's the truth.'

'Maybe, but you just said a minute ago that you wish you hadn't found out. So how will it help them?'

Lockyer picked a grass stem, scattered the seeds. 'He blamed me. That's basically what Joe said. Chris was stuck on the farm because I'd left, and given him no choice.'

'Yeah, well, Joe Cameron always was a bit of a knob,' Kev said. 'Look, Chris was growing up. Not just your little brother any more. And people cock up; it's what they do. He won't have blamed you for any of it.'

'No?'

'Look, one thing I know about siblings is that if they've got a gripe, bloody hell, you'll know about it. Chris was a great bloke, and he thought the world of you. The rest is just . . . stuff. Not important.'

'I just wish he'd talked to me about it. That's what's getting to me – the secrets. The lying.'

Kevin thought about that for a minute. 'You know why

people lie to the ones they love? 'Cause they're scared, mostly. Scared of disappointing them. Scared of ruining things.' He took a swig of beer. 'Chris was always the glass-half-full one, right? I bet that was bloody knackering, after a while.'

'You think he was unhappy?'

'Sometimes. Same as anyone. Christ, Matt, you know what farming's like in winter.'

Lockyer did know. The constant wet, the endless mud and slurry. Cold hands and feet from dawn till dusk. No money – never any money. Every day the same, and a feeling, at times, of being utterly marooned. That feeling was a big part of what had made *him* want to leave.

'Jody says I'm just like Dad,' he said. 'And I shouldn't stress about not being able to cheer them up. I don't *know* how to make things better but I try, all the time, because Chris isn't around to do it.'

'Fuck, mate,' Kevin said. 'She's right. You are *not* cut out for that.'

Lockyer smiled ruefully. 'Thanks.'

'You can't fill his shoes, Matt,' Kevin said. 'And if *you'd* snuffed it, he wouldn't have been able to fill yours, either.' He reached down and fetched another can from a plastic tub of ice beside him. 'You think too much. Always did. Now cheer up, have another beer, and tell me more about this Jody bird. In detail.'

Broad spent Monday morning watching the YouTube footage from the Soul Tree Festival and the Old Hat solstice party. Everything from 2011. She paused it on a shot of the stage at Old Hat Farm, where the group were hailing the eternal spirits, and turned towards Lockyer. 'Cosmic Bauble,' she said, with a grin.

'Pardon?' Lockyer said.

'Look at the banner – the band's called Cosmic Bauble. Bit daft.'

'Right.'

Clearly disappointed by his non-reaction, Broad carried on watching.

Lockyer was trying to think around the roadblocks, looking for another way in. Trying to remember the things he'd seen and heard that had stirred his subconscious. But there was too much noise in his head, and he couldn't make them surface. Still, he refused to accept the possibility that he was going to fail Lee Geary – or Holly Gilbert.

After lunch he made a tenth call to Jason's mother, Chantelle Stevens, and this time she picked up. She sounded furtive, as if she'd taken the call outside and didn't want to be overheard, but she confirmed everything Jason had told them about the funeral.

'My Will's no killer,' she said tersely. 'That's why he got out of here – that's why we got him out, right? He's *special*. He wasn't meant for this world.'

Impossible to say if she meant the world in general, or the specific sphere into which he'd been born.

More importantly, she was able to email them photographs date-stamped 18 November 2011, showing Jason by her side at Benjamin's wake. Chantelle in an immaculate black suit, her face heavy with a lifetime of disappointments.

Another picture was from two days later, taken at a café somewhere, her arm around Jason's shoulders, their heads together; smiling with love.

'That pretty much nails his alibi for Lee Geary,' Broad said.

'*If* Lee died on the eighteenth. But it doesn't rule out Old Hat Farm still being the place where he got that head wound.'

When there was no more video footage to see, Broad closed her notebook with a snap. 'I'm pretty much lost with this one, guv.'

'I know,' he said. 'It either all adds up to a murder – or more than one murder – that we can't prove, or else it adds up to nothing at all.'

'Forensics might still come up trumps,' Broad said.

'They might. But if that blood is Jim Fitzmorris's, we've basically got nothing.'

Broad chewed her lip, staring at her desk. Their big case, the one everyone would hear about. She looked flat, and Lockyer hated to see it.

'Motive,' he muttered. 'Talk to me about Holly Gilbert, Gem. Are the McNeils right to blame Ridgeway and the others?'

'Hell, yes,' she said.

'You're certain?'

'You aren't?'

'One thing bothers me. Why say Holly got out of the Land Rover and went back to the farm? Why tell *that* lie – a lie twenty-five eye-witness statements and a vehicle check could easily disprove?'

'Don't know, guv. But she *must* have been with them. There's no other way she could've got to Amesbury.'

'Isn't there? Let's suppose they were telling the truth. She got out at the end of the track and went back. Perhaps she changed her mind *again*, borrowed a vehicle from Old Hat Farm and set off after them.'

'But no unexplained vehicles drove either route south.'

'No unexplained vehicles drove either of the *direct* routes south,' Lockyer corrected. 'Holly wasn't from around here. She didn't know the roads well, and she was drunk. She could easily have got lost. That would explain the extra time it took her to get down there.'

'And then she just found the footbridge? By fluke?'

'It's possible. She could've hit her head at any point between getting out of the Land Rover and falling onto the lorry. Maybe on her way back up the farm track in the dark. Maybe if she went off hunting for another vehicle.'

'So what happened to that vehicle?' Broad countered.

'No idea. Abandoned somewhere in Amesbury or en route. No connection made to her death. Look, in spite of what we've been told about Holly throwing off the shackles, you don't get over the loss of a parent that easily. Least of all if it'd been just the two of you for a long time. Her sudden change in lifestyle, dropping out of her degree, experimenting with drugs, those are signs of crisis, not liberation.'

'But the McNeils didn't want to believe it?' Broad ventured.

'Right,' Lockyer said. 'They thought their love and acceptance was enough, that Holly was happy. And when a loved one dies, the idea that you're somehow to blame is terrible.

There's nothing worse than feeling like you didn't really know them. Or what was going on inside their head.'

Lockyer realized he was talking about himself. He felt Broad's scrutiny.

'So finding someone else to punish could be a kind of . . . deflection?' she said. 'We're talking about Vince and Jason, though, right? I didn't get the impression Trish felt that strongly about her niece. And she told us outright she agreed with the coroner's verdict of suicide.'

'Perhaps it suits her to believe that. We know she'd do anything to protect Vince and Jason.'

'Yeah. All those lies they tell each other . . .'

'Right.' Lockyer thought back to his conversation with Kevin. 'There's fear there, Gem. Fear that if they're completely open with one another, things will fall apart.'

He reflected on it for a moment. 'Vince started the fire that killed Trish's parents. Most people wouldn't want anything to do with that person ever again.'

'Trish said . . .' Broad flicked back through her notebook. 'Yeah – "We were both in love with him, but I was only fifteen." So she's basically been in love with him her whole life?' She sounded sceptical.

'Right. So maybe what Imogen did, that Trish couldn't forgive, was *have Vince first?*'

Lockyer thought again of Holly's photo of Vince and Trish: Trish looking up at Vince, and reaching for his hand; Vince looking away. The pain in Trish's eyes when they'd spoken about Jason's unrequited love for Holly. *That can be very painful.*

'Have you ever read "The More Loving One"?' Lockyer asked.

'Eh?' Broad said.

'W. H. Auden.'

She raised her eyebrows. 'We're doing poetry, now?'

'Sorry, don't mean to sound like a knob. I did it for A level. Auden says it's better – or easier – to be madly in love with someone, even if they don't love you back, than to be the object of that adoration.'

An unwelcome recollection of his message to Hedy. Of all his unwritten messages to Hedy, when she clearly just wanted to be left alone. Was what *he* felt really the easier half of the deal?

'You think Vince doesn't love Trish?' Broad said.

'I'm sure he does. But perhaps not with the same devotion. Maybe he loved Imogen more, and that's why Trish can hardly stand to hear her name mentioned.'

'Well, nothing says, "I love you," like burning down the family home.'

'But you might just be right there, Gem – an act of desperation like that might seem irresistibly romantic to a mixed-up teenager.'

Broad swivelled her chair back and forth. 'So maybe Jason's love for Holly was causing a bigger problem than he's letting on. Spoiling their friendship. Getting to be a burden on her.'

'Which would add to any sense of guilt Jason had when she killed herself.'

'So where does it all leave us, guv?'

Lockyer looked at his watch. 'Pub?' he said.

Broad looked surprised. 'On a Monday afternoon?'

'Live dangerously.'

They sat at a picnic table in the beer garden at the British Lion, Lockyer's favourite pub. The outside space was tucked behind the buildings, with the air of a secret hideaway.

Lockyer took a gulp of his pint, then felt his stomach rebel. He'd drunk took much, lately.

'Have a proper drink if you want, Gem,' he said. 'I'm stopping after this one; I can drive you back later.'

'Sure?'

'Course.'

She went up to the door, came back with a pint of Black Rat cider and two bags of crisps. They talked through the case again, in case any insight surfaced. None did. The fact remained that if the blood in the workshop wasn't Lee Geary's, they'd have nothing concrete against the McNeils, or anyone else. Considine would almost certainly write it off, and Lockyer would have to admit to Karen Wilkins that all their work had got them precisely nowhere. No justice for Lee Geary. No answers for his sister.

The evening drew on, the sun softened, and the beer garden filled with people still giddy, after lockdown, to be out drinking with friends. Lockyer thought of Róisín Conlan. Someone else he seemed poised to fail.

'Gem, are you still in touch with DC Cookson?'

'Niamh? Yeah. Why?'

Niamh Cookson was an Irish copper. She'd been on the

Wiltshire force until a few years after Brexit, when she'd moved back to Ireland and rejoined the gardaí.

'Is she . . . Do you trust her?' Lockyer asked.

'Trust her to do what?' Broad looked perplexed.

'Would she run a quick inquiry for you, and keep it quiet?'

Broad studied him, then looked away uneasily. 'You can't ask me that, guv.'

Lockyer kicked himself. 'You're right. Forget I said anything.'

'It's not that I don't trust you,' she said. 'You know I do. It's just, after—'

'Honestly, forget it. It's nothing bad. My head's a bit all over the place.'

Broad glanced up. 'Worried about your mum?'

'Yeah. Among other things.'

'Why not just tell me what it's about, this quick inquiry? I might be able to help.'

He wondered where to start. *Whether* to start. 'It might be better if you heard it from the horse's mouth.'

'All right. Who's the horse?'

'My next-door neighbour.'

'The little old lady?'

'Yeah.'

'So you want me to come round to yours?'

'Oh, yeah?' said a voice that made them both jump.

It was Pete, who'd appeared by their table with a mirthless smile pinned to his face.

'Propositioning my other half, DI Lockyer?'

'No, Pete, nothing like that,' Lockyer said evenly.

'What are you doing here?' Broad said, made tactless by two pints of cider.

'I've been trying to ring you,' he said, in a jovial tone that rang completely false. 'Then I got worried, so I came to find you.'

His phone was in his hand. It took Broad a second or two to twig. 'You *tracked* me here?'

'Well, like I said, I was worried. And I was in Devizes anyway.'

Lockyer noticed that Broad didn't ask why he was in Devizes, given that they lived seven miles away in Semington, and he was still working from home. Her cheeks flamed.

'My fault,' Lockyer said. 'I thought a post-work drink might help us sort through this case.'

'And did it?'

'Nope,' Broad said.

'I was going to run Gemma back later on,' Lockyer told him.

'Oh. Well, I'm here now,' Pete said.

'Join us for one,' Lockyer challenged.

'No, thanks, Matt.' That empty smile again. 'Not when I'm driving.'

'A Coke, then.'

Pete ignored him, and without further discussion Broad got to her feet, clumsily picking her way out from behind the bench, getting her bag strap caught between the slats, dropping it twice.

'Whoops,' she said.

'Come on, Gem,' Lockyer teased. 'Don't be a cosmic bauble.'

She burst out laughing, and quickly stifled it.

'Care to share the joke?' Pete said.

'Just something we saw today. A band,' she said.

'You saw a band today?'

'No, it . . . Never mind. Lost in translation.' She shot an apologetic glance at Lockyer. 'Night, guv.'

Lockyer watched them leave. At the gate Pete glanced back, wearing an expression of haughty propriety, and Lockyer had the momentary impulse to punch him. He reminded himself firmly that it was none of his business. It just felt like his business.

Lockyer's phone buzzed with an email from Cellmark, and as he skimmed it, the noisy chatter of the pub garden receded beneath the sudden thumping of blood in his ears. A surge of adrenalin. He rang the scientist back immediately.

'You're absolutely certain?' he said.

'Yes.'

The scientist, who was working very late, sounded weary. 'We double-checked against your suspect. The blood samples taken from the workshop site at Old Hat Farm do not belong to Lee Geary. But the database *has* returned a clear match.'

'No chance of a mix-up?'

'None at all. The samples you sent us belong to Holly Gilbert.'

16

Day 16, Tuesday

The forensic results felt like a thunderclap. As though they ought to change everything. But Lockyer took a sleepless night to think it through, and by morning was chafing with frustration.

When he told Broad, she wanted to go directly to Old Hat Farm and confront them with it. It had been his gut reaction as well, but he'd been back through everything, moving the pieces around in relation to what they now knew and, maddeningly, it still wasn't conclusive of foul play. There was a lot more smoke, but still no gun. And it meant they had no evidence at all of how Lee Geary had died.

'But the McNeils have obviously been lying to us,' Broad protested.

'There were maybe four hundred people at the farm that night, Gem,' he said, watching her deflate. 'No doubt bringing a lot of cars.'

They'd already speculated about the possibility that Holly

had hit her head at the farm and then chased after Ridgeway, getting herself to Amesbury somehow.

'And I guess she can't have got back into the Land Rover *after* hitting her head,' Broad said. 'There'd have been a lot more blood – normal blood, not *lady* blood,' she added awkwardly.

'Exactly.'

'But there's another possibility, isn't there?'

'That someone at Old Hat Farm deliberately attacked Holly?' Lockyer said.

'Right. Shouldn't we go and ask them?'

'*Connections*, Gem. The lies this family tell each other. We need to understand why, first – we need to understand *them*.'

Broad sighed. 'Plus, if she was attacked at the farm, and then deliberately dumped on the A303, how did they get her there?'

Lockyer thought about that. Vehicles borrowed, unregistered, stolen. If there was any possibility that a circuitous route could have got someone from Old Hat Farm to Amesbury without going through any traffic cameras, a defence team would tear the case to shreds. They would have to map every route possible within the two and a quarter hours between Holly being seen alive at the party and being hit by the lorry.

'Connections,' he muttered again. 'And you're right, Gem. I think they have been lying to us. Did you get anywhere with Nina Thorowgood? She of the mysterious Facebook messages?'

'Yes, actually,' Broad said.

'Has she agreed to talk to us?'

'Not exactly.'

Broad had been watching Nina Thorowgood's Facebook page assiduously. Someone had tagged her in a photo, sitting in a tepee at the Stonehenge Action Group camp, which was in woodland just west of Amesbury. Her response to Broad's suggestion that she and Lockyer simply present themselves at the camp to talk to her was *No fucking way*.

After a few more threats to do exactly that, Nina agreed to meet them in a lay-by.

On the drive south, Lockyer said, 'I hope I didn't get you into trouble last night. With Pete.'

'Oh – no.'

Broad kept her eyes straight ahead. The ugly fact of her boyfriend having tracked her to the pub hung between them.

'He's just been a bit ... I dunno ... twitchy, since the whole Covid thing. He's still hardly been out at all. Not even to a shop.'

'He walked right into a busy pub garden to retrieve you.'

She didn't answer.

They parked in the lay-by and waited. Lockyer squinted out at a plastic picnic table, where punnets of strawberries sat sweating in the heat, just like the man who was trying to sell them. Nose-to-tail traffic crawled past – the road shrank to single carriageways just as it passed Stonehenge, which always brought it to a virtual standstill. They were about three miles west of where Holly Gilbert had fallen, and been thrown onto the riverbank to die in the long summer grass.

Broad was getting cross. 'I think she's winding us up, guv.'

'Let's give her five more minutes . . . There.'

Lockyer pointed across the road at a figure striding along the field edge.

Nina ducked nimbly through the barbed-wire fence and marched between the slow lines of traffic. She was tall and long-limbed. She'd shaved off the pink dreadlocks, leaving a soft, honey-blonde crop. Every bit of skin was golden brown, and her eyes were very dark. She strode towards them as they got out of the car, looking so ferocious that Broad recoiled.

'God,' Nina said. 'Could you two look any more like the filth if you tried?' She glanced over her shoulder, then disappeared behind the strawberry-seller's van.

'Nina Thorowgood?' Broad said, as they followed her.

She rolled her eyes. 'No, the Virgin Mary.'

Lockyer and Broad exchanged a look as they showed their ID.

'Thank you for agreeing to speak to us,' Lockyer said.

'You've got five minutes. Then I need to get back. And I need some money.'

'Money?'

'Said I was going to buy strawberries, didn't I?'

'Oh, right.' Lockyer looked at Broad, who fetched her wallet.

'I've only got a twenty-pound—'

'That'll do fine.'

Nina snatched the note from Broad's fingers and tucked it into her bra. She sneered at Broad's shocked expression. 'I'm sure you can afford it.'

Irritated, Lockyer snapped, 'Perhaps you could drop the attitude, just for the next few minutes. It might speed things up.'

Nina glared at him.

'We're investigating the death of a man named Lee Geary. He was questioned in relation to Holly Gilbert's death, but released without charge. Shortly after Holly's death, you posted on her Facebook page that "they" had stolen from Holly and then "stolen her". What do you know about what happened that night?'

Nina folded her arms. 'What's the point? You lot don't *ever* get it right.'

'So help us,' Broad said. 'You were at Old Hat Farm that night – the night of June the twentieth 2011?'

'Yeah. I was there on and off all that year, until Trish kicked me out.'

'And you got to know Holly?'

'Yeah. We bonded.'

'You got close?'

'We just clicked, right? She seemed so bloody bourgeois when she first arrived, but actually her heart was wide open.' Nina glanced from Lockyer to Broad. 'She'd let go of all the bullshit, and wanted to help other people do the same.'

'By smoking *Salvia divinorum*?' Lockyer said.

'No, it wasn't about altered states. And no *way* was she suicidal. No way.'

'Things like that aren't always obvious—' Broad started to say.

'We *bonded* – do you even know what that means? We really *talked*. Lived side by side for months, like sisters.'

'So what did you mean when you said she'd been stolen?' Lockyer said.

'Just . . .' Nina gave a sharp sigh. 'I don't know, exactly. I don't believe she jumped, and I don't believe it was an accident. And when Stef said Holly got out of the car, and didn't go to Amesbury with them, I knew it was true. So somebody was lying. Somebody *is* lying. Holly had all that joy, all that life, and somebody—'

'You believed Stef?' Lockyer interjected.

'I didn't need to *believe* her, I knew she was telling the truth. I saw Holly get into Ridgeway's car, then later on I saw her come back up the track by herself.'

Lockyer and Broad exchanged a look.

'Why didn't you come forwards with this at the time?' he said.

'I *did*,' Nina snapped. 'Fat lot of good it did me. They decided I was off my head. "Had a bit to drink, love? Popped a few pills, have you, love?"' She sneered. 'They just wanted it pinned on Ridgeway and Stef.'

'You definitely told the investigating officers what you'd seen?' Lockyer said.

'Yep. And they wrote it all down. I told the McNeils as well, but they didn't believe me either. Trish said it was too raw, too painful, and I should shut the fuck up, basically. They all thought I'd got it wrong, but I know what I saw.'

'Well, you did the right thing by speaking up,' Broad said.

'Whatever. They were all so ready to believe she'd jumped,' she said angrily. 'It was bullshit. I went back a few times after she died, but it wasn't the same. In the end Trish told me to clear off. Then I got to thinking maybe they were in it together, but ...' she hesitated '... I don't know. I just know it wasn't suicide.'

'How well did you know Ridgeway Kingsley-Jones?' Lockyer asked.

Nina's gaze sharpened again. 'Well enough. He was a privileged alpha twat. If there was something he wanted, he genuinely saw no reason why he shouldn't just take it.'

'Trish McNeil described him as troubled. She said he'd been through a lot.'

'Seriously?' Nina scoffed. 'The only thing Ridgeway had been through was a private education. Worst he'd ever had to deal with was being used as a toast rack by the prefects.'

'Really?' Broad was sceptical.

'What? You think because he was a wannabe gangster, and hung out at Old Hat Farm, he must've been an honest peasant like the rest of us?' She was scathing. 'Born with a silver spoon firmly up his arse, that one. It just amused him to slum it.'

Lockyer remembered Ridgeway's weird accent in his interview. The way it had wavered between Home Counties and West Country yokel. 'Was he selling drugs at Old Hat Farm? At the party?' he asked.

'What do you think?'

'Do you think Ridgeway attacked Holly? Was *she* one of the things he wanted?'

'Wouldn't have been the first time.'

'There's nothing like that in his police record,' Broad said.

'So?' Nina said. 'There was a girl at a festival the year before Holly died. Sixteen years old. Your lot bullied her into dropping the charges because Ridgeway had an alibi.'

'Stef Gould?' Lockyer guessed.

'Bingo.' Nina crossed her arms defensively. 'She followed Ridgeway around like a dog. Said she was with him that whole night, 'cept she wasn't, unless she stood by and watched him rape that poor kid.'

'You think she gave Ridgeway a false alibi?'

'I *know* she did.'

'What makes you so sure?'

'Because I know the girl he raped. And I knew him and Stef.'

'If what you're telling us is true, I'm sorry your friend was persuaded to drop the charges,' Lockyer said. 'Serious sexual assault is very difficult to prosecute successfully.'

'Doesn't mean you shouldn't try, though, does it?'

'No,' Lockyer agreed. 'It doesn't.'

Broad hadn't spoken for a while but she'd been listening closely, jotting a few things in her notebook. She cleared her throat politely. 'Miss Thorowgood, I'd just like to be clear. You obviously have a low opinion of Ridgeway Kingsley-Jones. You've suggested that he might have assaulted Holly, sexually or otherwise. But by stating that you saw Holly come back to the party after he'd left you're essentially giving him an alibi for any involvement in her death.' Broad looked up from her notebook. 'Are you able to clarify that for me?'

'Look, I'm just telling you what I know, all right? I don't have all the answers – that's supposed to be *your* job. Ridgeway was a piece of shit, and a danger to women. Stef would have done *anything* to help him out, stupid cow. But I saw Holly come back to the party that night, and she looked properly raging. So maybe he'd tried something, I don't know.'

Nina sounded exasperated. 'And, yes, I was a bit pissed and, yes, I was a bit stoned and, no, I wasn't wearing a watch. I've no idea what time it actually was, but I remember the sequence of events perfectly well. Holly went off with them. I knew she had the hots for Ridgeway and I tried to talk her out of it, but she wouldn't listen. I was pissed off with her about it. There was a really great band coming on, Cosmic Bauble, and I wanted her to see them. But off she went. And I saw her come back while that band was on. Get it? That made it, like, a quarter of an hour later. Twenty minutes, tops.'

'You're certain?'

'Completely fucking certain.'

'Did you speak to her when she reappeared?' Lockyer asked. 'Were there any signs of an injury – any blood on her face or clothes? Did she seem dazed?'

'I didn't speak to her – I called out, but she didn't hear me over the music. And, I mean, obviously it was dark, but she wasn't dazed, she was storming. Moving with a purpose. There was no sign she'd hurt herself or been hurt – else I'd have gone after her.'

'All right, Nina,' Lockyer said. 'Thank you for talking to

us. If you think of anything else at all, please get in touch. Here's my card, and you know how to reach DC Broad.'

'That's it? Are you going to do something about it?'

'If we can find out what happened with any greater certainty, then we absolutely will. And we'll let you know, if you like. I'd like you to come in and make a statement about what you saw that night. I think your original one must have been misplaced.'

Nina snorted.

'Will you do that?' Lockyer pressed.

'Fat chance. I'm allergic to police stations.'

Lockyer and Broad turned to go, but then Lockyer thought of something. 'One other thing. You said Trish McNeil asked you to leave Old Hat Farm. Was that for good?'

She shrugged. 'I've not been back.'

'Why? What did you fall out about?'

A cynical little smile. 'Seems the whole everyone-is-welcome thing only lasts until she feels threatened.'

'How do you mean?'

'She didn't like the way Vince looked at me.'

'Vince? He was attracted to you?'

'Most men are,' she said, with zero false modesty. 'Nothing happened, or anything, but it didn't matter. Trish McNeil is basically still an insecure school-kid when it comes to her man.'

With that, Nina stalked away – taking Broad's twenty-pound note but no strawberries.

*

Back in the car Broad turned to Lockyer, looking wary.

'So I guess that's why Ridgeway and Stef told such an improbable story,' she said.

'Right. It was the truth.'

'There's no statement from Nina in the original file. Nothing but the twenty-five others that say Holly got into the Land Rover and left, end of.'

'No. Her statement never made it into the file.'

'That's . . . I mean, that's pretty bad police work, isn't it?'

'Yes.' Lockyer wondered whether the omission had been a deliberate shaping of evidence, or merely an oversight. He wondered if it was worth the aggravation of confronting Steve Saunders about it. It was a distraction, and gave Lockyer the familiar feeling that he was overlooking something – had missed something in what Nina had just told them. He knew not to chase it too hard but to wait, and hope, for it to surface.

'In her interview, Stef said that Holly was kicking up a fuss,' he said. 'That she "freaked out". Ridgeway said the same thing – Holly was "dialling up the drama" about something. And Nina just said she was "storming" when she came back to the farm.'

'Does that mean anything much?'

'I don't know. But if she was angry . . . Well, I don't think angry people tend to kill themselves. Anger has a purpose.'

'She got that head injury in the workshop,' Broad said. 'That's where her blood is.'

'Right. So why did she go there? Who was she looking for?'

*

Back at the station, Lockyer watched the taped interviews again, to make sure he'd missed nothing. He watched Jody's YouTube clips from the Old Hat solstice party again, Trish standing to greet the sunrise, apparently blissfully unaware that her niece was dead by then. Where was Vince? And Jason – he claimed to have been away altogether, but he'd yet to prove that. In the six-minute clip he hit pause on a shot of Cosmic Bauble performing. The time stamp was 21.06.11 01:44. About fifteen minutes after twenty-five witnesses had seen Holly get into Ridgeway's Land Rover, just as Nina had said. Time enough for them to have driven to the end of the track, and for Holly to have walked back. *She was moving with a purpose.* Had she been meeting someone in the workshop, not just looking for them?

'Maybe Jason,' Broad said, when Lockyer asked that question. 'Maybe he *was* there. After all, his aversion to crowds didn't stop him following Stef to the Soul Tree Festival.'

'I definitely want some solid corroboration of his alibi for the solstice party,' Lockyer agreed.

'Maybe he thought they were going to hook up, but Holly told him it wasn't going to happen. He couldn't accept it, and hit her with something.'

'Plenty of potential weapons in there.' Lockyer considered it. 'Even if Holly ran off afterwards, and ended up on that bridge somehow, Jason would still be in trouble. Attempted murder, or GBH as a bare minimum.'

'And if her DNA is on the carver's mallet?' Broad said.

'The CPS might think it was enough to charge him. But they both use that mallet – Jason and Vince. Both their DNA will be all over it. And given that nine years have passed, we won't ever be able to say which of them hit her with it.'

'But Vince would hardly have done it,' Broad said incredulously. 'His own *daughter*.'

Lockyer pictured Vince up in Holly's bedroom, watching through the window as the SOCOs searched the workshop. 'Holly's room is sacred to Vince, like a shrine,' he said. 'He goes in there a lot.'

'Lots of parents do that when they lose a kid.'

'Sure. But parents who've only known that child as an adult, and for only six months? That level of devotion . . .'

'You think it was maybe the wrong kind of devotion?'

'It just seems a little off to me. Too intense.'

'But Vince *is* intense,' Broad said. 'You don't mean something sexual?'

'I'm not saying that. But we can't rule it out. And even if it wasn't sexual, it could still have been unhealthy. For both of them.'

Broad looked thoughtful. 'Holly might not have been meeting either of them, of course,' she said. 'It could have been any random person she'd met at the party – or at Old Hat prior to the party. The assignation went wrong, then whoever it was drove her around in a panic, until they thought of that bridge.'

Steve Saunders had said the same thing: *That farm is basically a revolving door for drifters and weirdos.*

'We'll never find them, if that's the case,' Lockyer said.

'Well,' Broad said, 'we'd better hope the mallet has Holly's blood on it. Or Lee Geary's.'

'We need motive as well.' Lockyer paused. 'And that's the other thing, of course.'

'What is?'

'If one of the McNeils attacked Holly, why would Jason go after Ridgeway and the others?'

'Maybe he didn't know,' Broad said. 'Or maybe they'd seen something.'

'But they left the party before Holly got injured.'

'Or knew something, then. Something else that was going on at the farm?'

Lockyer pictured Holly, agitated, kicking up a fuss. Grieving, mixed-up Holly, changing her mind about going to Amesbury, and storming back to the farm instead. Looking for someone. Maybe wanting to talk to someone in particular. And Lee Geary had had something he needed to tell someone. At the thought of it Lockyer got that niggling feeling again. The suspicion of having missed the significance of something Nina Thorowgood had said.

'I want to know what Holly knew,' he said abruptly.

'About what?'

'About her dad and her aunt. All that lying about who Trish and Holly were ... why? What was the point? Holly grew up believing Graham Gilbert was her real father, then her mother died, and she found Vince. How? How *much* did she find out about him – and when?'

'Guv, how are we *ever* going to figure that out?' Broad said.

Lockyer drummed his thumbs on the desk. 'You found Holly and Imogen's old address, right? See if you can find a current phone number. I want to talk to whoever bought the place. And her laptop has got to be *somewhere.*'

Lockyer couldn't put off going to Westdene any longer. He found his father in the big barn, tinkering beneath the bonnet of the Hilux. The smell of the barn was the smell of his childhood: hay dust, dried muck, rusty metal and red diesel.

'Mum doesn't seem . . .' he began, but stalled. 'Have you managed to get anything more from the doctors?'

'Waiting game now,' John said. 'She just wants some time to rest.'

'To rest? Dad, she's practically in a coma.'

'That's enough,' John said firmly.

His fretful expression startled Lockyer.

'I know she's poorly. I can *see* she's poorly. Don't bloody well keep on about it. It doesn't help.'

'I just—' Lockyer cut himself off. 'Sorry.'

'What is it you want me to say, son?' He was almost pleading.

'Nothing, Dad. I guess I just want to hear that she's going to be all right.'

John turned back to the Toyota. 'Well, I've been saying that from the start.'

'Yeah,' Lockyer said softly. 'But I suppose I want it to be true.'

'You and me both, Matt,' John said. 'I'll not manage without her.'

Lockyer doubted that the farm would either, with nobody to run it but an old man and the son who'd chosen to leave. Perhaps the time had come to surrender. He knew then that he'd never say anything to his parents about Chris's pills, or any of it. Kevin was right: they didn't need to know. He felt better for the decision.

'Any idea where I might find Jody?' he asked.

'She went off a while back, riding the fences.'

The quad bike wasn't in the garage, so Lockyer shielded his eyes and stared into the distance. Half hoping not to see her, or to have their first awkward post-coital conversation. Sleeping with her had been a blissful moment out of his own head, but it had left him wondering if he'd made a promise he couldn't keep. He'd never been much good at reading women.

Before long he picked up the sound of an engine in the distance, and saw a plume of pale dust moving along the track back towards the yard. He waited for her to pull up.

Jody eyed Lockyer appraisingly as she climbed off. 'All right?'

'Yes. You?'

'Dandy.' She scuffed the dust from her fringe with one hand. Then simply stood in front of him, waiting.

Lockyer found the scrutiny hard to bear. 'Jody—' he started, but drew a blank.

'Right,' she said.

'What?'

'You're the type of bloke who makes it weird afterwards. Waiting for me to freak out about it – which is simply your way of freaking out about it.'

'I can't imagine you freaking out about much.'

'You got that right,' she said easily. 'Don't sweat it. I'm going in for a shower. And before you ask, that wasn't an invitation.'

'It's just, I'd hate for you to . . . There's someone else. I mean, she's not around, but—'

Jody rounded on him. 'I said, don't sweat it. I'm not looking for a *boyfriend*.' She put a scathing emphasis on the word. 'And if I was, it wouldn't be you.'

'Right. So we're cool?'

'I don't think you've *ever* been cool, Matt.'

'No. You're probably right. I just . . . I wouldn't want you to leave because—'

'Jesus, you really don't know when to shut up, do you?'

She flicked her eyes over him, as though wondering why she'd bothered. 'I'll leave when I'm ready. And it'll have *nothing* to do with you.'

She turned away, leaving him under no illusion of having made the situation any better. If she'd been starting to like him, she'd apparently changed her mind. And he wasn't sure he blamed her.

There was a faint ping, and Jody pulled her phone from her back pocket. She unlocked it, then caught her toe on the doorstep and stumbled. The phone flew out of her hand, and landed by Lockyer's feet. As he reached down for it he saw the email she'd been about to read – just a glimpse of the sender's name. It looked like *Trish*. Jody snatched her phone back without a word, and carried on inside. Lockyer almost went after her, but decided he'd probably imagined it – the name Trish was at the forefront his mind, after all, and Jody had already told him she wasn't in touch with the McNeils any more. So he ignored the unease it had triggered, and walked away.

17

Day 17, Wednesday

The terraced cottage in which Holly and Imogen had lived was on a quiet lane in the heart of Guildford. It was Victorian, small and pretty, the brickwork painted white, the windows and doors a Farrow & Ball sage green. The thirty-something man who opened the door to Lockyer and Broad was in good shape, with smooth skin and very white teeth.

'Mr Drummond?' Lockyer said, as they showed their ID.

The man smiled politely. 'Simon, please. Do come in.' He led them along a hallway to a sleekly modern kitchen at the back. 'I suppose I can't offer you anything to drink, what with the dreaded Covid.'

'No. But thank you.'

Simon indicated four large cardboard boxes on the floor in the corner. 'Well, that's the lot. All a bit dusty – sorry. I hauled them down from the loft, but that was as far as I got.'

'Thank you,' Broad said.

'What made you keep any of it?' Lockyer said.

'I'm not sure, exactly,' Simon said. 'It just seemed wrong to chuck it. Stu, my husband, thinks I'm morbid – peeping at relics of someone else's life. But I couldn't just bin the personal stuff. All the papers and photos.'

'How much do you know about what happened?' Lockyer asked.

'Nothing at all. But it's awful that two people could die like that with nobody to care enough to come and sort out their belongings. I suppose part of me thought that one day someone might come looking for answers.'

'Answers are exactly what we need,' Broad said.

'Did you find a laptop? Or any mobile phones?' Lockyer asked.

'No. The TV was still here, the stereo, and the girl's iPod. But the only computer was absolutely ancient. I'm afraid I took it to the tip with the rest of it, but I made a copy of the hard drive first – it's in one of those boxes. I hope that was okay?'

'Absolutely,' Lockyer said.

Back in the car, as they reached the motorway, Broad shot Lockyer a sideways glance. 'So . . . when would you like me to come round and talk to your neighbour?'

Lockyer hesitated. Her reaction to him asking if Niamh Cookson might run a search on the sly had been an abrupt reminder that she didn't have his equivocal approach to the rules. She did her job carefully and diligently, and she was still on the bottom rung of the ladder. He had no business dragging her into anything problematic. 'Forget about it, Gem,' he said. 'It's not important.'

'Come on, guv, it obviously *is* important.'

'No, really.' He cast about for a way to explain, but there wasn't one. 'Wouldn't want to get you into hot water with Pete,' he tried.

'It's not up to him,' Broad said, with imperfect conviction. 'I'd like to help, if I can.'

Lockyer said nothing. It was so tempting to accept. He desperately needed to break the stalemate he was in, needed something to nudge him one way or the other.

'I could come back with you this evening, if you like,' she pressed.

Lockyer kept his eyes on the road. 'Well. Let's see what time we get finished.'

'Okay.'

He changed the subject. 'So, what the hell happened to Holly's laptop, if it wasn't sent back to her? It's definitely not in our storage somewhere?'

'If it is, I can't find it,' Broad said. 'You don't think they could've sent it back to her university address by mistake?'

'Anything's possible.'

'I'll call them,' Broad said. 'It was Bournemouth, right? And her phone – where's that?'

'Where's Lee Geary's?' Lockyer added. 'But it was nine years ago, and they could both have dropped them en route to where they ended up. We'll never prove they were taken by a third party.'

'Unless we find them,' Broad said.

'Right,' he said, with no hope of doing so.

They were both sweating by the time they'd hauled the boxes up to their office. Broad flopped into her chair and hit the switch on her fan as she looked up the number for the University of Bournemouth. While she was passed around and put on hold, Lockyer heaved one of the boxes onto his desk.

Simon had packed the papers every which way, wasting no space. The first thing Lockyer fetched out was about seventeen years' worth of bank statements. He scanned one, from 2010, seeing nothing out of the ordinary. Then he found a framed photograph of Holly and Imogen, smiling, with their foreheads together.

The family resemblance was obvious. Holly looked about sixteen in the picture, which put Imogen in her mid-thirties. They had the same highlighted hair, the same pointed chin, the same nose and dark eyes. Imogen's genes had stamped out Vince's electric-blue irises, but Holly had his smile. Lockyer wondered if Imogen had been reminded of him, every time she saw it.

'You have?' Broad said loudly. 'Yes, great. I'm going to arrange for someone to come and collect it. Tomorrow. Yes, thank you.'

She hung up. 'They've got her laptop. Must've been sent back there in error after the inquest. The uni staff put it in storage with the stuff they'd cleared out of Holly's room, thinking someone would come and collect it.'

'Good,' Lockyer said. 'Well done.'

He carried on with the box he'd started, and found some childhood artworks, including a portrait of a family of three, done with red tissue paper and glitter. He studied Holly's depiction of Graham Gilbert, and wondered about their decision not to reveal to her that he wasn't her biological father, not even once she'd reached adulthood. Had they hoped she'd never find out? They must have known it would only make the shock more profound when she did. And to leave it until Imogen had died, when there'd be nobody left to answer her questions, could only have made it worse.

But perhaps it was exactly those questions that Imogen had hoped to avoid. Perhaps she hadn't wanted Holly to make contact with Vince, after what he'd done. But could Holly really have reached the age of twenty without ever having to produce her birth certificate for some reason? It was possible, Lockyer supposed; as long as she'd had a passport.

'Guv,' Broad said, waving a slip of paper from a different box as though reading his mind. 'Holly's birth certificate.'

'With Vince's name on it?'

'Nope, that part's blank. He could hardly go and sign the paperwork since he was already in jail.'

'And didn't know Imogen was pregnant,' Lockyer added. 'So, if Holly saw this after Imogen's death, it might be how she found out Graham Gilbert wasn't her real dad.'

Broad held up another paper. 'And this. Graham legally adopted her when she was eighteen months old.'

Lockyer tried to imagine how hard it must have hit Holly to find these documents with no forewarning. To discover that those closest to her had essentially lied to her all her life, however good their intentions. The seismic shock of that.

'Vince said Holly had found letters he'd written to Imogen from prison,' Lockyer said. 'I'm keen to read them. See whether they talked about the fire at all. Keep digging, Gem.'

There was a lot of medical communication dating from Imogen's first tests, then her diagnosis of lung cancer, back in August 2009. By then she'd had a little over a year left to live. Then he came across a large manilla envelope, the paper soft and dog-eared. He tipped the contents onto his desk, and found a very young Vince McNeil staring up at him. He'd posed astride a motorbike, wearing stone-washed jeans and a Guns N' Roses T-shirt, tight across his muscular chest and arms. Black hair curling down around his collar, stubble along his jaw. Blue eyes unmissable in spite of the grainy photo and faded colours. The glare he'd aimed at the camera bordered on belligerent.

Lockyer held up the picture to show Broad, who nodded in appreciation. 'Hot,' she said.

'Yeah?'

'Definitely. And if you were a straight teenage girl? *Unbearably* hot.'

Lockyer turned the picture over. On the back, Imogen – he assumed – had written *V.M. & I.S. FOREVER*, and drawn a heart around their initials.

'This would have given Holly a *big* clue,' he said.

He sifted through the rest of the envelope's contents – more photos of Vince, including a few of him and Imogen together. Then some early newspaper cuttings about the fire:

Police have arrested a local man, 19, known to the Simm family, in connection with the fire. Imogen Simm, 17, remains in hospital where she is being treated for smoke inhalation. The youngest child, Patricia, 15, remains in the care of a friend's family, with whom she was lucky enough to be staying that fateful night. 'Trishie's coping as well as can be expected, given what's happened,' says Yvette Collins, 41. 'Obviously her life won't ever be the same. It's such a terrible tragedy, we're all really struggling to take it in.'

After that Imogen had apparently stopped collecting the cuttings. Or she'd got rid of any others before she died. Perhaps shocked and horrified by what Vince had done. But she hadn't hated him enough to throw out her photographs of him, or the letters he'd written her from prison. Had she still loved him? Then something else struck him. He held up one of the other photos. 'Gem, look at this one.'

Broad squinted from ten feet away. 'Holly?'

'Imogen, aged nineteen, just before she married Graham Gilbert. Spitting image, right?'

'God, yeah. Holly definitely took after her mum.'

'So how the hell did Trish not realize she was Imogen's daughter? When Holly turned up at Old Hat Farm she was almost the same age Imogen had been the last time Trish saw her, before their big split. And I don't care how many years had gone by, she wouldn't have forgotten. If someone walked in now looking that much like my brother, it'd shock the hell out me.'

Broad frowned. 'Trish told us she didn't realize until after Holly's death, when the solicitor got in touch.'

'She's lying. And I want to know why.'

'Shall we go and ask?'

'No. We need *facts* – something they can't just talk their way around. I want to see what's on Holly's laptop and Imogen's hard drive. Hopefully something will fill in the blanks.'

Broad nodded. 'Must have been a shock for Vince too, don't you think? I mean, he loved Imogen enough to lose his head and light that fire. She cuts him off, and then in she walks, twenty years later – Holly, I mean. Looking *exactly* like Imogen did when he last saw her.'

'You're right. It *must* have been a shock, and possibly confusing for him. Emotionally.' Lockyer let that settle for a beat. 'Have you found anything useful?'

'Maybe.' Broad held up a box file. 'Imogen did some CBT in the last six months of her life – cognitive behavioural therapy? To help her cope with her diagnosis, I guess. She started journalling.'

'That's her diary?'

'Not exactly. She's done some exercises, identifying a thought or a feeling, then questioning where it might come from, how true it is, that kind of thing. And there's some more freehand stuff too – like this.' She passed him a sheet of paper.

A list ran down the left-hand side of the page: *I am angry. I am sad. I am to blame. I want this to stop. I want to go on living. I want to stay with Holly. I want to go back in time. I want to know why. I want to be forgiven.* Right down to the bottom of the page, where it ended, *I am so scared.*

'God,' Lockyer muttered.

'Yeah,' Broad said softly.

'I wonder what she wanted to be forgiven for.'

'I guess if you know you're going to die, you might want forgiveness for every crap thing you've ever done,' Broad said. 'Big or small.'

Lockyer lifted an external hard drive out of the box he'd almost emptied. 'I'm going to take this down to Tech.'

On the stairs, he ran into Steve Saunders.

'Farmer Giles,' Saunders said, cheerfully enough. 'I was on my way up to see you. I went back into the Holly Gilbert stuff. Turns out we *did* check up on vehicles at Old Hat Farm, and we searched the place as well.'

'You got a warrant?'

'Didn't need to. They had nothing to hide, and all that.'

'And?'

'And there weren't any vehicles. None on the premises, and none registered with the DVLA, other than a motorbike belonging to Vince McNeil. Doesn't mean they didn't have something parked up with mates elsewhere, or that they couldn't have borrowed one. But there was no evidence of it. Plus we had Ridgeway and the other two in for questioning by then, so we left it at that.'

Lockyer steeled himself. 'What made you check so carefully?'

'Professional curiosity. There was one witness at the party who contradicted all the others – I only thought of her after you asked. She said she saw Holly come *back* again. I thought we'd better check it out in case she was right, and after that Holly maybe tried to catch up with them after all. Hit her head somewhere *en route.*'

The exact same thought he and Broad had had.

'Nina Thorowgood,' Lockyer said.

'What?'

'Nina Thorowgood saw Holly come back to the party. Her statement backed up Ridgeway and Stef's version of events. Want to know how I know?'

'How?'

'We found her. Or, rather, DC Broad did, from social media posts she'd written about Holly. Know how we didn't find her?'

Saunders's face was settling into heavy lines.

'By reading her statement,' Lockyer said. 'Because it's not in the file.'

No reply.

'Why isn't it in the file, Steve?'

'Must've got lost. Things do.'

'That's bullshit, and you know—'

'Look, she was pissed at the time, and probably stoned too. Plenty of people confirmed *that* for us. She got the time wrong, that's all. She saw Holly *before* she went off with Ridgeway, not after.'

'That's not what she says, and she seems to remember the specifics pretty well. And you took it seriously enough to check the farm for vehicles.'

'*I* did, but my DI wasn't interested,' Saunders protested. 'It was twenty-five against one, for God's sake. I was only a DS, and Brent said I was wasting our time. Plus he—' Saunders cut himself off, glowering.

'He didn't want the waters muddied by anything that backed up Ridgeway's story?' Lockyer said.

'Didn't make any difference, anyway. She got it wrong – must've done. Holly went to Amesbury in that Land Rover, then off that bridge. Whether Ridgeway or any of the others helped her off it, we just couldn't prove.'

'We've found Holly's blood in the workshop at Old Hat Farm,' Lockyer said. 'Lots of it.' He watched the significance of that sink in.

'Now, hang on a minute—'

'Holly sustained a life-threatening injury at the farm that night, *after* Ridgeway and the others had left. I don't yet know whether it was an accident or a deliberate attack, but I know what I think. And it's entirely possible that the omission of Nina Thorowgood's evidence has helped a murder go undetected for the past nine years.'

Saunders's shock morphed into sullen anger.

'That statement *should* have been in the file, Steve!' Lockyer was furious. 'Christ! All the *shit* you've given me for the past year, all that holier-than-thou crap about bent officers!'

'This is *not* the same—'

'You concealed evidence.'

'I did as I was told!'

'You could have taken it over Brent's head. Instead you buried it, because you were ambitious and you wanted to get ahead. Because you're a team player, Steve, and you didn't have the guts to stand up to your DI, and make yourself unpopular.'

'Yeah, well, fuck you, Lockyer. It's nothing *like* what you—'

'It was shoddy police work, and you know it.'

They faced one another, unblinking. Saunders's neck had mottled deep red. Lockyer stood his ground, waiting for whatever was coming. A moment later Saunders shoved past him without a word, and thumped back down the stairs.

Broad looked awkward, almost nervous, in Iris Musprat's filthy, cluttered kitchen. Her youth and vitality made the old woman's frailty all the more obvious. Lockyer had strong misgivings about her being there at all, but she'd been determined to come, and obviously curious. So he'd let the temptation to share the problem override the suspicion that he would almost certainly regret it.

'Will you tell Gemma everything you've told me, please, Mrs Musprat?'

'What for?' Iris snapped.

'She's clever. She might come up with a solution.'

'Police, is she? Is this the start of it, then?'

'Yes, she's police, but she's also a friend.' Lockyer glanced across at Broad. 'You can trust her.'

Eventually Iris sat down at the table, and Lockyer gestured for Broad to do the same. There were only two chairs so he leant against the worktop, taking care not to topple a teetering stack of unwashed crockery.

Broad was a good listener. She didn't interrupt as Iris gathered herself, and began to talk about Róisín, the young woman brought over from Dublin to marry Patrick Conlan, an older man and a violent bully. That Róisín and Bill Hickson had fallen in love, in spite of the terrible danger of being found out. That Róisín had broken down one day, and run away. With no relatives in the country and no money for a ticket anywhere, she'd gone straight to Bill – where her husband had soon come looking for her.

'They didn't even have time to bring her round to mine,' Iris said, eyes glassy, staring into the past. 'Might've got away with it if she'd been with me and not him. I heard Paddy shouting and I didn't dare . . . Couldn't call the police – I had no phone back then. And our local plod was a mate of his, anyway; they drank together down the Plume of Feathers.'

She picked at some drips of wax on the table.

'I heard him thumping about next door, smashing things up, threatening to break both their necks. But he didn't find her. He told Bill he'd be watching, and if Rosie came anywhere near him he'd gut them both. It was no empty threat. He put one of his lackeys out on the track to keep watch, sent another to lurk in the woods. Always watching. Weeks, it went on.'

'But where was she?' Broad asked.

'Up in the loft,' Iris said. 'There wasn't a ladder, else Paddy might've checked up there. Bill lifted her up. Only she couldn't come down, see. Not while they were watching the house. So he'd wait until dark and pass food up to her. Cups of tea. A bucket for . . . the necessary.'

Broad was rapt. 'How long was she up there?'

Iris didn't answer. She'd gone very still. 'Quiet as a mouse,' she said eventually. 'Bill and I had to go on as normal, while poor Rosie . . .' She drew a sharp breath. 'I was so scared I could taste it. Paddy was the Devil himself. Some fella from the pub was late paying him back a loan the year before. Just a day late, and he ended up with two broken legs and his house cleaned out.'

'You must've been terrified,' Broad said.

Lockyer sensed that she was preparing to forgive the old woman anything. But she hadn't heard the worst of it yet.

Iris gave her a haunted look before she spoke again. 'Rosie grazed her leg, getting up there that first day. Caught it on an old nail.' She paused. 'I didn't *see* her, you understand? I didn't dare go round there. I could feel their eyes on me, all the time. Watching. It was summer, and warm. I remember fretting about how stuffy it must be, up in that loft.'

Another pause. 'Rosie must have got an infection in her leg. She got sick, but Bill never said. I suppose he wasn't worried, since nobody ever died of a scratch on their leg, did they?'

Broad had gone very still.

'If I'd seen her, it might've been different, but . . . I don't know when she died, exactly. Paddy called off his dogs after three weeks, give or take. I suppose he was convinced by then that Rosie'd got clean away.' Iris sucked her teeth. 'I wish to God she had, but she'd lain up there, all alone, getting sicker and sicker. "You'll have to come and help me," Bill says to me. He was standing on my back doorstep as it got dark, looking like someone had yanked his guts out with a hook. I thought he meant help Rosie down, help her to a bath, that sort of thing. I was glad it was all over. But when I got round to Bill's, the *smell* . . .'

Broad shot an open-mouthed glance at Lockyer.

'I couldn't go up there. I *couldn't*. So Bill went up, with a bedsheet to wind her in. I was supposed to catch her. Make sure she didn't go crashing straight through the floor. But I *couldn't*. She was too heavy.'

Lockyer saw the shame in her eyes.

'Oh, my God,' Broad whispered.

'I never saw her, not once Bill had wrapped her up. Just her hand, which fell out as she came down. Not the colour a hand should be. I remember seeing her wedding ring and thinking, Poor Rosie, she'll never get that off now. Not with her fingers all swollen up like that. She was always taking it off when Paddy wasn't around, wishing she could go back and never marry him, I suppose. *Forever Mine.* That's the inscription he'd put on the inside of it. *Forever Mine*, and the date they wed. Came to seem like a terrible curse, those words did. I think I fainted when I saw the ring, and her hand all . . . Not that fainting did any good.'

A short while later, Lockyer led Broad across the back garden and into the trees. She was frowning, and kept swallowing.

'You all right?'

'Yeah.'

They halted by the old yew tree.

'Here?' Broad said.

He nodded. 'Mrs Musprat told me exactly where to find her.'

'Jesus *Christ*, guv!' Broad swore. 'Sepsis?'

'That'd be my guess.'

'If they'd called a doctor, got her some antibiotics . . .'

'They'd have given the game away to Paddy Conlan. You heard what he was like.'

'So Bill just let her *die*?'

'He wouldn't have known the danger, not back then.'

'And nobody ever came looking for her? What about her family?'

'Nobody came. If Conlan was some kind of big man, he could've made up any story he liked. It was a different era. He probably told Róisín's parents she'd run off with another man. They might have been frightened and ashamed enough not to ask any questions.'

They stood in silence for a while, gnats zigzagging around their heads.

'She had a younger brother and sister,' Lockyer said, at length. 'They'd be in their seventies now. The girl's name was Gráinne Carey, but she might've got married.'

'That's who you wanted me to get Niamh to search for?' Broad said.

He nodded.

'Surely you weren't planning on telling her relatives about any of this, without initiating a proper investigation first.'

'I thought . . . maybe, if there were no relatives left, if nobody was wondering what had happened to Róisín, then I could live with knowing she was buried out here.'

'And do *nothing*?'

'I don't know. Maybe not.'

Broad's eyes were wide with disbelief. 'I don't understand, guv. Where's the dilemma? Why aren't SOCOs here right now, digging her up? I thought you were going to ask me to help find someone for Mrs Musprat – a long-lost relative, or something like that. Not conceal a crime!'

'I *know*. But Iris could be charged with manslaughter or conspiracy to conceal a death, maybe false imprisonment, perverting the course of justice.'

'Yes, she could! Because she did all of those things!'

Lockyer had never seen Broad angry before. She couldn't look him in the eye, and the regret he'd been expecting was coming on thick and fast. He took a breath. 'But did she? Is that fair?'

'Fair?' Broad echoed incredulously. 'What has *that* got to do with it? We *have* to call it in! I could lose my job – you could lose *your* job!'

'I know,' Lockyer said. 'But even if they broke the law, was a *crime* actually committed?'

'That's not up to *us* to decide.' Broad was emphatic. She stared at the roots of the yew tree. 'The body could be gone by now,' she said. 'Animals, decomposition—' She cut herself off, seeing his expression. 'You've already looked.'

'I had to know.'

'So now the SOCOs'll know that the ground has been disturbed. Recently.'

She turned away, and he knew he'd been selfish to involve her. There was no one else he could have shared it with, but that just meant he ought to have kept it to himself. The choice he was giving her was completely unfair.

'You should've called it in straight away, guv,' she said, 'before you started digging, but at least as soon as you found anything.'

'She's terrified, Gem.'

'But that— It doesn't *matter* where your loyalties lie!' She spoke in a hoarse whisper. 'We serve the law, and due process. You know that. We might be able to use discretion for an ounce of cannabis, but not *this*!'

'You're right.'

'So do it now. Call it in.'

'I can't.' As he said it, Lockyer realized it was true. *That* was the decision he'd already made. 'I'm sorry, Gem, but I won't. Not if it means she'll face charges.'

'Come *on*, guv. I doubt the CPS would bother.'

'You're certain of that?'

Broad hesitated. 'It's hardly in the public interest. But it's not up to us! You wouldn't have to say whose body it is,' she said. 'Or that Iris told you where to dig. You could say you were just—'

'Out digging in the woods of an evening? No.'

With a short sigh of exasperation, Broad walked a few paces away, then stood with her hands on her hips, head down. She stayed that way for a long time.

Lockyer waited. He already knew she'd back him up, but was realizing just how wrong it was to abuse her loyalty in that way.

'You must care a lot about her, guv,' she said eventually, turning to face him.

He saw a trace of pity in her eyes, as well as the disquiet. 'I suppose I do,' he said. 'But, look, Gem, if you need to call it in, I won't blame you. Honestly.'

'Like I could do that,' she muttered.

Her cheeks coloured. She still wouldn't look him in the eye.

'She's carried this around for *decades*,' Lockyer said. 'And she was obviously traumatized by what happened. But she never left. All she had was Bill, and this terrible secret they shared. Then Bill died, and I came along, and she finally decided to do right by Róisín and confess. As though she was to blame for any of it.'

'That's if she's telling the truth,' Broad pointed out.

'I believe her. And I want to give her an ending to it all – Róisín's family, too. But I won't see her hauled out of her home and charged. It's not fair.'

Broad took a deep breath, and sighed it out again. 'Why couldn't you just follow the rules, guv? Especially after last year, and that dodgy arson at the pub. If they find out about this . . .'

'I know.'

She stared silently down at the leaf litter for a while longer. Then: 'Have you checked whether or not Patrick Conlan is still alive?'

'No,' Lockyer admitted.

'Would Mrs Musprat lie, if you coached her? Just by omission?'

'She might. As long as it meant Róisín was taken out of here. Home to her people.'

A slow nod, and Broad looked up, her expression deeply troubled.

'Then I think I know what to do.'

18

Day 18, Thursday

There was nothing revelatory on Imogen's old hard drive. Latterly she'd visited a few online forums for people undergoing cancer treatment, but hadn't posted much. *I'm not interested in the Grand Canyon or getting a tattoo*, she'd written in one thread about bucket lists. *All I can think about is everything I should have done differently that I'll never get the chance to fix.*

If she'd been examining her past, she'd found it wanting.

Mid-morning, a courier arrived with Holly's possessions from Bournemouth University. Lockyer took her laptop straight to Tech, to get the battery charged and her password bypassed. Meanwhile, he and Broad went through the rest of her things, finding nothing out of the ordinary with one notable exception: a stack of letters, still in their envelopes, held together by a brittle rubber band. There were around sixty. The postmarks showed a span of 1990 to 1993, and the envelopes were all stamped *HMP Bedford*. Vince's letters to Imogen.

Lockyer split the stack and gave half to Broad, who'd barely spoken to him all morning. He sensed no anger beneath her quietness, which left the unpleasant conclusion that it must be disappointment. In him.

He'd have far preferred her to be angry.

He started on the earliest letters, from when Vince was newly incarcerated. He'd been nineteen years old, soon to turn twenty. An arsonist, an inadvertent double murderer, unknowingly about to become a father. They were written on official prison paper. At the top of each first page were three standardized fields that had been filled in: *When replying to this letter, please write on the envelope:· Number: C5572ATF Wing: F P-22 Name: Vincent McNeil.*

As Vince had said, this was how Holly had found out her father's name.

I love you so so much Imo. Missing you is driving me mad. I don't sleep at night, I just lie there thinking about you and about what could of happened with you there in the house that night. They won't tell me how you are or whats going on and its doing my head in. Please please write and tell me your OK.

The first several letters were like that, begging her to write to him, giving a few details about prison life, but not many. Perhaps it hadn't been so bad compared to his chaotic home life.

Later:

Kelly came in, she told me your living at your nans now so

I'll send this there. I hope they gave you my other letters, your family always hated me and were against me and I won't stand for it no more. Write to me Imo or better still come and see me I'm begging you. I'd do anything for you, you know that. Forgive me forgive me forgive me for what I did. I was out of my head, I must have been. I love you and only you for ever.

Later still:

I've been thinking lots about what happened, and about that night. I just don't know what you must think and I wish you'd write and tell me and stop me wondering because its killing me. Remember I told you about the time I took the car without asking and the old bastard shut me in the garage three days straight, and the rats ran all over me when I fell asleep? Well its like that not knowing what you think about it all and about me. Sitting in the dark with rats running over me. When I think you might not love me any more it makes me want to die. Its all for you. All of it.

Lockyer read them all. Vince got angrier, and more desperate, then more depressed. Gradually, the gaps between his letters got longer. At no other point did he mention the fire, or try to explain why he'd done it. At no point did he apologize to Imogen for killing her parents. He frequently begged for forgiveness, but Lockyer wasn't sure that was the same thing. It began to bother him. *I'm doing this for you, Imo. That's what I tell myself when I'm going mad and it feels like my heads going to explode. I'm doing all this for you, so I can see you again and kiss you and be with you for ever.*

Lockyer frowned at those words. 'Anything?' he asked Broad.

'I don't know,' she said, in a subdued voice. 'He flips between anger and despair, especially when he hears that Imogen's got engaged and is moving away. He keeps asking her if what he did was really so bad – to which I would argue that, *yes*, Vince, it really was. Then he starts doing woodwork and meets that guy he told us about, Mitch Dolton. The letters get a lot more spread out. Then they just stop.'

'Any indication in the final letter that it's going to be his last?'

'Yeah. He says: *I won't write any more Imo, not if you don't want me to. You of all people know what really happened that night, and you know who I really am. You know I'll always love you, no matter what. I only want you to be happy.* That's it,' she said. 'And it was probably for the best. I can't imagine Graham Gilbert was happy about Imogen getting letters from him – maybe that was why they moved again, over to Guildford. That was around the time Graham adopted Holly.'

'So perhaps Imogen drew a line under it at that point,' Lockyer said.

'But *why* did she keep his letters after what had happened?' Broad said. 'She never replied, and she clearly didn't plan to get back together with him when he got out.'

'No idea. Still in love with him, in spite of it all? She was so young. She was grieving, and pregnant, and the father of her baby had done this horrific thing. I expect she was pretty mixed-up about it.'

You of all people know what really happened that night.

Lockyer frowned. 'Unless . . . Does Vince mention the fire, specifically, in those later letters?'

'Not a lot. Just once, I think.' Broad flicked through the stack of pages. 'Here it is: *I can't think how scared you must have been as that fire took hold and you realized you were trapped. I can't stand to think of you being scared like that. I'd kill anyone that hurt you, you know that. But I can't, of course, not this time.*'

Lockyer swung back in his chair, turning to stare out at the ash trees. A seed of suspicion had germinated in his mind.

'What is it, guv?' Broad asked.

'So, after that last letter reaches Imogen, Vince does four more years. Then he's out at the age of twenty-seven, a free man with a much better grip of himself. He's come to terms with a lot of things. He doesn't know where Imogen is or how to find her. He doesn't know he has a daughter. But he finds Trish, or Trish finds *him*. Either way, two years later they get married, and set up at Old Hat Farm, Imogen forgotten.'

Broad looked sceptical. 'It's weird, isn't it, guv?'

'It is,' he said. 'But people *are*. Perhaps marrying Trish when Imogen had abandoned him was the next best thing for Vince. Or maybe it was some kind of penance.'

'That's messed up. Surely Trish would've guessed, if that was the case?'

'Possibly. But if she loved him, perhaps she didn't care about being second best.'

'Do you think Holly took these letters to Old Hat Farm?' Broad said.

'You mean, could Trish have read them? I doubt it. Holly didn't take much with her.'

'I hope you're right, because if you were insecure about your husband's long-lost ex, then these would really hurt.'

'I expect Holly's face hurt just as badly. Looking so much like her mother – the sister Trish hated.'

'I just don't get why she's lying about that?' Broad said. 'Why lie to Vince and Jase? Why lie to us about when she found out? It can't only have been because Vince said so, can it?'

Lockyer shook his head slowly. 'No. It's more than that. It's a total disavowal of her family. She didn't *want* to be Holly's aunt,' he said. 'She didn't *want* to be Imogen's sister. She didn't want them to exist.'

The notes of confusion in Vince's letters. The way he rarely mentioned the fire, and never apologized for it. The regret in Imogen's journalling, her bitter words about betrayal and injustice. About wanting to be forgiven. Lockyer remembered something Vince had said, right back at the beginning of the investigation: the *rookie mistake* of constructing the Molotov cocktail so that the incriminating T-shirt hadn't burnt away completely. *Imogen hated them as much as I did . . .* And then, in his last letter to her: *You of all people know what really happened that night.*

'What if *Imogen* started the fire?' he said. 'What if that's what Trish couldn't forgive her for?'

'What . . . *seriously?*'

'Their parents were determined to separate Imogen from Vince – forcibly, if necessary. Imagine how they'd have reacted to the news that she was pregnant. I doubt very much they'd have allowed her to keep the baby. Think about it, Gem. Think about all the things he says – for one thing, how could Imogen have seen the fire "take hold" if she was asleep upstairs at the time?'

'God . . . *maybe*? Plenty of teenagers hate their parents, but to *kill* them?'

'She may not have intended it to go that far. What was it Vince said?' Lockyer rummaged for his notebook. 'You asked him what he'd hoped to achieve by setting fire to the Simms' house, and he said, "I don't think you can apply that kind of logic to a lovesick teenager, when nothing will ever be as important as getting who they want." We assumed he was talking about himself, but he could easily have been talking about Imogen.'

'But why would Vince not just say it wasn't him, when he was arrested?'

Lockyer smiled sadly. 'Because he loved her, of course.'

'Okay, but the fire was started with one of Vince's T-shirts, and his whiskey bottle,' Broad said. 'Imogen would hardly incriminate him like that, would she?'

'She probably thought they'd burn to nothing.'

Broad considered this. 'Teenagers often *do* have one of their boyfriend's T-shirts kicking about. But what does it *mean*, guv? For Holly, and Lee Geary?'

'I don't know. But if I'm right then Vince's feelings for

Imogen – and perhaps for Holly, by extension – *must* have been complicated. No matter how Zen he'd got in prison.'

'But he was obviously devastated by Holly's death. Still is.'

'Still is,' Lockyer agreed. 'After all this time, when he knew her for just six months.'

You get this hard place inside you that sometimes has a mind of its own.

'What if all that grief – all that devotion . . . what if *guilt* is fuelling it?' he said.

'Because *he* hurt Holly?'

'Self-control doesn't mean the feelings aren't still there. Maybe we've been underestimating just how disruptive Holly turning up at the farm was. And if she was looking for Vince on the night of the party, where's the first place she might try?'

'The workshop,' Broad said quietly.

With a silent nod, Vince agreed to be interviewed under caution in relation to Holly's death. Trish stood in the doorway of the farmhouse as they walked him to the car, her fists clenched, her eyes wide with fright.

In the interview room, Vince gave them the steady stare Lockyer was getting used to – neutral, but not at all friendly.

'Well, say what you've got to say,' Vince rumbled.

Lockyer knew he'd have to rattle him to find a chink in his formidable armour. 'We've found a large quantity of Holly's blood on your workshop floor,' he said. 'A reliable witness saw her return to the solstice party after Ridgeway and the others left. Holly may not have died at Old Hat

Farm, but she received a potentially fatal injury there. We believe that somebody from the farm then took her down to the A303, and dumped her.'

Vince stayed very still but his face changed subtly. His eyes widened and his jaw softened as though, had he been a lesser man, it might have sagged open. 'No.'

'No what, Mr McNeil?' Broad asked.

'You're wrong.'

'What makes you say that?'

'Nobody at the farm would've hurt Holly. No one had any *reason* to hurt Holly.'

'The initial injury could have been accidental,' Lockyer said. 'Perhaps an argument that got out of hand, and ended with Holly either falling or being knocked over. Is that what happened, Vince?'

'What? No – how should I know?'

'The witness saw Holly walking with a purpose. She went to the workshop. We think she was either meeting or looking for someone there. Was it you, Vince?'

'No.'

'Jason, then?'

Finally, Vince moved: he put one hand to his mouth, then rubbed it slowly along his jaw.

'Talk to me, Vince,' Lockyer said tersely. 'What happened?'

'I don't know,' he said. 'Holly . . . She didn't go to Amesbury with Ridgeway?'

'It would appear not. He and the other two had nothing to do with her death. Where was Jason that night, Vince?'

'Away,' Vince said vaguely. 'He doesn't like crowds.'

Lockyer thought fast. Vince was steadily regaining his composure, and he wanted to find out everything he could before that happened. 'When did you last see Holly, that night?'

'I don't know for sure. It was just getting dark. Ten o'clock? Sometime around then. She came to get some food. I'd been doing the barbecue.'

'No later than that? It was another three hours before she got into Ridgeway's Land Rover.'

'She wanted to hang out with people her own age, not with her dad.'

'Did Holly know you'd started the fire that killed her grandparents?'

Calmer now, Vince lowered his hand. 'Imo had never told her anything about the fire, not until she got lung cancer. The smoke inhalation might've been a factor. She told Holly it'd been accidental – faulty wiring or something – but Holly found newspaper cuttings in her mother's things, after she died. And my letters from prison. So, yeah. She knew.'

Lockyer went for broke. 'Did she know it was actually her *mother* who started the fire?'

Vince looked up sharply. 'How did you—? *Nobody* knows that! How the *fuck* do you know about that?'

'It was just a hunch, until about five seconds ago.' Lockyer felt a tingle of excitement. They exchanged a long look.

'How did *you* know it was Imogen?' Lockyer asked.

'Because I knew it wasn't me. And that T-shirt . . . It was mine, but it was Imo's favourite. She wore it in bed after lights out, so her parents wouldn't see.'

The memory caused a pained expression.

'On the night of the fire I was sitting on a park bench the other side of town, working my way through a two-litre bottle of White Lightning. The police arrested me as I staggered home the next morning.'

'And Imogen let you take the blame.'

'She – she hadn't been herself. It was my fault. She was angry with me, and she had every right to be.'

'Oh? Why?'

'None of your fucking business.'

'Did Holly know it was Imogen?'

'Not for definite, but she'd guessed. From my old letters and maybe from things her mum had said. Same way you worked it out, I suppose.'

'Did you talk about it?'

'I told her to leave it. There was nothing to be gained by raking it all up.'

'Did she get upset, Vince? Is that how she ended up getting hurt?'

'No. The past –'

'– stays at the gate. Right. Except it doesn't. How could it, Vince? You did *seven years* for Imogen, and when you came out she'd moved on and started a whole new life without you in it. You must have been angry.'

'I was, for a while. But I learnt to let go of it. Took my share of the blame. Trish found me, and we started a new life, too.'

'But Holly turning up must have stirred up a lot of those negative feelings. You didn't even know you were a father until then.'

'Holly brought me nothing but joy.'

'But you could have been a father to her.'

'I *was* a father to her.'

Broad was keeping very quiet. Lockyer braced himself.

'Holly looked very much like her mother at that age, didn't she?' he said. 'The age Imogen was when you last saw her. That must have been . . . confusing.'

Vince's expression darkened, as though daring Lockyer to carry on down that road.

'I suppose Trish recognized at once who Holly was, given their resemblance,' he went on.

Vince looked troubled, as though this hadn't occurred to him before. 'No . . . I don't think so.'

'Come on, she must've done. Was it like having Imogen back, after all that time? Was some of your instant affection for Holly perhaps unresolved feelings for her mother?'

'What are you saying, you sick bastard?'

'Was it too much for Holly? Too intense? Did you cross a line, Vince?'

Vince shifted forwards, setting his fists on the table. His face didn't move but his eyes blazed. There was still anger in Vince McNeil, straining at the leash. 'No,' he said.

'Somebody at Old Hat Farm knows what happened to Holly that night.'

'You're wrong. Nobody there is capable of violence like that.'

The impenetrable calm was back. Lockyer knew he wasn't going to get anywhere.

'I think *you*'re wrong,' Lockyer said. 'Did it bother you that Jason fell in love with Holly?'

Vince stared at him with the silent implacability of a monolith. Then he stood up. 'That's enough, now.'

'We'll need to speak to Jason again,' Lockyer said. 'Please ask him to get in touch with us. Or we'll keep coming back until we find him.'

'Vince *must* have been hacked off with Imogen, though, right?' Broad said, as they climbed the stairs after the interview. 'He took the rap for her. Did *time* for her. And what does he get in return?'

'Her little sister,' Lockyer murmured.

'And then, twenty years later, a daughter who looks *exactly* like her mum, who Vince adores on sight . . . It *must* have been a shock for Trish.'

'I'm sure it was,' Lockyer said. 'But I'm also sure that Trish wouldn't do *anything* to upset Vince.'

'You think she's frightened of him?'

'Perhaps. Maybe more frightened of losing him. Him and Jason.' Lockyer paused on the top step. 'I think she'd put up with pretty much anything as long as Vince was happy. He clearly needn't have bothered lying to her about who Holly really was.'

Broad looked thoughtful. 'Do you think she'd have helped him if they'd needed to get rid of Holly?' she said.

'I'm certain of it.' He thought back. 'Vince isn't in the dawn footage of the solstice party. Trish is there, greeting the sun or whatever, but not him. Or Jase.'

'But, guv, even if all this adds up to a motive for Vince killing Holly, there's still a big problem.'

'Transport,' Lockyer said. 'How they got her down to the A303. And why.'

'But we've just established why, haven't we?'

Lockyer wanted to be convinced, but he wasn't. Not yet. 'I think we're getting a better idea of what's driving these people, and how a row might have broken out. How Holly might have ended up being knocked over, or even hit. But taking her down to the dual carriageway and chucking her under a lorry, instead of getting her to a hospital? Whoever did that wanted her dead. It was cold-blooded. Calculated.'

'You don't think it could've been panic?' Broad said. 'Perhaps they thought she was already dead.'

'Someone panicking would leave her where she fell. Maybe make an anonymous call to emergency services. But taking her to Amesbury – the last place she was supposed to have gone – and disposing of her in a way that convinces a coroner she killed herself . . . that's not panic.'

'You think all that was planned?'

'I do. Not necessarily in advance, but by someone thinking *very* clearly.'

'Not somebody who'd been drinking or taking drugs, then,' Broad said. 'Someone who couldn't risk their involvement being found out by the others?'

They exchanged a look.

'Someone with a lot to lose. We need to find Jason.'

'And the *how*?' Broad prompted.

'How they got her down there?' Lockyer felt a rising

frustration. 'We need something we can *prove*. Fast. Else the whole thing's going to fall apart.'

Which was basically what DSU Considine said, when she dialled in for an update.

'The forensics don't prove that Holly Gilbert died at the farm,' she said. 'Are you any closer to proving she didn't fall and hit her head, then somehow make her own way to Amesbury?'

'No, ma'am,' Lockyer was forced to admit. 'But the balance of probability—'

'Won't get a conviction,' she interrupted. 'And let's not forget this is supposed to be an investigation into the death of *Lee Geary*. Where are you on that?'

'If we find out what happened to Holly, we'll find out what happened to Lee,' he said. 'There are clear similarities between the two deaths. Two blunt-force head wounds that might not have been instantly fatal, the victims either left for dead or dumped in a way that made sure of it. In neither case can we work out how the victims were moved from Old Hat Farm, the last place anyone saw them alive, to where they were subsequently found.'

'And you're thinking same MO means same perp?'

'Yes. Possibly.'

'Surely the person who killed Holly would have no motive to kill Geary.'

'Unless Lee saw something that night, even if he didn't understand it. The forensics aren't back on the carver's mallet yet, ma'am, and we haven't looked at Holly's laptop – that might tell us something.'

'Didn't the 2011 investigation give it a thorough going-over?'

'They might have missed something. The McNeils *all* had strong feelings about Holly, and they've all been lying to each other about it for years. If I could just see the full picture, I'm certain—'

'But you're *not* certain, are you?' Considine interrupted again. 'I'm not going to let you spend months on this when you haven't proved definitively that a crime was committed, in either case.' She pressed her lips together. 'I'm sorry, Matt, but if the forensics draw a blank, I'm going to have to call time. Even if Holly or Lee's blood is on that mallet, you'd be no closer to proving who wielded the thing.'

Lockyer fought to keep his tone even. 'Give me a week. If we still haven't got enough, we'll have to rethink.'

Considine hesitated. 'All right. Keep me updated.'

Lockyer sat in the empty meeting room long after the call ended, trying to quell the flickers of anger in his gut – his usual reaction to helplessness. His mother's decline; Hedy's desertion; Chris's drug-dealing; Róisín Conlan. A series of painful problems he'd failed to solve, all clamouring for attention. But he'd thought he could close this case, and get justice for Lee Geary. And if he couldn't even do that, then perhaps, as Saunders had said, he shouldn't be in the job at all.

He sat there until the urge to smash something was back under his control.

*

The forensic report on the carver's mallet came in at the end of the day. Tense with anticipation, Lockyer opened the email.

'Well?' Broad said, looking up from a pile of Imogen's paperwork.

'It's clean,' Lockyer said grimly.

Her shoulders sagged. 'Oh.'

'No blood on it at all. No proof it was ever used a weapon.'

19

Day 19, Friday

A colleague from the Tech team returned Holly's laptop to them first thing in the morning.

'Her password is "Golightly",' he said scathingly.

Lockyer opened it up and started to look through. Reams of photos, all from before Imogen's death. A lot of college and university work. Nothing unusual, or relating to suicide, in her internet search history. Nothing to shed any light on her death. Frustration boiled up inside him.

'Any good?' Broad asked tentatively.

'No. And I can't see the video message from her mum.'

She spun her chair towards him. 'Have you looked under imports or downloads? Imogen might have sent it as an email attachment, or on a USB.'

Frowning, Lockyer did as she suggested. And there it was.

'Fuck's sake,' he muttered. 'What would I do without you, Gem?'

'Well.' The word was heavily loaded.

'Come and watch,' he said, and waited until she was beside him before hitting play.

Imogen appeared in full-screen.

For a few seconds she said nothing at all. She was so close to the camera that not much background was visible, but it didn't look as though she was at home. Sitting on a bed with white tubular bars, a glint of metal behind her that might have been the stand for an intravenous drip. Hospital, or perhaps a hospice.

The chemo had caused her to lose her hair. She was wearing a blue silk bandanna, and had pencilled in her eyebrows. Her face was much thinner than in any of the photos they'd seen: cheekbones and eye sockets chiselled out of the flesh, and not enough colour in her lips. She looked straight at the camera, and Lockyer noticed that one pupil was bigger and blacker than the other. The cancer had spread to her brain, he remembered. A good twenty seconds of silence elapsed before she spoke.

'Holly,' she said.

Her laboured breathing made that one word sound strenuous.

'I'm so sorry, sweetheart. I should've . . .' She trailed off. 'The doctor said this cancer might not be because of the fire, but I know it is. I *know*. And I haven't been angry about it, not in the longest time. But, my God, I'm angry now.' Her eyes widened as she said this. She was trembling. 'I kept telling myself this cough was just my normal one. Just the normal wheezes, you know. But if I'd started treatment sooner . . . I'm just so *angry* with myself, Hol. But perhaps I'm finally getting what I deserve.'

She stared down the lens, her mismatched eyes gleaming.

'I wasn't going to do this. Leave a last message telling you to have a brilliant life, and to shine your light and,' she made air-quotation marks, '"Live, Laugh, Love", right? Sorry. I wasn't going to do this. I know you'll have a brilliant life, my *brilliant* girl. I – I don't know what to say. It's difficult to – to say anything. All this therapy I've been having . . . it hasn't helped at all, Hol.'

She gave a little laugh, then coughed. Gasping for air.

'All it's done is remind me *exactly* what I lost. What I did *wrong*. But then I got *you*, Holly. So I won, didn't I? In spite of it all.' She leant even closer to the camera. 'There are things you're going to find out, sweetheart. Things . . . after I'm gone. I'm sorry. I . . . I meant to explain it all, but I never found the right time, or the right . . . way. Then I decided to clear it all out, so you'd never find anything. But I . . . Perhaps I owe him. Perhaps that's it.'

She sat perfectly still but for the quick rise and fall of her ribs.

'Do you remember that time we went to Deal? To the seaside? And there was that man on a motorbike . . . Do you even remember that? You were so little but you gave me the strangest look, and I thought, *She knows*. I nearly swallowed my own heart. I think Graham realized. Oh, poor Graham. But how could *you*? And it wasn't him, in any case. Just a stranger.'

She heaved in a breath. 'You'll find things out, Hol. I

can't . . . It's too late to do anything about it now. But, please, don't go looking for him. Promise me. Don't go looking. It – it could be dangerous. Remember what Dad used to say? What's done is done. Only *now* matters. Lock the past in a box and chuck away the key. Don't mark the spot with an X, because some things are the opposite of treasure . . .'

Tears brimmed in her eyes. 'I can't believe I'm about to lose you for ever. I'm so *angry*. I . . . Oh, God, I think I might've known all along. Right from the start. But it's too late now, and I—'

Another hiatus, during which her chest spasmed and tears slid over her stark cheekbones. She seemed confused, as though her thoughts had scattered and she couldn't quite join the dots. Lockyer wondered how much of that was the emotional strain, and how much was the effect of her illness.

'He must have thought that it . . . that I . . .' she murmured, almost too quietly to hear. 'How could I not see? He did it for me, and I . . . I . . . And afterwards –' she skipped some words, like a scratched record '– I saw Suki Collins at Mum and Dad's funeral. She couldn't look me in the eye. Most people couldn't. People get funny about loss. You'll find that out. But I think I knew *right then*. But I was such a coward. You were there too, Hol. Do you remember? You always loved that song, didn't you? "All Things Bright and Beautiful". Oh, this isn't what I wanted to say!' Imogen moaned. 'None of this is what I wanted to say.'

She found a tissue and wiped her face, then looked right back into the lens. Close enough for them to see the reflection of the camera in the glossy depths of her dilated eye.

'You are the best thing in the whole wide world, Holly Golightly. I know you'll be sad when I'm gone. We've always been a team, you and me. But go forwards, sweetheart. Don't go back.'

The picture became a blur of skin and shadow, as Imogen fumbled to halt the recording.

Lockyer and Broad sat in silence for a moment afterwards. There was something shocking about the footage, even though Imogen was a stranger to them. Seeing someone struggle like that; about to lose the fight.

Broad took a deep breath. 'God. Poor woman. And poor Holly. That won't have been how she wanted to remember her mum.'

And Holly had watched it at least two hundred times.

'No,' Lockyer agreed. 'So, Imogen knows she's left papers behind that are going to tell Holly she wasn't Graham Gilbert's biological daughter. And enough clues for her to identify Vince McNeil as a likely candidate.'

'It doesn't sound like Imogen wanted her to find him, though,' Broad said. 'All that "don't go back" stuff.'

'But she couldn't quite bring herself to get rid of the evidence. It sounds like she wrestled with it, felt she owed him, and ended up doing nothing.'

'Well, she *had* sent him to prison for seven years, and hidden the fact that he had a child,' Broad said. 'Maybe she also thought Holly had a right to know. In case she ever . . . needed a kidney, or something.'

'Maybe.'

Lockyer reflected for a moment, then hit play. Watched it again.

'"Don't go looking,"' he quoted. '"It could be dangerous."'

'But Holly *did* go looking,' Broad said quietly. 'And ended up dead. Perhaps Imogen knew a side to Vince we haven't seen yet, even if he didn't start the fire.'

Lockyer thought about it. 'If Imogen was scared of him, perhaps she used his T-shirt on purpose. Perhaps the arson was about getting rid of Vince, and she didn't mean it to go as far as it did.'

'That makes more sense to me than her deliberately killing her own parents.'

'Is there any mention of Trish in any of the stuff we've read? I don't think she's in any of the pictures, is she?'

'Well . . .' Broad went back to her own desk '. . . she's mentioned in the newspaper article about the fire. And there's this one picture . . .'

She riffled through her pile of potentially useful documents, and pulled out a photo in a blue cardboard frame – the default choice for generations of school photographs. In it Imogen and Trish, aged perhaps eight and six, were grinning with a muddle of infant and adult teeth.

'Would Holly have recognized Trish from this?' Lockyer said.

'Doubt it,' Broad replied. 'You're wondering if she knew who Trish McNeil really was?' She paused. 'I mean, Vince must have told her *something*, right? Some reason why they needed to lie about her mother.'

'Right. So Holly either knew already, or Vince told her, and they agreed to keep her real identity from Trish.'

'And Trish went along with it for Vince, and to keep the past outside the gates,' Broad said.

Lockyer considered that. 'I wonder if Holly went along with it.'

'You mean she and Trish might have had conversations that Vince didn't know about?'

'Maybe.'

Lockyer glanced at the notes he'd made during the video. 'Who's Suki Collins? Imogen says she saw her at her parents' funeral. Why does that name ring a bell?'

He shut his eyes, thinking back, then searched his desk for the newspaper cutting about the fire. Checked it briefly.

'The family Trish slept over with on the night of the fire were called Collins,' he said. 'Could Suki have been the friend? Let's see if we can find her.'

'Okay, guv.' Broad sounded sceptical. 'But do you really think it's worth—'

'Just do as I ask, Gem!'

Broad flinched and turned her attention back to her desk at once, moved some papers around, clicked her computer to life.

Shame flooded Lockyer. She had every right to question him, and he had no right to take his frustration out on her just because she was nearest, and wouldn't push back. He thought of Pete, extracting her from the pub garden. Her anxious anger when she'd realized what had happened to

Róisín Conlan. The way she put up with it from both of them, and would apparently keep on putting up with it.

'I'm sorry, Gem.'

She didn't look up. ''S all right, guv.'

'No, it isn't. It's not your fault. I just ... It's ...' He ran out of words.

Broad glanced across, the tension easing. 'It's all right, guv.'

His desk phone made them both jump.

'DI Lockyer?'

'Got a walk-in for you, Inspector. Down at Enquiries.'

Jason McNeil – or, rather, William Jason Stevens – sat in the interview room, radiating tension. As Lockyer and Broad sat down he raised his hands and performed his short, balletic centring ritual.

'What do you see when you do that?' Broad asked curiously.

Jason gave her a wistful look. 'Lovely as your colours are, Constable Broad, some situations are ... too much. But my own hands, the smell of my own skin? Boringly, reassuringly *brown*.'

Broad smiled, then checked herself.

'Thanks for coming in to talk to us, Jason,' Lockyer said. He started the tape, ran through the formalities. 'We were concerned you might have gone on the run.'

'I'm done running,' Jason said.

'Have you got something to tell us?'

'No. I – I just meant, that's how I got to Old Hat Farm in the first place. Running away.'

'How did you find it?' Broad asked.

'I walked.'

'From Swindon?'

'No, we were in Chippenham the night I decided to go.'

'How did you know the way?'

'I didn't. I just walked.'

'For how long?'

'Not sure. A few days. Then I found the farm, and they fed me. Let me stay, didn't ask me anything. Do you know how *rare* that is? I didn't know places like that existed – or people like that. Old Hat Farm was beautiful.'

'What changed?'

'Holly,' he said simply.

'Holly ruined it?' Broad sounded surprised.

'She made it perfect. And then she died. And what had been enough before she'd ever come just … wasn't any more.'

'I'm not sure what you're trying to tell us, Jason,' Lockyer said.

'Me neither,' he said. 'But you wanted to see me.'

'It's been nine years since Holly died, but her room has been kept just as it was. Does that not seem excessive, to you?'

'Vince doesn't want to let her go,' Jason said simply. 'Neither do I. If I shut my eyes, it's almost like she's still there.'

'Have the McNeils told you we've found Holly's blood in the workshop? And a witness who saw her return to the farm on the night she died, after Ridgeway and the others had left.'

Lockyer watched closely. Jason's face twitched. A hollow, hunted look came into his eyes.

'They told me,' he said.

'Can you explain how her blood came to be there?'

'No.'

'Where were you that night, Jason?'

'I went away.'

'To your mother's house?'

'No. Just to friends.'

'Who?'

'Travellers. A guy called Warwick and his kids. I stayed the night with them on my way to Old Hat that first time. We kept in touch. They were back in the area that summer, near the Avebury stones.'

'And where are they now?'

'I don't know. They're always on the road.'

'Can you get in touch and ask them to speak to us?'

A shake of his head. 'They know where I am, but not the other way around.'

'So what you're saying is that you don't have a verifiable alibi for the night Holly died,' Lockyer said.

'Should I lie? Invent something?'

'We believe Holly was either looking for or meeting someone in the workshop. Was it you, Jason?'

'No. I was sixteen miles away, at Avebury.'

'You took Vince's motorbike?'

'Yes.'

More traffic-camera footage they could have used, by now certainly wiped.

'Did you ever take Holly on the back of the bike?' he asked.

'Once or twice, but it made her nervous. Some kid at her school had been killed in a crash.'

'Did you take her anywhere that night? After she hit her head? Did you take her south, to Amesbury? Perhaps by some roundabout route, avoiding anywhere you might be seen?'

Jason stared at Lockyer for a long time. 'Like I said, I wasn't there. I don't know how she got hurt, and she didn't like the motorbike.' Jason looked down at his hands. 'She quite liked going round the fields on the quad bike, but never on the road. It was against the unwritten rules, wasting fuel like that, but I took her a few times. And it wasn't a waste, to see her so happy. Her face all lit up. Man . . .' He twisted his head, shutting his eyes as though to see her better. 'She was brighter than the sun.'

'Jason—'

'I'm telling you how she made me *feel*, Inspector,' Jason interrupted. 'I'm telling you I *loved* her. And it didn't matter if she loved me back in *that* way. I was still just happy she'd come into my life. And I wanted her to stay.'

'Was she planning to leave? Was that what she told you that night?'

'You're not *listening* to me! I'm saying I'd *never* have hurt her! I went after Ridgeway and the others for answers, because I couldn't get my head around someone doing that to her! Throwing her onto a road . . .' His eyes glittered. 'I can't prove it, but I'm not lying. I wasn't there that night. And maybe if I had been, she'd still be alive. I could've helped her. Instead I've got to live the rest of my life knowing I wasn't there when she needed me.'

That struck a chord. If Jason was telling the truth, Lockyer knew exactly what that felt like.

'Four people connected to Old Hat Farm died that year, Jason,' he said. 'And you had a motive for all of them.'

'I never harmed any of them. Yeah, I wanted answers from Ridgeway; but I never got the chance.'

'What about Vince?'

'What about him?' A flicker. 'You can't think . . . Holly was his *kid*, man. He adored her.'

'We'd gathered that.' Lockyer chose his words carefully. 'He's a passionate man. A man who internalizes his emotions. We think he might also have some issues he's never resolved to do with Holly's mother.'

Jason said nothing. But then, Lockyer hadn't posed a question. He brought out a picture of Vince and Imogen as teenage sweethearts.

Jason looked closely. 'That's Holly's mum?'

'Yes. Imogen Simm. They look very much alike, don't they?'

'Seriously.'

'Few things are as powerful as first love.' Lockyer paused. 'Jason, did you ever see Vince behave in a way you found . . . inappropriate towards Holly?'

The gaze Jason levelled at Lockyer registered first shock,

then disgust. Then he pushed the photo back across the table. 'I'd like to leave now.'

'Are you scared of Vince?'

'I'd like to go.'

They had no choice but to let him, and watched him walk across the car park beneath a sky of glaring white cloud. The day was stifling, inside and out.

They still had nothing definitive, nothing but theories. Nothing they could prove.

Broad switched on her desk fan. 'I'll get on and find Yvette or Suki Collins.'

Lockyer got the feeling she was humouring him. She was loyal, that much he knew, perhaps far too loyal. So he needed to be careful. The case was foundering – *he* was foundering – and Broad had apparently decided to go down with the ship.

Suki Clarke, née Collins, was now forty-five, the same age as Trish McNeil; a quantity surveyor, divorced and living with her children in Edinburgh. When the video call connected they saw a smartly dressed woman with fading auburn hair and startled grey eyes.

'Officers,' she said nervously.

People unused to talking to the police often sounded that way.

'Thank you for talking to us, Ms Clarke,' Lockyer began.

She gave a little shrug. 'I don't know how much help I can be. You said you wanted to talk about Trish Simm, but

I haven't seen her in decades. We didn't stay in touch after school.'

'That's actually the era we're interested in. The time of the fire at the Simms' house.'

Lockyer was sure he saw Suki's face tighten. 'What was Trish like as a teenager?' he asked.

'Well, she was ... I don't know. Not the easiest, but she was my best friend, I suppose. Our houses were only a few streets apart, so we were always at the school bus stop together, went up to big school together.'

'Was she happy at home?'

A pause. 'I think less so the older we got. Her parents were kind of ... relentless. She and Imogen didn't have much freedom. They always had to do their homework or their extracurriculars before anything else, and they were *always* the first to be picked up from a party. Paul – their dad – would just come marching in and get them. No grace period. That kind of thing is mortifying to a teenager.'

'What extracurriculars did Trish do?'

'She had to have extra maths and French tuition. She did tap dancing, and they were making her learn the violin. She hated it. She failed her grade-six exam about five times in a row.'

'What was Imogen like?'

'Nice.' A quick shrug. 'Two years older, so we didn't hang out together, but she was always kind to me. Maybe not as bright as Trish, but sort of gentle and dreamy.'

Selfish and manipulative was how Trish had described her sister.

'Did she and Imogen get along?'

'They did when they were little, but the older they got . . . They were chalk and cheese, really. And you know how oppressed people will often turn on each other, when they daren't turn on their oppressors?' Suki said. 'I read that somewhere. And then there was Vince McNeil.'

'We understand Trish had a crush on him.'

'A crush? Well, you could call it that.'

'What would you call it?'

'She was *obsessed* with him. Said she was in love with him, which I just accepted at the time. Looking back, it just wasn't healthy. She went on about him *all* the time – I got sick to death of it. She used to make me go to places he might be and hang around, in case we saw him. Like a groupie. Went on and on about how he should be with *her*, not Goody Two Shoes Imogen. How he'd see it eventually, and on, and on . . . I mean, we all had crushes. Mine was Keanu Reeves – still is, frankly. But that seemed so innocent, compared to Trish with Vince. Maybe because Vince was *real*, you know? He was right there, in her life – in her home, sometimes, when their parents were out.'

She looked away, thinking back.

'She used to have this box – it was just an old wooden jewellery box, but it had a little lock and key. She'd had it since we were kids, and filled it with things she'd found – her "treasures". Feathers, seashells, lost bits of china and marbles she'd dug up. Nothing valuable, you understand, just pretty things. But once she'd set eyes on Vince, the only things in that box were about him.'

'What kind of things?'

'Oh, God, tragic things. The wrapper from a Mars bar he'd eaten. Seriously. And one of the leather bootlaces he used to tie around his wrists, which snapped off one day. A picture of him she'd taken in secret – she cut him out and glued him onto a photo of herself, so it looked like they were together. Like I said, pretty desperate stuff.'

'How did Imogen and Vince meet?' Broad asked. 'He doesn't sound like the sort of friend their parents would have encouraged.'

'Ha! Ironic, really. The Simms insisted on the girls doing the Duke of Edinburgh's Award. Imogen was volunteering at the tertiary college in town as part of hers – helping adult learners in the literacy class. Vince was there two days a week, as part of some probationary scheme, I think. Doing an NVQ in something or other. Maybe welding. I can't remember.' Her face fell. 'It was bad luck for both girls that they met.'

'You mean the fire?'

'Well, yes, that. But . . . He was just bad news.'

Lockyer went out on a limb. 'Ms Clarke, do you think anything actually *happened* between Trish and Vince?'

Suki gave him a frank look. 'Well. *She* said so. I didn't believe her at first – we kind of fell out over it. She said she'd lost her virginity to him, and I was just shocked. I mean, I suppose I didn't *want* it to be true. We were so young – I was *years* away from wanting to have sex with anyone, in spite of all the crushes and the school-disco snogs. When she told me, it scared me. So I said she was lying, and she flipped.'

'You had a row about it?'

'A big one. Trish didn't talk to me for ages, until I caved in and asked her what it was like. Then she spent a happy *six hours* or so telling me every detail.' Suki pulled a face. 'I still didn't know whether to believe her. I mean, it was rape, wasn't it? If they did have sex?'

'If Trish was fifteen at the time, then yes, it was statutory rape,' Lockyer said.

'Did you meet Vince back then?' Broad asked.

'Not really,' she said. 'I saw him plenty, and he made me nervous. He *was* gorgeous, don't get me wrong, but I just sensed he came from a different place to us. Like there was always something going on underneath.'

'You didn't trust him?'

'No. Not at all.'

Lockyer decided to go for broke. 'Would it surprise you to hear that Vince McNeil *didn't* start the fire at the Simms' house?'

Suki sat in silence for a moment, but Lockyer saw that she wasn't surprised. She just hadn't wanted to be asked about it.

'No,' she said eventually.

'Why is that, Ms Clarke?'

'Because Trish lied about it. She lied about that night.'

Her words landed like a punch. Broad stiffened beside him, and a silence rang in the wake of the words.

'I'm sorry,' Lockyer said. 'She did what?'

'We had a sleepover because Paul and Diane had taken Imogen up to London for her birthday treat. Trish was left behind because she'd been argumentative, or something like that. We camped on the sitting-room floor and watched videos till we fell asleep, same as always. But I woke up in the night because Trish was coming back *in*. She couldn't see what she was doing in the dark, and she sort of stumbled into the side of the sofa and woke me. I thought she must have been along the hall to the loo but she was taking off her shoes and coat. I watched her do it.'

'You said it was dark?'

'It was, but with the door open there was always light from the kitchen window – there was a streetlamp outside. And she brought a cold draught in with her. You know how people do, when they've been outside and come in.'

'So you're saying that Trish went out that night?'

'Yes. But, I mean, she could've been sleepwalking, or staring at the moon. Or anything. The police came round late morning to tell us about the fire, and after that it was chaos. You can imagine the shock of it. It went right out of my head until they came back again – the police – to talk to Trish about Vince. She said he'd never do such a thing, of course, when everyone else thought the opposite. But I heard her say she was at our house all night, asleep, and I knew that wasn't true.'

'How far apart were your houses?'

'About a fifteen-minute walk. I never saw Trish leave that night, so I don't know how long she was gone. And I just put it out of my mind. Until . . .'

'Until what, Ms Clarke?' Broad said.

'Until I saw Imogen at the funeral. How *devastated* she

was. I don't think it'd been real to me until then. I'd been to see the house, of course – we all went to see it. It didn't look that bad, really. It wasn't like the whole place was a smoking shell, or anything like that. Just the ground floor on one side. But then, at the funeral, it hit me. They were *burying* Paul and Diane. Vince was in custody, and Imogen looked as though the world had ended. She and Trish wouldn't even *look* at each other.'

'Really?'

'As far as I know, they were hardly ever in the same room together after that.'

'It must have been a terrible time for them,' Broad said.

'God, yes. Well, I assume so.'

'Then you and Trish drifted apart as well?'

'I didn't know how to talk to her about what had happened. And I just didn't get her any more – she *still* wanted to talk about Vince all day long.'

'What do you think happened that night, Ms Clarke?'

'I think she went out and met up with Vince. I think they started that fire together.'

'Why would they?'

'I have no idea. I've no idea who Vince really was, but Trish would've done *anything* for his approval.' Suki looked down at her desk. She opened her mouth as though to add something, but closed it again.

'Did you tell anyone about that night?' Lockyer asked. 'About Trish leaving the house?'

She sighed. 'No. I just wasn't sure about any of it. And nobody ever asked me. Not until Holly showed up.'

This landed another blow. Lockyer's heart thumped. 'Holly Gilbert?'

'That's right. Imogen's daughter.'

'You spoke to her? When?'

'I met her, gosh – ten years ago now? She just turned up at the office one day. She'd found me on the company web-site, and come all the way up by train. The poor girl was obviously in a state – her mum had just died.'

'What did she want to see you about?'

'We had pretty much the exact same conversation as you and I have just had. She wanted to know about her mum and Trish back then, and about Vince, her dad – I think she'd only just found out about him.'

'And you told her about Trish leaving your house that night?'

'I did.' A shadow passed over Suki's face. 'I wondered afterwards if I shouldn't have. She seemed upset. But we do that, don't we? When someone we love dies, we want to know *everything*. We want all the answers at the exact moment it becomes too late to find out. Holly said she wanted the truth – she was adamant about that. I got the impression she thought *Imogen* had started the fire.'

'But you don't think so?'

'She could have done. Or Trish could have done. Or Vince, or all three, or none of them. Someone else who wanted to set Vince up and get rid of him; maybe even Paul Simm. But I *am* sure Trish knew more about it than she ever said.'

'Ms Clarke, do you know whether Trish was aware that Imogen was pregnant at the time?'

'Oh, yes. She couldn't wait to tell me.'

'How was she about it?'

'Jealous, I suppose. Upset. Said Imo would be in so much trouble when their parents found out, and that there was no way they'd let her keep it – she seemed pretty pleased about that, and I remember thinking it was spiteful of her.'

'When exactly did Holly come and see you, Ms Clarke?' Lockyer asked.

'I don't know, but I could try to find out, if it's important. I never throw away my old desk diaries, and I know I didn't have much time for her that day – I was giving a presentation later in the afternoon.'

'If you could please check, I'd really appreciate it.'

'All right.'

Suki seemed about to leave the call, then said, 'Should I not have told Holly? I mean, it doesn't *prove* anything, does it? But should I not have said anything to her?'

'There was no reason for you to keep anything from her,' Lockyer said carefully.

'Why are you interested in all this now? Has something happened? I never heard from Holly again after that.'

Lockyer was surprised Suki hadn't heard about Holly's death, but she'd been living in Scotland by then. It wouldn't have made half as much noise there as it had locally.

'I'm afraid we can't discuss the investigation,' Broad said evenly. 'But you've been very helpful, Ms Clarke. Thank you.'

'I'll get back to you with the date, if I can find it.'

When the call had ended Lockyer sat back with an explosive exhalation.

'We're on the *exact* same trail Holly was on nine years ago!' he said. 'We're practically in her footsteps, Gem, following all the same clues – the stuff in her mum's journals and papers, the hints in the video message . . . Holly wanted to know what had happened back then as much as we do.'

'Guv, do you really think Trish had something to do with the fire?' Broad said.

The idea made the back of Lockyer's neck prickle. If she had, it was motive for murder. 'I don't know. It's possible.'

'But would she really *do* that?' Broad said. 'I just can't picture it.'

Lockyer was thinking fast. 'No one was meant to be home, remember? She'd been left out of the trip to London. Vince had had sex with her, but was still in love with Imo, who was pregnant. She might have been hurt and confused enough to do something drastic.'

'Vince said Imogen was angry with him.'

Broad turned and searched her desk until she found what she was after. 'Here – this was in one of Imogen's CBT journals.' She held it out to him, marking the place with her finger.

When I think about T she's a stranger. A character from a book, not my own sister. She was still a child, still picking up treasures for her little collection. Such a baby. But I suppose I was, too. You of all people know what really happened that night, he said. But what did I know about anything? What could have been a worse thing to do? How could he? Is that love? So why is this all I can think about when it's too late to change anything? All I want is to stay with Holly a little longer. Lock the past away.

'When I first read it I thought she was talking about the fire,' Broad said. 'Now I think she was talking about Vince having sex with Trish.'

'I think you're right.'

'*That*'s what Vince was begging forgiveness for in his letters to Imogen,' Broad said. '"Forgive me forgive me forgive me for what I did." And it might explain why he was able to let her go when he came out of prison, right? He understood *why*.'

'So you still think Imogen started the fire?'

'I just can't see Trish setting Vince up for it,' Broad said. 'Like, sending him to jail.'

Lockyer wasn't so sure. 'She might not have thought it that far through. I can absolutely believe a traumatized, guilt-ridden fifteen-year-old wouldn't know how to put her hand up for it. Implicating Vince might have been purely accidental.'

'Imogen had Vince's T-shirt, though,' Broad said.

'But Trish could have found it – and the whiskey bottle. She might've taken them for her box of treasures.'

'Vince thinks it was Imogen.'

'He does,' Lockyer conceded. 'But perhaps Imogen suspected otherwise. There's that bit in her video, remember? She says, "He must have thought that I . . ." So, if she's talking about the fire, and we assume that she initially thought Vince was guilty, mightn't his letters have gradually made her realize he'd taken the rap because he thought *she*'d done it?'

Broad reread the passage in the journal. 'The bit that Imogen's underlined – "You of all people know what really happened". That's from one of Vince's letters.'

'Exactly.'

'So, if Vince thought it was Imogen, and Imogen thought it was Vince, maybe Imogen realized it couldn't have been either of them.' Broad paused to think it through. 'I dunno, guv. I still feel like we're just guessing. There's nothing to prove Trish was involved in the arson. Maybe she went out for a walk that night, and didn't go near the house.'

Lockyer pushed his hands through his hair. 'Of course we're guessing! What else can we do when we've got no *facts*? A statement from Suki Collins about something she saw when she was half asleep in the middle of the night thirty years ago is hardly going to stand up to scrutiny.'

'No,' Broad said tentatively. 'But then again, the most important thing is that Suki told Holly about it. Right?'

'Maybe. But there's nothing to prove *any* of this, not now, if there ever was. If we ask Trish she'll deny it, just like Vince and Jason have denied it. We've got no bloody *evidence*! No leverage over *any* of them!'

So . . . we keep looking?'

Lockyer pinched the bridge of his nose hard. 'Proof is what we need,' he said quietly. 'But I don't know how we get it. Or where we go from here.'

20

Lockyer left early. A headache was building behind his eyes, growing with a steady implacability. He knew it was cowardly but he couldn't face the hospital, in case Trudy was no better. He thought about going to see Jody and getting drunk with her again, if she'd have him. But he didn't want company, he wanted answers. He wanted to *get somewhere.*

Mrs Musprat was dragging a bag of rubbish out to her wheelie bin as he pulled up, and after a moment's hesitation, Lockyer went over to help. The bin stank after all the hot weather. He supposed it would be teeming with maggots inside, and couldn't help thinking of Róisín Conlan's body, swollen and discoloured. Far enough gone to have left a stain on his ceiling.

The old lady eyed him expectantly as he slammed the bin shut, but neither of them spoke.

Lockyer went inside, fetched a beer from the fridge and saw Hedy's postcard pinned alongside the photo of Róisín. Hedy, Iris, Jody, his mother. All the women in his life seemed keen to leave it, and all of them confounded him.

He couldn't help them. He couldn't bring them back, or fix things for them. Or for Holly Gilbert, or Lee Geary. He sank the beer quickly but it only made his headache worse.

Was it horses, not zebras, all over again? Was he looking for murders where there were only human tragedies, and a family who might never recover from him raking over their past?

As the sun set, Lockyer went out walking. The evening was as mild as many British summer days. Tiny insects eddied like dandelion seeds on air that smelt of dry grass. He crossed the stream that ran through Orcheston and went north, past the old mill, to the point at which the road ended. That was to say, it continued in its original form: an old chalk track that had never been tarmacked. Lockyer walked a few metres along it, his boots instantly covered with white dust. Then he stopped. Stood stock still.

The answer was staring him in the face.

Jason had given it to him, and he hadn't even noticed.

He turned and hurried back, jumped into the car and swerved out of the driveway with a scatter of gravel and dust.

He couldn't believe he hadn't seen it sooner, that he'd made the same fenced-in assumptions a stranger to Salisbury Plain might make, when *he* knew it was a single, sweeping landscape, in spite of how it appeared on modern maps. He knew it had been crossed every which way by human feet for centuries before tarmac roads were laid. The answer had been right there when he'd walked out to the army's sham village at Copehill Down. All those lost ways.

He parked in the exact spot where they'd begun their investigation, nearly three weeks before. About a mile south of Old Hat Farm, as close to where Lee Geary had been buried as it was possible to take a car. Then started walking.

A bright half-moon lit the track with a ghostly glow. He headed south. The hollowed-out mound where Lee had died rose up on his right, then fell behind him. He checked the OS map on his phone. The track even had a name: Old Marlborough Road. It was a byway now, crossing the MoD danger area, closed during exercises, but otherwise open. The parallel ruts left by modern tyres told Lockyer that plenty of army vehicles, farmers and off-roaders still used it. But because it no longer appeared on any road map, it had been overlooked by both investigations into Holly Gilbert's death.

He passed the shadowy bulk of Sidbury Hill, marched through patches of woodland where the darkness was like a physical thing. His headache eased, then vanished altogether. He knew where the track would take him, but wanted to walk it anyway. It felt like the most purposeful thing he'd done in a long time.

Holly had liked riding pillion on the quad bike, Jason had told them. A serious slip, given that Trish claimed to have bought it with money from the sale of Imogen's house *after* Holly's death. Who had Trish been covering for? Vince or Jason? Lockyer still wasn't sure. All three of the McNeils had motive.

He thought about his brother. About the roles filled by each member of a family, willingly or not. How hard some people fought either to shake off that role or to maintain it. Chris had always been the sunny optimist, with boundless good humour and a knack for connecting with people. Had it been simply too hard for him to step out of that role – to let them down – by telling them how he really felt? That he wanted to go away? Had *that* put him on the path to his early death, and left Lockyer floundering to take his place?

The McNeils all had their roles as well. Trish the loving mother, the generous, forgiving matriarch. Vince the strong but silent type, the good father, protective of women. Jason the phoenix, the *beautiful soul*, someone who touched the lives of others and made them better. But Trish had been a troubled teen who'd coveted – and eventually got – her sister's boyfriend. She'd possibly set fire to her family home, smashing everything apart to get what she wanted. Vince had a dark and abusive past. He'd been betrayed by one of the Simm girls, locked up for a crime he hadn't committed, and must have harboured dark feelings for Imogen. Jason also came from a violent background, and all of his goodness and talent hadn't been enough for Holly. He'd wanted her, and been denied.

And they *all* lied, to each other, to the world and to the police. To hide the darknesses, and to keep each other close; to maintain those invaluable roles. How far would they go to protect themselves? To keep the others from seeing the truth?

Because Lockyer knew how shocking it was to uncover secrets like those. The painful, seismic shift in perception that had caused him to question his every interaction with Chris, and everything about their relationship.

After about eight miles the Old Marlborough Road began to lose its identity. It narrowed, and paths joined and crossed it from either side. Then, finally, he passed alongside a run-down industrial yard of some kind, and came out onto a tarmacked lane. He was on Sheepbridge Road, very close to where Karen Wilkins lived. Lockyer crossed the lane to where the path continued. He checked the map regularly, zigzagging via farm tracks and field margins until he hit tarmac again.

The unmarked lane alongside the A303 that led to Ratfyn.

With a rush of satisfaction, Lockyer walked west along the lane to the point at which the bridleway cut off to the left, rising steadily to the bridge across the dual carriageway. The bridge from which Holly had been pitched.

This could be how he was going to prove what had happened to her, and clear Lee Geary's name. You could get to the bridge from Old Hat Farm by barely touching a road, let alone a road with any kind of surveillance. Perhaps not in a Land Rover, in the latter stages, but certainly on a quad bike. Lockyer walked right up onto the bridge. A car passed beneath him, its headlights cutting a lonely swathe through the darkness. He checked his watch; it was nearly one a.m. The weight of traffic would be much the same now as when Holly was killed. Whoever took her onto the bridge had probably had to wait for a lorry to come along. The deliberate brutality of it was shocking.

Lockyer retraced his steps for about three miles, until he

reached the rundown industrial yard he'd passed on Sheep-bridge Road. A hand-painted, bad-tempered sign attached to its metal gates read: *Private NO Public Access*. He peered past it, mentally crossing his fingers, and on a pole inside saw a CCTV camera, blinking its tiny red eye at five-second inter-vals. It looked as though it was angled to cover the gates, and possibly the approach along the lane. The entrance to the path that ran alongside the premises, back onto the plain.

Lockyer sat down in the poppies and wild barley on the verge, leaning his back against the gatepost. He was calm in a way he hadn't been for weeks. He shut his eyes, and dozed.

A squeal of hinges woke him, and a man was looming over him, features hard to make out against the brilliant sky.

'Hello,' Lockyer mumbled.

'Stag do?' the man said. 'Good night, was it?'

'No. I was just . . .' He wasn't sure what explanation to give.

'Go on,' the man said affably. 'Hop it.' He turned away, coughed messily and spat into the dandelions. Perhaps in his seventies, with a paunch and a slow, arthritic way of moving. He fastened the gates open then limped away across the yard.

Lockyer got to his feet, stiff from the hard ground and damp with dew. He picked a spider out of his hair, and followed.

'Excuse me, sir,' he called. 'Could I have a quick word?'

'Got no work for you 'ere,' the man replied, without

turning. 'Nothing to steal either. Best you head back into town.'

'I'm Detective Inspector Lockyer, Wiltshire Police.'

At this the man shot him a dubious look. 'Got some way of proving that, 'ave you?'

Lockyer reached for his ID, which was in the pocket of a jacket he wasn't wearing. He let his hand fall with a sigh. 'No. But I can come back with it later, if you like.'

The man looked him up and down, then grinned. 'Ha! Really were a rough night, weren't it?' He jerked his chin. 'Come on. Kettle's on.'

Lockyer followed him past the rusting hulks of several HGVs into the corner office of a huge, corrugated-iron barn. A calendar of topless girls hung on the wall, stuck at August 2014. There was a strong smell of grease and WD-40, a clutter of unidentifiable bits of metal, rubber and rags.

The old man made him a mug of instant coffee, which Lockyer would normally have turned down, but it was hot and caffeinated.

'Thank you, Mr . . .?'

'Dimmage. Frank Dimmage. This is my yard, me and my boy. Sit down. 'Ave a biscuit.'

He nudged a packet of economy Malted Milks towards Lockyer, then dropped into an armchair that was worn to the webbing. 'What's the story, then?'

'I'm reviewing an incident that happened several years ago. A girl called Holly Gilbert was killed on the A303 down at Ratfyn. She fell from the bridge.'

Frank raised his wiry eyebrows. 'I remember. Poor lass.'

'The assumption at the time was that she'd found her way onto the bridge from the Amesbury side. But I think they got there from this direction, across the plain.'

'They?' Frank echoed astutely. 'You reckon someone was with 'er?'

Lockyer gave a nod.

'An' you're hoping they're on my camera, whoever it was.'

'Yes. That's exactly what I'm hoping.'

Lockyer's pulse picked up at the possibility. But Frank Dimmage shot him down a moment later.

'Sorry. It keeps what it records for fourteen days then records over itself again. It's all digital these days, see? My boy set it up. All goes into the one box, on a loop.'

'I see,' Lockyer said. It had been too much to hope for, after all this time.

'We used to 'ave one that went onto tapes, but you could only record over 'em a handful of times before the footage was good for nothing.' He paused to think. 'When was it? The girl?'

'Nine years ago. The night of the twentieth of June 2011.'

Frank grunted, then got up and stuck his head out of the office door. 'Dexter!' he shouted. '*Dex!*'

Seconds later a younger man appeared, wearing overalls and a hunted expression. 'What?'

'When did we change the camera over? To the new one?'

Dexter eyed Lockyer. 'Who wants to know?'

'Rozzer.'

He looked shifty. 'Dunno. Seven, eight years back, maybe. Why?'

The old man wagged a finger at Lockyer. 'You might be in luck, PC Worzel,' he said, grinning at his own joke.

He limped over to a metal locker, kicked a pile of newspapers out of the way and heaved at the door. Inside were VHS tapes. A lot of very dirty old VHS tapes, none of which was labelled.

'I kept the ones that caught anything on 'em, see,' Frank said, 'especially when we'd 'ad stuff nicked. Just in case your lot ever wanted to do a damn thing about it, not that you ever did. Can't say whether what you're after's anywhere in this lot, but you're welcome to take 'em.'

'Thank you,' Lockyer said sincerely. 'I'll write you a receipt.'

He packed the heap of tapes into some old carrier bags, then went outside to call Broad to come and collect him. Just in time he remembered that it was Saturday, still very early, and that his clothes looked very much as though he'd slept in them. In a hedge.

He dialled a different number instead.

'Yep?' was Jody's perfunctory answer.

'Jody, it's Matt.'

'Yep?' Same neutral tone.

'I wonder if I could ask a favour.'

'Well, you can ask.'

'I'm standing on Sheepbridge Road down by Bulford, in last night's clothes, with nothing on me but my phone. Could you come and pick me up, please?'

A startled pause, then: 'You could call a taxi, get them to drive you to wherever your wallet is.'

Lockyer said nothing, and she relented.

'Fine. But only because I want to hear how the hell you ended up there.'

'Thanks, Jody. I'm at the breaker's yard. You know where I mean?'

'Yep. See you.'

While he waited Lockyer couldn't resist texting Broad to say he'd had a breakthrough. He thought her phone would be on silent and she could read it when she woke up, but she texted straight back.

What is it??

Got hours more video footage for us to trawl through. You can thank me later.

U going 2 the station guv?

Yes, will crack on. No need to come in, enjoy yr weekend.

No is fine. Give me 1hr.

Twenty minutes later Jody pulled up in the Hilux. She climbed out and rested one arm on the roof, engine running, as Lockyer loaded the three large plastic bags of cassettes into the back. Frank Dimmage came out and eyed Jody's blue hair, her tattoos, her obvious attitude.

'She a copper too, is she?' he asked, then gave a bark of laughter.

Lockyer smiled. 'No. Jody's just . . .' he glanced at her '. . . a friend.'

He climbed into the passenger seat. Jody shot him a quizzical look, then swung the pick-up into a U-turn. 'This I have to hear,' she said.

Lockyer told her about his midnight hike. How it might

finally crack the case open, after they'd found Holly's blood in the Old Hat Farm workshop. Jody absorbed it all quietly.

'You think it was one of them, don't you?' she said.

'I don't know yet.'

'But you *think* it was?' Jody looked troubled. Her hands gripped the wheel with white knuckles.

'What's up?' he asked.

'Nothing.'

Only then did he remember how keen she'd been that nothing she told him would come back to bite the McNeils. Remembered how fond of them she'd seemed. Remembered, with misgiving, seeing an email on her phone from a sender that looked like 'Trish'.

'I guess it's just finding out things aren't what you thought they were,' she said. 'People. Makes you doubt all sorts of stuff.'

'I know exactly what you mean.'

Lockyer sensed something else. Something she wasn't saying. 'Jody—'

'If you apologize for us shagging again, I swear to God I'll break your nose.'

Lockyer smiled ruefully. 'I believe you. And I wasn't going to.'

'Good.' A pause. 'What, then?'

'I was going to say thank you.'

'No probs. It wasn't exactly far to come.'

And because his head was oddly clear from lack of sleep, and the thrill of new evidence, he went on: 'No, I mean thank you for all you've done. You're the best thing that could've happened to the farm. Anytime, but especially now.'

Jody didn't reply for a long time. Then: 'What can I say? I'm fucking amazing.'

'You are.'

'Don't be a kiss-arse. It won't make me stay. I don't stay on anywhere. I move around.'

'I know. But I hope you won't go yet. And I hope you'll come back.'

She glanced at him again, face troubled. Then changed the subject.

He was already in the media room when Broad joined him.

'You should take your weekend off, Gem,' he said. 'We won't get paid for the overtime.'

'Are you kidding me? Do you know how few times I've heard you use the word "breakthrough"? Besides, Pete's washing his car. He won't even notice I've gone.'

She looked down at the bags of videos. 'What's all this, then?'

'It's either proof that Holly Gilbert was murdered, and who by, or it's a lot of wobbly footage of lorry parts being nicked from Sheepbridge Breakers.'

'Sheepbridge? Where's that?'

'Not far from Ratfyn. I went for a walk last night.'

He opened the OS map and showed her. 'I should've clocked it at the start,' he said. 'I walk byways like that all the time. I *live* at the end of one, for God's sake. But I've been distracted.'

'I don't think you should beat yourself up about that too much, guv,' Broad said quietly.

A technician hooked up a second video player so that they could work side by side.

The footage all dated from between 2003 and 2012. Lockyer said silent thanks that there was even a chance of finding something from 2011, but as they made their way through the bulging carrier bags, it seemed less and less likely they'd find what they needed.

When there were only five tapes left at the bottom of the last bag, their eyes met. Broad's still showed dogged optimism. Lockyer's, he was sure, reflected a growing sense of defeat. He chose a tape and rattled it into the slot. Hit play.

'Gem,' he said at once.

In the now-familiar night-vision shot, the lane was pale between thick summer hedges. Moths zipped in front of the lens now and then, and in the bottom right-hand corner, in white digits: 21/06/11 01:48. There were potentially two and a half hours of footage on the cassette. Holly had been hit by the lorry at around three forty-five in the morning. If Lockyer was right about how she'd got onto the bridge, the evidence ought to be on that tape. Broad leant across to stare at the screen alongside him. He wound it forwards to twenty past three, seeing nothing in the intervening time to make him pause. At three twenty-seven two badger cubs crossed the lane, nipping at each other's heels.

Then, at three twenty-eight, something else appeared. Lockyer held his breath.

The quad bike's headlights dazzled the camera as it

turned onto the lane from the footpath, all but obliterating the image. But as it passed the gates the driver's face was captured clearly, for perhaps two seconds. Lockyer knew who he'd been expecting to see. It gave him no pleasure to be right.

'Oh, my *God*,' Broad whispered.

The trailer was hooked to the back of the bike, carrying something under a rumpled tarp. When it came back the other way, at three minutes past four, the tarp was rolled up in one corner. Whatever had been in there was gone. Lockyer wound it back again, to the first sighting. Paused at the point where the image was clearest, as the bike was about to disappear from view.

'There,' he said, pointing to the screen.

Broad leant closer, squinting. 'Is that . . .?'

It wasn't immediately obvious, but the more you looked at it, the more the small object sticking out from under the tarp looked like a foot, wearing a white Converse trainer. Just like Holly's.

Lockyer shut his eyes. Gathered himself.

He ejected the tape and dropped it into an evidence bag Broad had fetched. 'Get Sam to make a copy of that, and get it logged as quickly as you can, Gem. I'll meet you out the front.'

'Hadn't we better update the DSU, guv? She might want us to hand over to the MCIT at this point.'

'No,' he said. 'We're going right now.'

21

Day 20, Saturday

Lockyer drove fast, gripped by a sense of intense urgency. His pulse kept up a rapid tick in his throat. Beside him DC Broad sat in silence, radiating tension. She'd come to like Old Hat Farm, Lockyer could tell. There *was* something seductive about it, and about its residents, but there was also something rotten at its core.

He sped the car eastwards, so focused on their destination that when they reached the track to the farm and a dirty white pick-up came hurtling out of it, he didn't recognize it at once.

It swerved into the road, and he slammed on the brakes so that they didn't collide. The other driver did the same, a slithering shudder of wheels, throwing up a huge cloud of dust.

As it cleared, Lockyer stared.

'What the hell?' he breathed.

'What is it, guv?'

'That's . . . that's my dad's car.'

'You what?'

The last of the dust swept away and Lockyer saw Jody at the wheel. The Hilux had stalled and she was trying desperately to get it started again, thumping the steering wheel in frustration. She didn't notice him until their eyes met. Then she froze. Shock and guilt flooded her face, like nothing he'd seen before. She tried even harder to start the engine, and when she managed it yanked at the wheel to go around him. To flee.

Lockyer rushed out of the car and stood in front of her. Thumped his hands down on the bonnet.

'Stop! *Stop!*' he shouted. 'What the hell are you doing here, Jody?'

'Get out of the way!'

'No. Switch off the engine. Do it!'

Jody didn't do as he said, but she stopped trying to get past him and sat motionless at the wheel, chest heaving. Lockyer heard Broad climb out of the car and come to stand a little way behind him. He went to the driver's side window.

'What's going on?' He was still too shocked to be angry. 'What are you doing here, Jody?'

'Get out of the fucking way.' Her voice was shaking. 'Just let me go.'

'Not until you tell me—'

'For fuck's sake! *Nothing*, okay? I just . . . I wanted to ask . . .'

'Ask what? Ask who?' Now the anger was building. The sensation that he'd been played for a fool. 'What's happened up at the farm?' he demanded.

No answer.

'Who *are* these people to you, Jody?'

'They're nothing! All right? Not any more.'

'Explain.'

Jody gave him a furious look, belligerence finally trumping her distress. 'I don't have to tell you a *single fucking thing*! Now, are you going to arrest me? No? So get the *fuck* out of my way!'

Lockyer glared at her. He knew better, by then, than to expect Jody to follow orders. It would have to wait. 'I'll find out what this is all about, Jody. And if you run, I'll find you, too.'

'Fuck off, Matt.'

He stepped back and she put her foot down, swerving around them and roaring away up the road. Lockyer was suddenly afraid that it would be the last time he – and Westdene – ever saw her.

'What was *that* about?' Broad asked tentatively, as they got back into the car.

'I don't know.'

'That's the Jody who gave us her footage of the Soul Tree Festival?'

'Yes.'

'Did you know that she knew the McNeils?'

'Yes.'

He clenched his teeth. *In a past life*, she'd said, and he'd believed her. But maybe that email *had* been from Trish. She'd insisted the McNeils were good people, but in the car that morning, in the strange numbness of fatigue, he'd told her *way* too much about the case. Told her that they finally had concrete evidence against them.

'Shit,' he muttered.

From the beginning, Jody had made no secret of where her loyalties lay. He'd been stupid to think they might, at some point, have transferred to him. The police.

'*Shit*,' he said again. Lockyer restarted the car and lurched it clumsily onto the farm track, almost clipping the ancient gatepost with its mysterious carving – the *oXo*, with the scalloped line above it. He'd never got around to asking what it meant.

Jason was standing in the middle of the yard, looking lost. His strange, slightly stooped posture radiated a kind of terrible indecision, the need to do something, without knowing what. Lockyer slammed the car to a halt beside him and was quickly out. 'Jason? What's happened?'

At the sight of Broad, Jason relaxed visibly. He raised one hand as if to reach out to her, and instinct made Lockyer step between them.

'Someone came to see Trish, and – and I don't know what happened,' Jason said. 'But when I tried to talk to her afterwards she was different. I've never seen her like that. She filled my mouth with ashes. I can't explain it to you.'

'Where are they now, Jason?' Broad asked.

He swallowed hard, nodded towards the farmhouse. 'In there. She won't let me in.'

'All right,' Lockyer said. 'Stay where you are.'

They hurried over to the farmhouse and, for the first

time, found the front door shut. After a cursory knock, Lockyer shoved it open.

'Mr and Mrs McNeil, this is DI Lockyer and DC Broad. We're coming in.'

There was no reply, but once they were in the hallway Lockyer froze.

Broad barrelled into the back of him. The kitchen door was closed, and the greyhound was standing outside it, tail swinging anxiously. No doubt the smell that had made Lockyer pull up short was even stronger to the dog. The unmistakable reek of petrol. It was everywhere.

'Trish? Vince?'

Lockyer's heart was thudding, his head very clear. He tried the kitchen door. It was locked.

'Just stay away!' came a ragged shout from inside. '*Go away!*'

The voice had a hysterical edge that made the hair stand up on the back of Lockyer's neck. He turned to Broad. 'Gem, go outside. Call for back-up – and the fire brigade. Wait with Jason. And take the dog with you.'

Broad was pale, but calm. She hooked her fingers through the greyhound's collar and it walked obediently beside her, away from danger.

Once they were clear Lockyer spoke, close to the door. 'Trish? Can I come in, please?'

'No! Go *away*! Why did you have to come?' Her voice broke apart, became a sob of anguish.

'I'd just like to talk to you. Please, Trish.'

No reply, just uncontrollable sobbing.

'I can smell petrol, Trish. Have you got petrol in there?'

'*Why* did . . . you have . . . to come here?' The words were a garbled mess.

Lockyer ran his hands over the ancient wood of the door, pushing, trying to work out where it was secured. He put his eye to the keyhole. Vince was sitting on the bench but had slumped forwards over the table. Blood was trickling from his scalp down into his eye, and pooling against the bridge of his nose.

'Trish, what's happened to Vince?' Lockyer tried to keep his voice calm. 'It looks like he's hurt. Should I call for some help for him?'

'*No!* It's *you!* You're the one hurting him! But I won't let you! I *won't!*'

Lockyer saw liquid shining on the table top, and spattered on the floor around Vince. Petrol.

Trish paced into view at the far end of the room, turning sharply to go back the other way, then halting, raising one hand to her mouth. In her other hand was a box of cook's matches.

Without another thought, Lockyer stepped back, as far as he could, and hurled himself at the door. The parched wood around the lock splintered on impact, and he staggered into the room. Trish turned towards him with a gasp, a swirl of hair and skirts, her face streaked with dirty tears as her makeup ran. She immediately scrabbled to open the matches. Her hands were shaking violently, but she got hold of one and held it ready to strike, gaping at him. Terror and defiance and desperation.

'*Stay back!*'

Lockyer held up his hands and went no closer.

'Trish, don't. Don't do it.'

'I – I won't let you tell him.' Voice quavering. 'I won't let you take him away from me!'

'You're frightened, I understand that. But look – look at Vince. He's hurt. We need to get him to a hospital.'

Trish shook her head emphatically. 'No. He – he'll leave me. I won't let you tell him! He'll *hate* me!'

'Don't you think he deserves to know the truth, Trish?'

'No!'

'You'd rather *kill* him? That doesn't sound like love to me, Trish.'

'Not love? What do you know? I've loved him *all my life!* There's never been *anyone* but him.'

'So let me help him,' Lockyer said. 'Let me get him to a doctor—'

'*Stay where you are!*' she screamed, raising the match, poised to strike.

The petrol fumes were overpowering, stinging Lockyer's eyes.

'Okay. All right, Trish. I'm staying here.'

There was a pause. Vince groaned faintly, but he didn't move. Lockyer saw shards on the floor around him. Hitting someone with a bottle wasn't like in the movies, he knew. The glass didn't explode into tiny fragments, and cause the victim a moment of befuddlement in a fight. In fact, it was often fatal.

Trish gazed at Vince, her face a mask of horror, and Lockyer doubted she would ever let him wake up.

'What happened at the solstice party?' he asked, to distract her. 'What happened with Holly?'

Trish's face twisted. '*Holly*,' she spat. 'She had no business coming here! Just turning up like that, expecting – expecting to have *everything*! Just like her mother. She was *just* like Imogen!'

A shudder went through her. Gradually, absently, she lowered the box of matches.

'"We've all got secrets, haven't we, Auntie Trish?" That's what she said to me. And she – she *smirked*. And I *knew* she was going to try and take him from me.'

'She'd been to see Suki,' Lockyer said. 'She knew you'd started the fire at your parents' house, all those years ago. She figured it out from what Suki said, and from her mother's papers.'

'*Imo* told her! She'd have done anything to hurt me – *anything*! Even after all this time!'

'No. Your sister never told anyone. She blamed herself for what had happened as much as she blamed you. Holly worked it out.'

'I don't believe you!'

'I understand how frightened you must be of Vince finding out – of *anyone* finding out. I get it. I do. But Vince *loves* you. And he'll go on loving you, I'm sure.'

After all, Chris could have done far worse than deal drugs, and Lockyer would still have loved him. Some things were immutable.

'No.' Trish sobbed. 'He *won't*.'

'What happened the night of the party? Did she threaten to tell Vince?'

'She – she'd come to find me earlier in the day. *I know what you did*. That's what she said. She – she didn't want Vince to go on thinking it'd been Imogen. Her precious, sainted mother. And she blamed *me* for Imo getting sick! Said the cancer had started in her lungs because of the fire.'

Trish shivered, eyes fixed on Vince. Lockyer clenched his teeth, willing Vince not to move, not to trigger her.

'I *begged* her not to tell him! It was all so long ago. We'd come to terms with it, moved on. And the house was supposed to be *empty*! They weren't supposed to be *in* there! And she . . . Holly *agreed*. She said she wouldn't tell. But I – I couldn't trust her.'

'So when she came back to the party?'

'I saw her. I saw her come marching back. She went straight to the workshop, and I *knew* she was looking for Vince. I knew she was going to tell him!'

'So you followed her?'

'She'd smoked *Salvia*, earlier on. Said she'd seen it all clearly. She said our life here – she said it was all bullshit, and Vince had a right to know who I really was.'

Trish looked at Lockyer with frantic eyes. 'But this *is* me! *This* is who I am!' She gestured around at the farm, and Lockyer wondered at the two versions of herself she must have been wrestling with: the kind, welcoming, loving woman she wanted to be, and the killer, about to commit another murder.

'She – she called me a *murderer*,' Trish breathed. 'Said she was going to find Vince right then, and tell him everything. So I—'

'What did you do?'

'I just wanted to *stop* her. To make her *see*. But she pushed me away. She said I was insane, and I just – I didn't mean to hurt her!'

'What did you hit her with, Trish?'

'Something. A piece of wood. Not hard, but she fell, and there was a lot of blood, and I thought . . . I thought . . .'

'You thought she was dead?

A shaky nod.

'What did you do next?'

'If she'd just gone to Amesbury with Ridgeway, like she was *supposed* to – like she said she was going to! – it would never have happened. She'd *said* that was where she was going, so why did she come back? If she'd stayed away . . .'

'What did you do with her, Trish?'

'The quad bike was right outside. I . . . put her in the trailer. Covered her up.'

'Then later on you drove her across the plain on the Old Marlborough Road. We have you on camera.'

'Jody said you'd figured it out. She told me where you'd been, and I knew . . . I *knew* you must've worked it out. But I won't let you tell Vince. I *won't*!'

'Trish, *please*, don't do this . . .'

Lockyer thought he heard sirens approaching. He cursed inwardly, wanting nothing to force her hand.

'I can't live with him hating me!' she gasped. 'I can't live without him!'

'Vince forgave Imogen for letting him take the blame for the fire, didn't he? He'll forgive you, too.'

'For the fire . . . I don't know. But not for Holly.' Trish's head shook convulsively. 'No. He couldn't. And I – I'll *die* before you tell him!'

'Trish, *no!*'

Lockyer started forwards as she scrabbled with the matches again, and at that moment Vince stirred. He groaned again, rolled his head and tried to sit up.

Trish froze. Setting fire to Vince when he was out cold was one thing, but perhaps this – Vince awake, maybe talking, maybe screaming in agony – was another.

'What . . .?' he mumbled thickly.

'Vince,' Lockyer said. 'It's going to be okay. An ambulance is coming.'

'Oh, no,' Trish moaned. 'No, no, no . . .'

Lockyer heard the rasp of the match.

He threw himself at Trish, grabbing at her hands, sending them both flying.

She screamed as they crashed against the Rayburn and onto the floor. A sharp pain in Lockyer's side told him he'd landed on glass. He screwed his eyes shut and waited for the roar, for the sudden blast of heat. There was a faint smell of sulphur, but that was all. No instant wall of flame. The match hadn't caught. He hurled the box away from Trish as he turned her onto her front, holding her hands tightly behind her back.

'Patricia McNeil, I'm arresting you for the murder of Holly Gilbert on the twenty-first of June 2011, and for the assault and attempted murder of Vincent McNeil. You do not have to say anything, but it may harm your defence if you do not mention when questioned something you later rely on in court. Anything you do say may be given in evidence. Do you understand?'

Trish just sobbed. She sobbed as if her heart was broken. But Lockyer thought of Holly, still alive after the initial assault, tumbling into the path of an oncoming lorry. He felt no pity for Trish.

'Gem!' he shouted. 'Cuffs!'

Vince was wiping the blood from his eye.

'What?' he said groggily. 'The murder of . . . What did you say? What's going on?'

'*No*,' Trish moaned.

Broad rushed in and tossed a set of cuffs to Lockyer. He secured Trish's wrists then got to his feet, pulling her up with him. She moved towards Vince but he stopped her.

'Back-up's coming,' Broad said. 'Ambulance too.'

Behind her, Jason had appeared in the doorway, his face blank with incomprehension. When Trish saw him she twisted away, hiding her face.

'She was going to tell you!' she said.

'What?' Vince said.

'Holly! She was going to tell you about the fire. That it – it was *me*! She wanted to drive us apart! Just like Imogen did!'

Vince's face had gone slack. '*You* killed Holly?'

'It was an *accident*! She was going to take you away from me!'

'I don't . . . How could you do that? *Holly?*'

'She was going to tell you!' Trish wept.

'But I *know* you started the fire!' Vince cried. 'I've known for *years* it was you!'

Trish was aghast. 'Wh-what?'

'I knew it was you, Trish!' Vince grimaced in pain. 'But you killed Holly to *hide* it?'

There was a silence. The stark horror of the truth rang around the room.

As Lockyer walked Trish out, she locked eyes with Jason. He looked at her as though she were a stranger, and she sagged against Lockyer, grey-faced with shock. Watching everything she'd built collapsing around her.

Vince's head wound wasn't serious. It needed stitches, and he was concussed, so the hospital kept him in for observation.

At the station, Trish gave a full statement. She sat hunched at the table in an interview room, still smelling faintly of petrol even though she'd been allowed to shower, and had changed into a grey custody suite tracksuit. With her damp hair combed back and no makeup, she looked older. Vulnerable. In a flat voice, she talked them through it again for the video cameras. A strange new emptiness in her eyes.

'I thought she was dead,' she said again. 'I had to leave her for quite a long time, until I could get away and . . . take her off the farm. She hadn't moved at all. She was still just lying there, where I'd left her. In the trailer.'

'If you'd taken her to a hospital, she might have lived,' Broad told her.

Trish turned that empty look on her.

'But you couldn't let that happen, could you?' Lockyer said. 'You had to make sure she was gone. It must have been difficult to lift her over the railings of the bridge.'

A nod.

'How did you manage it?'

'I stood on the saddle of the bike. Hard to balance, but she was small. Like Imo.'

It hadn't been Lee Geary. He *hadn't* been a liar. The first he'd heard about Holly's death had been during his own interview, when Saunders and Brent had told him.

With an effort, Lockyer kept an even tone.

'You knew a lot of people had seen Holly get into Ridgeway's Land Rover. Was that why you went south? To try to pin it on them?'

'Ridgeway was a dangerous man.'

'Lee Geary wasn't.'

Silence.

'I think you're a dangerous woman, Trish,' Lockyer said. 'Imogen tried to warn Holly about you. She told her not to go looking for her father, told her it could be dangerous. But I don't think it was Vince she was warning her about. I think you'd had your eye on Holly from the moment she arrived. You hid it from Vince, but not from Jason. He told us the colour of your voice changed.'

'It was an *accident*.'

'Driving her down to that bridge? Throwing her under that truck?'

After a loaded pause, Trish said, 'She was going to take Vince away from me.'

'Is that why you never told Vince he was a father? You knew, and you never told him.'

Trish blinked. 'He'd have gone looking for her.'

'Of course he would. And then perhaps he and Imogen would have got talking again. And you couldn't have that.'

'Please . . . please don't tell Vince I knew about the baby.'

'I think that's the least of your worries, Trish.'

When the interview wrapped up Lockyer came out to talk to DSU Considine, who'd been observing. She eyed him severely from behind her PPE visor. 'This should have been handed over as soon as you had firm evidence, Matt.'

'She and Vince would probably be dead right now if we hadn't gone straight there.'

Considine acknowledged that with a grunt. 'What on earth set her off?' she asked. 'How did she know you were on to her?'

For a split second, Lockyer thought about lying. Keeping Jody out of it. But it was only for an instant.

'It was my fault, ma'am,' he said. 'It was a stupid mistake. I disclosed to a witness that I'd worked out the murderer's route to the bridge. I should have been more careful. I guess she tipped Trish off.'

Considine raised her eyebrows. 'Well, that could have been a costly mistake, couldn't it?'

'Yes, ma'am.'

'Be a *lot* more careful next time, Matt.'

'Ma'am.'

'I take it you'll be inviting this witness to come in and make a full statement?'

'In the strongest possible terms, yes.'

'Then we'll say no more about it.'

Lockyer still had no idea how much Jody knew, or what exactly she'd meant to achieve by going to the farm. But he intended to find out.

'There *is* the other matter, of course,' Considine went on. 'You assured me that finding Holly's killer would give us Lee Geary's as well.'

'It's linked. I know it is. We just . . . still haven't got the evidence we need to progress it.'

'Well, you'd better get on with it, hadn't you?'

In the afternoon Broad took a call from Suki Clarke, which she put on speaker phone for Lockyer to hear.

'I just wanted to tell you when it was Holly came up to see me. I've managed to find the diary. It was the seventeenth of June that year, 2011.'

'That's very helpful. Thank you, Ms Clarke,' Broad said.

Where Suki might have said *You're welcome*, and rung off, she left a gap instead. Lockyer had sensed before that she was holding back.

'Is there something else you want to tell us, Ms Clarke?'

'I Googled Holly after we last spoke. So I know she's dead. She died just a few days after coming to see me.'

Lockyer heard the tremor in her voice. 'It wasn't your fault, Ms Clarke.'

'Oh, I don't know about that. The thing is . . . it was a really long time ago, I can't be sure – but, no, I *am* sure, that's the thing. But I've never said, because, well . . . how could I?'

'What is it?'

'All that stuff about how the family weren't supposed to have been home on the night of the fire. That they were still up in London as far as anyone knew – and maybe Vince *did* think that. Paul always closed the gates and put the car away in the garage, you see. If it'd been dark and all the lights were out, he'd have been none the wiser.' She took a breath. 'But *Trish* knew.'

For a second time, her words left a ringing silence in their small office.

Lockyer and Broad's eyes met.

'I'm sorry,' Lockyer said. 'Could you please repeat that?'

'She knew they were at home. My mum drove us to the garage to rent a video, and we came back past their house. It was on the left. Trish was sitting on that side, and she suddenly craned her head as we went past. Turned right around to look. I only caught a glimpse but the gates were open. And I – I saw Paul, shutting the garage doors. Mum didn't, she was watching the road, but I *know* Trish saw him, too.'

'So Trish may have deliberately started the fire *knowing* they were inside?'

'Maybe. Yes. I think so.' It was almost a whisper. 'But I never said anything.'

Lockyer heard the weight of self-recrimination in those words. 'You were just a kid, Ms Clarke,' he said. 'Did you tell Holly this?'

'No. I've never told anyone.'

Once they'd cut the call, Broad said, 'But *why*? Why attack her family? Or do you still think it was an impulsive gesture that escalated badly?'

Lockyer pictured the emptiness in Trish's gaze during her interview. He shook his head.

'I think she meant to kill them – all three of them. She didn't know how much Suki had told Holly, and she *couldn't* have Vince finding out. That was why she was ready to kill him first – to keep him from finding out who she *really* is.'

'Jesus. But *why* try to kill them?'

'Her parents were getting in her way. And her sister was about to have a permanent hold over Vince – their baby. Imogen had Vince for life, unless Trish did something about it. She needed them all out of the way before she could reinvent herself for him.'

Only with her family gone could Trish step into her sister's role – kind, generous, beloved of Vince. A desperate move, extreme, compared to Lockyer's feeble attempts to take over from Chris.

'Is she . . . I mean, she's *nuts*, right?' Broad said.

'Definitely unbalanced in some way, I'd say.'

'Do you think she killed Lee Geary, too?'

'It's possible. He might have known something about the night Holly died.' Lockyer tried to pick through it. 'But by November Trish would have known the police had nothing,' he said. 'The coroner had ruled suicide. So why kill him? Why take the risk?'

'I don't know, guv. But we've got her for Holly.'

'It's not enough.' Lockyer was emphatic. 'I want to know what happened to Lee. So does his sister. He was a victim in all this – he was *innocent*. We can't just drop it.'

Vince was on a busy ward in Salisbury District Hospital, one for people whose lives weren't in danger. He lay propped up on pillows with his head wound dressed, and didn't blink as Lockyer pulled the curtain around them for the illusion of privacy.

'How's the head?' he said.

Vince regarded him steadily, as inscrutable as ever. 'Kicking like a mule,' he rumbled.

'I need to ask you a few questions, if you're up to it?'

'The damage is done. Ask what you want.'

'How long have you known that Trish was responsible for the fire at her family home?'

'Since Holly came. She told me what she'd read in Imogen's journals, about her doubts. And saying she owed me something . . . And that line from one of my letters she'd picked up on – "You of all people". I figured it out. But I think I've suspected it for a lot longer. Should've known right from the start – Imo would never have done a thing like that, and she'd never have let me take the blame if she had. That sweet girl *loved* me.'

'You never said anything to Trish about it?'

'No point.' He turned his head away. 'Besides, I *owed*

Trish. I wasn't right back then. I was a mess. I had this *rage* at the heart of me . . . Later on she helped me get rid of it, but . . .'

Vince shut his eyes for a second. 'I had sex with her, not long before the fire. She was just a kid . . . God help me. I loved Imogen like – like I hardly knew what to do with all that feeling, you know? And I knew Trish was pie-eyed over me – and jealous. I thought it was funny, I guess. Made me feel like Billy Big Bollocks. Then one night I found her hanging around outside the pub when I came out. I was pissed. She grabbed my arse with both hands, and I . . .'

'Couldn't resist?' Lockyer said coldly.

'I *chose* not to resist. Smash it all to pieces – back then, that was all I knew how to do.'

Slowly, wincing, he turned his vivid gaze back towards Lockyer. 'I was rough with her. Up against the wall behind the pub. A fifteen-year-old virgin.' His voice was heavy with self-loathing. 'I got her pregnant. Did she tell you that?'

'No, she didn't.'

'Didn't tell me either. Not till I came out of jail. She lost it sometime after the fire, and there were complications. Ones that meant she couldn't have another baby.' His brows knotted. 'She didn't tell me straight away. She knew I wanted a kid more than anything. But we lost one after another in the first few years. After the fifth time, she told me why. What I'd done.'

'I see.'

'Do you?' Vince challenged. 'Do you see that if Trish is broken, it's because *I* broke her? I did *so much* damage.'

'The violence of her obsession with you would indicate that she was unstable to begin with.'

'I made it much worse. The fire was a cry for help. I understood that, as soon as I figured it out. I'm not saying she was right to do it, but I understood. And I *forgave* her.'

'What if it wasn't simply a cry for help?'

'What do you mean?'

'There's evidence to suggest that Trish knew her family were at home that night.'

Vince paled. 'What? No, she didn't—'

'I'm afraid she did. She'd seen her father earlier in the evening, when Mrs Collins drove her past the house.'

'No . . .' Vince breathed.

Lockyer gave him a moment to absorb it. 'I believe she started that fire with the intention of killing her family,' he went on. 'Particularly Imogen and her unborn child. Perhaps she knew she'd never get to have you while her sister was still around.'

'Wait, she . . . Trish knew Imo was pregnant? She *knew* about Holly, all along?'

'Yes. I'm sorry, Vince.'

Vince shuddered under the weight of it. Decades of lies. A daughter he might otherwise have seen grow up.

Something else occurred to Lockyer then. 'If Trish was also pregnant at the time she started the fire, she had even more reason to want her parents out of the picture. They'd have gone after you for sex with a minor, as soon as they found out about it. And Trish would do *anything* to protect you, Vince.'

After a second, Vince's face crumpled in anguish. 'My Imo, and *Holly* . . .' he whispered.

'I'm truly sorry.'

'But I don't *understand*! We've built a whole life . . . And Jase! How could she . . .?'

'The thought of losing you *terrifies* Trish. She was willing to kill Holly *and* you rather than risk that.'

'She wouldn't have struck that match,' Vince said, though his eyes lacked conviction.

'I think she would.'

'Oh, God . . . *Holly*. She was the best thing. She made everything *perfect*!'

'Not for Trish,' Lockyer murmured. He thought back to something Trish had said, the day she'd come to the police station: *What matters is who we are now . . . a mistake made once, in the chaos of childhood.* Ostensibly, she'd been talking about Jason, but quite definitely about herself as well.

But that defence fell to pieces when it came to Holly. Trish couldn't blame immaturity, or impulse, for what she'd done to Vince's daughter.

'What about Lee Geary?' Lockyer asked.

'What about him?' Vince said dully.

'Have you told us the truth about that day? That Lee left the farm alive and well, having spoken to you and bought some SD?'

'Yes. That's what happened.'

'Trish didn't talk to him? Or overhear anything he said to you?'

'No, she was nowhere around. None of the others were.'

Lockyer got up and pushed the curtain back. 'You know where I am if you want to talk to me about anything, Vince. I'll keep you informed about where Trish is being held, and what's happening. You still have your son,' he said.

'Yeah. Me and Jase . . . I guess we're in this mess together.'

As he walked away, Lockyer realized that Old Hat Farm might be taken from them. The court might go after the money from the sale of Holly's house under the Proceeds of Crime Act, and if there wasn't enough left in the bank to repay it, the farm would have to be sold. But now was not the time to break that to Vince.

Lockyer dialled Jody's number as he climbed the stairs. It went straight to voicemail, just as it had the first ten times he'd called. With a sinking feeling, he guessed she was long gone. He dialled the landline at Westdene but it rang out, unanswered. And as he stood at the door to his mother's ward, his breath clouding the glass with its cross-hatching of safety wires, he realized what it was that Nina Thorowgood had said, four days ago, that had sparked in his subconscious mind and then been lost beneath the welter of everything else.

Vince McNeil had just said the same thing.

Lockyer ran back down the stairs, and out to the car.

22

He rang Broad as he drove north towards the A303. 'Gem, can you get a message to Nina Thorowgood? Tell her I'm coming to see her.'

'Okay. When?'

'Right now. I'm on my way to the camp. Twenty minutes. Tell her if she doesn't come out and talk to me, I'll walk straight in there flashing my badge.'

'Has Vince said something?' Broad sounded startled.

'In a way. He reminded me of something Nina said when we saw her. It could be important.'

'I'm messaging her now, guv.'

'Thanks.'

Lockyer rang off and sat impatiently in the queue past Stonehenge, drumming his thumbs against the steering wheel. That flash of anger at himself again. He'd been slow to make the connections in this case, had failed to notice small, important things – just like with Chris. He'd risked failing Lee Geary, and leaving Karen with no answers.

Lockyer looped through Amesbury to the lane that slipped

back onto the westbound carriageway of the A303. As he drew closer to the protest camp, tents and vans became visible between the trees, and smoke curled up from a few cooking fires. Lockyer pulled up sharply, climbed out and stood with his hands in his pockets. Two minutes, then he'd go in and get her.

At one minute fifty, Nina came marching out with a face like thunder. 'What the fuck are you playing—'

'Save it. This is a murder investigation, and I don't have time.'

'Well, maybe I don't have time to talk to *you*,' Nina snapped, making to turn away.

'Would it help if I said I'd caught Holly's killer?'

At this, Nina let some of her front drop. 'Who is it?'

'I can't tell you until the suspect has been charged by the CPS, which won't be long now. It'll be in the press by the end of the week, but I can inform you sooner. If you talk to me now.'

'What do you want to know?'

'When we last spoke you said you went back to Old Hat Farm after Holly's death. You said you were trying to get some answers about what had happened, but in the end Trish McNeil asked you to leave.'

'Yeah?'

'You said to me something like you'd started to think they were "in it together". Do you remember saying that?'

She folded her arms. 'I suppose.'

'Can you explain to me what you meant?'

'Well . . . like, the McNeils and the others. Ridgeway and Stef, and the giant.'

'Lee Geary. And you were talking about Holly's death? You thought for a while they might have been colluding somehow?'

'Yeah.'

'What made you think that?'

'Saw them together, didn't I? After the inquest said it was suicide, and it was all done and dusted.'

'Nina, who *exactly* did you see? Where, and when?'

'So, I'd been staying at the farm for a few weeks, right? One day I was at the kitchen sink, getting a brew on, and I saw Lee out in the yard, going here and there. I figured he was looking for one of the McNeils. He went into the workshop, and then Vince came out with him, and they stood chatting for a bit. Five minutes, max. Then off they went.'

'Off they went where?'

'I don't know. Just off, out of the yard and down the track. Looked very friendly, and that's what got me thinking. *Why* would they be friendly? I knew all that stuff about them killing Holly was bollocks, but everyone else still thought it was them. It felt *off*, to me.'

'In what way were they friendly?'

'Vince had his arm around Lee – well, not *around* him, like with a normal-sized person. But one hand on his shoulder, sort of . . . pally. Smiling a lot.'

'Where did they go?'

'No clue. Vince didn't get back for hours, and there was no sign of Lee when he did. I didn't ask. I was keeping my head down because Trish didn't like me much, but the lecky'd been cut off at my flat, so I wanted to stay for Yule.'

'Can you remember when this was, Nina? When exactly?'

'I'd been there maybe two or three weeks – I went for the feast of Samhain, and stayed on.'

'Samhain is Halloween, right? The thirty-first of October?'

'Yeah. So it was the middle of November, something like that.'

Lockyer looked away for a moment.

I don't expect you to understand, but I admire him. He's the kind of person I wish I could be.

But Lockyer did understand. He knew exactly what Vince was prepared to do for Jason. The relief at finally understanding what had happened was still somehow leaden. Saddening.

'How long after that did Trish ask you to leave?' he asked.

'Not long. Jealous cow. Might even have been that night, or the day after . . .'

Because Trish knew that Nina had seen Lee there, Lockyer supposed. It had been nothing to do with Vince fancying her.

'Thank you, Nina. I'll need you to come in and make a formal statement about what you saw.'

'What? Why?'

'Because I think you were the last person to see Lee Geary alive. Other than the person who killed him.'

Nina was speechless for once.

'Can you come this afternoon? Can you come with me now?'

'What? No!'

'Monday morning, then?' Lockyer fixed her with a hard stare. 'This is important, Nina. I'll come and fetch you, if I have to.'

'All *right*. God,' she snapped. 'Monday morning, then. Someone'll have to pick me up from the lay-by, like before. I've got no petrol.'

Lockyer went to the station to update Broad, and to collect her for the drive back to Salisbury.

'What prompted you to go and talk to Nina again, guv?' Broad said. 'She didn't know anything about Lee's death.'

'But we didn't *ask*,' Lockyer said. 'Not really. She was all about Holly, and we focused on that. But she said she thought they might've been "in it together", and I suddenly realized which *they* she might've meant. Then Vince said that "none of the others" had spoken to Lee the day he came to the farm, when Trish had told me there was nobody staying. No one who could support her story of having seen Lee leave by himself, of his own accord.'

In the hospital car park, Lockyer spotted a familiar motorbike. 'Isn't that Vince's Harley?'

Sure enough, when they reached Vince's bedside Jason was already there, looking tired and extremely tense. He stood up when they approached, subtly inching away from them.

'Back again so soon, Inspector?' Vince said.

'I see you got the Harley going, Jason,' Lockyer said.

'It took a while,' Jason said. 'But I needed to see Vince, and there's no bus at the weekend. I still don't have a licence. Or any insurance. And it's not taxed, either.'

'Well, I'll forget you just said that,' Lockyer replied. 'Under the circumstances.' He turned to Vince. 'There were people staying at the farm the day Lee Geary came looking for Jason. Weren't there?'

Vince held his gaze for a long time. Lockyer saw realization dawn, then resignation follow quickly.

'A few had stayed on after Samhain,' he said.

'You said that Lee asked to see Jason, then bought some *Salvia* and left. But he didn't buy *Salvia*, and he didn't leave by himself. Did he, Vince?'

'You've found one of them?' he said. 'Someone who saw him that day?'

'Someone who saw you leave with him, yes. And who saw you come back later. Alone.'

Vince's whole face sagged. Beneath the sudden exhaustion, Lockyer was sure he saw relief.

'I recently found out that my little brother had been caught up in something illegal,' Lockyer said. 'I can't do anything about it – he's been dead a long time. But I felt for him the way you feel for Jason, and I know I'd have done almost *anything* to get him out of it.'

'What's he on about, Vince?' Jason said.

Vince gave his adoptive son a look of sorrow and love. Tears sparkled in his eyes. 'I'm sorry, Jase,' he whispered. 'I – I had to *protect* you.'

'Protect me from what? What do you mean?'

'From what you'd done.' He grasped Jason's hand tightly.

'I *understand*, Jase. I do. You weren't to know what had actually happened to Holly . . . Neither of us could have known! All we knew was that Ridgeway and the others took her away that night, and gave her back dead.'

Before he could say anything else, Lockyer arrested him for the murder of Lee Geary. He needed this confession to be admissible.

'Wh-*what*?' Jason stammered.

'A witness saw you talking to Lee, and they saw you leave together,' Lockyer said to Vince. 'Nobody saw Lee again after that. Not alive. Did you have a plan? Did you know where you were going?'

'Vince, don't say anything!' Jason cried.

'It's all right, son. People have to pay for what they do. We've taught you that, haven't we?'

'No! You've taught me to forgive, and move on!'

'For the things we do as kids, *yes*! Things we can't help, absolutely. But not this. This isn't in the past,' he thumped one fist against his ribs, 'it's right here. Like a millstone. People have always thought I was a killer, but I *wasn't*. Not until that day. But I did it for the best *possible* reason. I did it for love.'

He smiled brokenly at Jason.

It was so close to what Iris Musprat had said: *What was done was done out of love. How can that be a crime?* But killing Lee Geary had most definitely been a crime. A wholly despicable one.

'I can't live with it,' Vince said. 'I have to do what's right.'

Jason looked terrified.

'It'll be all right, son,' Vince whispered. 'You'll be all right.'

'I don't understand.'

'He did it to protect you, Jason,' Lockyer said. 'Lee wanted to see you, to plead his innocence. Right, Vince? He told you he'd seen Jason at Culver Street car park the night Ridgeway died.'

A silent nod from Vince.

'And you already knew Jason had gone to the Soul Tree Festival, on your motorbike, to look for Stef. So I can imagine what you thought when you heard she'd died there. Then, as the last man standing, Lee turns up at the farm wanting a chance to explain. A chance to beg Jason for his life.'

'That poor, sweet lad.' Vince's throat constricted. 'I told him we all knew it wasn't his fault, that I was sure we could get it all ironed out. I told him Jason was out picking mushrooms. I'd go with him, and we'd get it all sorted.'

Vince looked up, eyes stark with misery. 'He was so relieved.'

'You – you thought I'd done that?' Jason said quietly. 'Killed Ridgeway?'

'Jason—'

'You thought I'd *drowned* Stef? What the *fuck*, Vince!'

'I know how much you loved Holly! Like the way I loved her mother. I know what that feels like! And I know what I'd have done, if I'd thought her killers had walked free.'

'But I'm not you! I'm . . .' Jason faltered. 'I'm not a killer.'

He wrenched free of Vince's grip and clamped his hands in his armpits, hunching in distress.

'So you walked Lee out to the hollow,' Lockyer went on. 'Why there?'

Vince looked down at his big scarred hands, dark against the hospital sheet. 'I knew the place,' he said. 'I knew we'd be out of sight.'

'What did you hit him with?'

'A big lump of flint. There are lots of them just lying around.'

Quite possibly the rock Lockyer and Broad had seen at the foot of the hawthorn tree, on day one of the investigation.

'How did you hit him?'

Lockyer was careful not to feed him information. Just to be sure.

'Hard. From behind. It was ... kinder that way. Didn't want to scare the lad.'

'*Kinder?*' Broad burst out, making Jason flinch.

'Then you buried him,' Lockyer said.

'Tried to. It wasn't much of a grave – the ground was all chalk and roots. All I had to dig with were bits of stone, and my two hands. But it was a good place to leave him, a sacred place, with Brigid's hawthorn tree to keep watch. She's the goddess of healing, and protection ... I thought he'd be peaceful there.'

'Did you check that he was dead?' Lockyer asked tightly.

'What?'

'There was some evidence Lee might've been alive when he was buried.'

'What? Jesus – *no*. He was dead.'

'But did you check?'

'I didn't need to check, I heard the sound his skull made when I hit him,' Vince said. 'It was over in seconds. What he knew – what he'd *seen* – would've put Jase in prison. I couldn't let that happen. Not to him, and not to Trish. He's the only child she's ever had.'

He looked up at Jason. 'You just weren't yourself after Holly died – it wasn't your fault. Grief like that can change a man.'

'But I *didn't* kill the others!' Jason cried. 'I was there when Ridgeway died, but I never touched him! And Stef . . . God, do you really think I'd do that? Drown a girl like a – a *rat*?'

'Jase—'

'Why didn't you just talk to me about it? I could've told you. I could've explained it all to Lee! He didn't need to be frightened of me.'

As though finally starting to accept it, Vince's eyes widened. 'You – you *didn't* kill Ridgeway?' he said.

'*No!*'

'I believe you, Jason,' Lockyer said. 'But even if I didn't, we wouldn't have had a strong enough case to convict you. Even with Lee to testify that you were there that night. There's no DNA evidence against you, and the hand print wasn't a conclusive match. I doubt the CPS would have brought charges. There was never a strong enough case against *anyone*. That was why the original investigation stalled.'

With a choking sob, Jason walked away.

'Jase!' Vince called after him. '*Jason!*'

He didn't turn back.

'When you're discharged from hospital you'll be brought

into custody to make a statement, and for your arrest to be processed,' Lockyer said. 'We can arrange for legal representation, if you'd like.'

'Will I get bail? And be allowed back to the farm? There are the bees . . .'

'I doubt it. Not for a premeditated murder. But that's for your legal counsel to discuss with you.'

Lockyer called it in, and requested a uniformed officer to stand guard. Not that Vince seemed inclined to escape: he appeared willing to take what was coming to him. As though that might atone for the needless killing of an innocent – a murder as unnecessary as Trish killing Holly to keep a secret that was no such thing. Yet another tragic similarity between the two deaths.

'If they'd only *talked* to each other!' Broad said, echoing his thoughts as they left. '*None* of it needed to happen.'

'It's a God-awful mess,' Lockyer agreed.

'Now Jason's alone. He's got no one.'

'They're *all* alone.'

'You don't believe Jason killed Stef, either?' she said.

'No. I think the inquest got that one right. I think she went in for a swim and it was a mistake, that's all.'

'Me too. I never thought Jason seemed like a killer.'

'Don't go relying on feelings like that, will you? Don't ignore them, but don't bank on them.'

'Thanks, guv. That's helpful.' She shot him a wry look. 'But I was at least half right about the ritual witchcrafty stuff, wasn't I? At least in relation to *where* Lee was killed.'

'Yeah. I'll give you that.'

Outside, Jason was sitting motionless astride the motor-bike, feet on the ground, helmet dangling from one hand. Broad hesitated, looking conflicted.

'I'll bring the car around,' Lockyer said. 'You say what you need to say.'

When he reached the car and glanced back, they were talking. Broad put her hand on Jason's arm. Lockyer busied himself with pointlessly phoning Jody again, ignoring a prickle of what he decided was natural protectiveness. Not jealousy.

When she eventually got into the car beside him, and feeling as if he might regret it, he cleared his throat. 'I was thinking about something you said, Gem.'

'Oh? What did I say?'

'About having kids.'

She was immediately uneasy. 'Right?'

'It got me thinking. Feeling the way you said about it – claustrophobic – well, obviously, that could mean you're just not there yet. Age-wise, or life-stage-wise.'

Broad was staring straight ahead.

He ploughed on. 'Or it could be to do with commitment. I mean, having a child keeps you tied to the person you're having it with for the rest of your lives. When you think about it, that's pretty scary. It scares *me* . . . It's *way* more permanent than a marriage certificate, these days. I mean, that's partly why Trish acted so disastrously when she found out Imogen was pregnant with Vince's baby, right?'

'We're talking about the McNeils?' Broad said woodenly.

'No. I just . . . Never mind.'

'Okay, guv.'

For a second Lockyer thought about sticking his oar right in, and saying he thought Pete was a waste of space. Mercifully, some survival instinct made him shut his mouth. She seemed to have forgiven him for the Róisín Conlan situation, but he wasn't going to push his luck. He knew, with sudden clarity, that he couldn't afford to lose Gemma Broad.

There was no one around to clap facetiously, or throw sweets, like when they'd solved Hedy's case the year before. Least of all at the weekend. This time their success was met with the curt approval of DSU Considine, and that was about it. But Lockyer would get to tell the one person it mattered to most. Lee Geary's little sister. And that was far more important than broadcasting their success to colleagues. He'd be able to tell Karen that her brother *hadn't* been afraid in his final moments. He'd been reassured, by someone he trusted, that everything was going to be all right. It was small comfort, but Lee had had no idea he was walking to his own death, like a sacrificial lamb, with Vince's friendly hand on his shoulder.

23

Day 22, Monday

Lockyer went to Westdene Farm on Sunday, hoping to find Jody there. The air inside the farmhouse hung motionless, torpid with heat.

'She was here yesterday morning,' John told him. 'She'd just started work when she said she had to go and pick you up, or something like that. Took the Hilux, and she's not been back.'

'You've not seen her since? And she hasn't called?'

'No.'

They stood in the doorway to Chris's room – *Jody's* room – with their hands in their pockets. Staring at the few things she owned, still scattered about the place.

John turned troubled eyes on his son. 'Where's she gone off to, then?'

'I wish I knew.'

'Is she coming back?'

'I don't know, Dad.'

'Well, what happened?'

'It's . . .' Lockyer shifted uncomfortably. 'I don't know, exactly. I think she was involved in things we didn't know about. From years back.'

'*Police* things?'

'Yeah. Maybe.'

John stared at him for a moment. Then his face clouded and he turned away, closing the door to her room behind them. 'Jody's a good girl,' he said firmly, and stumped off down the stairs. 'Have you tried phoning her up?'

'Thanks, Dad,' Lockyer said wearily. 'That's a good idea.'

He sent her a text: *Just come in and talk to me about it. Please, Jody.*

Nina was collected from the lay-by on the A303 first thing on Monday morning, and gave a full statement about everything she'd seen at Old Hat Farm. After that they started to put together everything they had, to hand over to Major Crimes and the CPS.

Late in the afternoon there was a call for Lockyer from the front desk.

'Got another walk-in for you, Inspector,' the sergeant informed him.

He went down, expecting to see Jason McNeil – the only person he thought might still want to talk to him – so he pulled up short when he found Jody instead, pacing the foyer in front of the desk.

She fell still when she saw him. Arms folded, feet set wide in her dusty rigger boots. They exchanged a long look. Jody blinked first. Without a word, Lockyer ushered her through to an interview room.

'You going to record this?' she asked, sitting rigid in the plastic chair, her normal nonchalance entirely absent.

'No. You're not under arrest or caution. I want to hear what you've got to say, first.' He gave her a hard look. 'Before I decide whether or not to charge you with attempting to pervert the course of justice.'

'Oh, come off it, Matt—'

'It's DI Lockyer in here. Start talking, Jody.'

'It's Miss Upton in here,' she replied acidly. But, faced with his stony silence, she relented. 'Look, I'm sorry, all right? I don't do well with authority, never have. It's been a bit of a head-fuck for me, getting friendly with *you* . . . But the McNeils were good to me. They took me in when my folks kicked me out. Let me earn some money—'

'Selling drugs.'

'A *legal* high, as it was back then. They gave me a second chance. So, when you said something dodgy had gone on there, my first thought was that it couldn't have been them. I really *believed* that. We've all had run-ins with you lot. We all know you see a banged-up van and a few piercings and get itchy for an arrest.' She flicked her eyes at him. 'So, yeah, I was careful what I said to you. I didn't want to help you . . . get at them.'

'I was investigating two murders, Miss Upton.'

'I know. And I gave you my photos, didn't I? Pointed you to the YouTube clips as well. But I didn't think the McNeils would've had anything to do with it.'

'That wasn't your call.'

He caught an unpleasant glimpse of his own hypocrisy as he said that, given what had happened with Kevin last year, and was happening now with Iris Musprat.

'I'm here now, aren't I?' she said. 'And I was kidding about the Miss Upton thing, for fuck's sake.'

'You've been in touch with them all along. Haven't you? When you dropped your phone I saw an email from Trish.'

'Not much. But when you started asking about them, I just wanted to . . . check in.'

'I told you I had evidence implicating them. I shouldn't have, but I suppose I thought I could trust you. And you went straight there to tip Trish off.'

'I didn't!'

'Jody, I saw you—'

'But I didn't go to tip her off! I went to . . .' She looked away.

Lockyer noticed her right leg jiggling uncontrollably. 'What?'

Jody searched for the right words. 'She . . . I . . . helped her that night.'

Lockyer went cold.

'Helped her with what?'

'The blood. In the workshop. I'd gone looking for Vince – people were asking for Sally D, and I'd sold out. He and Jase often took time out in there. Instead I found Trish, on her knees, scrubbing the floor.'

'Jesus Christ, Jody—'

'I know it sounds bad, but I trusted them! I *liked* them.

And I had no reason to think it was *anything* other than what she said it was.'

'Which was?'

'A miscarriage. They had no kids of their own, and I knew she'd miscarried before. She told me this was the eleventh, and it was very early on. It'd taken her by surprise and she'd just . . . hurried to the nearest safe place she could find. She was in a bad way, crying, blood all over the place. I said I'd take care of it. Told her to go inside, get cleaned up, and go to bed. And I guess she did, because I didn't see her again until sunrise, and . . .'

Jody trailed off, perhaps realizing where Trish had actually been in those absent hours. Lockyer just waited, and after a while she leant closer. 'I *believed* her, right? So I stayed there and finished scrubbing the floor. And then *you* tell me you have evidence that that girl died in there, and I—'

Tears glimmered in her eyes. Not something Lockyer had ever thought he'd see.

'I felt so *stupid*. If it was true, if it was *her*! I just needed to ask Trish about it. I needed to hear that she *had* lost a baby that night, and that *was* what I'd scrubbed off the fucking floor! Not some murdered girl.'

'And what did Trish say?' Lockyer asked.

'She said of course it was true about the baby. But, my God, her *face*. I *knew* she was lying.'

She looked up, as two tears finally slipped down her face. 'I was going to tell you,' she said. 'But when I nearly rammed into you on the road I thought you'd come after me, or something. Followed me. And I flared up.'

'You did.'

She fished out a filthy tissue and blew her nose. 'So, there you go,' she said. 'That's it.'

'Did you see Holly at all that night?'

'No. I hardly knew her – I told you the truth about that. I might've seen her early on, before it even got dark. But not after that, I swear.'

'And you didn't see Trish again until dawn?'

'She came out for the sunrise in a different dress, looking lovely, and I thought she was amazing. I thought, She's been through so much and yet there she is, bouncing back. Giving back. God, I'm a fucking idiot.'

'No, you're not,' he said. 'She's very convincing. Is there anything else you can tell me about that night? About where any of the McNeils were, or what they did?'

'No. Well, Jason wasn't there – he never was, for the parties.'

'Right. Anything else at all?'

'No. I swear it.'

Lockyer sat back. He believed her, and his anger had burnt itself out.

'So, are you going to charge me with obstruction? Or whatever it was?'

'No. But you should have told the police at the time, Jody. And you should have told *me* sooner.'

'I know, all right? I fucking know! But I had no idea any-thing had gone on at the farm, did I? I left the next day, before anyone had even heard about Holly – I didn't find out about it for *weeks*. And then it went from Ridgeway having done it to her committing suicide, and I just never made any kind of connection to . . . the blood.'

'I need you to make a formal statement about what you saw and did that night.'

'Okay. Then what?'

'Then you can go home.'

'Home?'

He caught himself. 'Back to Westdene. You still work there, right?'

Jody sniffed loudly, scrubbing at her nose again. 'Yeah. I still work there.'

Lockyer arranged another interview with Trish while she was still in their custody suite, prior to her magistrate's hearing. She was still in a grey tracksuit, bare-faced, her long hair tied back. Almost unrecognizable. Her legal counsel sat beside her: a crisp young woman in a navy blue suit.

'Tell me about the day Lee Geary came back to the farm,' Lockyer said. 'The eighteenth of November 2011.'

Trish gave him a careful look, then glanced at Broad, who was poised to make notes. 'It was like I already told you,' she said. 'Lee came and spoke to Vince. Bought some Sally D, then went on his way. That's all.'

'Mrs McNeil, your husband has been charged with the murder of Lee Geary. He's made a full confession.'

Lockyer watched this sink in.

Trish shot a startled look at her counsel, who gave a single nod of confirmation. 'So I – I can't even do that for him,' she murmured. 'He'll go back to prison?'

'Yes. He will.'

'He served seven years for a crime he didn't commit, back in the nineties.' Trish's voice shook. 'Can't that be taken into account?'

'I'm afraid it doesn't work that way,' Lockyer said. 'However, if you wish to confess to the arson, and the manslaughter – or rather, the murder – of your parents, his lawyer might seek to have his conviction overturned. It wouldn't affect the outcome of his murder trial, but he might be in line for some compensation on his release.'

'It'd be a pension by then,' she said bitterly.

'The only pension he'll have,' Lockyer pointed out. 'Did you deliberately frame him, Trish? Did you use Vince's T-shirt and whiskey bottle on purpose?'

Her empty stare told him she had.

'But why?'

'I didn't know what would happen,' she murmured.

'Come off it, Trish. You're cleverer than that.' Lockyer thought about it. 'Oh. I see. You mean, you didn't know they'd die? Or which of them? And if any of them survived, you couldn't have them knowing it'd been you. Right?'

Silence.

'And Imogen *did* survive. So, if you'd owned up and been sent to prison, she and Vince would have been together, with a baby on the way, and nothing to come between them.'

At this, Trish's face twisted as though in sudden pain. She sat hunched in on herself for some time.

'He was gone *hours*,' she said eventually. 'I saw him leave with Lee, and I . . . thought it was strange. When he got back he was dog tired and filthy. When I asked him, he said he'd been digging rocks for a wall.'

'You knew he was lying?' Broad said. 'Did you challenge him?'

'If he didn't want to tell me, he must have had a good reason.'

'You didn't suspect he might've harmed Lee?'

'He had no reason to.'

As she said this, confusion filled her face. 'I don't know why he . . . Lee wasn't to blame for any of it. But Vince has confessed, you said?'

'Yes, when we presented him with certain evidence regarding the crime. But he seemed relieved to come clean about it. It must have been weighing on him.'

'Yes. My poor love . . . He's not a killer. I've always known that.'

'But you made him one, Trish,' Lockyer pointed out, 'by killing his daughter, and lying about it. By letting him and Jason think Ridgeway and the others were responsible.'

At this a look of sheer terror stormed Trish's face. But it quickly vanished, as though it was too much, and her mind had rejected it entirely. Lockyer wondered about that. Whether a psychiatric assessment would be needed. The defence would doubtless call for one.

'It was that bitch Nina, wasn't it?' Trish said, with quiet fury. 'I *knew* she'd seen Lee that day. I sent her packing, but . . . Vindictive *bitch*.'

Neither Lockyer nor Broad made any reply to this.

Trish leant towards them. 'We've built something *good* there, don't you see? We *love* each other! We've healed each other.'

'No,' Lockyer said. 'You've lied from the very beginning, and now people are dead – innocent people. Because you've been pretending to be someone you're not for the past thirty years. And now there's nothing left.'

'There's Jason,' Trish said. 'Our son. We gave him a whole new life, a happy one.'

'That might have been true,' Lockyer said. 'But now he's alone. And he's not at all happy.'

Trish flinched. 'Stop it,' she murmured. 'Just shut up. You've ruined *everything*.'

'*You* ruined everything when you started that fire,' Lockyer said. 'Vince took the blame to protect your sister, the woman he loved, and he killed Lee to protect Jason. But everything *you* did was for yourself.'

They stood up to go.

'One other thing, if I may,' Lockyer said. 'The symbol that's carved onto the gatepost at Old Hat Farm. What does it mean?'

Trish smiled faintly. 'It's the old hobo code. For travellers. It means "This is a good place to stop."' The smile vanished. 'All I wanted was for that to be true.'

Jason also came in to make a formal statement about everything he'd known and not known about Lee Geary – mostly the latter. He spoke softly, as though his head was hurting. The prolonged beep of the tape recorder made him wince. His DNA results weren't back: they hadn't yet checked for matches in the database that might link him to any other crimes. Lockyer sincerely hoped they'd draw a blank.

Afterwards, Lockyer drove him back to the farm. He pulled to a halt on the yard, and the quiet when they climbed out was striking. A soft, hot breeze, the gentle ticking of the engine as it cooled.

'Pascal and Melody?' Lockyer asked.

'Moved on,' Jason said. 'Can't blame them.'

'No. I suppose not.'

The old greyhound wandered out from the house and came to lean against Jason's legs. He crouched down to rub its shoulders. 'We've been sleeping in the barn,' he murmured. 'Can't get the stink of petrol out of the house.'

'I'm sorry, Jason,' Lockyer said.

Jason squinted up at him. 'Not your fault, is it?'

Lockyer felt it was, in part.

Jason straightened up, gazing around at the parched land and the ramshackle buildings, the swifts cutting the sky.

'What do you do?' he said softly, almost to himself. 'When the people you love turn out to be not who you thought they were?'

'I don't know.'

The horrible sensation of things you were certain of turning out to be wrong. Cracks zigzagging through the foundations of your world. Lockyer could hardly imagine

the scale of what Jason must be wrestling with. He didn't
know what to say.

'I'll have to leave here. Won't I?' Jason said.

'You might. But not right away.'

'Part of me wants to go,' he said. 'This place is *them*. It'll
never be the same now. But ... Holly.' He hung his head,
heaved in a breath. 'Holly's here. If I go, it'd feel like I was
leaving her behind. Losing her all over again.'

'She's not here, Jason,' Lockyer said. 'I get it, I really do. I
know how you feel. But she's not here. And no one can ever
take away your memories of her.'

'I wish she'd *talked* to me!' He spoke with quiet passion.
'If she'd told me what she knew about Trish and her mum
back then, we could have sorted it out. I know we could.'

'Holly couldn't have known how Trish was going to react.
Or how *you*'d react—'

'She knew I'd never turn on her. Not ever.'

'Perhaps she thought the same about Trish.'

Jason gazed at the distant rise of Pewsey Hill, golden in the
afternoon sun. 'I guess none of us knew Trish at all,' he said.

Lockyer had his card in his hand and was waiting for a
good moment to give it to Jason. He was thinking about
taking his leave, and heading home. He didn't know what
else he could say to help this gentle man, who'd lost
everything. He was still thinking about it when Jason shuddered, and started to cry.

Lockyer went home. They'd solved two murders, one that
had been ruled a suicide, the other on the verge of being

left unexplained. It was satisfying, and a relief, but left him curiously empty.

Perhaps Old Hat Farm *had* been a good place, for a while. For Jason it had been a sanctuary, a chance to live an entirely new life. For Vince, too, it had been a place to start again. Neither had foreseen the grief that was coming. And perhaps if Holly had never gone there – if Imogen had destroyed all the evidence of her real father's identity – it would have carried on being a good place. Built on lies that would never come to light.

Lockyer couldn't escape the feeling that *he*'d torn it all down. It wasn't true, but that didn't seem to matter. In his heart was a kernel of guilt that was partly to do with Old Hat Farm, and partly to do with his own family. They'd all kept things from one another. They'd hidden parts of themselves from the ones they loved. The realization came with faint but unavoidable sorrow.

He went out to the back garden, and gazed into the shadows beneath the trees. He'd stalled for too long. The case was finished. Lee Geary and Holly Gilbert would get the justice they deserved. It was time to do the same for Róisín Conlan. A weird sensation ran over his skin. He looked down, saw goosebumps on his arms. The air was cool – far cooler than it had been for weeks. In the distance came a faint rumble of thunder, and moments later the first fat drop of rain landed on his face.

Day 30, Tuesday

A week later there was a cordon of blue-and-white crime-scene tape along the edge of the copse, and a tent had been erected as a forensic team excavated the skeleton of Róisín Conlan. Lockyer, who'd been removed from the investigation as soon as he'd called it in, stood on his back doorstep and watched. Broad, as they'd agreed, had gone into the station as usual, leaving Merry at home this time.

So far, Mrs Musprat had stuck to the plan and stayed indoors. Lockyer had no idea if she'd continue to do so, but he'd done what he could. He'd tried to impress upon her that he'd probably lose his job if his orchestration of the 'discovery' of the body came to light. He *thought* she'd understood.

An hour or so later, Steve Saunders came out of the trees carrying a small evidence bag. Lockyer's pulse picked up. He went over to the remains of his back fence.

'This should help,' Saunders said, waving the bag.

Lockyer took it, held the plastic taut to see the contents clearly. Felt a rush of relief.

Beneath a few crumbs of clinging earth, the gold ring was as brightly yellow as the day Paddy Conlan had slipped it onto Róisín's finger. The swollen flesh that had held it in place had long since decomposed. Lockyer peered closely, and picked out the words on the inside surface: *Forever Mine 22–7–1961*. A summer wedding for a young bride with no idea of the torment to come. Now Iris could legitimately identify the body for them. She could tell them what a brute Paddy Conlan had been. She could tell them all of it, omitting just one thing: that Róisín had come to Bill's the day she ran away.

'It was still on her finger,' Saunders said, giving Lockyer a look. 'Stroke of luck that the Girl Guide's mutt sniffed her out, isn't it?'

'Merry does love to dig,' Lockyer said neutrally.

'Does she usually bring her dog with her when she comes visiting?'

'She doesn't come visiting, as a rule. It was to discuss the case.'

'Course it was.' Saunders sniffed. 'SOCOs did say the ground was more churned up than they'd expect for a Jack Russell. More like a Great Dane.'

'Well, Merry's pretty industrious.'

'Hm,' he grunted. 'Looked to *me* like someone had been digging. With a spade.'

Lockyer said nothing.

The two men locked eyes.

Saunders had been avoiding Lockyer since their row about Nina's testimony. Now he cleared his throat.

'I took a look at your report on Holly Gilbert as it went by,' he said awkwardly. 'Good result, that.'

'Thanks,' Lockyer said.

'I'm glad it wasn't Ridgeway, not when we'd had to let him go. And I'm glad us arresting them for it wasn't what got the three of them killed. Not directly, anyway.'

'No,' Lockyer agreed. 'Your investigation wasn't wrong. It just didn't go back far enough.'

'All right, don't hurt your shoulder patting yourself on the back, you twat.'

'Why not?' Lockyer said. 'You would.'

Saunders made a face, looked away, sniffed. 'No reference to that girl's missing statement in there,' he said.

'No,' Lockyer said. 'Nina didn't mention it when she came in, so neither did I.'

Another awkward pause.

'Maybe I'm more of a team player than you give me credit for, Steve.'

'Maybe,' Saunders conceded.

Lockyer guessed it was as close as Saunders would ever come to saying thanks. Sure enough, he changed the subject.

'Reckon the old bird next door'll know whose ring it is?'

'She might,' Lockyer said. 'She's lived here a long time.' He turned to look at the dark reflections in Iris's windows. 'Be gentle with her, though, won't you? She might not look it, but Mrs Musprat is a sensitive soul.'

'So am I, Farmer Giles,' Saunders said, which made Lockyer smile.

Saunders took the evidence bag from him. 'Why aren't you at the station, anyway? We can work a scene without you watching over us, you know.'

'I was due some leave. And this is better than TV.'

'Is that right? Well, I'm going to talk to the old dear, see if she recognizes this.' Saunders waved the ring again. 'Stick the kettle on, would you?'

'Just don't call her "love", Steve. She'll take your head clean off.'

Lockyer left them to it once Saunders had emerged from Iris's cottage with the victim's name, and no immediate urge to either arrest her or denounce Lockyer for any involvement.

He went and sat at his mother's bedside, mostly in silence, as he'd grown used to doing, but now and then telling her something about the case, or about Chris, or the farm.

'Jody knew more than she ever let on,' he murmured. 'I mean, Trish lied to her, like she lied to everyone. Jody didn't realize the significance of what she'd seen, but . . . We slept together, and she still didn't trust me enough to tell me. Why is that? Why don't people feel like they can talk to me?'

He gazed out of the window.

'She'll probably leave. I think we've made up over the police stuff, and the sex, but I still think she'll go.'

'What was that?' Trudy mumbled.

Lockyer started in shock. Without thinking, he broke the two-metre rule and reached for his mother's hand. Slowly, she rolled her head towards him, opened her eyes just a little.

'Hello there,' he said. 'How are you feeling?'

'Oh, you know. Not too bad.'

Her voice was quiet and thin. For several seconds, she stared fixedly at the hand Lockyer was holding. Then her fingers squeezed his. A light flutter of pressure.

Relief stormed through him. He grinned foolishly at her. 'You'll be back slinging bales in no time.'

She twitched her eyebrows. 'The legs are less cooperative. But Dr Lorne is optimistic.'

'That's great, Mum.'

A huge weight was lifting from him, leaving him shaky. 'I haven't managed to speak to the doctor for a couple of days,' he said. 'But—'

'You slept with Jody?' Trudy interrupted.

Lockyer winced inwardly. 'Do you think you might be able to forget you heard that?'

'I doubt it, Matthew. I'm clearly very out of the loop. Just don't go and—'

'Please, please, don't give me any advice about it. I beg you.'

'All right. But you *did* confide in me.'

'I thought you were asleep. I was just . . . thinking out loud.'

'Fretting, is what you were doing. You always were a worrier.'

'Well, there have been things to worry about, lately.'

In silence, she squeezed his fingers again. 'I've been having the oddest dreams,' she said. 'I dreamt you'd found a body in your back garden.'

'Well, actually, I have. But I'll tell you about it another time.'

Lockyer said silent thanks he hadn't spoken out loud about Chris's unhappiness, or the pills, while she was sleeping. He'd never tell either of his parents, and whether that was right or wrong, he didn't care. It wasn't a lie, and if it was a secret, it was a kind one. It didn't mean they hadn't known him. It didn't alter the love they'd all felt.

'Well,' Trudy said, 'if I can't ask for gossip about your love life, then you'd better tell me more about what you've been up to. And your father. How's he doing?'

'All right, I think. The heat's been wearing him out, but Jody's more than picked up the slack. She's a force to be reckoned with.'

'Is she indeed? I think I'd like to meet this girl. You will try to get her to stick around, won't you?'

Lockyer looked down. 'Yes. I'll try.'

Trudy's face fell. 'Oh, Matthew, sorry – I didn't mean . . . Hedy . . .'

'I know. It's okay.'

'Any word from her, lately? I've lost track of time in here.'

'No word, no,' he said. 'But I think I hear her loud and clear.'

Trudy's smile was sad. Seconds later, her eyelids slid shut again.

*

At Westdene Farm he found his father in the barn, cleaning various tractor parts with an oily rag. The place felt subtly bereft without the pervasive heat, now that the weather had broken. Lockyer went to stand next to his father. Watched but didn't try to help. John gave him a nod.

'Don't you go upsetting our Jody again,' he said.

'It's all right, Dad. It's all sorted.'

'Better be,' John muttered. 'If she walks out because of you, I'll have something to say about it.' His father eyed him suspiciously. 'Not fallen for you, has she?'

'Jody? Fallen for *me*?'

John grinned. 'Ha! Not likely, I suppose.'

'Guess who I just spoke to?'

'Your mother.'

'Yeah. She woke up while I was there.'

A nod. 'Rang me this morning. Said she was feeling better.'

'Doctor Lorne says she's out of danger,' Lockyer said. 'But it could take weeks, or even months, to find out how much movement she'll get back. Whether she'll be able to walk unaided, or manage without help.'

'If she needs help, we'll help her,' John said gruffly.

'I suppose the main thing is she'll be coming home.'

'Of course she's coming home.'

'Not of course. We didn't know she would.'

Lockyer wasn't sure why, but he wanted his father to acknowledge the danger she'd been in. The danger they'd all been in.

With a frown, John rubbed hard at what looked like a tie rod end. Then he stopped, and in his face Lockyer saw what he'd needed to see. The perfect mirror of his own fear and relief: evidence of their shared experience.

'We didn't know,' John agreed. 'But she is. That's the point.'

Lockyer wanted to hug him, but they hadn't hugged since he was a boy. He made do with clasping his shoulder.

John patted his hand brusquely. 'Now go and make things right with Jody.'

'They are right—'

'Don't argue with me, son.'

He found her sitting at the dining-room table, surrounded by heaps of paper. She'd thrown a battered jumper on over her habitual vest, and looked tired. She took off her reading glasses as he came in. Her expression was complicated. She waved a fistful of paperwork at him.

'Your dad's accounting is *batshit*,' she said. 'Why haven't you done something about it?'

'Me? Dad's always done all that.'

'Yeah. Except he hasn't. God knows what he put on the last tax return – I mean, seriously.'

'You don't have to do it, Jody. I'm pretty sure it's not your job.'

'No? What *is* my job, exactly?' she challenged.

'Well,' he smiled, 'keeping everything together, I suppose.'

A startled look flickered over her face. 'Right, well. If there's ever an audit, you're screwed. So.'

'Thanks, Jody.'

'You're not welcome, Matt,' she muttered grouchily.

'My mum's woken up. She managed to squeeze my hand.'

'Yeah, your old man told me,' she said. 'I'm really glad.'

'Will you stay, Jody?'

'Look, I already said—'

'I know. You don't stay anywhere. You move around.'

'Right.'

'Only . . . why?'

'What do you mean, *why*?'

'You used to have a car, you used to have a flat, and when Danny died you got rid of it all and went back to being a nomad.' He shook his head. 'All that stuff about moving on and not dwelling on loss, not building shrines, or whatever. That's all fine. But if you spend your whole life running just to *avoid* doing that, isn't that the same thing, in the end?'

'Don't *analyse* me, Detective—'

'You know, laying out a loved one's bones might not mean people are letting themselves be *enslaved* by grief,' he said. 'It might also be a way for them to live peacefully *with* their grief. A way to keep the lost close.'

'Whatever.' Jody didn't look at him.

'Where's Danny buried? You could go and see him. I'd go with you, if you ever wanted company.'

Silence.

'They'll still need help here, even once Mum's home,' Lockyer said. 'They've needed help for years, and she's not going to just bounce back from this.'

'Stop trying to guilt me into doing what suits *you*.' Now Jody eyed him. 'I stay for ever so you get to wash your hands of helping out around here? Is that the idea?'

Lockyer bridled. 'That's not it at all.'

'No?'

'No. Well ... Okay. Maybe it is that, partly.' He sighed. 'Look, I never thought my dad would accept help from *anyone*, not after Chris died. But he just sent me in here to make sure you don't leave.'

Jody's eyes roved across the papers in front of her, alighting on nothing.

Lockyer pushed on. 'All I'm saying is, he likes having you here, and so do I. Mum will too. Maybe you don't have to keep moving for the rest of your life. Maybe this is a good place to stop.'

'I don't want to stop. I ... can't.'

'How long has it been since you tried?'

Jody didn't reply, so Lockyer turned to go. 'Please, just think about it,' he said. 'Even if it's only for a few more months.'

'Matt?' she called after him. 'Milk and four sugars.'

After a week of digging, Saunders's team had collected five first-hand accounts from people who'd either lived in Orcheston in the early 1960s or had known Patrick Conlan from elsewhere. Along with Mrs Musprat's statement, a picture was emerging of a violent man and an abusive husband. One witness hinted at Róisín's affair with Bill Hickson, which, when pressed, Iris admitted to having known about. Bill was not around to be questioned, of course, and Iris described him as a gentle, decent sort of man.

The evidence all pointed to Paddy Conlan having found

out about the affair and killed his wife in retribution – especially since he'd never reported her missing. He'd told her family she'd run away with another man, but had told neighbours in Orcheston that she'd gone back to Dublin to nurse her sick mother. Paddy had died in 1978, in what might safely be termed suspicious circumstances: his body had been pulled out of the Regent's Canal at Camden Lock, with his hands tied behind his back and a bullet in his head. The murder had never been solved.

Saunders had located Róisín's younger sister, Gráinne, and her brother Sean. They still lived in Dublin. Róisín's body was to be repatriated for her funeral and interment, but Gráinne wanted to visit the burial site.

Lockyer left work at lunchtime the day she was due to arrive. As he got up to go, Broad gave him the wide-eyed, anxious look she always wore at any mention of Róisín. She had no poker face whatsoever. She wasn't cut out for even the mildest of deceptions, and Lockyer was ashamed to have found that out.

'So . . . it's all good?' she said quietly.

'It's all good. Steve's wrapping up. There isn't enough evidence for further action, and the chief suspect died decades ago.'

Broad checked that the corridor was empty. 'And Mrs Musprat hasn't said . . .?'

'Anything she shouldn't,' Lockyer confirmed. 'Look, I'm really sorry, Gem. I'm sorry I made this into more than it needed to be. And dragged you into it.'

'You wanted to protect her,' Broad said. 'I get it. And you

could drag me pretty much anywhere, guv.' She blushed, not unexpectedly.

Lockyer believed her, and decided to be more careful, in future, not to do it again. 'Well, it's over with now,' he said, and she looked relieved. 'Unless I find another body. Maybe out in the coal shed, next time.'

Broad laughed. 'It'll be me calling you next. I'll have killed Pete.'

The joke landed like a sour note. She turned even redder, and stared at her computer screen.

Lockyer pictured her talking to Jason McNeil at the hospital, and the way she'd touched his arm. Someone who saw indigo and gold when they looked at her, and tasted orange sorbet when she spoke. With a sudden spasm of frustration he wished she'd ditch Pete, with his tidy garage, faux-chumminess, and rules about dogs, and go immediately to Old Hat Farm to see how Jason was doing. Let Merry run around with the greyhound.

'Well,' he murmured, 'as and when that day comes, I'll be at your service. See you tomorrow, Gem.'

'Yeah. See you, guv.'

He watched discreetly as Gráinne walked slowly from the hire car into the woods. She was a good decade younger than Mrs Musprat, but still elderly and unsteady on her feet. A younger couple were with her – perhaps some configuration of offspring and in-law. The woman carried a huge bouquet of roses.

There *was* a rightness to it. The story they'd told might

not be completely accurate, but it *had* been Paddy Conlan who'd killed Róisín – indirectly, by his actions – far more than it had been Bill or Iris.

Finally Lockyer was free of it. It was, in some ways, another case solved. One that had involved a manipulation of the truth, and him operating beyond the proper parameters of his job. Which made it twice he'd done that. He'd have to make sure there wasn't a third time. Three times was a habit.

A fitful breeze tossed the trees. After half an hour the sombre trio emerged, and found Iris Musprat standing by the back fence. Lockyer couldn't hear what was said, but when Iris turned, Gráinne went with her into the cottage next door. The younger couple waited, arms folded against the wind. Another fifteen minutes or so passed before Gráinne reappeared. She wiped her eyes several times as she was helped back around to the car.

'Are you okay, Nana?' Lockyer heard the young man ask, as he held the door for her.

'Oh, yes. Just me, getting weepy.' Gráinne spoke in a musical Irish accent.

Lockyer had his suspicions. When they'd gone he went to see Mrs Musprat. 'You told her, didn't you?'

'She'd a right to know,' Iris said. 'A right to hear exactly what had happened to her sister.' She eyed him, noting his worried expression. 'She's not going to tell a soul, so you can stop looking so frit.'

'How do you know?'

'She said so, and I know when someone's telling the

truth. She was grateful. Far better that Rosie slipped away knowing she was hidden safe, and Bill was watching over her, than that Paddy had got his hands on her.'

Lockyer considered that. He supposed that, as long as Iris hadn't gone into too much detail, it did paint a more peaceful picture. 'And you?' he asked.

'And me what?'

'Are you satisfied?'

A curt nod. 'I am.'

'Don't go dying on me now, just because you've got it all off your chest.'

'Ha! We'll see.'

After that Lockyer went to the spot where the bones had lain. Looked down at the empty, disordered ground, where the wind was now scattering rose petals. He stood there until his mind was clear.

After sunset he decided to walk, but paused on the front step when he heard a car coming up the track. It was a rare occurrence, and his first thought was that it must be Jody, or perhaps Kevin, in his perennially knackered Citroën. But it wasn't the Hilux or Kevin's old banger that came into view. It was a vintage, mint green Austin Allegro.

Lockyer recognized it at once, and was shocked into stillness. Not until it had pulled up right in front of him, and he saw who was at the wheel, did he believe it. Serious grey eyes in the elongated oval of her face. Elegant, bony fingers gripping the steering wheel.

Hedy Lambert.

Nearly six months after she'd left without a word, and just like that she was back. Their eyes met, but he couldn't read anything from hers. He was stunned. Felt a flare of happiness that quickly vanished behind clouds of confusion and resentment. After a while she opened the door and climbed out, awkwardly, carefully. As she turned Lockyer noticed that she'd cut her hair, and changed shape. On her narrow frame, the outward curve of her abdomen was obvious. It took a few seconds for him to grasp that she was pregnant. Maybe about six months pregnant.

'Hello,' she said.

ACKNOWLEDGEMENTS

My sincere thanks to former Police Constable Jenny Freeman, Police Sergeant William Monk, Police Constable Charlotte Sartin, and Detective Inspector Simon Child, of Wiltshire Police, for talking to me about their work, answering my stupid questions, and being kind about the results.

I am enormously grateful to Jane Wood, Florence Hare, Emily Patience and all the wonderful people at Quercus, for their vision, skill, and dedication in bringing Lockyer into the world; to my brilliant agent, Mark Lucas, whose input is never less than pure gold; and to Niamh O'Grady, also at the Soho Agency, for all the help and support she's given. Thank you all so very much.